THE
BOND

KAYE DOBBIE

THE BOND

Print: 978-0-6483745-9-6
eBook: 978-0-6483745-7-2

Cover Design and Interior Format

ALSO BY KAYE DOBBIE

For my family and friends, with many, many thanks.

AUTHOR'S NOTE

The Bond was first published in 1995. Although the story remains the same, this new version has been completely re-edited. I have tried to be sensitive in writing about the white settlers arriving in the Port Phillip District, and their interactions with the original Aboriginal inhabitants. Looking through the eyes of people who lived in the 1830s and 1840s is not always consistent with modern sensitivities. I have chosen to use the tribal name Djadjawurrung in the book, although at the time there were many different spellings.

RACHEL

1835

PROLOGUE

Midsummer Eve, Richmond Bridge,
Van Diemen's Land

RACHEL WRAPPED HER ARMS ABOUT her narrow body, huddling herself against the chill. The fury of the mid-summer storm had lessened, the wind abating and the wild, whipping rain easing to soft drizzle. The branches above her head were dripping water down onto her hair. She shook her head and pushed the leaves aside, breathing in the cool, fresh smell of the earth.

Before her, through the long grass and reeds, she could see the swirl of the river, swollen now with the rain. Ducks were venturing out from their hiding places for a last foray before night-fall. A moment ago, she had watched with interest as a man with a cart came down and watered his horses, before heading on across the bridge. But he hadn't seen her, hidden as she was by the grass and the low scrubby bushes at the river's edge.

Behind her, Rachel could see the tangle of dark smoke rising from the chimneys of the buildings that made up the township of Richmond. The orphanage was there among them and Rachel turned her eyes determinedly away. The sun was dropping lower, and its fading gleam struck a rainbow on the shifting storm clouds. For a moment she let her eyes rest on the mingling colours, wondering if it were true what they said.

About rainbows and pots of gold.

She could do with a pot of gold. It would solve all her problems. She hugged herself again, resting her chin on her bony knees and closing her eyes. Since Pa had gone—she still did not like to think of him as dead—there had been no-one to care about her future but herself. Once Pa had made plans and decisions, once Rachel had no thoughts in her head but the sunshine and the flowers and the warmth of Pa's coat as she lay sleeping, rocked by the trot of his horse. But now Pa was gone, life had taken a different, grimmer turn. These days all she could think of was her narrow bed at the orphanage and her tasteless meals and the other girls with their eyes too big in their little faces.

It wasn't fair, she thought, and blinked savagely at tears. Why had Pa had to die? When he was all she had? He had been a good man. Mrs Roadknight said so, and Mrs Roadknight knew all her 'boys'. She fed them and dried their coats, wet from the rain, and told the police she hadn't seen any of them in months with such a solemn, honest look in her eye they couldn't help but believe her, even when they knew she was lying.

'He never stole from the poor man.' Mrs Roadknight told Rachel. 'Only the rich, and then he were so courteous, they had no complaints. That's why it took so long to catch him, you see. No one wanted him caught. But the reward . . .' and she shook her head, 'ten pound is a lot of money, Rachel. And some men being what they are . . . One of them bounty hunters it was, finally tracked him down.'

So Pa's gallant career on the road had come to an end. He had been shot while resisting arrest, and so there was one less bandit to swoop down on the little settlements and the lonely travellers, one less bandit to annoy the authorities of Van Diemen's Land. Not that there weren't plenty of others to take his place! But Pa had been special. Even Mrs Roadknight, who ran the End of the World Inn on the road between Pitt Water and Jerusalem, and to whom they were all special, thought he was a cut above the rest. The inn was a notorious bushrangers' stopping point, although the police could prove nothing and were usually so undermanned they did not even try.

When Pa had been killed, Mrs Roadknight had taken Rachel in. The little girl was only five, and for the next three years she remained there, slightly neglected, but loved well enough and treated like a little princess by all the 'strangers' who called on Mrs Roadknight at odd times of the day and night. Rachel learned from an early age to view the law with suspicion, and believe wholeheartedly in the myth of the bushranger—the gallant man ill-used and ill-treated by a cruel society, who was compelled to escape into the bush and live by pillage and theft, evading the police as best he could.

In some cases it was true enough, but in others the men who called themselves bandits or bushrangers were savage and without conscience of any kind, sometimes even a little deranged by the cruelty they had endured in the convict camps and roadgangs. Not that the child Rachel comprehended such things. She just knew that there were some men whose eyes frightened her, and she stayed away from them.

The police finally decided they'd had enough of Mrs Roadknight and closed down the inn on the Jerusalem road. And Rachel, eight then, had gone to the new orphanage in the growing township of Richmond. She was no longer treated like a little princess; she was just one of many little girls who had been abandoned.

Rachel swallowed, lifting her head again. Her hair had come loose as always and was wild down her back. A thick, black cloud. The rain shone in it, like droplets of silver. She loved the weight of it, pulling at her neck. There was a rule at the Orphanage that hair should be kept up under a bonnet at all times. But there was no-one here to see.

'Gypsy black.' That was what Pa had called her hair. It shone in candlelight with a blue sheen. Her face was pale and would one day be a perfect oval, but now it was too thin, too angular for beauty. Her nose was straight, perhaps a little long, and her eyes were dark and secret, slanting at the corners, as black as her hair.

'There's Spanish blood in us,' Pa used to tell her. 'One of our ancestors was wrecked from the Armada, in Drake's time, and found his way to Devon.' It sounded more romantic than being called 'gippo' or 'black' as they travelled about Van Diemen's Land. For, when he wasn't being a gallant

highwayman, Pa was a hawker ... a tinker, selling
to the lonely wives and women of the settlements
throughout the island. Pa had a way with women.
Even then Rachel knew it. And knew some of
them came willing to his bed. But it was never
more than that. It was Rachel who was his companion, his friend, his apprentice.

The light was fading fast. She would be missed
soon at the orphanage. She had her duties to perform—helping with the cooking and the cleaning,
helping the smaller ones. Because Rachel was thirteen. It was eight years since Pa had died, although
at night when she closed her eyes she could still
feel him close. The tears stung again. Usually she
held them back, but because she was alone in the
twilight, this time Rachel let them come.

She wept for a long time. It was so unfair! Pa
had been all she had and, although life had been
sometimes hard and uncertain, at least she had had
someone. It was the sense of belonging she missed
more than anything. The orphanage was so cold.
They were fed and clothed and generally looked
after, physically as well as spiritually—on Sundays
they made a long crocodile and walked to church
for their worship—but emotionally . . . she felt as
empty and desolate as the great craggy mountains
to the west. And for someone like Rachel, so warm
and eager to love, so desperate for love in return, it
was sometimes so unbearable she just had to escape.

Like now.

Just to be alone with her memories and her
thoughts, to regather her inner strength. To remind
herself who she was, a person in her own right,
rather than just another nameless body in an

orphanage uniform . . .

Suddenly behind her, a twig crunched. Rachel glanced swiftly and nervously over her shoulder. At first, she could see nothing. The darkness had grown thicker in the moments she had been grieving for the past. And then a shape moved, a figure on a horse. The animal wickered softly, nuzzling the long grass, and Rachel's heart began to beat with frightened thuds. It was dangerous out here alone. There were ruffians; thieves and murderers not so gallant as her father. Rachel crouched, ready to run.

'It's all right,' a voice said, soft and low with a drawl she found familiar, a little like Pa's. 'I came to water the horse and I heard someone cryin'. Are you hurt?'

Rachel watched, wide-eyed, as the man urged the horse closer. He was a dark shadow in the evening shadows. She could not distinguish his features at first, and it was only when he dismounted that she saw him better, but still not well enough to colour the hair flopping over his eyes. His shoulders were broad from hard physical work, and his mouth and jaw had a straight, stubborn look at odds with the concern in his voice.

'Are you hurt?'

She shook her head, and wiped her face with her sleeve, scrubbing at it roughly, as if to eliminate all traces of her weakness. 'I was just thinking sad thoughts,' she told him warily.

He looked at her again, and the hard mouth softened into a flicker of a smile. 'What sad thoughts would they be, darlin'?'

'I was thinking of my Pa.' She looked at him again,

slyly out of the slanting eyes, to see what effect that was having. 'He's dead and I'm an orphan.' Comprehension came into his face. 'You're from the orphanage,' he said. 'Should you be out here by yourself?'

Rachel shrugged indifferently, but fear wormed its way into her mind again, and she glanced rather nervously towards the smoke from the town, now a grey smudge in the dark sky. She would get into trouble. There would be no supper for her tonight, and probably she would be birched if Mrs Hewett, who was in charge of them all, was angry enough with her. And yet, she rarely got to speak to a man. The orphanage was for girls only, run by females. She missed the male attention she had had at Mrs Roadknight's inn, and she missed her Pa. This man sounded rather like her Pa. She could not bear to leave him just yet.

He was standing so quietly, as if lost in his own thoughts. She looked at him curiously. 'Are you from the town? Have I seen you at church?'

He smiled. 'Well, I don't go all that often. Have you always lived here?' he added, shifting the subject.

'We travelled all over, Pa and I,' she murmured softly. 'He was a friend of Matthew Brady, or so Mrs Roadknight said.'

She felt the man stiffen. 'You mean the bushranger, Brady?'

'Yes.' she sighed. 'And my Pa was a gentleman, too. He didn't hurt anyone. He only took what he had to, and he was always polite and always kind to the ladies. But they caught him one day, the police troopers and their hired killer, and shot him dead, and so I was left all alone. I stayed with Mrs Road-knight for a time, up at the End of the World Inn, but the police closed her down, and she went to her sister in Hobart Town. There wasn't room for me. So I came to the orphanage to live.'

He was silent for so long she wondered what he was thinking. Usually, when she spoke of Pa and Mathew Brady, there were cooes and murmurs of excitement and admiration. But when the stranger spoke again it was only to say, 'Have you any other family you might go to?' His voice was a murmur in the darkness, as though, she thought with a plea-surable shiver, he was part of the darkness itself.

'Not that I know of,' she told him cheerfully. 'Pa never spoke of any, if I do.' A breeze stirred the leaves above her head, and she lifted her face to its coolness. There were a few, faint stars now. 'My mother died when I was only a baby,' she added, and tried without success to feel sorrow. She had never known her mother, and so could not miss her. 'Pa said she was already married to someone else when he met her, and they lay together for seven nights and then her husband returned and Pa went away. But when I was born, my mother died and told her husband the truth before she did. He found Pa and handed me to him like a bundle of old rags, so he said.' And she laughed, for Pa had made it sound so funny when he told her. 'So I have no Ma and no Pa, and that makes me an orphan. That's why I was crying.'

'I can understand that,' he said. 'It's not easy being alone.' There was bitterness now in his voice.

Perhaps he was one of the convicts, exiled from home and loved ones, sent to be punished with lash and hard labour? Or perhaps he was a settler, who had travelled halfway around the world looking for fortune and found only misery?

'Have you any family?' Rachel asked gently.

'Not any more,' he told her, and it was the sheer expressionlessness of his voice that touched her heart. His hand was resting on the branch near her, and some impulse made her put her own small palm over it.

'Then we are two of the same,' she told him, in what was meant to be comfort.

He seemed surprised. She felt his hand twitch, and then relax again under hers. 'Maybe we are,' he said, and amusement warmed his voice.

'Where are you from?'

He pushed back his fringe, and it flopped immediately back over his brow. 'I've been working over Sorell way. I'm on my way home at last,' and he laughed with a mockery she couldn't understand. But she felt compassion and a sense of companionship overcome her wariness for a stranger. For whatever reason this man was alone and unhappy, and something in him reached out to her as if they were truly, as she had said, two of a kind.

Rachel looked up at the stars again, and suddenly her mood lightened. 'Do you know what night this is?' she asked him in a whisper that barely suppressed the excitement in her voice. As though she were about to present him with a gift.

He shook his head without answering.

'It's my birthday,' she said. 'I was born on Midsummer's Eve. My Pa used to say that Midsummer's Eve was a magic night—you know, old magic. He said I could make a wish and it would come true.'

'Have you ever made one?' he asked her, and she felt him move closer and squat down beside her.

'Sometimes,' she murmured, 'but they didn't come true. Maybe I wished for too much.'

She saw him smile, bending his head, and tossed her own indignantly. He looked up at the movement and his eyes gleamed with a moist sheen that made her wonder if he had tears in them. Was he a ghost, a lost soul, uncared for and unwanted, come to haunt the river bank? There was supposed to be a ghost here, but she had forgot exactly what it was. Rachel felt her skin prickle.

'Don't you believe Midsummer's Eve is magical?' she asked him quietly, her voice full of fright.

He took a moment to answer her. 'My father used to say I was a Moonraker, so maybe I do.'

Rachel tilted her head to one side, her fears forgotten. 'What's a Moonraker, sir?'

He laughed, and it was a warm laugh, the laugh of a friend. 'That's someone who sees the moon's reflection in a pool of water and thinking the moon itself is floating there, tries to fetch it out.'

Rachel sniffed. 'A fool, you mean! Well, I will make my wish, whatever you think.' There was a silence, while she did—I wish to see this man again—and then wondered, irritably, why she had wasted it on such a thing. She should have wished for something like a pot of gold, or a loving home and family.

'What did you wish for?' he asked her, trying to make his voice serious.

Rachel bit her lip. She would not tell him the truth. He would laugh at her. Instead, she spied the horse, still cropping the grass, and smiled. 'I wished you would take me for a ride on your horse,' she told him slyly.

He seemed to be considering it, and then he stood up. 'Why not?' he mocked, as if to himself. 'It's not often I can make someone's wish come true!'

Rachel's heart leapt. He mounted, and held out his hand, reaching for hers. Without a second thought she gave it to him, feeling his fingers close hard, and then he had pulled her up into the saddle before him, his strong arms either side of her. She felt his breath in her hair, and turned her head to meet his eyes. His hands tightened on the reins, and the muscles in his arms hardened. 'Where do you want to gallop to?' he asked her evenly. 'Will we go to Hobart Town and back, or on and on into the sea?'

Rachel laughed, hearing the edge of excitement in his voice, although he strove to hide it, matching her own. 'The sea!' she cried.

He kicked his heels savagely into the horse's flanks and set it speeding away, down the road. The wind was in her face, streaming her hair out behind her, making her cheeks sting and her eyes smart. Neither of them spoke. The rain had cooled the air, and it was delicious and so exhilarating, she felt as if she were flying. In all her young life she had never felt like this, riding like the night wind with this stranger. The excitement twisted in her, making her laugh out loud, and his arm tightened about her so that she was pressed hard against him. The horse stumbled, but somehow he held it upright, and she felt the power of his body with a sense of wonder. She felt small and protected, as if her father was with her again, only different in a way she couldn't understand. Rachel pushed her hair out of her eyes and smiled to herself. I'll never forget this moment, she thought. Not as long as I live. When I'm old, I'll still hug it to myself, and remember.

After a while, she realised he had slowed the horse to a trot. It was puffing and blowing, its sides heaving. It could not be an easy thing, she thought, carrying the two of them. In dismay, she saw the lights of Richmond before them, and knew their journey had come to an end. He kicked the horse into a canter again, and its hooves flicked up mud and grass along the riverbank. Some water birds flew up, squawking their displeasure at being disturbed so late, and Rachel turned, laughing, to meet his eyes.

He paused a moment, hesitating, and then suddenly he leaned forward. His lips brushed hers in the darkness, warm and soft. Rachel was so surprised, she did not move, and felt his smile even though she could not see it. 'You're a lovely girl,' he told her. 'I'm glad I could make your wish come true. Now you'd better be going, or you'll be in for trouble.'

Reluctantly, Rachel slid down. 'Will I see you again?' she asked him. 'Will you come back again?'

He smiled. 'Maybe I'll be here next Midsummer's Eve to grant you another wish, darlin'!'

She laughed, as he had meant her to. She moved away, backwards, still watching him darkly silhouetted on the horse against a sky which was now full of stars.

'What's your name?' he asked her suddenly.

She had started to run, back the way she had come. 'Rachel, it's Rachel,' she called, her voice fading in the darkness. And she ran on, skipping and laughing, not caring that when she returned there would be angry faces and she would go to bed sore and hungry. It was her special secret, and she hugged it to herself, and thought of it often and never forgot it. And although she was by the river the following Midsummer's Eve, waiting in the darkness with fast beating heart, he did not come. And she wondered if he had been a ghost, after all.

RACHEL

&

WILL

1839

CHAPTER 1

'ARE YOU SURE SHE'S QUITE suitable?'
The young woman walked around Rachel, eyeing her up and down as if she were, Rachel thought to herself, a cow brought to market. The woman had tawny hair, scraped back into a bun, and her face was pale and pinched and bad-tempered. The baby in her arms wailed and she jogged it impatiently. They said her name was Martha Potter, her husband owned a farm beyond Richmond, and she wanted a girl to help her with the children.

'She has had three children in five years,' Mrs Finn had murmured, as they made their way to the parlour where Martha Potter waited. 'And she is a second wife, so maybe there are others from the first marriage. She heard of my girls from some friend or other who was very satisfied, so . . .' She met Rachel's shining, and openly curious, dark eyes. 'I am sure you will be perfect for her, Rachel. Although you know how much I value your presence here, in the orphanage. If only Emily hadn't gone to the Talbot's last week and Suzanne wasn't ill again!'

Rachel smiled. 'Yes, Mrs Finn.'

Rachel had been in the Orphanage when Mrs Hewett was running the place, and everyone knew what a terror she had been. Things were different now, of course. Mrs Finn was in charge, and Mrs Finn was sober, industrious and wonderfully suited to her job. She believed in female education, and all her girls were literate. Rachel was seventeen now and the oldest girl there, but that was no fault of her own. Mrs Finn had kept her on, as though loath to let her go. Until now.

'Be polite, Rachel,' she was saying, 'and do keep your eyes lowered. You know how intimidating you can be, when you stare at people. They do not like it, my dear!'

Rachel smiled again, and lowered the offendingly frank gaze. She knew Mrs Finn valued her. She was a good worker, and a good teacher too, and all the children loved her. Mrs Finn called her 'a treasure' and Rachel knew, with a feeling of pride, that she meant it. But she also knew that, deep in her heart, Mrs Finn had always hoped that one day someone would come along whom she could send Rachel to with the happy knowledge that another of her 'girls' had been 'well placed'.

'She is very . . . dark,' Mrs Potter murmured. 'My own children all have the Potter blue eyes and blonde hair!' As if, Rachel thought, that were somehow better than her own black hair and black eyes. But she kept her eyes down, her hands clasped before her, looking suitably meek and mild.

'Rachel has learned all the skills of managing a house,' Mrs Finn went on smoothly. 'All my girls must learn to perform general household tasks. And she has cared for many children over the years. She can read and write and do sums, and sews beautifully. You would not do better than to take Rachel into your home, Mrs Potter, I do assure you. There is no comparison between Rachel and one of the convict girls they try to foist upon us.' She took a deep breath and then added more delicately, 'Now, if we can agree upon a suitable wage . . . ?'

Mrs Potter jogged the baby again, more through habit than necessity, Rachel decided. 'My husband can pay,' and she murmured a sum for Mrs Finn's ears only. 'Not a penny more!' she snapped, and there was no room for argument in her voice.

Mrs Finn smiled. 'Of course, I understand. These are difficult times for us all. I believe yet another bank in Hobart Town has closed its doors, and what is to become of its patrons?' Then, with a nod, 'Yes, Mrs Potter, that would be most satisfactory.' It was little enough, but it was better than they had hoped for. Mrs Finn had learned through bitter experience not to aim too high. And in due course, Rachel may find something better or—Mrs Finn's hope for all her girls—make a good and happy marriage.

'When can she come?' Mrs Potter demanded.

'Tomorrow morning. Bright and early. Can you send some conveyance, Mrs Potter? Only we keep nothing here at the orphanage. I believe you live out at Greengage?'

Mrs Potter nodded. 'Yes. At Down Farm. I'll send the cart for her tomorrow.' She looked at Rachel, as if expecting something, and Rachel gave a little bob of a curtsey. It seemed to satisfy her, for she went out with Mrs Finn, the baby beginning to wail again. After a moment, Mrs Finn returned and gave Rachel her cool, calm smile.

'That is settled then,' she said. For a moment she looked uncertain and then she took a breath. This was not exactly what she had hoped for Rachel, but . . . it would have to do. 'It may take a little time, Rachel, but I am sure Mrs Potter will come to realise how fortunate she is in you.'

Would she? Rachel sincerely hoped so. She felt suddenly sad. The orphanage had been her home, her only home, for nine years. And now she was leaving a home again, but this time, she was going out into the world. At seventeen she was bright and friendly. There was a warmth and liveliness about her that was very appealing, so that few people realised that beneath it all was still the desperate, lonely little girl, feeling the loss of her father like a betrayal, searching for the love so cruelly taken from her. Perhaps that was why she was so good with the younger children—she understood their feelings so well. She would miss them very much, but Rachel knew in her heart that the orphanage had never taken the place of a real home. For her, a home was not so much four solid walls and a roof. In her early years there had rarely been such a thing, for she and Pa had travelled constantly. And yet she had been happy, secure . . . No, for Rachel, a home would always mean a man's warm arm about her shoulders, and a man's warm smile, and the sort of unconditional love her Pa had given her.

'I'm sure everything will be all right,' Rachel murmured softly, her voice a mixture still of Pa's Devon accent and Mrs Finn's careful training. 'And if it isn't, why . . .' with a half smile, her black eyes sparkling, 'I can always come back here!'

Mrs Finn clicked her tongue, but she couldn't be angry. The girl was enchanting. Sometimes, she worried for her. That openness, that lovely inviting smile. People would take advantage of her, perhaps even hurt her. And yet Rachel must learn that for herself, for no amount of telling would prepare her for life. 'You know, Rachel,' she said briskly, 'there will always be a welcome for you here. But I do hope this is a new beginning for you, a new life.'

She was right in that! Even in the sad moments that evening, when she was saying her goodbyes to the little ones and promising to visit, all the while hugging them tightly, Rachel knew she had not begun to live yet. These nine years had been a waiting time, as though she were a player in one of the orphanage's Christmas plays, waiting in the shadowy wings, waiting to go on the bright stage and play her part. And she had been waiting for a long time.

'The cart's here!'

One of the girls was calling up the stairs. Rachel hurriedly finished cramming the last item into her trunk and slammed the lid. She was neatly dressed in her dark gown, her black hair twisted up into a heavy bun under the white bonnet. She looked clean and neat, the perfect employee, she thought, glancing into the mirror. But she did not see the glow in her cheeks and eyes, the irrepressible smile pulling at her lips, the warmth and sparkle all about her.

"I'll give you a hand with it,' Betsy muttered, pushing up her sleeves and bending to grip one of the handles. She and Rachel struggled down the narrow stairs into the hall, where Mrs Finn was standing, waiting.

'Rachel, I know you do not need my good wishes, for you will do very well without them. But you have them, nevertheless!' And she embraced the young girl warmly and smiled her goodbye.

Rachel blinked tears and laughed, and with one last look over her shoulder, went out with Betsy, the trunk again between them. She was leaving, she told herself, and still could not believe it.

The driver sat waiting, his back to them, and with a grimace at Betsy, Rachel heaved her end of the trunk up onto the back of the cart. 'Goodbye,' she breathed. 'I'll visit when I can. Promise.'

Betsy hugged her tearfully, and stepped back. 'I'll miss you, won't be the same without you,' she muttered, and wiped her cheeks with her hands. Rachel went to the seat and climbed up beside the driver, twisting to wave her arm as they started off. She continued to wave as the orphanage slid out of sight, beyond the Court House, its eager faces blurred by distance and tears. Only then did she allow herself to slip the handkerchief from her sleeve to mop at her eyes.

The tears did not last long. Rachel took a deep breath. She had always known this day would come, and so she had been prepared for it. For although Rachel loved the other children, they knew as well as she that nothing at the orphanage was permanent. New girls were always arriving, and old girls were always leaving; some wrote back happy letters, some wrote back sad letters. But no one could remain forever, whatever the fate that awaited them.

Rachel shivered and suddenly realised how cold it was. Winter held the countryside in relentless, icy fists. The sky above Richmond was a grim grey, promising no let up to the chill winds that made Rachel's eyes water now for reasons other than sadness. She pulled her cloak closer about her ears, glad of the gloves Mrs Finn had given her last Christmas. There might even be snow before the day was out.

The driver shook the reins, urging the dawdling horse on along the street. Rachel turned to look at him—a thickset young man, dark haired, face closed with his own thoughts—before dismissing him and gazing about her again with a growing, scarcely contained excitement.

She knew Richmond well enough. The orphanage girls walked to St Luke's every second Sunday for the church service. And often one or two of the girls were required to go out on a message for Mrs Finn, to various tradesmen and women in the township. Rachel had seen soldiers marching their chained, convict road gangs to spend the night at the gaol in Bathurst Street. She had seen the coach pass through from Jerusalem on its way to Risdon Ferry, and Hobart Town. There was a mill to grind the settler's flour, and a bakery and a butcher and wheelwrights and blacksmiths and hotels and inns and every other amenity required by a thriving community.

At this time of the morning the road was quiet.

Just some farmers' carts and drays, rumbling along the rough, dirt streets, avoiding the potholes that everyone complained about but no-one mended. The driver of Rachel's cart several times raised his hand to answer the greeting of others. 'George!' they called him, and once, 'Young George!' Rachel couldn't help but wriggle with excitement as they reached the edge of the town and passed the last inn.

Soon they were out in the country. Rachel accustomed herself to the swaying of the cart as they travelled the road to Greengage. If road it could be called! More like an animal track, she thought with scorn. But the driver of the cart did not seem to be bothered. They passed by a few cottages—small holdings—and a couple of children who were playing by the road waved as the cart rumbled past. Rachel waved back, laughing, her black eyes shining. She caught the driver's glance at her and the amused twist of his lips. It made her stop, folding her hands tightly in her lap. She looked at him under her lashes, and supposed he thought her silly.

'You been at the orphanage long?'

Rachel eyed him suspiciously for a moment, but he kept looking straight ahead.

'Nine years,' she told him primly, and then spoilt it by adding, 'and six months, two weeks and four days.'

He grinned.

She examined him for a moment. He wore an old shirt, open at the neck, and worn trousers. His boots were dusty and also worn. A convict labourer, perhaps, or a ticket-of-leave man, working for Government-set wages. There was a hardness about him, a toughness, that made her think his life had not been easy. She had known plenty of such men in her early years; perhaps that was why she felt an affinity with them.

Suddenly, ahead of them, the uniform of one of Richmond's field policemen caught her eye against the grey bush. He rode swiftly towards them, his mount's hooves pounding the hard, cold ground, and then he was past. The driver turned and spat onto the ground, not bothering to hide his contempt. Rachel glanced at him curiously. Mrs Roadknight had hated the police, and although Mrs Finn had done much to temper such views in Rachel, she still could not help a shiver of dislike when she saw a policeman's uniform. 'Ex-convicts the lot of them,' Mrs Roadknight used to say. 'I've never yet seen a policeman who wasn't half-drunk and ready to be bribed!' But worse than the police, worse by far, were the men who did their hunting and killing for them. The bounty hunters. 'Scum,' Mrs Roadknight would say, her lips twisting as though the word were bile in her throat. Once, in Richmond, Rachel had seen the police come riding proudly into town with two dead men in the back of a dray, the bodies jolting lifelessly. 'Bushrangers,' the people around her whispered. The two men were dirty and unkempt, their hair and beards long and scraggly, their clothes a mixture of rags and kangaroo skins... and blood. There had been another man riding with the police, laughing and joking, looking very much at home in the saddle. Someone in the crowd had murmured, 'Bounty hunter,' as if it were a curse. And Rachel had stared at that man, until she felt as if he must feel her eyes stabbing at the back of his head. How could a man, she asked herself, hunt and kill another, like an animal, for the sake of the bounty on his head? Surely, such a man was far worse than those he hunted.

George, the driver, had said nothing all this time. They had travelled in silence. The wind, if anything, was getting colder. A crow flew, cawing harshly, into the trees, its black wings snapping twigs and rustling leaves as it settled. Rachel's eyes began to flicker with weariness, until she almost fell into a doze—she had been up very early that morning. Her head nodded and she sat up with a start when the cart jolted over a dip in the uneven track. The driver was whistling to himself under his breath, as if he were very much used to his own company.

Rachel watched him a moment, secretly. She had thought him sullen, but now she realised it was just that his expression was serious. Brown eyes gazed ahead, while he rested his arms on his knees, the reins slack in his fingers. The horse must know the way by heart, for it plodded along, one feathery hoof after another.

'Have you been long at the Potter's?' she asked him, and had to clear her throat, her voice was so rusty from disuse—Rachel was rarely quiet for long. He appeared to be considering the question for far longer than it warranted.

'A few years now,' he said.

'They pay you then?' she dared, trying to discover his status.

One corner of his mouth lifted. 'They pay me.'

Would the Potters be good employers? She wondered. She hoped very much she would like Down

Farm: she hoped her letters back to the orphanage would be happy ones. 'What happened to the
nursemaid before me?' she asked the driver suddenly.

George looked at her sideways. 'Nothing happened to her. She's still there. But it's not for me to
talk about.'

Rachel pulled a face. 'Oh please! I'd like to know.
What did she do wrong?'

He relented. 'Suzy and Mrs Potter didn't get on,
that's all. She didn't do nothing wrong.' Remembering Mrs Potter, Rachel could well believe that.
There was amusement again in his eyes. 'You ask a
lot of questions,' he said. 'Sometimes it's not wise to
ask so many questions.'

Rachel bit her lip. He was right. One shouldn't
ask too many questions in Van Diemen's Land.
Too many people had secrets to hide and pasts
they would rather keep from the light of day. But
Rachel couldn't help herself. She glanced about
and realised how isolated they were on this lonely
road. Too many questions might get her murdered,
her body tossed into the scrub for the wild animals to eat. She shivered and then jumped when
he touched her arm.

'Sarah'll have a fire to warm you, when we get to
Down Farm,' he told her, and there was concern in
his eyes. 'Here, this is it now.'

Rachel looked up in surprise, and realised they
were turned up a track and that the land was cleared
here, with paddocks fenced for crops and animals.
In common with most farmers in Van Diemen's
Land, the Potters were mixed farmers—only a
few wealthier landholders had the amount of land

necessary to specialise. The track ran up to a farm house. A verandah encircled the house itself, and there were narrow windows in its shadow, as well as upper windows jutting out of the steep slant of the roof. Hens ran about the yard and some horses galloped in the paddock beside the house. There were a number of out buildings—a barn and a small stable, as well as wood shed and various other sheds, built higgledy piggledy. Behind the farm rose the bulk of a square shaped hill, topped by a dense covering of trees.

Rachel had been so engrossed in the view of Down Farm that she did not realise the cart had rumbled to the end of the track, and stopped at the gate to the yard. There were two men standing there, one older. The older man grinned at the driver and said, 'A right little charmer, eh, George?'

George grinned back. 'Aye, we've taken on trouble this time.'

It took a moment for Rachel to realise they were speaking of her, and then she sat, fuming, while the cart passed on into the yard and drew to a halt. A rooster came to strut amongst the hens, as though showing off just for Rachel.

'In there,' George said, and pointed to the door. 'I'll bring the trunk.'

Rachel threw him a flashing black look, and climbed down, turning her back. She heard him laugh as she climbed the verandah to the door, and then the vehicle was moving, leaving her. As she waited for her knock on the door to be answered, Rachel glanced about her. The place was tidy enough, though the front garden was non-existent. She let her eyes wander across the rise of the paddocks to the road beyond and the grey sky above. Down Farm was a world of its own.

The door had opened. A maid stood there, perhaps a few years older than Rachel but many inches shorter. She blinked up at Rachel for a moment, before saying into the room to her left, 'Tis the new girl, Mrs Potter! I'll send her in then, will I?'

Mrs Potter must have made some answer, for the maid glanced back at Rachel and said in a breathy voice, 'Wipe your feet, then, and go through. Mrs Potter is waiting.'

Rachel wiped her feet, and went in. There was a room to the right of the door which she guessed to be the front parlour, reserved for visitors. For Mrs Potter had a visitor now.

Reverend Jones was someone Rachel knew well from church on Sundays and his little talks to the girls at the orphanage. He was an elderly man, with a long face, who rode a grey mare about his large parish. Rachel made a bobbing curtsey to them both.

'This is the girl I spoke of, Reverend,' Mrs Potter announced importantly. She was dressed in a good dark gown, her hair neatly bound up beneath a lace cap.

'Ah yes, Rachel Naish,' Reverend Jones smiled toothily. 'I know her, of course. A good girl, very capable.'

Rachel was relieved he had forgotten, or perhaps he chose not to mention, her few transgressions. Mrs Potter looked pleased with herself. 'Well, I'm sure she will be of use to me. I know it is a wife's duty to give her husband children, but really, sometimes . . .' her eyes blinked rapidly, and she gave a little cough. The Reverend looked down at his hands.

'Quite so,' he said.

'And Suzy was quite impossible. She was more interested in the yard men than my children!'

Reverend Jones cleared his throat, glancing at Rachel whom Mrs Potter had clearly forgotten. She patted her hair and murmured sharply, 'That will be all for now, Rachel. Sarah will show you where you will be sleeping, and then you can go and meet the children.'

'Yes ma'am,' and Rachel bobbed her little curtsey and went out.

Sarah was waiting beyond the door, and whispered, 'This way. Someone'll bring your trunk up in a minute.'

'This way' was along a short, cluttered hallway and up the narrow staircase to a cold little room poked away at the back of the house under the eaves. 'Mrs Potter says you're to sleep here, so's to be close to the children in the night. They're just down the end there.' Sarah's blue eyes were wide.

'Does she indeed,' Rachel murmured. Sleepless nights would probably be her lot. But then, she had had them before, at the Orphanage. She went to the casement and looked out. There was a view over a vegetable garden—rather bare in this season—and the barn and then beyond to the glowering hill. The sky was a dark steel grey—a 'snow sky' Mrs Finn would have called it.

'Do you like it here, Sarah?' she asked the other girl, flashing her a friendly smile over her shoulder.

Sarah eyed her warily, as though she had learned to mistrust friendliness. 'I like it well enough, though I've no choice but to stay on, I was assigned here twelve months ago from Hobart Town. Not that Captain Potter isn't always kind to me, even when she . . . I mean, Mrs Potter, when she says I'm useless.'

Rachel laughed. 'Mrs Potter sounds as if she runs the farm and everyone on it. What is her husband like?'

Sarah glanced over her shoulder again, as though expecting the Potters to be ranged behind her. 'He lets her have her way with the house, I know that. I wasn't here before he married for the second time, but I've heard said everything changed a lot. She soon smartened things up.'

I'll bet she did, Rachel thought to herself. But all she said aloud was, 'Are there any other children? From the first marriage, I mean?'

Sarah shook her head. 'Only the three that belong to Martha. Isn't that enough for you?'

Rachel smiled. 'It's quite enough, thank you, Sarah.'

Sarah nodded her head and backed away. 'I'd better go. I've the vegetables to peel. Mrs Potter likes the dinner on the table at one sharp, when the men come in.'

And she had gone, the door closing behind her.

Rachel sighed, and sat down on the bed. It was too firm, but that didn't worry her. She was not concerned with small, cold rooms and hard beds. Rachel had never known luxury and did not hunger after it, rather people interested her, and there seemed quite a deal to be interested in at Down Farm.

A thud on her door heralded her trunk. George

stepped into the room and dumped the luggage on the floor. Rachel glanced at him uneasily. 'Thank you,' she said stiffly. He grinned at her, and closed the door behind him, leaving Rachel staring silently at the empty room.

Rachel ate her dinner with the Potters—she was expected to supervise the children. Mrs Potter held the baby, but the other two, Martha for her mother—but called Matty—and Francis for his father—called Frank—were Rachel's province. The baby was called Victoria, after the new Queen in England, and so far had not descended to Vicky.

Captain Potter was about forty years old; a large, quiet man who let his wife speak for him while he murmured monosyllabic replies. His hands were red, scrubbed clean for the table, but there was a ring of grime about his wrists under the cuffs and his hair was standing on end. A handsome face had sunk into weatherbeaten folds, but he was still handsome. He had looked at Rachel once, a hard penetrating look, and did not look again, but she felt that he had seen more in that one look than his wife would in a hundred.

Rachel already had *her* measure. Martha Potter wanted to join the ranks of the 'gentleman' farmers of the colony, the military who owned most of the land because they had been given preferential treatment by Governor Arthur, before he left the colony in 1835. Martha wanted to be a lady of leisure and refinement, with a house in Hobart Town and a manager to oversee her country property. She had already informed Rachel that the children would go to a school and she had heard of an excellent one from her sister in Hobart Town. Certainly, the parish school in Richmond was beneath them. Her sister appeared to have all Martha wanted herself and envy was laced with pride throughout her conversation.

The fact that Captain Potter took all this, nodding and agreeing and not uttering a single word made Rachel wonder if he even heard what his wife was saying.

'Matty has upset her dish, Rachel!' Martha Potter screeched.

Rachel, coming out of her reverie, scooped it up, wiping the worst of the mess with a napkin. Matty began to cry and the baby followed suit. Captain Potter glanced at the last of his meal, hesitated, and then rose swiftly to his feet.

'I will see you this evening, my love,' he murmured, and dutifully kissed the head of each of his young children, before closing the door thankfully after him.

Mrs Potter sighed. 'I think it is time for baby's nap,' she said. 'And I will show you where the children sleep and what your other duties involve, Rachel.'

The 'other duties' were endless.

Rachel listened, wondering how Martha expected all these tasks to be accomplished before nightfall. Matty and Frank sat, wide-eyed, gazing at Rachel. When their mother had taken Baby Victoria away, Rachel told them a story about a dragon, delighting in the way their eyes grew even wider, and how they chuckled at the end.

'Tell us some more,' Frank demanded.

But she shook her head. 'I will tell you a story tonight, when you're in bed. For now, you will both be good while I mend some clothes.'

They were as good as could be expected of two energetic children of four and two and a half. Later, Sarah brought Rachel a tray with some tea on it, as well as milk for the children, and a plump cake, still warm from the oven. The baby was awake by then and Rachel held it on her knee while Martha went about her own duties with a free hand.

'Cook says she hasn't heard a peep from the little ones all afternoon,' Sarah told her, wide-eyed. 'What have you done to 'em?'

Rachel laughed. 'I'm used to children.'

'Even a little imp like Master Frank here?' Sarah muttered, eyeing the little boy uneasily as he grinned back at her. 'He used to give poor Suzy 'ell! That's when the mistress caught her,' with a quick glance at the door, 'swearing fit to make a sailor blush!'

Rachel smiled and ruffled Frank's hair. 'I've seen naughtier than Master Frank.'

'Well, you're better at it than Suzy, that's for sure.'

Rachel looked at her curiously, suddenly remembering her conversation with George. 'What happened to Suzy?'

Sarah moved closer, lowering her voice so that the children strained to hear. 'Suzy's still here. She's all right, in her way, but Mrs Potter don't want her around the children. She's a bit lazy, and she's always making eyes at the men.'

Rachel looked forward with interest to meeting Suzy. 'Are there many men for Suzy to make eyes at?' she asked with a smile.

Sarah pursed her lips. 'There's Old George and Young George, you've met him. And then there's Jack and Rummy and Pat and a few of the convicts we get on and off from Richmond, when we want more land cleared. There are always strangers up at the inn in Greengage, passing through, and sometimes one will call in to see Captain Potter. His brother used to live here too, Captain Potter's brother I mean. He went off looking for some land of his own and I haven't heard where he ended up. But it's mostly Young George that Suzy wriggles her hips at. She likes George.'

Rachel's eyebrows lifted in surprise. 'George? Why him?'

Sarah stared at her. 'Haven't you seen him? He's handsomer than any of the others at Down Farm. Suzy drools at the mouth when he goes near her.'

Rachel laughed. George had not struck her as so desirable, but then perhaps she hadn't really looked properly at him—she had been too sad at leaving the Orphanage and too nervous about arriving at Down Farm. Next time she saw him she would pay him more attention.

Sarah had not spoken again and Rachel saw that she was deep in her own thoughts. The girl was tiny, like a child, although there was no doubting she was a grown woman. Her fair hair was so light it could more properly be called white-blonde, and her eyes were pale and blue, doll-like in their roundness. What could Sarah have done to be transported across the seas to Van Diemen's

Land? Rachel opened her mouth to ask and then didn't quite dare. George had told her she asked too many questions, and he was right. She would wait a little bit longer, until she felt Sarah trusted her, and then she would ask.

As the day drew in, Captain Potter returned to the house and she heard him calling out instructions to one of his men. Rachel washed and readied the children for bed, and then gave them their supper—they did not take their evening meal with their parents. She told them the promised story and tucked them up in bed. Outside, she heard the rumble of a horse-drawn cart and laughter. Down Farm men returning from their day's work.

Rachel went to the window, peering out, but it was too dark to see much. The silhouette of a man on a horse suddenly struck her as familiar, but he was gone in a moment, and the memory with him. The baby, which she had placed in a crib in the corner, began to cry and with a sigh Rachel went to pick her up. Victoria was fretful and difficult, and Rachel was glad when Martha Potter came at last to take the baby into her own room to feed and settle there. Even so it was late when Rachel was finally able to creep into her own bed. She was tired, but for some reason she found it difficult to sleep, perhaps because of the unfamiliar country noises. She lay listening to the sounds from outside, the infrequent lowing of a cow and the bark of a dog. Later, a horse arrived and there were more voices and laughter, and a snatch of a song. For a long time she lay there, feeling lost without the familiar noises of the town Orphanage and the long room, with its beds full of small bodies. It had been her home for so long.

Soon, she told herself firmly, I will feel just as much at home at Down Farm. Soon, I will smile to myself and think how glad I am to be here, how happy I am with my life. I will grow to love Captain Potter and Martha, and Matty and Frank and the baby, and Sarah and Suzy and George and all the rest. But as she drifted into sleep, it was Pa she thought of, though for some reason he was riding a horse, a black silhouette against the starlit sky, and she was riding with him.

CHAPTER 2

MRS POTTER HAD BEEN UP to the baby several times in the night and was not in a good mood the next morning. Rachel kept the other two children out of her way, dressing them and breakfasting with them, and then taking them outside to play.

It was cold again, but at least the sky was clear and the snow she had thought due any moment had not come down. Rachel managed to amuse Frank and Matty for a time, but when her attention wandered for a moment, Matty promptly fell over on the hard ground and began to wail, and then Frank started up in sympathy. Above the noise, Rachel heard a voice behind her.

'Not doing too well, are you?'

She turned her head and looked up at George. His eyes were tired and small, as though he had just got up. But his smile was warm and, unlike yesterday, somehow endearing. He was almost handsome, Rachel thought in surprise. Perhaps Suzy was right.

Behind her, the children had stopped crying and

had found some other form of amusement. Matty was pulling leaves off a shrub and Frank had discovered the ginger cat, sheltering by the wall in a watery patch of sunshine.

'I'm doing better than Suzy, by all accounts,' she retorted to George, and smiled back.

Rachel had had enough practise flirting with the butcher's boy to know how it was done. But the butcher's boy hadn't really appealed to her, just as George didn't really appeal to her now. No man had yet stirred in her more than a passing interest. And besides, flirting wasn't her way. Rachel was too direct.

'Suzy wasn't made to be a nursemaid,' George declared with a glint in his eye. Rachel wondered what Suzy was made to be, but decided it was wiser not to ask. 'I've been down to the inn at Greengage,' he went on, when she remained silent. 'Had to get some bits and pieces for Mrs Potter. Had a drink while I was there,' and he winked.

Rachel shook her head at him. 'Drinking rots the stomach and befuddles the mind.' She quoted a favourite saying of Mrs Finn.

George grinned. 'You and Mrs Potter should get on well,' he told her, and Rachel knew it wasn't a compliment. 'Don't you know this country was built on grog?'

Rachel only shook her head at him again. 'Where are you from, George?' she asked, her interest stirred.

He shrugged and his eyes became wary. 'Here and there.'

Rachel opened her mouth to try again, but before she could speak the ginger cat struck. Frank began to scream. Rachel shouted and sent the thing off with a well aimed kick. Then Frank had to be soothed, and Matty too, who was crying in support of her brother. When she had the situation under control again, Rachel found that Young George had gone.

During the midday meal, Mrs Potter did little but complain about Captain Potter's brother, who Rachel remembered Sarah saying had gone away to find land of his own. 'Not a penny,' Martha declared, 'after all he had from us while living at Down Farm.'

Captain Potter filled his mouth with a forkful of stew, and remained silent while he chewed. Martha eyed him with increasing irritation.

'Do you have any idea where he is?'

'None at all, my dear,' he mumbled, and kept on eating.

'He was always a liar,' she declared, and then looked as if she feared she had said too much. But Captain Potter did not even glance at her. 'I mean,' she went on, emboldened, 'there was that girl over at Jerusalem, who swore he was the father of her brat, *and* that widow at Richmond.' Her face darkened. 'I never liked him, Frank. I did not tell you so at the time, because he was your brother. But I never liked his manners or his ways. Some people are not to be trusted, and Israel Potter is one of them!'

But Captain Potter still said nothing at all.

'Are you going in to Greengage this afternoon?' she asked him sharply, giving up on the brother at last. 'Only George forgot to get the brandy I particularly asked for, for Cook's fruit cake. I don't know what he was doing all that time. I really think you need to speak to him.'

Captain Potter nodded. 'I'll speak to him. I have to get the mare reshod, so when I take her in to Will I'll get your brandy for you myself, Martha.'

Far from being pacified, Martha frowned and made an uneasy gesture. 'Do we really need to patronise that man?' she whispered loudly, while Rachel pretended not to listen. 'He's a drunkard and everybody knows it. Oh, I know it was all very sad, about his wife . . . she was my friend, too! But to allow himself to go to pieces like that,' and she grimaced. 'It isn't nice, is it?'

Captain Potter looked at her. There was something in his glance that made Rachel feel cold. Even Martha felt it. She touched her hair, her bodice, little birdlike gestures of unease. 'What is it? What have I said?'

Her husband stared at his plate, taking his time to answer. 'Will is not a drunkard. He is a man in torment. Besides, he's a friend.'

'But he is always at the inn Agnes says so—'

'Agnes is a gossip, Martha, and you shouldn't listen to her. Will drinks, yes, but he is not a drunkard.'

Not yet. The words were unspoken, but Rachel could almost hear them on Martha's tongue. Captain Potter shook his head and stood up.

'I must get back. Goodbye, my dear,' and with a smile which didn't quite reach his eyes he went out and closed the door.

Martha waved her hand irritably. 'I don't know,' she muttered to no-one in particular. 'Some people just don't like to hear the truth.'

Later, as they ascended the narrow stairs, Martha

informed her, 'I would rather you did the children's ironing, Rachel. Not that Sarah doesn't do an adequate job, but. . .' with a twitch of her lips. 'You can iron, can't you?'

Rachel agreed that she could, her heart sinking. More tasks. Life was easier at the orphanage. She glanced at the window in passing, and sighed for the crisp, cold day and the rolling paddocks down to the Richmond-Greengage road. She had hoped the world outside the orphanage would be more interesting than this. As it was, the afternoon dragged and by the time the supper tray had come and the children were in bed, there were moths fluttering at the casement and the dog was barking again.

Sarah came to collect the supper tray, and smiled, her face all hollows in the lamplight as she looked at the children. 'Lovely, aren't they, when they're asleep?' she murmured. 'Pity Frank's such a little demon.'

Rachel smiled back and went with Sarah to the door. The house seemed very quiet. 'Where is everyone?' she asked.

Sarah shrugged. 'Him and her are in the parlour, pretending to be gentry,' she said, and there was a malicious edge to her voice Rachel had not heard there before. 'Cook's gone home to Greengage and Suzy's out somewhere with George. I don't know what they're doing and I don't want to.'

'I spoke with George today,' Rachel murmured. 'He doesn't like to talk about himself much, does he?'

Sarah shrugged again. 'We all have our secrets. He's had a hard time of it, Young George. Prefers to put it behind him. There're some who like to go over and over their lives, and get rid of the pain that way. But those like George, they need to hide it away inside, and pretend it never happened.'

'What about you Sarah?' Rachel asked her gently. 'What do you like to do?'

Sarah glanced at her, the blue eyes almost startled for a moment. 'I'm not ashamed of what I did,' she said firmly. 'I stole because I was starving and that's a fact. Me parents came from the country—London drew lots of country folk. They thought it'd be better to be out of work and hungry in London than out of work and hungry at home. Well, they were wrong. We lived in Islington, and sometimes I can still smell that street. One day I woke up and looked about and there they all were, me sisters and me brothers and me Ma, all starving, all crowded into one room. There was no work for us, and Da had gone out a year before and never came back. So I went down to the market and I stole food and I were caught. Then it was prison and the Old Bailey and . . . well, now I'm here and eating well, and they're still there and probably still starving.'

She spoke quietly, without rancor, and yet Rachel could feel the anger in her at the unfairness of it all. Sarah shook her head and sighed. 'I'd best get on,' she said, and began to descend the stairs.

'What about Suzy?' Rachel asked. 'What did she do?'

Sarah turned and looked at her, her smile lopsided. 'You do ask a lot of questions,' she said mockingly. 'George was right in that at least.'

'What did George say about me?' Rachel demanded, and then laughed at Sarah's expression.

'Sorry. I only ask because I'm interested.'

Sarah smiled. 'George said you were as fresh and lovely as a daisy, but you asked too many questions for his taste, though he thought it'd not be long before one of the men took you away from Mrs Potter, and that you'd go willingly. And Suzy,' with a grimace, 'she was sent out for being on the streets and she don't care who knows it!'

Rachel felt the colour come into her face. She knew what 'being on the streets' meant. She had been respectably brought up at the orphanage, almost sheltered, but there were still girls there who gloried in imparting such knowledge to others. She was not completely innocent, just naive.

The day had given her much to ponder on, as she lay at last in her bed. There was Young George, who kept his secrets, and Suzy, who didn't care who knew hers, while Sarah was full of bitterness at life's injustice. And there was Israel Potter, the liar, while Will was a tormented man who drank too much . . . Rachel sighed and rested her cheek against her hand on the pillow. I like Captain Potter, she decided. There was something honourable about him, something honest that appealed to her. Like Pa, Rachel felt she could always trust him.

The following morning Mrs Barber called.

Mrs Barber, Rachel learned, was Martha's best friend, and her husband owned a farm on the other side of Greengage. So she tidied the children up and, hand in hand, they descended to the front parlour. Mrs Barber sat in the best chair while Martha Potter rose with a tight little smile, saying, 'Come and say good morning to Mrs Barber, my dears. See how they've grown, Agnes!'

Agnes beamed. 'On yes, yes indeed,' she twittered, and gazed at Matty with her bouncing blonde curls and big blue eyes and Frank with his sullen little face betrayed by a wobbly lip. 'You're so lucky, Martha.'

Rachel examined Agnes Barber. She was small and dainty, with neat clothes. Brown hair curled about a round, dimpled face and clear blue eyes the colour of cornflowers. She was pretty, but was already beginning to fade.

'This is Rachel,' Martha Potter was saying. 'She's the girl from the Orphanage. Rachel is helping me with the children. I don't mind telling you, Agnes, that they are just too much for me in my present state of health.'

Agnes's eyes melted with sympathy. 'I know how you suffer, dear Martha. And how brave you are sometimes. If only we all had your courage.'

Rachel blinked, wondering whether the woman was being sarcastic. But there was nothing of that in Agnes Barber's gaze. She meant it all right. Rachel felt her lips twitch and almost smiled.

Martha preened herself. 'Well, some of us are braver than others, Agnes. I was saying to Frank only yesterday that Will Trigg has let himself go to pieces.'

Agnes nodded, pursing her lips, and settled in her chair ready for a good gossip. 'It was a tragedy, dear,' she ventured cautiously.

Martha would have none of that. 'Oh yes, it was a tragedy,' she agreed dismissively. 'Hannah was such a sweet girl. But these things happen, and we must learn to rise above them. Will has to take a hold on his life, before it's too late.'

Agnes' blue eyes fixed on Martha. 'My Tom saw him down at the inn a week since—Tom had to collect some money owed him,' she added quickly, flustered, as Martha's eyes narrowed. 'And, my dear, Tom said Will Trigg could hardly walk!'

'I heard he was in Richmond last month, visiting that dreadful inn The King's Head, and you know what sort of women go there.'

Agnes's eyes popped like two boiled lollies. 'Shame! Of course, no decent woman will go near him while he—' she broke off, realising Rachel was listening with rapt attention, and cleared her throat in embarrassment.

'You may take the children out now, Rachel,' Martha said sharply. Rachel curtseyed and hand in hand with Matty and Frank, went back out and closed the door. But not before she heard Martha saying, 'He gets worse every day, Agnes! Frank still takes business to him, but others are beginning to go elsewhere—'

Rachel grimaced. Just as the conversation had become interesting she was sent away! Matty put her thumb in her mouth and began to suck it while Frank was swinging on Rachel's hand. Outside, the day was cold and grey. And it was raining, a misty, miserable rain that closed them in as effectively as a curtain. Rachel sighed and wondered what she could do to amuse the children.

'Psst!'

Rachel lifted her head in surprise. Sarah was standing in the kitchen doorway at the end of the narrow hallway, beckoning. The children broke away and ran to Sarah. She smiled down at them and presented them each with a biscuit in the shape of a little man. She winked at Rachel. 'Best way to keep 'em quiet,' she said.

The kitchen had a stone flagged floor and a large scrubbed table for preparing the meals. Cook usually sat in the rocker by the hearth, but today she was absent in Richmond, visiting her daughter. Cook, Rachel had learned, was married to Old George and they lived together at Greengage in a cottage beside the inn, which was, so Sarah said, handy for their daily 'dose'.

'Van Diemen's Land is sodden with grog,' Sarah muttered scornfully. 'I think they must shoot any teetotaller's, the same as they shoot savages.'

Rachel had begun to descend the steps when a sound from the table made her aware they were not alone. Suzy, she thought, and did not need Sarah's introductions. Suzy smiled lazily, showing large white teeth, her eyes were coloured hazel and darkly lashed and her hair was corn fair. She was a big girl, full bosomed and broad hipped, with rounded arms and plump little fingers.

'What are those two bitches talkin' about?' she asked, nodding towards the parlour as she took one of the biscuits for herself and bit off its head with relish.

Rachel sat down on the chair Suzy pushed towards her and wondered whether she should answer. Martha would not like her gossiping with Suzy, and yet the urge to do so was overwhelming.

'They were talking about someone called Will,' she replied carefully.

Suzy smiled, arranging her wrinkled skirts about her as if they were made of satin instead of rather dirty blue cotton. 'Will Trigg,' she said with a slow grin. 'He's drinkin' deeper every day, soon he'll drown in it and that will be that. A waste of a man if ever there was!'

Sarah tut-tutted and shook her head, glancing behind her. The children sat and ate their biscuits like angels.

'There were plenty o' women would have had him, after his wife died. And now they shake their heads over him and say they're glad they didn't make that mistake.' She laughed, spluttering biscuit on the table. 'Though I reckon if he gave any of 'em half the chance, they'd be in his bed like shot from a gun, ready to have their go at reformin' him.'

'Does he need reforming?' Rachel asked curiously. 'Perhaps he's happy the way he is.'

Suzy lifted her eyebrows. 'If he keeps going the way he is, he won't be much use to any woman, even the whores at the Kings Head. A woman wants more from a man than a rum-sodden kiss and a promise. If you know what I mean.' And she winked slowly and suggestively.

Rachel didn't know what she meant. Sarah tittered nervously, and obviously did. The children reached for another biscuit and Suzy handed them one each, her eyes softening. Whatever Frank had done to her, she harboured no grudges Rachel thought to herself.

'What happened to his wife?' Rachel asked with

interest.

It was Sarah who answered her. 'It was an accident. She was comin' back from Richmond in the gig, and it overturned. Crushed her, it did, and the child inside her. Both dead by the time they got her back to Greengage. Poor Will. It must have been the end for him. He just don't care any more.' And she sighed, her round blue eyes filling with tears.

Suzy took another biscuit for herself. 'Will is the blacksmith in Greengage,' she explained. 'But he's losing a customer a week. Because he drinks too much and looks like he's just in off a convict ship.'

Sarah made her face a study of innocence. 'George drinks too much and he is off a convict ship.'

Suzy shot her a narrowed glance. 'George is different,' she snapped. Her hazel eyes went dreamy and she smiled to herself. 'George is all right.'

Sarah glanced at Rachel and her eyes laughed.

'George reminds me of a man I used to know, back home,' Suzy went on, still gazing into space. 'He were a hard man too, and sometimes cruel, but there was a gentleness beneath it all. I think men have to grow hard on the outside, here in Van Diemen's Land. I think the soft ones drown in the grog and the misery, like Will Trigg. No, George would do me. We'd suit just fine, George and me.'

Suzy, Mrs Finn would have said, was a deep thinker. Rachel watched the other girl with interest, noting the tiny scar beside her left eye, and the sprinkling of pock marks marring her skin. Life had not been smooth and easy for Suzy, there was hardship and grief in the hollows under her eyes and the tightening of her jaw, and yet she had lived through it and was looking to the future, with Young George, if she could get him.

'What about you, Rachel?' Suzy's lazy smile was turned in Rachel's direction. 'Tell us about yourself.'

Rachel did, repeating her well worn tale of Pa and Mathew Brady, and how Pa had been shot for the sake of ten pounds.

'You're a one!' Sarah breathed. 'A bushranger for a father. I heard that Mathew Brady was a real gentleman, and even them ones he robbed loved him and wept when he hung in Hobart Town.'

Rachel sighed. 'Pa was the same. A gentleman.' Her eyes narrowed. 'They had no right to shoot him dead. Mrs Roadknight used to say that she had never seen a policeman worth a pinch of respect.'

Suzy laughed, and then shook her head at Rachel's angry glance. 'He was breaking the law,' she said matter of factly. 'Even though half of Vandemon would have said good luck to him, he was still breaking it. So the Governor sent out his men to track him down like a dog and shoot him. I've known a few bandits that deserved no better—they were near enough to wild animals.'

There was a silence, and then Rachel whispered furiously, 'Pa was different. He was good and kind. How can you know?'

Suzy shrugged. 'I knew one o' them trackers, in Hobart Town. One o' them bounty hunters. He knew the bush like a savage—at least as well as the men he was hunting. Some o' them bushrangers were bad men, and he told me things that made my hair curl. Maybe some, like your Pa, were good but most o' them weren't. They killed and stole and lived like animals, and that was how they deserved to die.'

Rachel gripped her hands in her lap. Anger rose up in her, but she held it in. Suzy knew nothing! It was Rachel who had lived among these men, Rachel who understood them. 'Bounty hunters,' she managed at last, and her voice shook. 'They're the worst of all. They kill a man for money, like a kangaroo to sell its skin. Only they cut off a man's head and bring that back, to save carrying the body. Murder is their trade. Like a ... a butcher or a baker or a nursemaid. How can that be right?'

Suzy and Sarah looked at each other. 'Not all o' them are murderers,' Suzy retorted, but Rachel wasn't listening.

'It was a bounty hunter killed my Pa!' she shouted.

The children had stopped eating and were looking at her, wide eyed, and she bit her lip, realising how her emotion had frightened them. She took a deep breath and forced herself to be calm.

'I'm sorry,' she managed, and laughed shakily. 'It still hurts me, after so many years. He was all I had, and they killed him for a ten pound reward.'

Sarah touched her arm. 'I know,' she whispered. 'I feel the same. Somehow things hardly ever turn out the way they should. I don't even know if my family are still alive. I think of them all the time, and I hope. But there's nothing I can do, over here on the other side of the world. I wrote once ... well, someone wrote a letter for me. But there was no letter back.'

Suzy smiled her lazy smile. 'We're a happy lot, ladies! Come on, eat up! Cook will be back soon, and then it'll be back to work for us all.' And she handed them each another biscuit with a flourish.

After the children were in bed that evening, and Martha had taken the baby to her own room, Rachel put aside her mending and went to the window. The clouds had gone, and the night was clear and cold, with masses of stars to light the dark, distant sky. Rachel felt restless and uncomfortable. Perhaps it was the talk with Suzy that made her so. She wished she hadn't got so angry, usually she didn't allow her feelings to get the better of her, but today she had burned with passionate anger.

Rachel sighed and knew she would never be able to go to sleep. After a moment of hesitation, she pulled her cloak about her shoulders and crept downstairs. The house was very quiet, although she thought she could hear soft voices from the parlour where the family usually went to while away the hours until bedtime—and they were few enough, for they kept early hours here at Down Farm.

Outside, the air was cold, taking her breath and making the skin on her face sting. Rachel wrapped her arms about herself and walked slowly to the yard gate, opening it enough to squeeze through and out, into the lane. The night was so still, her breath turned to white mist before her eyes and as she walked she saw more mist, pale swirling fingers of it, filling the hollows and the dips in the laneway and the paddocks, eerie and secretive.

The ginger cat ran past her, startling her so much she cried out, and then laughed at her own foolishness. 'Puss!' she called softly, but the animal ignored her, lying switching its tail in the grass through the fence, just beyond her reach. Lamplight wavered through one of the shuttered windows of the farm house, and then was extinguished. The dog was barking again, the sound echoing about the hills, and it was a moment before Rachel realised there was a horse coming.

At first, she thought it must be far away—sound travelled long distances on still nights. But it came on so suddenly that Rachel hardly realised the rider had turned up the laneway before he was upon her. She stepped sharply back, hard against the wooden rail of the fence, bruising her back. At the same time the beast flashed by, puffing from the hard ride, and Rachel felt the wind of its passing.

For a moment she was too startled to move. The horse and rider had cleared the yard gate and come to a rapid halt near the stable. Rachel took a deep breath, trying to still the shaking of her limbs, and watched the rider jump down and lead his mount inside the building. A light, faint and yellow, suddenly shone out through the small window high in the wall. Was it George? she wondered. The man, from the brief glimpse she had had of him, seemed of a similar size to Young George. No doubt he had been to the inn in Greengage again.

For a little longer Rachel stood leaning back against the railing, breathing in the night air. The mist was growing thicker, swirling about her hem and shoes now, clammy and cold and a little frightening. The cat had vanished into the darkness, and she was alone. The light in the stables beckoned her, and soon she gave up trying to resist it.

As she drew closer, Rachel could hear someone whistling under their breath. Cautiously, she reached the doorway and looked inside. A lamp hung from a hook on the wall, its light flickering over the man with his back to her, while leaving the further corners of the stables in thick darkness. He was rubbing down the horse with firm, strong movements. His dark hair was still untidy from the wild ride, and he was wearing old, dusty trousers, a stained shirt and boots, well worn beneath the dirt of the road.

At first she thought it was indeed Young George, and then as she watched the light play over his shoulders and arms, while he worked on the horse, Rachel realised that this man was bigger, taller, and his hair was darker and longer. It wasn't George after all, it wasn't anybody she had yet met at Down Farm.

'Does Martha know you're wandering around in the dark?' he asked suddenly, and glanced at her over his shoulder.

Rachel was surprised that he had known she was there. She made an awkward movement, embarrassed to be caught staring. 'The children are abed. I have finished my duties. Surely my time is my own, sir?'

He gave a short laugh. 'Don't be too sure of that.'

He had finished what he was doing. The horse was munching on some feed and he gave it a last pat before closing the stall. He turned, wiping his hands carefully on a piece of sacking, and looked at her. For a moment he just looked, his eyes ranging over her in a way she had never experienced before, as though he had the right. She took a breath to tell him he was rude, but before she could say anything he spoke again.

'Have you been assigned here?'

Rachel shook her head, her eyes flashing in the lamplight. 'Have you come to see Captain Potter?' she countered. 'Should I wake him?'

'God no!' he said sharply. 'Martha wanted the mare by tomorrow, so I brought her over tonight myself, just to impress her,' and he grimaced. 'I'll take the roan and George can pick it up when he comes in the morning.' And suddenly he smiled, as though sharing a joke with her. His voice, she thought, was dark and smooth, like the river at night, flowing under the stars and the shadowy bulk of the bridge . . . Rachel flushed for such a thought, hoping he hadn't read it in her eyes.

'You're the nursery maid then,' he murmured, when she didn't speak.

Rachel looked up in surprise. 'How did you know that?'

'George,' he teased. 'He described you in detail.'

George! She flushed again, feeling awkward and self conscious. Had he told this man she was as fresh and lovely as a daisy? Was that why he had stared so?

'You don't look the sort to stick it out here for too long,' the stranger went on.

'What sort do I look like then?' Rachel retorted, and then wished she hadn't.

'What sort?' he mocked. He came forward until he was only a step away from her and she had to look up to see into his eyes. They were grey, like a snow sky. And his dark hair was too long and needed a wash, as did the rest of him. She smelt the drink on him then, and felt such a stab of disappointment she was shocked. Gently, he reached out a hand to touch her cheek. Rachel felt the warm, calloused tips of his fingers on her skin and shivered. 'I meant only that you look made for better things,' he whispered. Then, suddenly, he had dropped his hand, turning away from her. 'Go back to bed,' he said sharply, not even looking at her over his shoulder. 'Girls like you shouldn't be wandering around out here anyway.'

He was moving to saddle the other horse. For a moment Rachel stood and watched him, the colour flooding her face, too surprised to do otherwise. And then she turned and ran, back to the house. What was wrong with her? Why had she stood there, as though her feet had taken root in the earth, while Will Trigg touched her as if he had every right? For it had been Will Trigg she had met this night, she was certain of it, and she didn't know whether to be sorry or glad.

CHAPTER 3

MRS POTTER WAS ILL.
And Rachel was left with all three children as well as the task of carrying messages to and from the bedchamber to Sarah and Suzy and Cook. Cook took it in very bad part.

'You're not the mistress here,' Cook told her roundly, 'I only take my orders from the mistress.'

'The mistress is ill,' Rachel retorted with strained patience. 'And if you want to go up and bother her, go on. But she was puking into a bowl when last I saw her, and she won't take kindly to being interrupted.'

Cook subsided with a mutter, but there were no more arguments. Suzy treated it as a joke and an opportunity to sit and rest in the wintry sunlight, flirting with George whenever he happened to pass. And he seemed to be passing a great deal that day. Rachel listened to them talking and laughing together in low voices. Once, when she was by the upstairs window, she saw George grab Suzy about the waist and kiss her thoroughly on the mouth. She didn't struggle. In fact she appeared to be kissing him back.

When Martha Potter was no better the next morning, Captain Potter sent for the doctor. Rachel, balancing the baby on one hip, waited in the parlour and when the doctor descended the stairs, she offered tea and some cake fresh from the oven.

'Thank you, my dear.' He was thirsty, he said. 'Four calls this morning and another three this afternoon. All the same complaint, I'm afraid. But I wouldn't have thought there was anything to worry about in Mrs Potter's case, she seems a strong, healthy young woman. Just keep her quiet and let her rest for a day or two, and she'll get over it.'

Rachel nodded, and glanced up as Captain Potter came into the room. 'Tea for you, sir?'

He hesitated, and then nodded with a smile. 'Thank you, Rachel, I will.'

The doctor made conversation—he seemed to know all about the Potters. Rachel supposed he couldn't help but know about the families in the district in his occupation. 'How's your brother, Frank?' he asked, biting into the cake. 'Doing well, is he?'

Frank Potter pulled a face. 'Haven't heard from him,' he replied. 'Last we knew he had taken passage to Port Phillip, to see what the land is like over there. Plenty of it, by all accounts. Enough to run sheep and make a good living, even in these bad times, if you have the capital.'

'Israel was always a restless one,' the doctor murmured. 'Perhaps the responsibility of farming will settle him down.'

But Captain Potter looked doubtful. He finished

his tea, and rose to his feet reluctantly. 'I've a calf looking poorly,' he said abruptly. 'I'd better see to it. Unless you want to, Jack?' with a feeble attempt at humour.

The doctor smiled weakly. 'I've enough patients at the moment, Frank, without turning to calves.' When he was gone, bolting down the last of his cake, Rachel sighed and looked at the baby. Victoria looked back at her with big, innocent blue eyes.

'At least the children are well,' Captain Potter said that evening. He had climbed the stairs to see them to bed in their mother's absence. The baby was gumming at a bowl of bread and milk and seemed to be enjoying the experience. 'I'm sure Mrs Potter will be well again soon,' he added. 'She's of a strong constitution. Not like my first wife, my Letty.' For a moment he looked so sad, Rachel felt tears sting her own eyes. Captain Potter was a kind man, and she had come to feel even fonder of him during these past days when Martha was locked away in her sickroom. She couldn't help but wonder why he had married someone like Martha. Had he loved her? For although he showed kindness and consideration to his young wife, Rachel had come to the conclusion there was nothing deeper. Sometimes he looked at her in such a way . . . as if he were observing a total stranger. Could love fade so quickly? It was a mournful thought.

Pa had said something to her once, when he

was speaking about Rachel's mother, Mary. How peculiar, Rachel thought, that she should remember it after all these years! 'Love can lead you into trouble,' he had warned her, and looked so sad. As sad as Captain Potter. 'Mary,' he said, 'was trouble. All golden and beautiful, but even knowing the trouble she caused me, I'd have her again without a second thought. That's love, Rachel. And when love takes you by the hand, you just have to follow where she leads.' And then he'd laughed long and loud in that way he had, as if life and everything about it amused him. A game, to be played to the end for the sheer enjoyment of it. I won't let love lead me anywhere I don't want to go, Rachel thought smugly. I'm too sensible for that!

During the following week, Rachel often thought of the orphanage with longing. Not that she couldn't manage—of course she could. Only she'd had hardly a moment's sleep, and she felt as if there was a great weight on her young shoulders, getting heavier by the hour.

By the following week, Matty had fallen ill, and needed careful nursing, but the others appeared well enough so far. Rachel stood in the nursery, rocking the baby while Matty slept and Frank ran about, pretending he was riding a horse.

'Frank, please . . .' she began for the hundredth time, but the little boy rushed past her, laughing, down the corridor. She heard his quick, running steps on the stairs, and sighed in angry exasperation. 'Frank come back here!'

Matty was still sleeping, so she carried the baby down with her. There was only silence here, apart from a clatter in the kitchen. Rachel poked her head around the door. 'Is Frank here?'

Cook sniffed. 'Not as far as I know. Run off has he?' with a certain malicious satisfaction. Sarah was more sympathetic. 'He'll have gone out to the horses. He always does.'

Should she leave him? Rachel knew she couldn't. She handed the baby to Sarah, 'Just for a moment,' and hurried out before Cook could do more than draw breath.

The yard was cold and bleak, and Rachel looked about her. There were voices from the stable. Rachel walked briskly across there, only to hesitate in the doorway. She remembered the night she came here and Will Trigg had touched her face so gently. Something in her stirred at the thought, but Frank's piping notes interrupted, and she stepped into the cool shadows.

'I'm four,' Frank was saying importantly.

'I know,' replied George.

Rachel moved closer, and the sound of her skirts brushing on the straw made them both look up, Frank guiltily and George with a grin.

'Frank,' she said firmly, 'it was very wrong of you to run away.'

Frank shuffled his feet. 'You can't tell me what to do. You're not Mama,' he said. And then with an uneasy glance at George, 'Can she?'

Rachel watched as George bent closer to the little boy. 'She can, Frank. You'd better do what she says.'

Frank muttered something, scuffing his feet as he came over to Rachel. She caught his hand with a sigh and met George's eyes. 'Thank you,' she told him, heartfelt.

He nodded with a grin. 'Pleasure.' His hair flopped forward, over his eyes, and for a moment something like recognition struck her a blow. Hope sprang up inside her, a hope she had carried with her for four years now. And then the certainty faded, as Frank pulled at her hand.

Rachel forced a small smile to her lips. 'Matty is asleep and I've left the baby with Cook and Sarah,' she said lamely. 'I'd best go back.'

He didn't reply, and Rachel let Frank pull her into the daylight. She could hear the baby crying as she reached the house. Did she really know the man? Hope surged again, and made her uneasy, edgy, as though she were afraid to believe. Afraid of being disappointed. Sometimes, in Richmond, she had looked at men in the street and wondered . . . *Is that him?* But she had never known, never been certain. The hope, the dream, had carried her through dark days. I will meet him again, she had told herself many times. That wish at least will come true.

'George?' Sarah answered her question curiously, pausing as she rolled the dough. 'He's been here about five years I believe. Why?'

Rachel shrugged, rocking the baby, which had stopped crying as soon as she took it back from Sarah. Frank sat quietly by the fire, stroking the ginger cat, which was desperately pretending to be asleep. 'I just wondered. I had a feeling I might have met him before.'

Sarah's eyes narrowed teasingly. 'Haven't lost your heart to him, have you? Suzy will scratch your eyes out. She's got her sights fixed on Young George.'

Rachel smiled. 'She can have him.' The uneasy feeling had gone, vanquished by the warmth and homeliness of the kitchen. 'What about you, Sarah?' she added with a grin. 'Is there anyone special for you?' Rachel had now seen most of the men who worked about the place, and in her opinion none of them were the sort to set a girl's heart on fire.

But Sarah paused in thought, taking the teasing question seriously. 'I'm particular,' she said at last. 'I'm not so easy to please as Suzy. I suppose I do sometimes look twice at Will Trigg. What woman wouldn't? But he was always beyond my reach and now,' with a sigh, 'well he's not interested in me. He's drowning, just like Suzy says.'

'He didn't seem to be drowning the other night,' Rachel retorted, and then bit her lip in vexation. She had told no one about her meeting with Will Trigg, and now Sarah was looking at her with big, curious eyes. 'He brought Mrs Potter's mare back,' she explained swiftly, before Sarah could ask. 'He said she wanted it the next day. I was taking a walk, and I happened to see him. That's all. He seemed all right, though.'

'He seems all right,' Sarah agreed, still watching her. 'But most nights he's half drunk. And in the mornin' he looks like death. He's getting worse, Rachel. Everyone can see it.'

It was a depressing thought.

'They'd only been married a year. She was no beauty, not the sort to fall blind in love with, but she was gentle and kind. I suppose one minute he had everything in the world he wanted, and the next he had nothing at all.'

Baby Victoria was snuffling, beginning to work up to a cry. Rachel shifted the baby's weight to her other arm.

'I hope Mrs Potter is up and about soon,' she murmured.

Sarah grinned at her. 'Poor Rachel. Is being the lady of the house not much fun then?'

Rachel poked out her tongue, and then grinned when Frank started to shriek with laughter.

Martha had emerged from her room. She looked pale and a little sulky, but resigned to taking up her duties again. 'I still feel so weak and so tired,' she complained, closing her eyes against the glare from the window. 'Do close those curtains, Rachel! My head is splitting.'

Rachel's jaw tightened, but she moved to close the curtains. The doctor said Martha was better, only Martha refused to believe it. It appeared she so enjoyed the role of invalid, she was loath to give it up.

'I will rest here a moment,' Martha went on, her voice fading. 'Go and tell Cook to send me up a tray of weak tea and bread and butter. I don't think I could eat anything more."

Rachel went, trying not to slam the door. Cook muttered, while she loaded the tray, and Sarah's blue eyes laughed. 'It's ladylike to be ailing,' she explained to Rachel. 'Mrs Potter is distantly related to gentry, you know. Near enough to a lady.'

'Maybe she's breeding again,' Cook announced.

Rachel blanched. 'Oh no!' she cried, before she could stop herself, and Sarah burst into laughter.

But when Agnes Barber came to visit later in the day, Martha seemed to perk up considerably and, when Agnes left, was even prepared to take the baby for an hour or so, while Rachel performed some of her long neglected tasks. That evening, Captain Potter informed his wife that he had felt increasing admiration for Rachel's efforts at keeping the household running smoothly, and he suggested it might be a good thing for 'the girl' to go down to Greengage in the morning, for a break.

'She can go with George,' he went on, oblivious to Martha's sullen mouth. 'A breath of air will do her good. And she's not seen the village yet.'

'Oh!' Martha gasped, trying not to look as put out as she felt. 'Do you think she has managed so very well, Frank?'

Captain Potter, sensing his mistake, was quick to rectify it. 'My dear, no-one could do as well as you. I just thought the girl deserved a break. She will work the better for it, believe me.'

Martha allowed herself to be mollified. 'Oh, very well. But she mustn't stay too long. I still feel quite giddy.'

Rachel was pleased, when Martha called her in to the parlour to tell her the news. 'I have decided you need some little time away from Down Farm,' she announced. 'A trip to Greengage will do you good, Rachel. You haven't seen Greengage, have you? Well, it will only be a short trip, mind, but still you will be glad to be away from the children for a time, won't you?'

Rachel answered cautiously, 'I am very fond of the children, Mrs Potter.'

Martha smiled. 'Of course! Nevertheless, you may go to Greengage with George in the morning. There is no more to be said.'

Rachel had not intended to argue, and bobbing her little curtsey, hurried out.

The next morning the sun was shining, though the air was cold. There had been a brief shower of rain in the night, but now the clouds were gone, and only the puddles in the road showed they had ever been. Rachel beamed, pulling her cloak tighter about her as she waited for George to bring out the horse and cart. Matty and Frank waved from the window, Sarah's anxious face hovering behind them. She could already hear Baby Victoria crying and hoped, nervously, that George would hurry in case Martha changed her mind.

At last they were out on the road, clomping along the narrow, rough track that led to Greengage. A chill wind blew in the trees, showering them with last night's raindrops. Rachel laughed, and brushed them off her cloak. George grinned at her. 'So you've been let out?'

'Mrs Potter is much better. She said I needed some time away from the children.'

George snorted. 'I heard it was Captain Potter's idea.'

Rachel frowned, but George said no more, as if the subject were a matter of indifference to him. The motion of the horse was soothing, and Rachel relaxed for the first time in a week. It was good to be out and free of the responsibilities which held her in such a vicelike grip. Perhaps it wasn't so unnatural for Martha to feign feeling worse than she was. Rachel could almost sympathise with her.

The inn was the first sign that they had reached Greengage. A jumble of low buildings, with smoke belching from the chimnies. Horses whinnied and an unseen cockatoo shrieked. Beyond the inn, were a number of cottages fronting the main street—the road widened as it ran through Greengage, before narrowing again beyond it. There was a store, with a number of sacks and barrels stacked under the verandah roof, and children teasing a mangey looking dog. George did not stop. They were almost out of Greengage again—a matter of a minute—before he pulled up the horse and cart, in front of the blacksmith's shop.

The big doors were opened to the fresh, cold air, and Rachel could hear someone hammering. There was a horse tethered at the railing along the front, waiting attention, and a customer had brought in a dray with a damaged wheel. The blacksmith in a place like Greengage would do all such repairs, from mending farm ploughs and wheels to reshoeing horses. Beyond the shop and up a slight rise was a small cottage, surrounded by a picket fence and an overgrown garden. It looked in need of paint and care and attention. Part of the fence had fallen down.

George had stepped down to the ground. He looked at Rachel. 'I'll only be a moment,' he said. 'You can stay there if you like.' But Rachel was already climbing down and following him to the big open doorway.

It was dark inside. A brief ray of sunlight shone on dust motes, dancing in the air. Beyond the gloom was the glow of fire, and the smell of coals and hot metal. Will Trigg stood with his back to them, hammering. Even on this freezing day the heat was such that he had taken off his shirt, and his bare brown flesh shone with sweat, the bands of muscle tightening as he moved, bending to his work. The long dark hair at his neck was matted and curling with moisture. Rachel couldn't take her eyes off him.

'Will!' George called.

Will turned his head slowly, and Rachel could see that he was frowning. Slowly, he put down the hammer and rose to his feet. He glanced at Rachel, and reached over to a bench and picked up his shirt, pulling it on as he came towards them. 'George,' he muttered, and didn't sound pleased.

Was this really the man she had seen in the stable that night? Rachel wondered curiously. He was dark haired, darker than George and older, with dark stubble on his chin. Grey eyes were squinting against the pale sun, as though the light hurt, but even so Rachel could see how bloodshot they were.

'Rachel here has come for a visit to Greengage,' George was saying. His eyes slid over the other man, a mixture of scorn and compassion in them.

But Will Trigg didn't seem to notice. He was look-ing at Rachel.

He closed his eyes a moment, as if the pain in his head were just too great to keep them open, and then looked again, 'Rachel?' he repeated. 'Do I know you, Rachel?'

George grinned. 'In your dreams, Will.'

Rachel felt herself colour with anger and embar-rassment. But Will was still looking at her, his tanned face sickly pale, and she realised he didn't remember their meeting in the stable. At last, as if pulling himself together, he said gruffly, 'What is it you want, George? Has Frank sent some message?'

'He said he'd like you to take a look at the gig, when you've the time.'

Will nodded, rubbing his face so that the whis-kers grated. 'I'll come over later in the week. Might have to be Sunday. I've a bit of work on just now.'

George looked back down the street, towards the inn. 'I'm going for a drink,' he said. 'Want to come?'

Will followed his gaze and his mouth tightened. 'I don't think so.'

But George only laughed, and somehow it was not a pleasant laugh. He looked at Rachel, raising his brows. 'I'll only be a minute or two. Do you want to walk around a bit? The store's over there.' And then, with a wink, 'Although the only thing worth seeing in Greengage is Will, and you've seen him now.'

Rachel wasn't sure whether or not it was a joke, but Will laughed. 'Get going then, George,' he retorted, 'but only one drink, mind. I'll not baby-sit her more than a few minutes.'

George grinned and set off, loping towards the

inn as though it was a pot of gold. Will laughed again, and squinted back at Rachel. 'Do you want a cup of tea, Rachel, while you wait?'

She didn't know what to say. She thought she should refuse, and silently cursed George for putting her in such a position. But Will Trigg had already moved into the smithy and she saw there was a kettle on the side of the hearth there, and he was searching around for a mug. Reluctantly, Rachel followed him in and stood watching him uneasily. The brief moment of humour had passed, and he looked tired and haggard, as though the life had been burned out of him. And yet he was such a strong man. It seemed a shame. Rachel half thought he would upend a bottle into his own mug, but he made them both tea with a deft, practised hand. Rachel sipped and glanced about her at the smithy. It was tidy enough, not the shambles she would have expected from a man sliding into an abyss.

'What do you do at Down Farm, Rachel?' he asked her, but she thought he wasn't really interested. He was just making conversation and wishing George would hurry back.

'I'm the nursery maid,' she said. 'You met me the other night, when you brought Martha's mare back.'

Grey eyes went to hers, startled, and he searched his memory. 'Yes,' he said at last. 'I remember now. You looked different. You had your hair down around your shoulders—black hair—and now it's all bound up under that bonnet.' He seemed pleased with the feat and took a deep drink from his mug. The tea appeared to revive him. 'I'm sorry,' he sighed, and gave her a lop-sided smile that was quite devastating. 'You must think me a Moonraker, Rachel, to have forgot you so soon.'

For a moment she couldn't even draw breath. That one word had sent her mind spinning, back over the years, back to the young girl and the man on the horse, riding in the darkness with the wind blowing her hair out behind them, like fingers reaching for the stars.

'Rachel?' he was frowning at her. She licked her lips and tried to pull herself together, but her hands were trembling, spilling the hot tea. She felt as if her whole world had just been split asunder, like an egg shell, and she could never put it back together again the way it was.

'That word,' she whispered. 'Moonraker. You've said it to me before.' Her voice was hard to get out, as though her throat had closed on it. 'We've met before, Mr Trigg!'

He stared at her in exasperation. 'You told me so, in the stables you said. I've remembered.'

'No, no,' she breathed. 'Before that. By the river in Richmond. It was my birthday. It was Midsummer's Eve.'

For a moment he didn't understand her, his expression blank, slightly irritated. She doubted. And then she watched his eyes spring wide open, grey as ashes, and the comprehension slid over his face, leaving it suddenly young and naked. As though the four years in between had melted and all that had happened to him since was erased. 'Rachel,' he whispered, and looked at her in wonder.

'You never came back,' she said angrily, the thirteen year old girl she had been berating him. 'I waited for you, but you never came back.'

'Did I say I would?' he closed his eyes for a moment, as though it were all too much for him. 'I'm sorry, Rachel. Life overtook me.'

Her mood changed, and she gasped, 'But don't you see what this means? It means my wish did come true after all! I wished that I would see you again, and I have. I have! Somehow I always knew I would. I was always waiting.'

His mouth softened into a smile. 'Were you?' And then, with a frown, 'But you said you wished to take a ride on my horse.'

Rachel moved uneasily. 'I didn't like to tell you the truth.' She flicked him a look under her lashes. 'And I did enjoy the gallop. On and on into the sea.'

He wasn't listening. 'Rachel,' he whispered to himself.

Almost, she reached out a hand and touched his face, but something stopped her. This wasn't how she had imagined their meeting. He was a stranger, after all, even though he had been with her in memory all these years. 'Were you living in Green-gage in those days?' she asked him instead.

He paused, and rubbed a hand over his unshaven face. He looked shaken. 'I bought the blacksmithy around then. It's my trade.'

'You were unhappy that night,' Rachel said. 'I felt it. Perhaps because I was unhappy too.'

He shrugged. 'It's old history, isn't it?' She felt him withdraw, as though other memories had returned to swamp those of the girl and the man, beside the dark river. You don't know me, he seemed to be saying to her. Don't presume that you know me.

Rachel heard a footstep behind her, and George peered into the shadows. 'Rachel? We'd best get back now, or Mrs Potter'll be foaming at the mouth.'

Rachel rose hastily, setting the half full mug down with a rattle. Suddenly she wanted to weep. So long she had dreamed of this moment, for so very long. And the reality was nothing like the dream. What had she expected? To fall into his arms? Perhaps, and she shuddered inwardly. Rachel admitted to herself that she had been searching for this man ever since the evening by the river—he had assumed enormous importance in her life. And all from just one—albeit magical—meeting.

Outside the cold air stung her cheeks after the heat of the fire, and she blinked, reaching up to pull her cloak closer about her throat. George was eyeing her curiously, but he didn't joke as she had feared, merely reached out a hand to help her up onto the cart. Only then did Rachel find the courage to turn and smile at Will Trigg, as he stood in the doorway of his smithy.

'Thank you for the tea, Mr Trigg,' she said cheerily. 'I enjoyed it very much.'

He nodded, but he didn't return her smile. He looked pale and shaken, as though he too had had a shock. And then she forced her eyes away, and they were off down the street, going home. She didn't turn back. She didn't want to see him standing looking after them.

George was in a garrulous mood, and Rachel smiled and pretended to listen. 'What did you think of Will?' he kept asking her. As though he were secretly amused at something. She had a feeling he had left her there on purpose, for some reason of his own. Thankfully, after a time, he lost interest, and fell to humming under his breath.

She didn't want to tell George what she thought of Will Trigg. How he would stare! Her 'lost ghost' had become lost indeed. His wife and child had been taken so brutally from him, and he had begun to drink heavily. He was drowning, as Suzy said.

I can save him, Rachel thought shakily. I know I can. And then wondered, with shame, how many other women had thought the same thing. He was handsome, no doubt of that. The sight of him, half naked, in the red gloom of the smithy, had made Rachel catch her breath. But it was more than that. It was as if she could see inside his body, to his soul, to the wretchedness within.

The cart jolted on. George glanced at the silent girl beside him and smiled in secret delight. The sky was clouding over again, but Rachel didn't even notice. She was locked into her thoughts, and George thought he knew what they were. He had brought them together this morning half in jest, just to see what would happen, and half in the hope something would. Will needed his mind taken off his troubles, and what better distraction than a lovely young girl. An innocent young girl, if George knew anything about it. And he did.

But things seemed to have taken a turn George had not foreseen. Rachel's face was white, as white as Will's had been as they drove away. Obviously this was no idle flirtation. It was as if they'd been struck by a thunderbolt, the pair of them. Now it just remained to be seen if either of them—or George— could do anything about it.

CHAPTER 4

MARTHA POTTER CONTINUED TO IMPROVE. She was well enough the next day to preside over the midday meal. Her husband appeared pleased to have things back to normal. Rachel, dealing with a convalescent Matty, was not so happy. Perhaps sensing that her mind was not concentrated as it should be, Frank led her a merry dance, running off at every opportunity. Once, Rachel apprehended him as he reached the stable, and caught sight of George and Suzy, locked in a passionate embrace in the shadows, before she was able to drag Frank away. They didn't even look up.

The memory of them, clasped together, kept intruding on her thoughts. It was mixed up, some-how, with the memory of Will Trigg. Rachel was attracted to him in a way she had never been attracted to a man before. And her head ached with trying to make sense of a thing that made no sense. How could a glance, a few words, suddenly assume such importance? How could the touch of his fingers on her cheek or the way he smiled, keep her awake at night? Rachel pounded her pillow in

miserable anger. I do not love him! she told herself. I just feel sorry for him. I want to help him.
How could I possibly love him? But Rachel knew
he fascinated her, and that fascination had begun
before she had discovered who he really was. The
knowledge that Will was the man she had met by
the river seemed to have taken possession of her.

One afternoon a farmer from Pitt Water rode
over to see Captain Potter, with a letter from his
cousin. The cousin had taken up land in the Port
Phillip District, and mentioned seeing Captain
Potter's brother, Israel. Martha was smiling and
gracious while the man was there, but spitting like
an angry cat when he had gone.

'Why couldn't he write to us himself, instead of
leaving us to get our news secondhand?'

Captain Potter tapped his fingers thoughtfully on
the arm of his chair. 'It sounds as if he means to stay
on the mainland,' he murmured. 'I've sometimes
thought, my dear, that we should look elsewhere
ourselves. I can't afford to extend the farm. Land
is too expensive.' He shook his head. 'Vandemon
is over populated. There just isn't enough land for
everyone. The mainland offers the chance to grab
a big holding. But we'd have to do it soon, Martha,
or everything worth having will be gone.'

Martha looked aghast. 'This is my home!' she
declared. 'I could never leave Vandemon. Go into
the wilderness and fight the savages for every acre?
I don't know how you can suggest it Frank! You
know how delicate my health is. . .' Her eyes glinted
with rage and self pity.

He comforted her, but there was a spark in his
own eye—Rachel felt certain that nothing Mar-

tha could say or do would quench that fire. She wondered, if it came to the point, whether Martha's delicate health would really weigh the balance against the scramble for more land.

The Potters had friends to visit in Richmond and Martha had agreed to Rachel travelling with them and spending an hour at the orphanage. The friends lived not far away, and Rachel was able to walk, her cloak wrapped closely about her against the cold, whipping wind. The river was reflecting the sky, the reeds blown sideways and the water tossed into little white waves. She thought of Will Trigg, but shut him determinedly from her mind. Thinking of him only made her feel strange, confused, and so unlike the Rachel she had always assumed herself to be.

Mrs Finn was pleased to see her, and the girls gathered around her. Rachel told them all about the Potters and Down Farm.

'So you're happy?' Betsy asked her, with a relieved smile.

Rachel smiled back. 'I'm happy.'

There was plenty of news to catch up on, and memories to laugh over, and the time went swiftly as they sat and talked. Rachel realised all too soon she would have to hurry, if she was to catch the Potters before they left. Kisses and breathless goodbyes, and she rushed out of the door, her head down and her cloak flying behind her. If she were late, Martha Potter would be in a rage, and such things, as Rachel knew, were best avoided.

She didn't even see the man until she collided with him. The hard contact of her head with his chest momentarily stunned her. Rachel stumbled back, tripping on the hem of her skirt, and would have fallen if he hadn't grabbed her upper arm in a bruising hold.

'Rachel!' She had been about to apologise, lifting a face flushed with wry humour. Both died in an instant. The colour left her skin and she felt the grip of his hand tighten. Grey eyes narrowed, as he bent towards her, peering into her face.

'Are you hurt? You're not faintin', Rachel?'

She must have looked like she might be, Rachel realised, and forced herself to straighten. She took a deep breath, shaking off his grip. Her hands trembled as she smoothed her rumpled sleeve. 'No.' She cleared her throat. 'No, I'm quite all right. I'm so sorry. I was in a rush to get back to the Potters. They're waiting.'

The concern in his eyes faded. He turned to look behind him, as if expecting Martha to be standing there.

Rachel couldn't help it.

While he was looking away, her eyes ran quickly, avidly over him, taking in every detail: the decent, if rather worn clothing, the dark, straight hair at his nape, the set of his shoulders. He still wore a wedding ring on his finger, his hand clenching over it. And he had polished his boots. He looked so good, oh so good—Rachel's mouth went dry. He was turning back!

Trembling with embarrassment, Rachel bent

her head, pretending to brush a speck off her cuff. Her hands were shaking, her heart rattling in her breast, while she waited for him to speak. But he was silent for so long. In the end she had no choice but to look at him again—a swift glance under her lashes. And it was then that she realised, with a sense of shock, that he was examining her in exactly the same way as she had just examined him. With quick, almost furtive glances, storing up the memories for later, for the long, dark, lonely hours . . .

'Rachel,' he began. Something in his voice triggered her voice into action. 'I was at the orphanage,' she began, breathless. 'It was so nice to see my friends. The time got away from me, I didn't realise it was so late. Mrs Potter will be cross with me if I'm late . . . They're waiting at the Richmond Hotel. I must hurry.'

But she didn't move.

He had waited until she was finished, watching her, the grey eyes growing even more concerned. Now his mouth twisted into a wry smile, as though he thought he knew what was the matter with her. He pushed back his fringe with awkward fingers. 'Rachel,' he began again. 'I didn't mean to upset you the other day. I ... fear I'm a great disappointment to you. Memories have a way of growing bigger and better as time goes on. You expected a hero ten foot tall. I don't measure up, do I?'

She was shaking her head. 'You're quite wrong,' she said, while her face coloured with mortification.

'I don't think so,' he muttered. 'I know what I've become. You made a wish, you said. I'm bettin' you're sorry now it came true.' There was bitterness and misery in his voice, enough to thrust through the fears that held her, and force her to speak with sudden, urgent honesty.

'No,' she gasped. 'Oh no, Mr Trigg! I'm not sorry at all. At least, not sorry about that. I'm only regretful I didn't come earlier, before things got quite so bad. It would have been easier, then, to set them to rights . . .'

Her voice trailed off. He was staring at her with wide eyes. As if he could hardly believe what he was hearing, as if he didn't know whether to laugh or cry. Rachel cursed her tongue. Will moved at last, reaching to take her arm again.

'Rachel . . .' he began gently.

But Rachel had had as much as she could take. She said loudly, 'I must go, really!' and bolted past him, almost running down the street towards the Richmond Hotel. He stared after her, frowning. As she reached the corner she threw back a look at him, a look that was almost hunted. As though she were afraid of him, he thought startled . . . or herself. The idea . . . everything she had said, crunched together in his mind. Was that it? He had been well aware of what he was feeling towards her, and had called himself every kind of idiot. But that she should feel the same towards him . . .

Will shook his head angrily. Don't, he told himself. Don't even begin to imagine what it would be like. The girl was like a lighthouse, surrounded by jagged, dangerous rocks—in other words he knew any move towards her would be disastrous for him. She was too young and too innocent. Bad news for Will Trigg. And more than that. Memories, terrors that he never spoke of now, but which would forever prevent him from finding happiness with Rachel Naish.

With a sigh, Will turned away. *Forget it!* he told himself curtly. But his feet seemed to hardly touch the ground; euphoria, not whisky, was making his head as light as a cloud. Desperately, he ignored the feelings that should have warned him it was already too late. That the light was shining full on him, and he was on the rocks.

Fool! Rachel told herself. You fool! Going on in that gauche, naive way. No wonder he had stared. He had probably been trying very hard not to laugh in your face. A man like that. And yet she had meant it, every word of it. And she believed it. She could help him, she knew it. Some devil whispered in her ear that others had probably felt like that too, but she ignored it. They don't love him like I do, she told herself. No-one ever has. There was no doubt Will was in a mess . . . his dead wife and his drinking . . . but something about him touched her as nothing ever had before in her life. Was that what Pa had meant, about love leading one into trouble? Rachel asked herself uneasily. Was Will Trigg trouble? And knew deep inside that even if he was, she was lost. Just as Pa had been lost. Will belonged to her and she to him, even if he didn't know it yet.

The Potters had only just arrived, and Rachel

realised, with relief, there would be no harsh words or recriminations or reminders of Martha's 'delicate health'. The ride back was uneventful and she was able to sit in silence with her thoughts.

On Sunday morning, the household gathered in the yard. Captain Potter cleared his throat and, glancing at Martha uneasily, read a passage or two from a battered looking bible. Rachel, trying to hold Frank still with one hand and Matty with the other, stood on the verandah. She was accustomed to Sunday sermons, and was surprised to see how some of the others treated it as a joke, or an intrusion.

'Will I go to hell when I die?'

The voice was soft—a whisper. Rachel gazed down at Frank, for a moment speechless. The blue eyes stared back, a little defiant as always, but with a flicker of fear behind them. 'Why, Frank, who put such an idea in your head?'

He looked sideways, towards Cook and Old George, and back again. 'No one,' he lied uneasily. 'What's hell like?'

Rachel put a hand on his head and smiled. 'You're not going there, my dear. Only very, very bad people go to hell. When you die, a long long time from now, when you're an old, old man, you'll go straight to heaven.'

He thought about that and then he smiled one of his angelic smiles. 'Cook's going to hell then,

Rachel! I heard Old George call her a bad old woman!'

Cook's head swung around and she glared, but Frank's smile only grew wider.

During the afternoon Rachel had a few hours free. She sat in her room for a time, concentrating on doing some mending for herself. Finished, she went to the window and looked outside. The sun was shining fitfully through the clouds. A cool breeze stirred the tree tops. The horses in the paddock were galloping about like foals, kicking up their heels. It would be spring soon, and they could feel it. Rachel could feel it too, and suddenly she could not bear to be inside a moment longer.

Down Farm was very quiet. Martha Potter and her husband had set out with the children after midday on a visit to the Barbers. The others seemed to have disappeared. Rachel felt herself alone in the world and was enjoying the feeling. It was not often she had her time to herself.

She walked down the laneway to the narrow road and stood a moment, listening to the silence. Then she began, slowly, to stroll along the road. She was thinking of the last time she had gone walking and the horse had come so suddenly, nearly running her down. When she heard the horse this time, for a moment she thought it was part of the memory. But it was no memory . . . Rachel's heart leapt, and she turned. The animal came from nowhere, around the corner. It had reached her before the rider was able to halt, so close that Rachel felt the hot breath in her face. The horse, obviously unnerved by the girl in her long cloak, tried to rear, front feet slicing the air, while its rider fought for control. Rachel cried out, stumbling back and sat down hard on the road. For a moment the breath was knocked out of her, and then she looked up. At Will.

Her heart was thumping. 'Do you mean to run into me again?' she gasped angrily. Angry from the fright he had given her, and angry because she was sprawled so inelegantly on the icey ground before him.

His look of astonishment gave way to laughter. 'I thought it was you who ran into me,' he retorted when he was able. And then he smiled and, bending down low, held out his hand steadily towards her. Without a second thought, she reached up and grasped it. His fingers closed hard over hers. She felt his strength as he tugged her to her feet, and then up into the saddle before him. Strong arms closed about her. Rachel felt his breath in her hair and closed her eyes dizzily. The past mingled dangerously with the present. Her heart was beating shockingly fast.

'Where were you going?' he mocked. 'To Greengage on foot?'

'I like to walk,' she retorted. 'It helps me to think.'

He didn't reply, only nudged the horse on towards the laneway. Rachel felt the warmth of his body behind her, the strength of his arms enclosing her as he held the reins. Why had she taken his hand? Why had she reached out to his fingers, as if it were the most natural thing in the world? After what she said in Richmond he must know how she felt. Was he laughing at her, even now?

'You rode faster the last time,' she managed at last, making her voice airy but gazing straight ahead.

Her hair brushed his cheek, the strands soft and

shiny and clean. Will resisted the urge to touch. He had not held a woman this close since Hannah—he discounted the women he had paid for, the bought comfort. Somehow that just wasn't the same.

'My head won't stand a gallop today,' he retorted wryly. 'I drink too much,' he added. It was the truth, wasn't it? he thought bitterly. And if she didn't know it already, it was his duty to tell her. And just how far, some inner voice mocked, are you prepared to go, to make her turn and run from you?

'Why?' she whispered. 'Why do you drink too much?'

He considered the question honestly. 'I don't know how it happened. After Hannah died, I began to slide downhill and there seemed no reason to pull back. It's so much easier just to keep going down. Easier not to have to think.' One of his arms slid about her waist, and he felt her stiffen warily. His voice came, soft and dark in her ear— the river at night. 'But today, because I was coming here, I washed myself up and put on clean clothes. Rachel, I even shaved.'

'You needn't have bothered,' she whispered, while hope and fear flared inside her.

He moved his arm upward ever so slightly, and felt the weight of her breasts. Oh, but she was a beautiful armful. His breath was warm on her neck, and he bent and kissed her nape. 'I can't stop thinking about you,' he murmured, and his mouth lingered.

Rachel felt a rush of heat through her that left her trembling. This was all beyond her experience.

She had never been so close to a man before, apart from Pa. She didn't know how to begin to handle her feelings or his.

'Someone will see,' she gasped.

'I don't care who sees,' he muttered, and kissed her again.

Did he mean it? she asked herself. What should I do now? Say no?

They had reached the yard gate, and he dismounted, reaching to help her down, But, frightened and confused, she slid down on her own, moving away from him, out of his reach. His smile mocked himself. 'I've a gig to look at,' he said, and leading the horse to the water trough, tethered it there, and walked away from her.

The gig was in the barn, and he stooped and examined the buckled wheel, trying to ignore the stabbing pain behind his eyes. Suddenly he knew she was there, with him. He didn't even have to look, he just knew. And it was a little frightening, to acknowledge such a thing.

'What was your wife like?' Her voice was soft and sweet, just like everything else about her.

Rachel saw his hand grip the spoke, and wished she had stayed silent. Perhaps he would tell her to go away now—she deserved it. It was cruel to stir up painful memories, and yet she wanted . . . needed to know. It was important.

'She wasn't beautiful,' he said at last, not looking at her. 'But she was kind. I needed kindness then, Rachel. When she died like that . . . it seemed like a punishment. Divine judgment,' and he gave that jeering laugh again. She opened her mouth to ask him what he was being punished for, but he was speaking again. 'So many plans we'd made, and none of them meant anything. I couldn't see the point of it.'

'But you've kept up your trade,' she replied softly. 'And here you are, looking at Captain Potter's gig. You haven't really given up, Mr Trigg.'

He looked up at her as he squatted down beside the gig, and his grey eyes shone with a savage light. 'I'm no hero, Rachel. My character isn't one to hold up as an example to others. You must know that now. Why do you care what I do, and what becomes of me?'

Rachel shook her head and said nothing.

He straightened. 'I want to warn you away. I know I must warn you away . . . but at the same time I want to do anything . . . say anything to bring you closer.'

He looked so grim and unhappy. She felt her heart overflowing with love and compassion. 'Ah, poor Will,' she breathed. Her feet took her forward and she let herself go, reaching out to lay her hand on his arm. She felt his muscles tense, and then slowly, slowly he reached out his own hand and put it on her cheek, sliding his fingers up into her dark, curling hair. She watched in a sort of wonder as he leaned closer, his breath warming her lips. And then his lips touched hers, at first so gently she hardly felt them. He kissed the corner of her mouth, and then the fullness of her lips, until she parted them slightly, and shivered as she felt his tongue moisten them.

Will lifted his head and looked down at her. Her eyes were closed, and she had swayed towards him. Her expression was wrapt, captivated. Now was the time to stop, now was the time to draw back. But instead he groaned with a need that was almost pain and pulled her hard into his arms. Rachel responded to his kiss without reserve. Her heart was thudding out a tattoo against her ribs. Her legs could barely hold her up and she leaned into the warmth of his body. She felt as if a great wall of water were swamping her, and although she floundered to reach the surface, her head spinning, her lungs bursting for air, all the while she knew that she didn't really care if she were saved or not.

'I'll say one thing for you, Will,' a voice drawled from the doorway. 'You're a fast worker.'

Rachel felt him pull away, though one arm still held her fast against his side, as though he couldn't quite bring himself to release her yet. She opened her eyes, the lids so heavy, and met George's amused brown gaze.

'Captain Potter'll be back in a minute,' he added, to no-one in particular. And then he slouched away, chuckling.

Rachel put a hand to her mouth, as though his kiss had left a mark, her dark eyes widening. He looked at her for a moment, watching as passion turned to confusion ... and a certain wariness. She was wondering whether or not George was right. The question was clear in her eyes. Was this just a game to him, another conquest? After a moment Will laughed softly, deliberately, without humour. 'You take these things too seriously, Rachel,' he told her, and watched her flinch. 'Haven't you ever been kissed before? Go on, you'd best get back to the house before Martha finds you here. Believe me, she wouldn't like it.'

'No,' she whispered, 'she wouldn't.'

He said no more. He didn't have to. His face was closed to her, offering no hope, no opening ... Hurt made her paler than ever, but she turned her back so that he wouldn't see. Rachel walked towards the doorway, her steps quickening as she drew closer. And he let her go without a word, watching her stumble as she crossed the yard before she reached the door. Had it been enough? Would she be hurt enough, angry enough to kill whatever it was she thought she felt for him? He hoped so, by God he hoped so! Because it had hurt him just as much as it hurt her. With a sift, savage curse, Will turned back to the gig.

George was right. The Potters were home only moments later, and Rachel was required to take the children while Martha 'composed' herself. Captain Potter went out to see Will, and to invite him in for tea—much to Martha's disgust. Rachel had a few brief moments to try and put her own feelings in order.

It had just been a game to him, she thought bitterly. And she had behaved like such a fool. Telling him she could help him. How he must have laughed! Her face flamed at the thought and she clenched her fists. Perhaps it had been a game between George and Will? A bet? To see how fast she would fall into the trap. Rachel put her head in her hands, wishing she could crawl into a cupboard and hide. She was so hurt and humiliated, it was unbearable. And besides that, her heart was breaking.

The door opened, and Martha came in to the parlour. 'Whatever are you doing, Rachel? Straighten

Frank's jacket. Matty! Hands in your lap, please!'

Voices. Rachel looked up, her dark eyes hunted. Through the window, she could see the two men coming across the yard towards the house. Hands shaking, she moved to withdraw, with the children, from the room.

'Wherever are you going, Rachel?' Martha gripped her arm. 'I need you to stay and help hand out the cups.'

Rachel opened her mouth to make an excuse, but her mind was a blank. Besides, it was too late. Will had followed Captain Potter into the room, bending his head under the lintel, and Martha was murmuring her good afternoons, the syrup in her voice not quite hiding the steel.

'Martha,' Will's voice was bland, and Rachel saw the gleam in his grey eyes as he read her expression correctly. Then those same eyes moved on to Rachel and, feeling the hot humiliating colour flooding into her face, she spun away to fuss about Matty, wondering how long she could stay in the same room as him.

'Rachel, please fetch the tea,' Martha instructed. 'Cook will have prepared it. I'm afraid,' with a shrug to Will, 'Cook considers that's where her duties end.'

Rachel went stiffly out, closing the door thankfully behind her. A reprieve, if only for a moment. In the kitchen, Cook was muttering, setting out the tea cups and some of her fruit cake which reeked of brandy. Sarah and Suzy were nowhere to be seen. 'Here,' Cook snapped, handing her the tray, 'and tell her ladyship I'm off home now. Old George is waitin' and he's none too pleased.'

Rachel carried the heavy tray up the hallway to the parlour. The door defeated her. In the end, she had to set the tray on the table by the front door, open the door, and then carry the tray in. She felt flustered and uncomfortable and she had never felt quite like that before. It was so unlike her. He had done that. She should be angry, furiously angry— instead she just wanted to cry.

At last the tray was set on the table, and Martha went about pouring with a set smile. Will and Captain Potter were talking easily enough about, as far as Rachel could make out, the situation in Hobart Town. The children were playing by the fireplace with some toys Agnes Barber had given them. The baby was cooing on her father's knee, pulling at the shiny buttons on his coat.

'Hand these out please, Rachel,' Martha said, and pushed a cup at Rachel. She took it over to Captain Potter, and then Martha was handing her another,

Rachel turned with it in her hands. Will was watching her, and his grey eyes were warm with something she knew must be derision. He was laughing at her expense. He knew what she was feeling, knew he had capsized her equilibrium. It amused him to have humiliated her and thrown her love back into her face. What a child she must seem to him! The cup in her hand began to shake dangerously.

He had reached her and removed it before she could draw a breath. 'Careful,' he said softly. And then, with a frown, 'You've burned yourself.'

Rachel looked down in surprise and saw that the tea had spilled onto her hand. She looked up again, into those grey eyes. They were still warm, but suddenly, she knew it was not derision in them after all. It was something else altogether. A raw, possessive emotion that made her catch her breath in wonder.

'Rachel!' Martha was irritated. 'What is the matter with you girl? Perhaps you'd better take the children upstairs after all.'

Rachel bobbed her little curtsey and gathered up Matty and Frank, stooped to relieve Captain Potter of Victoria, and then herded her charges towards the door. Will moved to open it for her.

She hadn't meant to look up at him, but she couldn't help herself. So it wasn't serious, eh? She teased him silently. So it was just a kiss? And her dark eyes were shining as she closed the door.

'Will Trigg has gone a little strange,' Martha said later to her husband. 'Rushing to open doors for servants. Whatever is the matter with him?'

Captain Potter looked thoughtful.

'And he was sober! Do you think he's on the mend?'

Her husband lifted his eyebrows. 'Who can say, my love?'

Martha sighed. 'Well, I am sure he can rely upon me to give him all the help I can. His wife was my friend, after all. And he is still eligible, despite everything. I am sure we could find some woman willing to overlook his reputation.'

Captain Potter lowered his eyes, hiding the gleam of laughter.

Sarah looked at Rachel again. The girl was pale and wan, as though she were ill. Could Suzy be right? She swore George wasn't lying, and that Will Trigg had been kissing Rachel half to death in the barn last Sunday. It seemed incredible, and yet. . . Rachel hardly looked like she was in the same country as the rest of them. Sarah shook her head. Why was it some women always went for the wrong men?

'Will Trigg,' Suzy had muttered to Sarah. 'I didn't think he still had it in him!'

Sarah frowned. 'He's young enough, isn't he?'

Suzy shrugged. 'Thirty, so George says. Bit old for our Rachel.' She grinned to herself, 'Maybe I'll go fishing over at the Greengage smithy next time I'm there, and see if I can get a bite.'

'Maybe Rachel's bait's special,' Sarah retorted.

But Suzy just laughed and sauntered away, her hips swaying.

Sarah looked again at Rachel and took a breath. 'I'm older than you, Rachel. I know how it is. Sometimes when you're seventeen you think you're in love, but it's not real. It doesn't last.'

Rachel flushed and said nothing.

'You'll see,' Sarah went on, more comfortably, sure she was doing the right thing. 'One morning you'll wake up and it'll be gone.'

Rachel couldn't help but laugh, while Sarah's expression changed to indignation. The laugh wavered and Rachel bit her lip. Her dark eyes were enormous, full of unhappiness. 'Sarah, if it's love, then it's not like they say. It makes me so confused. I can't sleep at night, I just lie there, thinking. Of him.'

Sarah eyed her curiously. 'It's serious, that's for sure.'

'Sometimes,' Rachel whispered, 'I feel like there's a great hollow inside me. As if I need him to make me whole again. I think about him all the time. Mrs Potter tells me I'm a fool because I drop things and forget things. But I can't help it. I don't even care! I need him, Sarah, but I don't know what to do . . . what to say. I've never felt like this before; I never thought I could.'

'Well,' Sarah sighed, 'I don't know what to say. I'll ask Suzy. She's had more experience with men than me.'

'No, don't ask Suzy,' Rachel cried, embarrassed. 'It's nothing to do with her.'

Sarah was thoughtful. 'Maybe he's as mad for you as you are for him,' she suggested. 'Maybe you should ask him.'

But Rachel only shook her head. Sarah didn't understand. Will didn't want to love her, that was the trouble. He had shut her out. Why? She lay in the darkness, eyes wide, wondering. Did he feel disloyal to his dead wife, was that it? She was sure that Hannah would never begrudge him happiness. How could Rachel make him understand that? 'Oh Will,' she breathed into the night. 'I know you feel for me what I feel for you. Am I so vain, to believe we are meant for each other?'

The night gave her no answer and no hope. She loved a man who did not want to love her. She feared he thought her too young and inexperienced to deal with the situation. And perhaps she was.

CHAPTER 5

ON THE FOLLOWING SUNDAY THERE was a church service in Greengage. The minister from Richmond, Reverend Jones, came to Greengage every fourth Sunday. On the other Sundays he held services in Richmond or elsewhere about his district.

Everyone attended.

The service was held outdoors, under a huge gum tree. Chairs and benches from the inn had been arranged around and the people huddled under their hats and coats, some praying it did not rain while others prayed that it would. The inn was always ready to provide shelter, and did a roaring trade.

Rachel looked about with interest at the congregation. The innkeeper was there, a ruffian with a ready smile, and his wife and great brood of children.

The Barbers were there, Agnes sweet in blue, while her tall husband wore a suit that was too big for him. There were lots of people from the cottages and farms in the district, the adults chatting, while the children played. The Reverend found his notes and cleared his throat and his flock settled to silence.

Rachel tried to concentrate, really she did, but her thoughts kept straying. She flicked a quick searching glance about her, unable to help herself. Of course he isn't here! a voice inside mocked. Why would he be?

George was leaning nonchalantly against the big gum tree, pretending not to notice Suzy's lingering glances. Beside Suzy, Sarah wore a faded bonnet and an air of righteous piety. And, Rachel felt herself stiffen, there was Will Trigg after all. He stood only a few yards away, but slightly behind her so that she had not seen him until now. Had he noticed her turning and twisting? Searching for him? The thought made her shrivel inside. But no . . . his head was turned the other way as he spoke to someone beside him.

Rachel gazed at him as if she were drowning.

'Rachel!' hissed Martha. Rachel rose hastily for the hymn, her face flaming. Out of the corner of her eye, she saw Sarah frowning, while beyond her Suzy began to sing in a surprisingly beautiful contralto voice.

After the service, there was more time to chat. Agnes Barber came to claim Martha. Matty and Frank ran about with the other children, getting more and more tired and over-excited, while the baby slept on in Rachel's arms, her sweet round face innocent of the fears and confusion which beset her nursemaid.

'Babies are lovely,' Sarah sighed.

'Bloody noisy things,' Suzy retorted, with a toss

of her golden head.

Sarah began a long-winded discussion on babies in general.

Rachel noticed that Will Trigg was standing with George now, beside the tree. They were laughing about something. Why hadn't he gone to the inn with the others? Even the Reverend had been eager to accept the offer of the drink for the long journey home.

Suzy sauntered over to the two men, and took George's arm possessively in her own. He rolled his eyes at Will, but didn't complain as she led him away. Will stood, smiling to himself, gazing down at his feet. Then suddenly he looked up and caught Rachel's eye. Something in his face changed, was held. Sarah's voice gradually dwindled to a halt. She looked from Rachel to Will in exasperation, and then sighed. 'Did you enjoy the service, Mr Trigg?' she asked him rather sharply.

He turned to look at her swiftly and his smile was wry. 'Not much.' he said. 'This is my first attendance in a long time, and now I know why I stopped.'

'Why did you come today?' Sarah retorted.

He looked at Rachel, and she saw the answer in his eyes. Rachel bent over the baby, fussing with its shawl, wrapping it more closely. Sarah sighed again.

'I think I'll go away now,' she said, and did.

Rachel smoothed the baby's bonnet, and then started when Will spoke, his voice so close that she realised he had come to stand right beside her. 'Nothing can come of this, Rachel, you know that.'

She didn't look at him. He wondered whether it was because he had embarrassed her or that he merely irritated her. She was such a beautiful girl. He had been watching her during the service. The straight nose, the way her lips pouted slightly when she was concentrating, the dark curl of her hair against her white skin . . . Colour ravaged her pale face and he realised he had been staring at her for too long without speaking. She wasn't like Hannah, he thought desperately. Not like Hannah at all. And yet he was drawn to her, like the tug of a big fish on a line, fighting all the way to the gaff.

Suddenly she looked up at him with her great dark eyes. The baby stirred in her arms and she rocked it without taking her gaze off him. 'Why are you afraid, Mr Trigg,' she breathed. 'Am I so terrible, that you have to shut me out?'

He blinked, taken by surprise. He put up his hand, pushing the straight, thick hair out of his eyes. 'What are you saying to me, Rachel?'

'I'm saying that I think, ever since that night by the river, ever since I made my wish, we've had a bond. A special bond. Even before I knew exactly who you were, I felt it. And . . . it's wonderful! But sometimes it frightens me, because it makes me feel as if I am no longer the mistress of my own emotions.' Her voice shook.

It was beginning to rain, and she didn't even know it. He knew he should tell her lies now, hurt her so badly she would never speak to him again. While at the same time he knew that he couldn't bear to hurt her. He had tried, in the barn, and been so wretched from it, he had agreed against his better judgment to take tea with Martha and Frank, longing to make it up to her. More than anything in the world—more than his own self-preservation perhaps—he wanted her in his arms.

'Are you free this afternoon?'

She nodded, watching him.

'Will you meet me again on the Greengage road? At around three? Just keep walking, and I'll be there. We can talk.'

Rachel hesitated. Was it wise to meet him alone like that? But wisdom seemed to have very little to do with the way she was feeling. Rachel nodded, and then, as if suddenly realising it was raining, glanced up. The droplets sparkled in her hair and she closed her eyes. Unable to help himself, Will touched her cheek, and then she was gone, moving swiftly over the grass towards the inn, holding the baby firmly in her arms.

It was easy enough to get away. Martha and Captain Potter were entertaining the Barbers and Rachel had pleaded a headache and retired to her room.

The sky was overcast and steely grey. There was a real storm brewing, she thought, and felt the same storm building inside her. She didn't dare to consider if this was right or wrong. She didn't dare to stop and hesitate.

The road was empty. She heard Will coming and stood waiting. For a moment they gazed at each other, as though both were a little afraid of the power of their feelings. And then Will reached down, and she put her fingers in his, and he drew her up effortlessly into the saddle. His arm came around her, blacksmith's muscles hard as iron. Then he kicked his horse into a canter, and soon they were galloping. The rush of the air cooled her skin. She felt her hair blowing out behind them, and closed her eyes, letting memory slide backwards.

For a time they just galloped. It seemed to calm her, centering her thoughts and emotions, so that at last she was able to turn and look at him without blushing. His grey eyes narrowed in a question, and then he smiled faintly, reassuringly.

'All right?' he asked her. His words were caught and tossed away by the wind, so that he had to repeat them, bending closer to her.

Rachel nodded, and smiled back, but didn't look away.

The horse was slowing. She felt his hand come up to cup and hold her face, and then, with a sigh, his mouth came down hard on hers. The sheer desperation of his kiss matched her own.

'Ah, darling,' he breathed.

Rachel touched his lips with her fingers. 'I don't understand why it is,' she whispered. 'But when you're with me something happens . . . you fill me up until there's only you.'

He looked down, searching her eyes, and she knew he felt the same. 'Sometimes it takes you like that, Rachel, and there's no escaping it. There's no running from it. You just have to lean forward and fall into it. Fall, Rachel.'

His words wove a spell upon her. She felt as if she was standing on the edge of high cliffs, leaning against the wind. Swaying, her feet teetering on the brink. And then she leaned forward, slowly, and slowly she was falling down, down, into the dark dangerous waters of Will's sea.

Her mouth clung to his. There was an outcrop of rock close to the road, and Will moved the horse behind it, dismounted and lifted Rachel down. She felt his arms tighten about her, and his warm breath was on her neck as his lips pressed against her soft skin. 'Oh Rachel,' he whispered, 'I want you.' And she knew she wanted him, too, or at least she wanted something. Every touch of his hands and lips pushed her deeper into those dangerous waters and she wasn't even trying to save herself. He was unbuttoning her bodice, and she felt him touching her breasts, stroking the soft, full flesh, filling his hands. She gasped out his name, and suddenly the sound of her own voice, unfamiliar and unrestrained, shocked and frightened her, jolting her back to sanity.

'Will,' she said. Then, when he didn't seem able to hear her or to stop, 'Will!'

He looked up, his eyes for a moment sightless. And then he blinked, and saw her, and the red marks from his hands and mouth on her white skin. His brows drew down in a dark frown.

Was he angry? she thought. Had he expected her to lie with him, like Suzy, like one of his King's Head girls? Surely he had not expected that! 'I must go now,' she said harshly, trying to draw her bodice together. He stilled her hands, slowly and firmly redoing the hooks and buttons he had been in such haste to undo moments before. His hands didn't even tremble, she thought bitterly, while her own were shaking like leaves in a gale.

'Don't cry.' Will pushed his hair back out of his

eyes, and then rested his head in both hands for a moment, as though he couldn't bear to face her. Or himself.

'I'm not,' she told him in a shaky little voice.

'But you want to!' he burst out, and looked at her. Then he began to walk back towards the horse. 'I'm sorry,' he shouted. 'I'm sorry! What else can I say? You know how I feel now, Rachel. You know that when I'm with you I'm a man with no control over his baser instincts. And if that frightens you then it's all to the good.'

Rachel trailed after him, trying hard not to shed the tears he'd accused her of.

Her hair was tangled, and she pushed it back at her nape. Her mouth felt bruised where he had kissed her. 'Don't you think it's the same for me?' she asked him softly.

He didn't turn. 'I think you're young with all your life ahead of you, and time to change your mind a hundred times. It's only when you get old like me, Rachel, that things get serious. It's my own fault, I should know better than to mess around with virgins.'

He had known how it would be, when he arranged to meet her. The desperate struggle with his feelings had been lost, briefly, but he'd strengthened his resolve again. For the moment.

Will glanced at her over his shoulder, and his smile mocked himself. 'Come on.' He was holding the horse steady and she watched as he swung himself up into the saddle and held out his hand to her. There was something impatient in the gesture, as though he wanted to be finished with her. It hurt, and Rachel gave her fingers quickly and felt herself pulled up behind him. Then her arms tightened about him involuntarily and she gasped as the horse sprang away, earth scattering behind it.

Oh Will, she thought. I love you, I do love you. But perhaps you're too complicated for me, too dangerous for me. You could break my heart into a hundred pieces and I'd never be the same again. She didn't say it aloud. He was riding like the devil towards Down Farm, and she could no longer pretend that he wasn't keen to be shot of her. The rain was coming down now; heavy, thudding rain. It stung her cheeks with a pain that was like pleasure, and she closed her eyes and lifted her face to it.

During the next few days Rachel was almost glad that Baby Victoria was teething. Her mind was taken up with frustrating attempts to settle the child's fretting and grizzling. By the time Martha came to fetch the baby in the evening, Rachel's head was aching. She would sit on her bed and brush her hair with slow, calming strokes, trying to empty her mind of everything.

She thought she had succeeded. Yet, as soon as she blew out the candle and lay down in the darkness, as soon as her eyes closed, she saw him before her, and began to toss and turn. Rachel wondered whether she was ill, with some lingering malady. But deep inside she knew it was a malady of the heart, and only Will could cure it.

Martha was ailing again, too. She said her head

ached and nothing would soothe it. The baby's cries hurt too much, and Rachel took Victoria as well as the others. The doctor called and went away shaking his head, uncertain what to make of it. Suzy declared Martha was pretending to be sick, so that she could do nothing all day. Rachel wasn't so certain.

'Sometimes she looks as white as a ghost,' she said. 'And she can hardly bare the light from the windows.'

'Found any gin bottles under the bed?' Suzy mocked. 'Sounds like a hangover to me.'

Cook clicked her tongue, but Sarah giggled. Rachel shook her head impatiently.

'She won't miss the dance,' Suzy added smugly. 'You wait and see.' The dance was a yearly event in Greengage, an important date on the district calendar. Martha looked forward to it, as did everyone else at Down Farm. It was held every year at the inn, and although when it came to mingling there were clear demarcations, all of Greengage society, from the humblest to the grandest, was invited. Rachel had been looking forward to it, too. She had already planned what she was to wear.

As she left the kitchen, Suzy moved closer, lowering her voice. 'I thought you might like to know,' she said. 'There's someone in the barn, workin' on repairin' the broken wheel on the gig.'

Rachel stared at her. 'Someone?' she breathed. 'Who is this someone?'

Suzy smiled slyly. 'Don't you know, Rachel?'

Rachel bit her lip. 'I don't believe you,' she whispered.

'Please yourself,' Suzy mocked. 'But I've a feelin''

this is a someone you might want to see.' And she winked.

Rachel stared. She was right of course, Rachel did want to see him, but she couldn't let Suzy know it. 'Thank you for telling me,' she managed, moving away, 'but I'm not interested.'

Suzy only shrugged. 'Please yourself.' But she smirked, as she turned her back. Rachel could protest all she liked, she saw the truth. George had been right. The girl was mad about Will Trigg, ripe for the picking! Well, good luck to him. It might, as George said, do Will good. George was a sly one all right. It had been George's idea, to drop the thought in Rachel's ear. Will would never have agreed to an arranged meeting. He'd decided he was no good for the girl, and when Will decided something it was like breaking rock to get him to change his mind. Will had a conscience, George said, that was his trouble. That had always been his trouble.

Rachel stood at the window of the children's room, biting her nails. Frank and Matty were occupied, and the baby was sleeping at last. Perhaps she could just slip out and . . . The thought was suspended. Captain Potter had come from of the barn and stood now in the doorway, looking back. He was talking to someone, and after a moment the other man stepped forward too, into the light. Will was nodding, squinting ahead as though the glare hurt his eyes.

Rachel's heart was thudding and her legs were trembling. This might be her only chance of seeing Will alone. He had not sought her out since that Sunday they met on the Greengage road, and she was beginning to believe he had meant what he said, that he had no intention of doing so again.

Captain Potter had moved off, across the yard to the house, and Will had disappeared back into the darkness. Rachel moved swiftly to the door and slipped out onto the landing. She heard Captain Potter's steps in the hall and then the door of his study closed behind him. After a long moment, she went to find Sarah.

'I'll give you my best bonnet,' Rachel promised. 'And the green ribbon. It's only for a moment to two. I just need to talk to him, that's all.'

Sarah hesitated. It was a lovely bonnet, and a pretty green ribbon. Worth any trouble she might get into from Martha. 'It's not right to go sneaking off like this,' she made a token protest, but Rachel knew she had won.

Outside, the yard was quiet. She could hear someone working in the trees beyond the house, an axe ringing rhythmically through the still air. Rachel took a breath, and fear gripped her. Her feet slowed, and then she quickened her step again, knowing she mustn't hesitate or she'd turn and run. Her determination took her on, through the doorway of the barn.

Will looked up at her, startled. And couldn't look away.

He had been dreading this . . . or hoping for it. He didn't really know which. Only that now she was here, standing against the light like that, she looked like an angel. And he felt more torn and desperate than ever. He had no right to her, he knew that. She should marry some stolid, well-set-up young farmer and go to her wedding bed a virgin. She should lie on white, sweetly scented sheets with all the glory that was her due.

'Will?'

He looked away, concentrating on what he was doing. That was the best thing, put her from his mind, don't look, don't feel. But she came closer, pausing only a few steps from him. He could smell the scent she put in her washing water. 'Will?' she said again, and there was something so appealing in the lilt of her voice. But he hardened his heart once more and bent to his work.

Rachel bit her lip, watching him. He looked awful, unshaven, pale, his eyes dark shadowed and bloodshot. Why was he punishing himself, why was he punishing them both?

'Have I done something wrong, Will?' she whispered at last, and there was a lump in her throat that threatened to overset her completely. 'Talk to me, please.'

'You've done nothing wrong,' he said grimly. 'I'm the one who's done something wrong. And now I'm tryin' to put it right.'

'You've been drinking again,' she said irrelevantly.

'I have bad dreams,' he retorted.

'Why are you being like this to me?'

He paused, his hands still, the dark fringe falling forward to hide his eyes. 'You don't want a man like me,' he told her quietly.

'Don't I?' she asked him after a moment, and her voice was high and shaking.

'I'd come home every night, drunk, and beat you,' he warned her angrily.

'Would you?' she moved slightly, but closer, not further away as had been his intention. 'Did you come home to Hannah drunk every night, and beat her?'

'Of course not,' he muttered impatiently, then glanced at her sideways, suspiciously. She was watching him, and he couldn't read anything in her face other than polite interest. 'You deserve better than me!' he cried. 'That's what I'm trying to tell you.'

'Hush.' She reached out, and held her finger against his lips. 'I know I'm only seventeen, Will. But I'm not a fool. I can make up my own mind.'

He shook his head, turning away from her. 'You don't know anything, Rachel. If you knew—' but he stopped.

'If I knew what?'

'There are things,' he hedged, and then laughed at the sheer stupidity of it. 'I'm putting an end to it, Rachel. For both our sakes.'

She said nothing, only bending her head. The toe of her shoe was moving, drawing a picture in the straw and dust on the barn floor. 'So,' she began quietly, 'you want me to turn and leave, and pretend I don't love you and you don't love me. And that for some reason—some maggot you have in your head—we can never do anything about it. Is that right, Will?'

'That's right,' he said stubbornly, watching her toe drawing in the dust.

'Can't you even come and visit me occasionally?'

'Martha hates me. If she knew . . . she wouldn't let me within a mile of you,' he retorted, but gently now, wearily. 'And how often could we meet in Greengage? Five minutes every second week when Martha could spare you? Best to pretend we don't feel like this, and after a time the feeling will go away, because it's hopeless, Rachel. It's bloody hopeless!' Frustration coloured his words. He was right of course, Rachel thought miserably. At least, he was right about Martha. She would make certain Rachel was never alone with him. He was not the sort of man, in Martha's mind, to trust with an innocent young woman. Perhaps it *was* hopeless, and yet Rachel could not. . . would not believe it.

She looked up, her eyes shy, but they didn't waver from his. 'I think things only seem hopeless to you because your life is a little . . . untidy. You need someone to put the pieces back together again, Will. Someone who cares enough and is patient enough to set things to rights. Why don't you let me try? I know you think I'm too young to understand or to know my own mind. But I'm not young really. You forget my Pa was a bushranger, and I've survived a life on the road, as well as life at the End of the World Inn with Mrs Roadknight and her 'boys'. And I've grown up in the orphanage, hungry all the time, until Mrs Finn came to run it. In some ways I'm old, Will, older than you. And I want so much to help you, I want so much . . .' her voice broke.

She hung her head, swallowing, willing herself not to cry in front of him. He didn't need her tears.

He touched her shoulders, lightly, smoothing the cloth, fingers running softly, gently down her arms to her wrists and then closing, warm and hard, on her hands. 'Ah darlin',' he murmured. He put his arms about her, drawing her gently into his chest. He felt her lean against him trustingly and almost gave in to her. Almost. But what she had said only reinforced his feeling that what he was doing was right, rather than the reverse, and he sighed and leaned his cheek on the top of her head.

'You don't have to marry me, Will.' she whispered softly into his chest. 'If that's the reason . . . if you still feel bound in some way to your Hannah. I would understand.' Will squeezed his eyes shut tightly. For a moment the image came to him, of holding her in his arms the long night through. He imagined the passion in her eyes, in her kisses. She was capable of passion, he knew that, just as he was capable of stirring it in her. And then he sighed again, knowing it was only a dream. He could never do that to her—put her beyond respectability. For without the mantle of marriage and the approval of Greengage society, her life could be no more than half lived.

'You don't know what you're saying,' he told her quietly. 'Don't let your feelings play tricks on you. You'd regret it, Rachel. Go back to the house and in a while, you'll be thinking how lucky you were to have escaped from Will Trigg with no more harm than a few kisses.'

Rachel lifted her face and he kissed her, tenderly, as if she were a child. 'I don't sleep at night any more,' she told him, and the tears slid down her cheeks.

'Neither do I,' he said. 'But it'll pass, believe me, Rachel. These feelings will pass.'

He pushed her gently towards the house, his kiss still burning on her lips, and she went without looking back. She had told him everything she had in her heart, and still he had been unmoved. There was nothing else she could do.

Sarah rose up from the chair by the window, blue eyes searching the other girl's face. Rachel shook her head and forced a smile. 'He says these feelings will pass, Sarah. He says they will pass.' The smile trembled at the corners, and then dissolved altogether. Rachel began to cry, softly and hopelessly, into her hands.

Martha was ill again. Captain Potter looked at Rachel, his eyes dark with concern. 'The doctor is coming as soon as he can,' he said. 'Tell me, Rachel, how do you find her?' And now his expression became almost guilty, she thought. Perhaps he, as much as the rest of them was skeptical about Martha's illness.

'Mrs Potter seems in great pain, sir,' Rachel replied. Victoria made a grab at her nose, but she fended off the little hand, letting the chubby fingers curl about her thumb.

Captain Potter nodded, seemed about to say more, then changed his mind. 'Will you take the doctor in to see her?' he asked her. 'I've work that won't wait.'

Rachel nodded, and he smiled briefly in her direction before striding downstairs.

The doctor came at last, examined Martha and prescribed the laudanum. He spoke quietly to Captain Potter about a change of scene. 'Hobart Town,' he suggested. 'Perhaps you should consider removing your wife there for a week or two. Give her a change of air, something new to take an interest in.'

Captain Potter shook his head impatiently. 'We're coming up to our busiest time on the farm. And then there's the expense.' He shook his head again, stubborn. 'I don't see how I can possibly manage it. Can't Martha go on her own?'

'Frank, I don't think you understand. Martha is very determined in this matter, and perhaps she is right. Perhaps it is what she needs. I believe she has a sister in Hobart Town she is very fond of. But you should go with her; she feels you put her a good second behind your farm, you know.'

Captain Potter stood up, his face flushed with anger. 'Put her . . .' he repeated. 'The woman knows that everything I do at Down Farm is for her and the children! So that she can live as well as she wants to! I'm sorry, I can't possibly, Jack. She is being unreasonable. If she wants to go to Hobart Town, then she can take Rachel with her. I'll be staying here.'

The doctor breathed a deep sigh. 'Very well, Frank. I understand, but I wonder if Martha will.' There was a twinkle of compassion in his eyes, as he closed the door softly behind him.

After he had gone, Captain Potter went to find Rachel. For one so young, she had been an amazing strength in the household during this time of upset. Slowly, carefully, he explained the situation, while the girl gazed back at him, her dark eyes full of empathy.

'You will need to go to Hobart Town with Mrs Potter.'

'Of course, sir.'

He nodded, and took a deep breath. 'Very well.

I'll arrange matters. I think it would be best to leave the two older children here, in the hands of Sarah, but Victoria will have to travel with you.'

'When will we be leaving, sir?' she ventured to ask.

Captain Potter paused. 'I couldn't manage it until next week. Is there a problem, Rachel?'

She shook her head hastily. 'I...I was thinking of the Greengage dance.' If she missed the dance, then she wouldn't see Will again.

He half smiled. 'Ah! No, you won't be leaving until after the dance. Martha has had a new dress made.'

Rachel stared into space after he had gone. Hobart Town! She had never, to her knowledge, been there. But she had heard of the many houses and the many people, and that sometimes there were so many ships in port the masts and riggings made a forest on the water. Perhaps the new scenery and new faces would help to clear away this melancholy within her. Maybe she could even forget Will Trigg once and for all.

'I may not come back,' she said aloud; trying out the idea on herself. 'Surely there are lots of positions to be had in Hobart Town, probably better paid than this?' Yes, that could well be the best course of action. 'Hobart Town is far enough away,' she added in a firmer voice. But the empty silence of the room mocked her and Rachel wondered, in despair, if there was anywhere she could run that Will's memory would not find her.

Sarah peeped in. 'Oh, there you are,' she announced, stepping into the room and closing the door.

Rachel made an exasperated sound. 'Yes, it's me Sarah.'

'Cook sent me to find you, she says if Master Frank says another word to her she'll scream.' Then, with a nod over her shoulder, 'How is Mrs Potter?'

'The same.'

Sarah rolled her eyes. 'Suzy says she just likes everyone running around after her, making a fuss. Makes her feel important.'

Rachel grimaced. 'Suzy would. I don't know. I think she really is ill.'

But Sarah wasn't convinced either. She tickled Victoria's cheek, cooing at the baby. Frank and Matty were in the kitchen with Cook, and Rachel knew she should go and get them. Cook was not the patient sort where children were concerned, but it was peaceful here with Sarah, and she rarely had any peace these days.

'Saw Will Trigg in Greengage yesterday,' Sarah said, her manner purposely careless. The blue eyes flickered to Rachel, noting the way the girl's mouth pursed up. 'He asked after you,' she went on, when it seemed Rachel would not speak.

Still Rachel said nothing.

'You're the only woman he's looked at, since Hannah,' Sarah went on. 'That's what George says. There were plenty hanging around after she died, offering comfort to the widower,' with a snort, 'but he didn't even look. Until now. George says he's real keen on you, Rachel.'

'George should mind his own business,' Rachel retorted and turned her face away.

'George says Will's just stubborn, that he's always been stubborn. But he'll come round. George says

Will's going to the Greengage dance next Saturday.'

'What, is George Will's keeper or something?' she asked angrily.

'You can't blame him,' Sarah said softly. 'Will Trigg is his mate.' And, she added to herself, you are mine.

'Well he can mind his own business from now on,' Rachel retorted stiffly. 'I'm going to Hobart Town. Martha's going next week, to stay with her sister, and Victoria and I am to go with her.' It came out so grandly.

Sarah's eyes popped. 'Rachel,' she whispered, 'do you mean it? Is she going to Hobart Town without her husband?'

'He says he's too busy,' Rachel replied, looking away.

'But how long is she going for?'

Rachel shrugged. 'I don't know. A week or two.' Then, biting her lip, 'I might. . . I may look around, while I'm there. For another place, I mean.' She sounded awkward, but Sarah didn't notice. She was staring at her in silent condemnation.

'You mean you aren't coming back!'

'I didn't say that.'

'But you meant it.' Then, with a disgusted shake of her head. 'It's Will, isn't it? You're going because of Will Trigg?'

Rachel said nothing.

'Why do two people who clearly love each other have to be so stupid about it?' Sarah demanded. 'What's wrong with you two anyway, that you'd rather be miserable apart than happy together? So what if it don't last forever? Does anything last forever?'

But still Rachel couldn't seem to think of anything to say. Sarah marched to the door, pausing
with her hand on the knob. 'Do you want me to
tell George you're going, is that it?'

'It won't make any difference whether you tell
George or not,' she said. But Sarah thought she had
her answer, and closed the door behind her.

CHAPTER 6

THE NIGHT WAS CLEAR AND sharp. Rachel lifted her face to the starry sky and tried to make her mind as clear and sharp as the night. She didn't need distractions; she had made her decision. The gig teetered its way down the road to Greengage. Behind them, the sturdier farm cart brought Sarah and Suzy and George and a couple of others. Rachel could hear their voices in the stillness, laughing and joking. By comparison, the gig was quiet. Frank and Matty were quivering with excitement, but were afraid to voice it. Their mother did not like their chatter, she said it made her head ache.

The arrangements to visit Hobart Town had been made, letters had been sent back and forth, seats on the coach had been booked. And Martha was feeling well, certainly well enough to attend this Greengage yearly event.

In fact ever since it became clear she was going to Hobart Town, her health had improved dramatically. Not so Captain Potter's temper. There was a general consensus at Down Farm that it was better to keep out of his way.

When they reached Greengage, Rachel looked about her in wonder as they took their place with the dozens of other horses and vehicles. People were everywhere, calling to friends, laughing. She felt herself caught up in the moment despite herself. Frank and Matty were clamouring to get down, and Rachel helped them to the ground while Captain Potter assisted his wife. Sarah was there beside her, squeezing her arm, her blue eyes shining. Martha Potter, very smart in her new green dress, was fussing, ordering Rachel to see that the children didn't run off, frowning as she scanned bobbing heads for her particular friends.

'It's a shame we have no proper hall for such functions,' she told her husband rather petulantly. The Greengage Inn was the only place with sufficient space to allow for a gathering of any size.

'One day we'll raise the money,' he soothed her through long habit. 'One day Greengage will rival Richmond.'

Martha merely looked long-suffering.

The inn had been cleared of chairs and benches, and lanterns hung from the walls. Coloured paper streamers floated in the breeze from the door, and there were jugs of ale and punch for the thirsty guests—Martha Potter eyed these with misgiving. She clutched her husband's arm firmly and made sure Rachel was within earshot. Sarah and Suzy were convict girls and although Martha knew her moral duty, she did not expect them to keep the same standards as herself. Rachel was another matter—she would make it her business to ensure that Rachel came to no harm.

Young Frank's voice piped with excitement, and Rachel smiled and bent down to listen to him. She was glad she had come, really she was. This might be her last time in Greengage. There were lots of other families, and soon they were mingling while the servants congregated at the other end of the room. There was an invisible line down the middle, and everyone was expected to stay within that boundary.

Rachel wore her best gown, of navy wool. Mrs Finn had presented it to her on her last birthday. The colour accentuated her pale skin and dark hair and eyes. She looked lovely and more than a few glances were sent her way. There was a young man smiling at her from near the refreshment table, the son of one of the farmers, and she blushed and looked down, conscious that Martha was watching her with approval.

When the dancing began, Rachel thought she would have to stay with Martha and the children, and Martha seemed content with that idea. But Agnes Barber shooed her away with, 'I'll watch them. You go and enjoy yourself, Rachel.' Rachel glanced at Martha, whose smile was hard and false, and hesitated. Agnes shooed her again, and Rachel went swiftly before she could change her mind.

The music had started and Suzy and George were dancing close, George's hand suspiciously low on her back as he held her. Sarah greeted Rachel warmly, rolling her eyes towards the other couple. The young farmer's son came and asked Rachel to dance and she agreed with a smile, enjoying his admiration and friendly conversation. He went to fetch her some punch, and then they were danc-

ing again. Rachel watched Martha make a stately
progress around the room with her husband, and
then Matty and Frank, with several other young
children, slipped through the dancing couples, gig-
gling, having their own kind of fun.

The evening moved on, but still there was someone missing.

Perhaps he won't come, Rachel thought. Perhaps he wants me to go to Hobart Town. And next
week that's where she'd be. Among new faces, new
voices, everything new. She would forget she had
ever known him, ever loved him. It was as Sarah
said, she was only seventeen and would fall out of
this predicament as suddenly as she had fallen into
it.

Suzy was standing beside her. Her sudden hiss
of breath startled Rachel out of her thoughts. She
looked up, following Suzy's gaze.

And the world stopped turning.

Will Trigg stood against the darkness beyond
the doorway. He was washed and clean, his clothes
pressed and smart, and so handsome she could
understand Suzy's astonishment. With his straight
dark hair combed back from his forehead and his
grey eyes narrowed against the light of the room,
he put every other man to shame. This was the
Will Trigg she had dreamed of meeting again for
so long. Not the shattered, hurt man in the smithy,
but the man of the river, four years ago. This was
how she had always imagined it.

Others were looking, too, as though wondering
why they had never noticed him before. And then
Suzy was pressing through the crowd, not caring
who she jabbed with her elbows, until she stood

right in front of him, forcing him to pay attention. He looked down, and she said something, making him laugh. A new tune had begun, and still laughing, he went with her into the crush of dancing bodies.

Rachel felt something pressing into her arm, and looked down with surprise to see Sarah's hand, gripping her tightly. 'George isn't happy either,' she murmured, and Rachel saw George glowering, leaning against the wall with a drink in his hand. 'He's a looker, isn't he?' she whispered, and she didn't mean George now. 'Suzy's lost her head.'

Across the room, Martha was staring with a frown at Suzy and Will Trigg, and Rachel knew Suzy would get a lecture when they were home again. The gimlet eyes fastened on Rachel, and Rachel was well aware that while Martha had approved of her dancing with the farmer's young son she would not approve of her dancing with Will Trigg. His reputation had made him an outcast in her eyes, and set Rachel beyond his reach.

Not that it looks like I'll have the chance, she told herself miserably. Suzy means to have him all to herself. And anyway, why should she care? Hadn't she already decided the stay in Hobart Town was to be a new start? The music was beginning again, and Suzy was still clinging to his arm. But he was shaking his head, smiling, and then George was there forcibly removing her. Suzy looked sulky, as he pulled her away towards the refreshment table, and Rachel could almost hear Will's sigh of relief as he straightened his jacket. He was moving closer, slowly, through the dancing bodies, stopping here for a word, smiling there, his eyes always searching.

Rachel caught her breath, for he had seen her now. He came on. And she couldn't move, just stood and waited, looking into his eyes. Grey eyes, like rain clouds with the sun behind them, shining with some secret of their own.

'Come and dance with me, Rachel,' he said, and his voice was brusque. Suddenly she realised he was as nervous as she.

She nodded, not trusting herself to speak, and he drew her into his arms. He looked like a stranger, but a dear stranger. He had gone to so much trouble. For her? Suddenly all of her practical decisions meant nothing. Her heart flooded with warmth and she smiled up at him in sheer happiness. He squeezed the fingers he held in his, and the corner of his mouth lifted in his lop-sided smile.

'You shouldn't be lookin' at me like that, Rachel.'

'I can't help it.'

'I'm too old for you. Too old in ways other than years.'

She shook her head, although the smile dimmed a little.

'Are you really going away, Rachel?' She tried to read his expression, but found it too difficult.

'Yes,' she whispered.

He made a sound like a groan, said harshly, 'I have to speak to you. But not here, not here. Everyone's watchin' us.'

Surprised, Rachel looked up, and saw that it was true. People were watching them, some in amusement, some like Martha, in censure.

'Outside,' he said close to her ear. 'Can you manage it, Rachel?'

Her smile was from the heart. 'Yes. As soon as I

can.'

The music had finished and he let her go, turning his back as if she meant nothing to him. Rachel made her way to Sarah. Sarah eyed her with a pleased grin. 'You look like you've just had your pardon,' she teased. Then, eyes narrowing, 'Look out, here she comes!' Behind them, Martha was making her way through the crowd, her gaze fixed unwaveringly on her young charge. Rachel turned desperately to the other girl.

'I have to go out. Just for a moment. Please, keep her here.'

Sarah stared at her as if she were a lunatic.

'Please,' Rachel whispered desperately. 'Say I was taken ill, Sarah, anything! Just for a moment.'

She left Sarah gaping after her, and pushed her way through the happy crowd to the door. The group of men lounging on the threshold, smoking, gave way good-naturedly. And Rachel was out. Out into the cold, still night. Her breath misted white before her and she spun around, desperately searching for him. 'Will?' An arm slid about her waist, and then Will was pulling her on, past the inn, towards the tall trees which shielded the banks of the creek behind it. Rachel went willingly, laughing, her feet flying over the uneven ground, buoyed up by love and Will's strong arm.

The creek was running fast. White fountains of water sprayed over the rocks. Leaves and debris swirled on the current. Will turned her to face him, his fingers hard on the flesh of her shoulders. In the darkness she could not read his expression, but she heard him draw in a deep breath.

'Rachel,' he said. 'Rachel, my darling girl. I've

been so sure, so strong . . . until now. And now I hear you're going away. And suddenly I'm askin' myself what's the point of it all. Ah, Rachel, isn't a pinch of happiness worth any darkness that follows?'

Rachel nodded, dazed.

'I want you, you know that. And you've said you want me . . . Tell me I'm goin' mad, Rachel. That it's all a dream, and you never really loved a wreck of a man like me. That I'm too old, with too many ghosts looking over my shoulder, that I'm a Moon-raker after all. And then I can go away again and drink myself into nothingness and put you out of my mind.'

Rachel closed her eyes tightly. Her pulse was racing, and yet her head was clear and sharp, like the night, and her heart was flooded with a great happiness as she lifted her face to his. 'You're none of those things, Will,' she whispered. 'And I love you, I love you very much.'

He pulled her against him so hard she lost her breath, and his mouth closed on hers. His hands ran over her shoulders and then down her back, before sliding around to cup the fullness of her breasts. As though he wanted to touch every part of her, to convince himself she really was his.

Rachel caught her breath again, and captured his hands, holding them fast between her own. His eyes glittered on the edge of losing control. 'Will,' she said shakily. Then, more firmly, 'Will, not here. Not here. I want you, too. You know I do. But not here in the creek!'

He laughed sharply. 'You're right. Sorry. I told you I was mad for you. I should take you back inside. Rachel . . .' He put his hand up to her face, tracing her features like a blind man. 'I won't wake up, will I, and find this was another of my dreams?'

She smiled, and rested her cheek a moment against his palm, turning her face to kiss the warm, calloused skin. 'Never,' she whispered.

Will felt the tension leave him at last. There was no more to be said. He'd lost the fight with his conscience, and maybe that was how it should be. Without Rachel he'd be dead anyway, and it'd taken the threat of her leaving to make him finally accept that, and whatever pain went with it. He slipped an arm about her waist, and drew her back towards the lights of the inn. She leaned against him trustingly, enjoying the closeness. Once or twice he stopped, to kiss her. And she laughed, tugging at his hand, until he pulled her back against him, kissing her again.

Sarah was waiting outside the door, her eyes big and anxious. She caught sight of them and ran over. 'Mrs Potter'll murder you,' she hissed to Rachel, ignoring Will.

Rachel laughed as though she didn't give a damn. Her face was soft and dreamy and Sarah wanted to shake her, hard. But Will frowned, and she saw that he at least understood the seriousness of the situation. Sarah caught Rachel's hand. 'Come on!' she hissed. 'An' you better think of something quick.' But as they moved towards the lighted doorway Martha was already there, her face like stone.

'Rachel!' Her voice grated as though the anger she was suppressing was physically hurting her. She reached out and gripped Rachel's arm viciously, perhaps afraid she might escape again. Captain

Potter stood behind his wife, looking cross and embarrassed.

Will sighed. He had done many foolish things and, because of his tragedy, the people of Greengage had forgiven him or borne with him. But this time he had gone too far. And he knew it.

'You will not speak with him again, nor see him again,' Martha was saying in a sharp, hissing whisper. 'Do you hear me, Rachel?' Behind her, the doorway began to fill with interested faces, their breaths steaming in the cold.

Rachel stood with her head bowed, unmoving, mutiny in every stiff line of her. The storm breaking over her might shake her, but she was unrepentant.

'He's a drunk and a lecher,' Martha went on, her tongue running over itself. 'Oh yes,' as Rachel moved to protest. 'A lecher. He takes his pleasures from whores because no decent woman will go near him.'

There was a deathly silence; Rachel felt her face go scarlet. 'You should put your wife on a leash, Frank,' Will said, his deep voice hard with anger. 'Until she learns how to behave herself.'

Frank's eyes narrowed dangerously. 'I find that ironic, coming from you.'

'I wouldn't harm Rachel,' Will retorted. 'I love her.'

Martha made a sound alarmingly like a snort, but the men ignored her.

'She is my employee and under my protection,' Frank Potter said in a voice which strove to be calm. 'She is seventeen years old, Will.'

Rachel's head was pounding, and her arm was aching where Martha was still gripping it. They were arguing about her, she thought in disbelief, as though she had no say at all in the matter of the rest of her life.

'I want to marry her!' Will shouted. Frank Potter stared at him, at first in amazement and then, his eyes narrowing, in speculation. But Martha was having none of it.

'You disgust me, Will Trigg. You're not fit to marry any decent woman—' but Frank shot her a sharp look that for once silenced her.

'Are you serious?' he demanded.

Will looked at Rachel and then away again, as though he were afraid of what he might see in her eyes. 'If she'll have me,' he said harshly.

Captain Potter looked at him a moment longer and then nodded. 'I can see that you're serious, and sober enough this time. Come and see me tomorrow, if you are still of the same mind. For now it is late, and we must take our children home.'

Martha swept past him, drawing aside her skirts and lifting her nose in the air. Rachel looked back over her shoulder, dragged along by Martha's hold on her arm, and her eyes were big and pleading. He forced himself to smile, in an effort to reassure her.

When they had gone, Will began to walk slowly home. He felt tired and drained of all emotion. The euphoria he had felt by the creek had fled, and he wondered just what he thought he was doing. Inside, there was a jug on the bench and he poured himself a drink. It was milk, and he nearly spat it out, but forced himself to swallow. He had a bottle of rum somewhere, but he dared not touch it. Not if he had to go and see Frank tomorrow. The sweat broke out on him, cold and clammy, and he swayed a little, closing his eyes. Was he mad to think of such a thing? He was unfit to be a husband, as unfit as Martha had said. And yet, Rachel's face came into his mind, and he knew he had no choice. She had been right all along. She was his salvation and he was terrified that without her his life would sink once more into the black oblivion he had once craved.

Rachel stood by the window for the hundredth time. Was he here yet? Would he come after all? Almost, she could understand if he did not. It must be daunting, to come and face Martha in one of her rages. And yet, if he did not come, Rachel knew she would be lost.

Martha had still been full of fury the morning after the dance, lecturing Rachel on her behaviour and telling her roundly what a fool she was to contemplate marrying Will Trigg.

'Men don't change because they have a ring on their finger,' she said hotly. 'He will be the same whether or not you are his wife. Think of that, Rachel. Do you want a man who spends his whole life drunk?'

That was something Rachel did not want to hear.

'How many women, Rachel, marry, thinking they can change their husbands to suit themselves? A man only changes if he wants to.'

Silently Rachel met Martha's eyes, until Martha's eyes darted away. She was speaking from the heart, Rachel realised in surprise. Perhaps she really did mean well. But that didn't mean Rachel could allow her to dictate her future. She straightened. 'He was not always like that, Mrs Potter. There's no reason why he should not change back again. Besides, I love him,' she added softly, and flinched when Martha laughed derisively.

'You love him?' she mocked. 'What does a seventeen year old girl know about love?'

Rachel angrily bit her lip, refusing to say anything which might spoil her chance of happiness.

Outside, a horse thudded up the lane. There were voices in the yard. Rachel stood up to rush to the window, but Martha caught her arm, hissing, 'Have you no shame, girl? Sit down and be quiet!'

Captain Potter's voice echoed in the hall, the door to the study opened and closed, and there was silence. Martha flicked her a satisfied look. 'You can go and ask Cook to make us some tea, Rachel,' she said. 'We don't serve anything stronger in this household.'

Rachel went, thankful to be out of her sight. Cook nodded at the instruction, muttering as usual, while Sarah grinned at her encouragingly.

'You're a miracle, you know? *Will Trigg!* Do you realise how many women have looked at him and wondered whether they might be able to turn him back from the brink? And now here he is, in with Captain Potter, wearing his best jacket and his hair combed and—I swear it!—smelling sweet as a rose.'

Rachel was laughing. Cook glared over at them, and flapped her hands. 'Out!' she said. Rachel flew back to the front room. The men were a long time coming, and when they did come Will was pale and Captain Potter stern. He cleared his throat as the two women looked up expectantly—Rachel was having difficulty keeping still.

'Rachel, Will tells me he is serious in this proposal. He has made certain promises to me concerning his behaviour in the future, and I believe he is genuine in his affections. I am willing to agree to his marrying you, if that is your wish?'

Rachel stood up. 'Oh yes, it is my wish,' she breathed, and looked at Will briefly, afraid her happiness would spill over if she looked longer.

Martha cleared her throat. 'I don't want to put a damper on the occasion, but—'

'Then don't,' Will retorted, and reaching out, took Rachel's hand in his.

'Come for a walk with me,' he begged. 'I am sure it's allowable this once?' with a lifted eyebrow at Frank. He nodded, with a small smile, and Will led Rachel out of the room and into the yard.

'Are you sure?' she asked him, as he led her along. 'I mean, I don't want you to. . . I know you were forced into saying what you did, last night. . . Will!'

He was laughing. He pulled her around the corner of the stable building and into his arms. 'No-one forces me to do anything I don't want to do, darlin',' he teased, and her mouth opened under his, while her arms slid around his neck as she kissed him as desperately as he was kissing her. He bent, his lips at the hollow of her throat, pushing down the neck of her gown so he could reach the swell of her bosom. 'So beautiful,' he murmured. Rachel leaned her head back against the rough wood and closed her eyes, enjoying his attentions.

'Do you think everything will be all right?' she asked softly.

He stilled, and lifted his head to search her face with serious grey eyes. 'I don't know. I hope to God it is. You know how much I want it to be.'

Rachel smiled at him, pushing the hair off his forehead with possessive fingers. 'I hardly know anything about you, Will. Only what other people have told me. I want *you* to tell me.'

He let her go, and she looked after him, puzzled, as he walked over to the fence railing and leaned against it. 'I can tell you about Hannah, if you like, though there's little to tell. I loved her, but not in the way I love you. She was soft, like gentle rain; you're a storm, Rachel.'

'I don't need to know about Hannah,' she whispered. 'I know you loved her, and how you must have suffered when she died. I meant what you were like when you were young, where you came from, what you've done.' She shrugged. 'Your past, Will, because that's what made you the man you are.'

He didn't turn around. 'I don't talk much about my past,' he said finally. 'But for what it's worth, I was born in Wiltshire, near Devizes, though I don't remember it. I came to Vandemon as a child with my parents. My father was a blacksmith, like me. They're both dead now. I'm alone, just as you are Rachel. That's all.' But there was something so even, something so studied about his voice it puzzled her. As though he had read a passage in a book and was repeating it from memory. She knew well enough that he was not a man to open up easily. But, Rachel smiled to herself, they had plenty of time.

Will had turned around, and his grey eyes slid over her. Her skin tingled. 'Can we get married soon?'

She smiled back. 'As soon as you like.'

'Tomorrow then,' he mocked.

'I'll need a dress,' she reminded him. 'And a ring for my finger.'

He sighed.

'Well then, Will Trigg, it can't be tomorrow. Besides, I have to go to Hobart Town with Martha. When I come back we can be married.'

'You're right, I know. And while you're away it'll give me time to . . .' he smiled wryly, 'To "pull myself together" as Frank puts it. I'm just afraid you'll change your mind,' he added softly. Something in his face made her come and put her arms about him, holding him tight.

'I'll not change my mind,' she promised. 'I'll never change my mind, Will.'

And she really thought she meant it.

'It's a mistake,' Martha said with a certain smugness. 'She'll regret it.'

Her husband pursed his lips. 'Perhaps. But Will's promises seem heartfelt to me, my dear, and I know him as well as any man knows him. It may just be the remaking of him. Rachel is a warm, loving girl. He needs some love in his life.'

Martha shifted angrily in her seat. Love? she

thought bitterly. What does Frank know of love?

Frank watched her, wondering whether he should tell her what he knew of Will Trigg, and then decided against it. Martha would take pleasure in spreading the story all over the district. Will's past was his business. As far as Frank was concerned, Will's life had begun four years ago, when he came to Greengage and took up the blacksmith's shop.

'She will live to regret it,' Martha said again, her mouth tight with anger and disapproval.

Maybe, he thought, watching through the window as the couple walked back across the yard. Their hands were clasped, and Will bent his head, smiling, to listen to something Rachel was saying. Maybe it was a mistake, but surely, for Will's sake, that was a chance worth taking?

CHAPTER 7

THE JOURNEY HAD BEEN TIRING and the weather unseasonably warm. Rachel was grateful when the coach finally reached the outskirts of Hobart Town. Martha had complained the entire journey, and when she wasn't complaining she was leaning back against the shabby cushions with eyes closed. The driver had done his best, but nothing could shorten the journey or improve the roads. Baby Victoria had been excited and exhausted by turns, and Rachel had constantly to quiet her, while the other passengers looked on, some indulgent, some indifferent and some sharp with annoyance.

Despite that, and despite the physical ache she felt, whenever she thought of Will Trigg, Rachel sat up straighter and looked about with interest. Hobart Town! When Rachel had been sent to the Orphanage in Richmond, Mrs Roadknight had travelled to her sister in Hobart Town. It was years now since she had seen that lady. Was she still alive? Was she still in Hobart Town? Suddenly Rachel had a longing to find out. She had no father, and no mother. Of course, Mrs Roadknight had never pretended to be her mother, but she was a strong link from the days with Pa.

They were now travelling through Hobart Town's busy, tree-lined streets and the buildings grew taller and more solid and more crowded. Mount Wellington towered over the scene, its great flanks covered in bush. The Derwent River was full of ships—Hobart Town, a fellow traveller informed her, was one of the world's busiest ports.

'Whale oil and seal oil,' he explained. 'There's a roaring trade in 'em. Ships from the most outlandish countries drop anchor here.'

'And yet,' another passenger ventured, 'there are some who say Van Diemen's Land is doing poorly, sir.'

'In some ways we are. Too many convicts, too many immigrants, too little land and too few jobs. And there is a slump in prices at the moment. Not good for farmers such as myself.' He sighed. 'To the north of us, across Bass Strait, lies the Port Phillip District. All that land, just waiting to be taken up and made something of. Why, last year, Port Phillip sent meat to feed us! Unthinkable, isn't it? And yet it is so. We have too many people and too little to offer 'em. I'm afraid, for those with money and ambition, the future lies across Bass Strait. As for the rest. . .' with a shrug, 'the ex- felons who leave Vandemon for a new start—well we're better off without 'em!'

Martha shifted uncomfortably; it was the sort of thing her husband had been saying for months. Beneath lowered lashes, her eyes shone with pain, or anger—Rachel could not decide which. 'How much further,' she murmured. 'I really cannot bear much more of this. Why didn't Frank hire a private conveyance, as I asked?'

Rachel bit her lip and didn't reply. Captain Potter had refused to 'waste more money', as he put it, on this foolhardy venture than was necessary. The servants had been amused by it all, but Martha's face had been white with anger.

Captain Potter had come to see Rachel before they left for Hobart Town. She had been uneasy in his presence, feeling sorry for him, and somehow disloyal that she was going to Hobart Town with Martha, and leaving him behind. But after all, he only wanted to give her some money. 'You'll want to do some shopping,' he explained, 'for your wedding.'

Rachel had blinked and smiled. 'Yes sir. Thank you very much, sir.'

Captain Potter had moved towards the door. 'Enjoy yourself.' With a smile, 'You may not get to Hobart Town again in a very long time. Will is not the travelling sort, I'm afraid.'

Rachel had smiled more naturally then. 'You know him well don't you, sir?'

Captain Potter paused at the door, his hand tightening on the knob. 'Yes, I know him well. He is a fine man, despite the mess he's got himself into. Don't let anyone tell you differently.' And with that, he left her to her thoughts and the sleeping children.

There was a trap waiting for them at the coach station, and Rachel was caught up in helping Martha, keeping track of their luggage, and holding the wriggling baby. And then at last, they reached

Martha's sister's house. A two storey stone building, with shuttered windows and a stolid, welcoming air. The sister, Mrs Kennedy, perfectly complemented her home. Solid and welcoming, she drew Martha into her arms. The childless widow of a shipowner, she led a comfortable life in Hobart Town, employing a number of servants, going to functions at friends' homes and generally doing very much as she pleased.

Once in her room, Martha took to her bed. The baby, too, fell asleep in that sudden way babies do. Rachel sank down with relief into a chair in the room set aside as the nursery. The chair was lumpy, but at least it wasn't moving! But she was young and the tiredness soon passed. Rachel went to the window and gazed out at Hobart Town. The curl of excitement inside her made her feel almost disloyal. She missed Will, she told herself, of course she did, but she couldn't help it. After all these years of sameness, she was seeing new sights. She was in Hobart Town! And she meant to make the most of it.

The Kennedy household seemed leisurely and restful compared with Down Farm, but nevertheless very well run. Martha rested the next day, but was ready that evening to accompany her sister on a visit with mutual acquaintances. Further invitations were forthcoming and Rachel saw very little of the two women after that. She was left with

Baby Victoria much of the time, and although the other servants were polite they were distant.

On Sunday, she went strolling. An afternoon church service had just finished, and couples and families in their Sunday best were out to enjoy themselves and stretch their legs. Rachel gazed up Macquarie Street, past handsome St David's Church and a great number of other impressive buildings, to the bulk of Mount Wellington. It was a wonderful sight, and the only thing which spoilt it for her, was that Will wasn't there to see it with her.

Rachel grew to know Hobart Town well during her first week. She explored the steep, cobbled streets and gazed into the small shop windows. She stared wide-eyed at the imposing warehouses and wharves, and the taverns where the sealers and whalers drank. It was in many ways a rough, boisterous town, and in others—as shown by Mrs Kennedy and Martha—one of quiet sophistication.

But no matter how many soirees were held, or how many honest citizens wrote 'home' of opportunities to be had in Van Diemen's Land, no-one could forget it was a penal colony. Convicts roamed the streets, in chain gangs from the barracks and prisons, or else on tickets-of-leave, going about their own business, which often included getting very drunk. At night, there were all manner of violent atrocities committed. The convicts and sailors could be evenly matched in their viciousness.

'Be sure to say hello to the Female Factory for me!' Suzy had told Rachel before she left. 'I've fond memories of the place.'

Sarah had scoffed. 'To be sure you have, I bet you

have fonder memories of the flesh-pots and sly grog shops!'

Suzy tipped back her blonde head and laughed. 'Ah, that would be tellin'.' After a moment she said, more evenly, 'There's others with a secret life, you know.' Something in her eyes made Rachel uneasy. 'George was with your Will Trigg, once in Greengage, an' a stranger came through. He wanted a horse shoed. George told me the stranger recognised Will, but he didn't call him that. He called him by another name.'

Sarah frowned. 'It was a mistake, that's all.'

But Suzy shook her head. 'This stranger seemed awful sure, George said.' And then, her eyes sly, 'Why don't you get Will to tell you about it, Rachel, before you wed him and it's too late to change your mind?'

Rachel stared back into Suzy's hazel eyes. There was a hint of jealousy there, and malice. Suzy thought she should be the one getting married. Sarah sprang to the aid of her friend.

'George! What would he know? He was probably drunk.' And she smiled determinedly at Rachel. 'Bring us back something from Hobarton,' she said.

The conversation had moved on, but later Rachel thought about what Suzy said. If there was anything to tell, Will would tell her in his own time. She could be patient, couldn't she? And if she couldn't then she must learn patience for Will's sake. Suzy was jealous, that was all. She was trying to spoil Rachel's happiness, and Rachel would not let her.

Rachel pondered it, as she lay in her bed in Hobart Town. As always, her thoughts stole inevitably back to Will, and their last meeting before she left.

He had been looking wan, and thinner. Sarah had whispered that he'd given up the drink altogether. 'Some say,' she breathed, 'it's like cutting off your arm.' After the first time, Rachel did not ask him about it—he would not tell her; 'My business, darlin'.' But she suffered for him, and was proud of him, and longed for the day when she could share everything with him.

'I know I have to show I'm worthy of you, Rachel, but I wish I could rush you to the altar before you leave,' he had told her wryly.

She smiled. 'Soon,' she had soothed. She had lifted her face for his kiss, and the sheer desperation of it told her all she wanted to know.

Soon, she repeated to herself. Soon . . .

Martha seemed a different person these days. The fussy, irritable woman had gone and in her place was a smiling, relaxed woman in fashionable clothing and a charming hat. Was this the Martha that Captain Potter had fallen in love with? Rachel asked herself. If so, a lot of things made sense. Martha didn't speak of Captain Potter, nor the two children, although she visited the baby every day. And it was not until she overheard the servants gossiping, that Rachel realised why Martha was so happy. There was a man, a ship-owner like Mrs Kennedy's dead husband, and he had been paying

Martha a great deal of attention.

The idea made Rachel uncomfortable, although she told herself it was nothing. Martha would return home to Down Farm, she had no choice. That was her reality; the rest was just a dream. She was playing a game with herself, in which she was a widow, perhaps, like her sister. Rachel realised again just how unhappy Martha was at Down Farm.

So the days passed. The fine weather continued, and she could take the baby for walks. There was still plenty to see in Hobart Town and Rachel was determined to make the most of it. It was during one of these walks that she decided it was time to find Mrs Roadknight.

Rachel visited the Post Office, and made some enquiries. As the postal assistant searched through the lists of names and addresses, Rachel felt her heart begin to thud with anticipation. And then there it was. *Roadknight, Mrs.* And an address in Veteran's Row.

For a moment she stared at the name, transfixed. And then she realised the man was waiting impatiently for her to speak, and a whiskered gentleman was glaring at her, and she hastily moved on. It was time to get back anyway. Victoria was due to begin her afternoon grizzle.

Veteran's Row, she repeated to herself over and over as she walked. She tried to remember Mrs Roadknight as she had been at the End of the World Inn, but the memory was blurred and faded. A large woman, Rachel decided, with sharp brown eyes and her hair braided. She remembered more strongly the smells and sounds of the inn—the drink and the unwashed bodies, and the noise . . . so much noise. Rachel sighed. Was it wise at this point to look over her shoulder? Did she really want to revisit her past? But it might be her only chance. She probably would not return Hobart Town again—her life was charted for her. She saw it with the unswerving certainty of the young: The blacksmith's wife in Greengage and soon perhaps a mother, keeping the white cottage spick and span, working in the garden, and involving herself in Greengage activities. The image was perfect, and if it was a little *too* perfect, it didn't occur to her.

Rachel shook herself. Veteran's Row, she repeated softly. Yes, it would be fitting to see Mrs Roadknight again. To bring together the little girl of the Jerusalem-road Inn, and the seventeen year old bride-to-be, before she began her future with Will in earnest.

Veteran's Row, Rachel discovered on her afternoon off, began where Murray Street and Harrington Street converged. She found it easily enough, after climbing the steep hill with her purchases. She had bought blue muslin for a new dress, with trimmings, as well as some fine cotton for nightdresses and underthings. Somehow, it did not seem right that a newly married woman should wear the old calico drawers issued to her at the Orphanage.

She had also found some ribbon for Suzy, and

some lace for Sarah. For the children she had bought carved wooden toys about the size of her hand. At least, she thought with a sigh, Victoria would enjoy cutting her teeth on them. The pocket watch she had found in a pawnshop. The old man had driven a hard bargain, his sharp eyes aware that she was set on it despite her attempts at nonchalance. In the end it took nearly all that remained of Rachel's money, but she knew she had to have it. It was perfect for Will.

The house in Veteran's row was a short walk from the corner. A stone cottage, with a newly painted green front door and red flowers in a windowbox. It looked neat and welcoming but for some reason Rachel's fingers tightened on her parcels. Should she go in after all? It was all such a long time ago. Once again she wondered if perhaps the past was best left undisturbed. Will's words hummed in her head—'I don't talk much about my past.' But having come this far it seemed almost cowardly to turn tail and run now.

The footsteps coming to the door were slow and heavy. Rachel smoothed her skirts nervously, tucking back a wisp of hair beneath her bonnet. And then the door was opening inwards and peering out at her was a round, curious face with bright, brown eyes.

'Yes?'

Rachel opened her mouth and shut it again. Mrs Roadknight—for that was who it was—had always seemed so large. A big, broad woman with a big, soft bosom against which Rachel could rest her head when she was tired and sad. But that had been the memory of a small child. The reality was shorter than Rachel, though broad enough, with a face as round as a pie beneath her braided grey hair. Only the eyes were the same.

'Well?' she added sharply, when Rachel didn't seem about to speak. Then, the bright eyes narrowing, 'Do I know you, girl? Come on, speak up now! State your business!'

'Mrs Roadknight,' Rachel whispered. And then, louder, 'It's me. It's Rachel Naish.'

The brown eyes went a little out of focus, and then suddenly a broad smile broke across the round face, and Rachel was gathered into a surprisingly strong embrace. 'My dearie,' she muttered. 'Come inside, come inside,' And she drew Rachel in and closed the door.

There was hot tea and raisin cake, and Mrs Roadknight beamed across the table at her. 'Now my sister's gone, I don't get visitors very often,' she told Rachel. 'And not ones as special as you! What are you doing here? Have you left the orphanage?' Then, her face tightening, her eyes darkening, 'Were they cruel to you, dearie? Oh God, that was one thing that made me turn cold in the night, the thought that they might be cruel to you. But I'd no choice.'

Rachel leaned forward to grasp the warm hand. 'No, the orphanage was well enough, and I have friends there I write to. I'm a nursery maid now, at Greengage. And I'm in Hobart Town because my employer's wife was ill and she needed a change of air. I just thought. . . I just wondered ... I couldn't leave without seeing you, Mrs Roadknight.'

The round face split again into that broad smile. 'Indeed not! Oh Rachel, I've missed you that much. I always felt I should visit, but. . .' with a sigh, 'I didn't want to come between you and any new life you might 'ave. And I'd nothing to offer you, dearie.'

You could have written, Rachel thought suddenly. A letter now and then would have made a difference. The harshness of the thought surprised her. Rachel hadn't realised she harboured a grudge until now. The knowledge made her uneasy as she tried to temper it, tried to see Mrs Roadknight's side of things. Mrs Roadknight had done what she thought was best, hadn't she? And besides, Rachel had not sought her out after all these years to have an argument.

'Your Pa was always my favourite,' Mrs Road-knight was saying now, her eyes unfocussed again. As though she were seeing and hearing some long dead scene. 'He could talk the birds out of the trees, so he could. It was like dyin' myself, when I heard he'd been shot. Scum, that's what they are, them bounty hunters.' Her face twisted. 'I read of such things in the 'paper sometimes. Big, bold men, they call 'emselves. I call 'em murderers.'

The familiar refrain. Rachel felt as if she were back at the inn again, on the Jerusalem road. None of Mrs Roadknight's bitterness had faded, and neither, Rachel knew, had her own. Pa had been taken from them, and they would never forgive the man who did it, nor any of his kind.

After a moment the old woman took a breath, her eyes filled with tears. 'Your Pa loved you, Rachel. He used to say to me, "It's the girl I worry about, if I get caught. But you'll look after her, won't you Cassie?" "Of course I will," I tol' him. And I did my best. Until them buggers closed me down.' She shook her head.

'I miss him,' Rachel replied after a moment. 'Even now. It's so lonely, somehow, being without any blood relatives. There's no one who has known me from the cradle. I envy those people who go on and on about sisters and brothers, and uncles and aunts.'

Mrs Roadknight nodded sympathetically. 'You've never thought to look for your mother then?'

Rachel stared at her, the cup frozen in her fingers. 'My mother died when I was born,' she whispered.

Mrs Roadknight pulled a doubtful face. 'Did she, dearie? Perhaps I'm getting a little odd in my old age, but I was sure she was alive. Your Pa took you after you were born because the 'usband came back and there was a terrible old scene. So off he went to get you, and that was that. But I always thought Mary stayed with her 'usband and went on living with him, just as if nothin' had 'appened.'

Rachel shook her head. 'You must be mistaken,' she said firmly. 'You must be.' It was so unthinkable, so unbearable. It must be a mistake.

The brown eyes were shrewd now. 'You don't like the thought of being cast off so easily, do you, dearie? But sometimes it 'appens. Perhaps Mary wasn't the type to be a good mother and knew it, and saw that your Pa'd do a better job of it. He loved you, and the 'usband would have hated you, and who can blame 'im for that? Or maybe it was just better for you to go, safer . . . There could 'ave been reasons. Don't judge her, Rachel.'

Rachel swallowed. 'If she's alive, I should . . . that is, what's her name?'

Mrs Roadknight tapped a finger against her chin. 'What was it now? Something churchy, I do believe. Hymbury, that's it.' And she laughed at her own cleverness. 'Yes, Mary Hymbury. Your Pa used to say she was one of the angels.'

Angels don't give away their children, Rachel thought heavily. The visit had started so well, so happily, and now . . . Rachel wished she had never come.

'Where is she now?' she murmured dully. 'Mary Hymbury, I mean.'

Mrs Roadknight shrugged. 'They were living in New Norfolk. Her husband was a landowner there —a magistrate as well. Quite the important man. Which was why it was so awful, I suppose, that she, that Mary, should 'ave a child by your Pa.' Mrs Roadknight grinned. 'It was a lark, wasn't it?'

A lark? thought Rachel. She was looking at Mrs Roadknight with new eyes today, and she wasn't very happy with what she saw. What had appealed to the child shocked the grown girl.

'What's it like now, Greengage?' the old lady went on. 'Nothin' but a few houses and an inn, when I passed through it last.'

Rachel forced herself to smile and put the unpleasantness from her mind. She would have time later to mull over these revelations. 'It's not much different. But my . . . my future husband is the blacksmith there, and I suppose soon it will be my home too.'

So then she must tell Mrs Roadknight all about Will—'Trigg, Trigg? No I've not heard the name before, dearie'—and receive her congratulations and a gift of some old, faded, embroidered towels that had been kept from Mrs Roadknight's own short wedded career.

'You have been very kind coming to see an old woman,' she said, when it was time for Rachel to go. 'Come back again, when you can.'

Rachel smiled, and returned her embrace warmly, telling Mrs Roadknight she must visit Greengage one day. And after all she was glad she had come, even though she had heard things she would rather not have heard, and thought things she would rather not have thought. She had a puzzle to solve, something which may hurt her more, but Rachel could not leave the mystery of her mother unpicked. She had to know. She must know the truth, whatever the cost.

In all, Rachel was nearly a month away from Down Farm—and she was homesick. The last week, Rachel was certain, Martha was perfectly well again, but enjoying the life and bustle of Hobart Town too much to want to leave. In the end Captain Potter wrote a curt letter, and Martha, her face pale and cross, prepared to return home.

'Why can he not come to Hobart Town? Why can't George run the farm?'

'He says the children are missing you,' her sister told her firmly.

Martha shrugged. 'He says that only to make me feel guilty.' And then she burst into tears. 'I don't want to go, I hate it! I hate everything about it!'

'You can come again,' her sister said. 'Come in the summer, and we will go to the races.'

Although Martha eventually allowed herself to be soothed, resigned to the fact she must return to her husband, she set out on the journey grudgingly, gazing longingly over her shoulder. But if Martha was unhappy, Rachel was not. She smiled to herself, and thought of Will. It was as well she, Rachel, did not hanker after the races and new dresses and weeks spent in Hobart Town. It was unlikely Will would ever be able to give them to her. And yet she loved him so much she did not care. Hobart Town was all very well for a time, but she was so looking forward to getting back to Down Farm . . . and to Will. The journey seemed to take forever, and then suddenly they were home.

Sarah beamed at her, breathless at the sight of the lace. 'I'll trim my black dress with it.'

Suzy slipped the ribbon between her fingers, and smiled lazily. 'You did think of us then, while you was enjoying yourself?'

'Of course I did.'

'Will's looking good,' Sarah whispered. 'Looks like he did before Hannah died. Suzy's that jealous. Wants him for herself.'

'Huh!' Suzy tossed her head. 'George'll go further in this world than Will, you wait and see. We'll be ridin' to town in a coach and four.'

Sarah scoffed and Rachel laughed. But her heart beat faster. She was so looking forward to seeing Will, she could hardly contain herself until he came. What, she thought, suddenly terrified, if he had changed his mind? What if the time apart had made him begin to wonder again if he was making

some sort of mistake? She shook her head, angry
with herself. She mustn't begin to doubt; she was
just so nervous. It would be all right when he came
. . . if only he would come soon!

Rachel leaned to peer out of the children's
window at the men returning home from the paddocks. There was George, and Old George, and the
others she knew by sight but rarely spoke with. The
light was fading, but still golden enough to throw
long shadows across the yard. The evenings were
stretching out as winter drew to a close. Rachel
smiled as the dog sent the ginger cat, spitting and
hissing, over the fence.

Then suddenly voices were raised, and George
was laughing, and when she looked back to the
group of men she saw that someone else had
joined them, reining in his horse and leaning
down to listen. Whatever it was they had to say,
it made Will shake his head with a laugh as he
dismounted. Rachel stepped back, away from the
window, suddenly afraid he might see her there.
She felt breathless and dizzy. Had she forgotten so
soon how handsome he was?

'She'll have changed her mind!' George called
out as Will walked towards the front door.

'Not my Rachel!' he retorted with certainty.

Rachel closed her eyes. Slowly, she released her
breath. And then she was out of the room and
half running, her feet hardly seeming to touch
the ground. Sarah was opening the door even as
Rachel reached the landing, and she came down
the stairs in a rush. Will looked up, and his grey
eyes shone, while his smile was as wide as her own.
And then she was in his arms and he was holding

her so tightly it was an effort to breath.

'Oh Will, Will!'

He released her long enough to look down at her, and then hugged her again.

Sarah clicked her tongue. 'Let the man inside the door, Rachel. Half the winged creatures in creation are comin' to join us.'

Laughing, Rachel stepped back, holding onto his hand and drawing him in. Behind them, Captain Potter said dryly, 'Come in, Will. You're looking well.' Then, with a flicker of a smile, 'Use the parlour there, if you want to speak to Rachel in private. I suppose it would be more proper to have a chaperone, but I have too much to do and I'm sure Sarah is the same.' And he closed the door of the study behind him.

'Go on,' Sarah added, pushing them towards the parlour. 'But only a few minutes, mind, or Martha'll be wanting to know what's goin' on.'

'Only a few minutes,' moaned Will, but she ignored him and closed the door. He sighed and turned to look into Rachel's glowing dark eyes. 'Oh darlin' when can we be married?'

Something in his voice sent shivers up and down her spine. 'Very soon,' she soothed. He looked so good. It was not just that the colour was back in his face, that he was the man he had been before tragedy took hold of him, but he was *her* man, and she wanted to be with him.

'I've painted up the cottage,' he went on. 'And mended the fence. There'll be things you want to do, curtains and the like.' He shrugged, as though such notions were entirely foreign to him. Laughter tugged at Rachel's lips.

Suddenly he sighed, and reaching out drew her against him, resting his face on the top of her head. 'I've missed you.'

'I thought Mrs Potter would never come home,' she breathed, and lifting her face kissed his lips softly. Martha's misery seemed to have passed, or she was hiding it well, and now she had thrown herself into the prospect of Rachel's nuptials. 'Oh Will, she has all these plans now for the wedding. She means to have a dress made for me, and then a "little gathering" as she calls it at the inn. To send me off in style, she says. As though I were a ship, going to set sail around the world.'

He laughed. 'Well, let her have her way. Make a grand day of it, Rachel.'

He kissed her, gently at first and then with growing passion. Then Rachel remembered she had things to tell him. She pulled away, and catching his hand in hers, led him to the cedar and horsehair sofa that was Martha's pride and joy. When he was seated, she told him about Hobart Town, about going to see Mrs Roadknight and about her mother, Mary Hymbury.

Slowly, Will pushed back his dark fringe, as though it helped him to think. 'The name seems familiar to me,' he offered. 'Magistrate, was he?'

'Why yes!' and she beamed at him, proud of his cleverness.

Will laughed with mockery. 'I know my magistrates, darlin'. But as for the rest. . . no, I haven't heard of Mary or what became of her. You'd best talk to Frank Potter.'

But Rachel felt uneasy about confiding in Captain Potter. He would tell Martha and Martha would be curious, and Martha was not one to keep secrets. Rachel did not want this one spread far and wide in Greengage. 'I'll speak with Mrs Finn, at the Orphanage,' she said suddenly. 'I must write to her anyway, about the wedding. She'll know what to do.'

He pulled her close against him. 'You don't hanker then, to be a magistrate's daughter, Rachel? I can't offer you that sort of life, you know that. You're so young,' and he moved restlessly, as though the fact distressed him. 'How can you really know your own mind?'

Rachel smiled and reached up to stroke his cheek. 'I don't want to live like a magistrate's daughter. Ever since Pa died all I've ever wanted was a home of my own, and someone to love who loved me. Someone like you, Will. You're all I want.'

Did he believe her? Something flickered in the grey eyes. Then he was smiling, and he bent and kissed her again. Sarah was knocking softly on the door, but for a moment they ignored her, holding onto each other, desperate to pretend the outside world did not exist.

CHAPTER 8

THE WEDDING DAY DAWNED AT last, fine and cool. It was September before they were able to marry, and then Rachel had been on tenter-hooks, thinking it would be delayed. The children were as excited as Rachel, and raced about, getting under her feet. The new nursery maid was a middle aged woman from Richmond and Young Frank had already decided she smelled and he hated her. It did not bode well for her future.

Mrs Finn had answered her letter, and promised to be at the church. She had had little to say on the subject of Rachel's mother except that Mrs Roadknight was correct and she hadn't died when Rachel was born. As far as she knew the Hymbury's had packed up and left for Sydney. Mr Hymbury Esq was an ambitious sort of gentleman, and keen to get as far as he could in the colony.

Mary had gone with him. She may even be dead by now, and Mrs Finn knew of no other relatives in Van Diemen's Land. So Rachel was forced to let it rest there, for the moment.

Martha had done her best for Rachel's wed-

ding—and let everyone know it—but somehow
Rachel did not find her as irritating as she once
had. Perhaps it was knowing the extent of Martha's
unhappiness which had mellowed her.

The blue dress was simple but perfect, a foil to
Rachel's beauty. Her black hair, left loose and tumbling down her back, was set with a simple crown
of flowers.

George drove her to the service, with Captain
Potter to give her away. Will was waiting near the
big gum tree, and she knew by the look on his
face that she was beautiful. He appeared pale, as
though he hadn't slept much, but when he smiled
Rachel knew that all the worries and the delays
had been worth it. Bits and pieces stuck out in
her mind after that. Sarah mopping her eyes, and
Suzy winking lasciviously. The children squealing
in excitement, and Victoria wailing. Martha leaning a cool cheek to hers, wishing her the best in a
consciously cheerful voice. Will bending to kiss her
lips. And afterwards, as everyone gathered around
with their congratulations, the way he held her
hand. So possessively that she was sure he would
never let it go.

There was food and drink at the inn. Rachel
danced in her wedding dress and smiled and smiled
until her face hurt. Until at last Will drew her close
and said their goodbyes, and they were out in the
cool of the evening.

'Come on, wife,' he mocked, and his arm
squeezed her to his side, as he grinned down at her.
The flowers in her hair had drooped and her eyes
were shadowed with tiredness, but she was lovely
and his blood stirred at the sight of her. He would

make it work, no matter how much it cost him. Nothing would take his wife from him, he promised himself, not if he could prevent it.

Inside the cottage, he lit the lamp. The soft light filled the room, and Rachel glanced about her. This was her home now. Happiness filled her to bursting, but like a child, she was afraid to believe in case she woke up and found it a dream. She looked across at Will, and read the same thought in his eyes. And somehow that made it all right.

He held out his hand to her, and Rachel went like an arrow into his arms.

'Let me undress you,' he whispered. And, when shyly she shook her head, 'Let me. I've been waiting so long for this moment.'

He kissed her throat, his hands lightly smoothing her back and shoulders. Rachel felt her head spin from his mouth and the wine she had had pressed on her time and again. 'Mrs Finn liked you,' she tried to say, but he kissed her long and hard, and she lost the thread. But Mrs Finn had liked him.

'Just the man for you,' she had told Rachel with a decided nod of her head. 'You compliment each other, my dear. I'm so glad to see you settled.'

Rachel smiled, remembering the words. And then a frown creased her brow. 'Mrs Roadknight didn't come though. I thought she might.'

He paused, stroking her arm, and his breath was hot on her cheek. 'Rachel, forget about Mrs Roadknight. She forgot about you.'

Rachel stiffened and tried to pull away. 'She didn't! She did what was best for me. How can you say that?'

But he held her, nuzzling her throat. 'She put you

with strangers, Rachel, and left you. Was that what was best for you?'

The tears pricked at her eyes and tore at her throat. It was only what she herself had thought, but loyalty still bound her to Mrs Roadknight, that last link with Pa, and she said stiffly, 'You're being unjust, Will.'

'Come to bed,' he whispered.

She resisted. 'I don't know if I want to.'

He smiled. 'I know I'm the first.'

Rachel felt a stab of anger, and didn't bother to hide it. 'I know I'm not.'

He laughed. 'I've had my share of women,' he agreed, and smiled at the look on her face. 'Are you jealous of that, darlin'? Don't be, Rachel, ah don't be. None of them was like you.'

His mouth slid over her averted cheek, down to her bared shoulder, Rachel shivered as he led her through the doorway into the bedroom. Her trunk sat chastely by the wall, brought over earlier by George, still to be unpacked and the contents put away. Rachel felt her breath tremble in her throat. Will had begun to open her bodice, undoing it button by tiny button so that he could kiss every inch of pale skin as it was revealed.

His mouth covered hers again, the beautiful dress slid down her arms and he sank down onto the side of the bed, pulling her onto his lap. He began to kiss her breasts, his head a shadow against her flesh— the room was lit only faintly by the lamp in the other room. Rachel gasped, holding him against her. His hands encircled her waist and he looked up, meeting her eyes.

'It's real, isn't it, Rachel?' he whispered, and

suddenly she saw through his control, to the vulnerable man beneath.

She smiled, touching his cheek, and all the fear was gone. Why had she been afraid? This was her beloved husband. 'It's real, darling Will.'

Their kisses grew hotter, wilder. Will pulled her down against his chest, her body warm and smooth against his. Her beautiful dress was tossed aside, and his hands were teasing her, his mouth tasting her, until she cried out, 'Oh Will, I can't wait any more,' and then was horrified at what she had said. But he only replied, in a taut, stranger's voice, 'Neither can I,' and covered her, his big body pressing her down into the mattress, making her his wife in fact as well as name.

For a time she lay still beneath him. The violence of his passion was passed—like a thirsty man, he had quenched his thirst. There was an ache, where he had thrust against her, but not so bad as some of the girls at the Orphanage had told her it would be. And he had been so grateful, so loving, afterwards. Even now he was gathering her against his chest, so that she lay more on him than the bed. His fingers curled possessively about her hip.

Rachel opened her eyes and half sat up to look at him, pushing her long hair over her shoulder so that she could see him properly. She loved the way his dark lashes framed his grey eyes, and his hair was so straight, still a little long. His nose was well cut and his jaw wide and strong, and there was not one tooth missing . . .

He was laughing at her perusal and rolled her on the bed until she was under him again. 'Well, am I handsome enough for you?' he asked her, but there was that vulnerability again beneath the teasing, as though he were afraid of her answer.

'You're beautiful,' she whispered, and her eyes slanted up at him, shy and yet provocative in a way she hardly yet understood. She was only just starting out on her journey into womanhood.

'So are you,' he murmured with soft wonder, and she could see that he meant it. He smoothed back a truant lock of black hair with his finger, and traced her dark eyebrows, running his fingertip down the bridge of her nose to her lips. She caught it between her teeth, pretending to bite, and he smiled. The joy was bubbling over inside her.

'Is this how it's meant to be?' she asked him softly. 'You know so much more than me, Will. Is it? Should I be so happy?'

His eyes searched hers. 'I can't tell you, darlin'. I just keep thinking how lucky we are.' Then he grinned and wrapped his arms around her once more. 'I've got months of waitin' to make up for. I can't waste time with talkin', woman!'

She kissed him back. And this time when he made love to her he was not so desperate, but slow and almost playful. Until she was squirming all over him—like, she thought hot-faced later, a cat on heat. But he didn't seem to mind. He wanted something from her, but she didn't know what it was. Only when he slid inside her, and she realised the friction of his body against hers was going to make her explode, did she understand. And only when she did explode, sobbing with the pleasure of it did Will allow himself to find his own ecstasy.

'Oh Will, oh Will,' she whispered in his arms, feeling the thud of his heart against her cheek. And couldn't believe any other man in the world could possibly make her body sing like it just had. Only Will could do that. Only Will was special.

Outside, the day was slipping away. And there was still so much to be done! The washing was drying and should be turned, the hearth needed cleaning, and the garden needed weeding. And then Will would be needing his mug of tea and piece of cake —he was always so hungry when he was working.

Rachel moved restlessly, thinking of all her undone tasks.

'Be still, Bella,' the accented voice was polite, with a hint of amusement. 'Not much longer, I promise.'

Rachel forced herself to be still although her skin was twitching with impatience. It was so silly, she thought, as well as a waste of valuable time. Will's idea, of course, but when he had heard that the artist from Hobart Town was travelling through Greengage, he had insisted. 'He's meant to be good,' he told her. 'I mean, he makes a good likeness. Not like some of them. Wouldn't recognise your own wife!' Then touching her cheek with his finger, 'Humour me, darlin'?'

Rachel had been unable to refuse him. It was sweet, really, she supposed. After a whole three months of blissful marriage, a husband wanting a miniature of his wife as a keepsake. 'What about you?' she'd retorted. 'Can I have one of you?'

He had laughed. 'I can only afford one, and you're

prettier, Rachel.'

The artist, a Signor Rossi, was a dapper little man, although Rachel noted his cuffs were rather threadbare and his jacket worn shiny in places. Perhaps there wasn't much money in painting portraits after all. And yet Greengage and towns like it often patronised such persons, eager to have their likenesses painted and hung on their walls, copying the habits of those richer than themselves. That was why Signor Rossi made his yearly pilgrimage from Hobart Town into the countryside.

'There,' he laid down the brush with a sigh.

Rachel sighed too, and rose, rubbing her arms and stretching her fingers. 'May I see it, sir?'

He smiled and nodded. 'You are a good subject, Bella. You have strength as well as beauty in your face.'

No doubt he flattered everyone the same, but Rachel felt obliged to thank him as she drew closer to his work. It was tiny, only about the size of her clenched fist. Later, he said, he would set it in Will's watch case, the one Rachel had given him and which he treasured so highly. The face was like her own, and yet not a mirror image. Rachel frowned, bending closer. Were her eyes so direct and fearless? Was her mouth so wide and ready to smile? She would not have thought so. And the nose ... it was wrong, she was certain. Her own could not be so long.

'Very fine, sir,' she managed.

He laughed. 'You don't like it,' he replied easily. 'Women rarely like their own portraits, unless I flatter them quite outrageously. Perhaps that is why I am so poor, eh? But I prefer to paint the truth behind the face, Bella.'

'Then I hope Will wants the truth,' she replied rather sharply, and then was ashamed.

But Will was pleased. He studied the portrait for a long time, while she waited impatiently, and then he looked up and met her eyes. 'I don't know what it is,' he told her quietly, 'but he's caught something of you, Rachel. More than just the colour of your eyes and hair and the shape of your face. Something of your soul.'

'I don't know why you want it,' she whispered, deeply touched. 'You know I'll never leave you, Will. You'll never need that to remember me by, because I'll always be here.' A lump rose in her throat, and he came and drew her into his arms.

'It's all right,' he breathed, kissing her wet lashes. 'It's all right. Sometimes I just can't believe I'm so lucky.'

Rachel held him tightly against her. Why, she wondered, was he afraid? As if at any moment he expected everything to be taken away from him. It frightened her, too, so that she strove even harder to make him happy, to make him understand this was forever.

'We're lucky because I made that wish on Midsummer's eve,' Rachel reminded him at last. 'That's been our luck, Will.'

Everyone said they were fortunate. To the people of Greengage, the Triggs were the happiest of couples. Will was a changed man, no one could deny that, and Rachel glowed like the moon, soft and gentle. In three months of married bliss they had had only one argument, and even now Rachel couldn't bear to think of it. So silly, really.

It had been over some news George brought—a group of desperate bandits were said to be terrorising homesteads in the Ross area to the north. George had said, 'Good luck to them,' and Rachel had laughed and agreed. Will hadn't said a word.

But when George was gone, Rachel, puzzled, had asked him what was wrong. And he had asked her why she wished thieves and murderers well.

'You don't understand,' she had begun.

'I understand,' he snapped. 'They have a right, it seems, to vent their spleen on the innocent. What about the rights of the innocent?'

'Those men have been forced to become bushrangers because of—'

'That's a myth, Rachel. You're thinkin' that way because of your past.'

'Pa was never—'

'For God's sake, can't you see your father for what he was!' he shouted at her.

Rachel sat very still, and then she said quietly, too hurt for anger, 'You mean a thief and a murderer, Will?'

The fury was wiped from his face in an instant. 'No, Rachel,' he whispered. 'No, Rachel.' And he came and put his arms around her.

They said no more, but it had never been resolved, and the pain was still there. And the puzzlement. Why had he said such things?

Then, of course, there were Will's bad dreams. She had told no one about them. And Will would not discuss them with her, although she had tried to make him talk.

'They're only dreams,' he'd told her, making a joke of it, refusing even to recount them. 'Turn

over and put the pillow on your head, Rachel, so
you can't hear me.' And although he'd teased her,
and made her smile, the dreams were a blemish on
what would otherwise have been perfection.

The dreams had begun soon after they were
married. Not every night, just now and again,
sometimes two nights in a row, sometimes not for
a week. Usually they began with Will tossing and
turning in the bed, and often after a time he was
able to wake himself up, soaking with sweat. But
sometimes he didn't, or couldn't wake up. And
then he would call out things Rachel hardly comprehended. Things which made her feel cold, with
a dread she never spoke out loud, not even to Will
himself.

'Blood,' he whispered once, his voice full of
horror. 'Blood all over them.' And then, one mem-
orable night, he spoke in so chilling a voice Rachel
sat huddled on the edge of the bed, watching him
and feeling quite certain that Will had gone away
and this was a stranger. 'Stand up,' he said, 'and stand
still. Stand up and stand still, you bastard. I've got
the gun now. It's loaded and I don't miss. Through
the head, maybe, or maybe I'll smash both your
legs and leave you for the wild dogs to finish off.'

Was this Will? Rachel asked herself. Her gentle,
loving Will? She could not recognise her husband
in that cold, ruthless voice. It must be a dream, just
a bad dream. And she tried to believe it, to convince herself of it, while within her the worm of
doubt burrowed deeper.

Captain Potter, being Will's friend, often called when he was in Greengage. Sometimes he sent George in with fresh meat or vegetables, if he had some to spare from the farm and garden. Rachel was grateful for that. Although Will's clients had begun to return, they were hardly making a fortune.

Martha called, too, once or twice. And although she nodded to Rachel at church on Sundays, her manner was cool now, as befitted the squire's lady to a mere blacksmith's wife, and cooler still to Will. She disliked him for what he had done after Hannah died, and disliked him more now he had reformed without any help from Martha.

Matty and Frank and Victoria were always pleased to see Rachel—as predicted, Frank did not get on with his new nursemaid. Baby Victoria was growing so fast. Rachel, looking at the big blue eyes and sweet round face, began to wish that soon she and Will would have a child of their own. He wanted one, she knew, as much as she.

Sarah called when she could, and Rachel looked forward to her visits. She had made acquaintances in Greengage, but no friends as close as Sarah. She missed the confidences they had exchanged at Down Farm and, though Rachel hardly liked to admit it, she missed Suzy, too. But, she told herself firmly, she had Will now, and their life together compensated for all else.

'It's a miracle what you've done,' Sarah told her.

'Will's the miracle,' Rachel retorted softly. 'He's the one.'

At night, in his arms, it was still a miracle. Her

body cleaved to his passionately, and she forgot herself in his kisses and his touch. Perhaps, she thought, it was Pa's Spanish blood in her veins that made her so hot for him, so eager to meet him halfway when it came to their marriage bed. He had only to touch her and she sparkled into flames, and even when she lowered her eyes, trying to hide it from him, he knew.

Sometimes, when Will had business in Richmond, Rachel visited the Orphanage and Mrs Finn. Once, they had discussed Rachel's mother, and Mrs Finn had spoken to her firmly. 'I think you must forget that, Rachel. You are happy and have your own life now. Put the past behind you.'

'But the past is part of me,' Rachel had argued. 'It's what makes me who I am.'

Mrs Finn shook her head. 'I think you are hoping for some sort of reconciliation, my dear. Just as you were with Mrs Roadknight. You will be disappointed again, you know.'

Rachel tightened her hands. 'I wasn't disappointed with Mrs Roadknight. I just expected too much. I have written to her, you know, asking her again to visit if ever she is near Greengage. Not that I expect she will. She is settled in her cottage, with her memories.'

And then Will came to fetch her, interrupting them, and when Rachel walked off on his arm, she knew the girls were all peeping out at them, enviously, from behind the windows.

Rachel straightened with a grimace, stretching her aching back, and surveyed the garden. It was looking lush and green, but it had been an effort. They really needed some rain. Not that today was rainy. Far from it. The sun was shining and a butterfly darted among the flowers, teasing the kitten Will had brought her, as it leapt and pounced, trying to catch its unwilling playmate.

Martha was saying she was ill again, seriously this time, Sarah had said on her most recent visit. Rachel remembered how unhappy Martha had been, and supposed illness was an escape, of a sort. And, Sarah went on, the new nursery maid was threatening to leave because Frank kept running away from her. 'She's a dragon,' Sarah told Rachel. 'Not like you.'

'Has Captain Potter called in the doctor?' Rachel said, her mind still on Martha.

Sarah nodded. 'He gave her laudanum, and she goes to sleep. She sleeps most of the time. Sad thing is, she can't abide having the children near her. Not that she was such a good mother, but she loved them in her way. They don't understand what's going on, poor little mites.'

'She was going to Hobart Town this summer,' Rachel murmured. Now it seemed unlikely Martha would be going anywhere any summer, Sarah told her, if she didn't improve.

The sound of a vehicle broke Rachel's reverie, and she lifted her gaze from the garden. There was a wagon pulling to a halt outside the smithy. A man and a woman sat together a moment, heads close. Rachel pushed up the brim of her hat to see them better, but did not recognise them. She watched as they climbed down and, after another conference, went into Will's shop. The sound of Will's hammer stopped its tapping, and there was silence. Customers, Rachel supposed, and made to turn away, when suddenly the woman gave a shriek fit to wake the dead.

For a heartbeat Rachel could not move. And then she was running, out of the gate and down the worn path to the smithy. Forgetting everything in the terrible fear that something had happened to Will. 'Will!' she called frantically, breathless as she reached the doorway. Her eyes, blinded by the sun, were useless for a moment. But, as painfully slowly her sight adjusted to the dim light, a strange scene unfolded before her.

The woman, Rachel realised with a shock, had her arms about Will. Hugging him to her, despite his bare chest and sweaty skin. She was laughing and crying, all at the same time. The man was standing a little distance behind her, and his smile was splitting his face in two.

'Will?' Rachel whispered. Confusion filled her, and suddenly her legs seemed too weak to hold her up. She swayed, and leaned hard against the door jamb.

Will looked up, his grey eyes so full of joy they were like a beacon in his grimy face. 'Rachel,' he said, laughing. 'Rachel, this is Zelda!' and he threw his arm around the woman who was, Rachel realised, almost as big as him. 'And this,' putting his other arm around the man's shoulders, 'is Benny,' Benny was small and wiry with twinkling eyes, whereas Zelda's eyes were as wary as Rachel's.

For a moment she was speechless. 'How do you do?' she asked at last, with incongruous politeness. Her glance to Will was questioning.

He dropped his arms and came forward, bending his smiling face close to hers. 'They're friends, darlin'. Old friends. Make them welcome and I'll be up in a minute.'

Rachel opened her mouth to ask questions, but his lips brushed hers—to silence her, she thought resentfully—and then he was saying over his shoulder, 'Go up to the cottage. I just have to finish this, and I'll be joinin' you.'

Zelda accompanied her, talking in a loud voice about their journey from Hobart Town, while Benny trailed behind. Will had never spoken of either of them before, but Rachel was unwilling to tell them so. She pretended to listen to Zelda, nodding, until they reached the door. Benny opened it with a flourish, and Rachel smiled as she passed through, ignoring Zelda's guffaws.

The atmosphere was tense. Rachel offered tea and cake, and busied herself preparing both. But it was all pretence, to avoid saying too much. She was desperate to hear Will's step at the door, and when at last she did, she turned with relief. But Zelda was there before her, hugging him again, as though she needed to touch him to convince herself he was real. And Benny was up too, shaking his hand so vigorously, Rachel thought it might come off. Will only laughed, as pleased as them.

'Sit down,' he told them sternly, but his grey eyes were smiling.

Rachel put his cup before him. Feeling like an interloper in her own home, she went to move back towards the hearth. But Will caught her hand and drew her down onto his lap, holding her with one arm while he drank his tea. She felt her face colour under the interested gaze of Benny and Zelda, and then wondered why she should care. Whatever these people were to him, Rachel was the wife he loved.

Benny began to talk about Hobart Town and how his business, unlike so many others, was flourishing. 'I'm a carriage-maker,' he explained to Rachel.

'The best in Vandemon,' Zelda boasted, and grinned at her husband. When her smile returned to Rachel it was not quite so friendly, and her bright eyes were speculative.

'How are things for you, Will?' Benny added.

Will said they had enough trade from the district to make a living, as well as passers through. Benny lifted an eyebrow, but Will wouldn't meet his eyes. 'Vandemon's a big place,' he said shortly, as though answering some unspoken question.

Zelda leaned forward. 'You're still taking a risk.'

Will said nothing, but Zelda's lips fastened like a purse, and Rachel knew that, behind her, he had shaken his head slightly. To stop further questions.

'We have to be in Richmond sometime tomorrow,' Zelda went on. 'And we've a room at the inn tonight. I hope you're going to ask us to stay over for supper, so's we can celebrate your wedding.'

'Nothing would please us more,' Will replied, and Rachel's heart sank.

They talked generally for a while and then Will returned to the shop, saying he had work to finish, and Benny and Zelda went with him. Rachel tidied up and set about preparing the meal. Resentment began to boil in her. They were his friends, she tried to reason with herself. Why should she care? And yet something in Zelda's manner made Rachel dislike her . . . and more. Made her afraid.

After a time, she heated water for Will to wash in, and at a loss to occupy herself further, made her way down the path to the smithy. She could hear their voices as she approached, but it was not until she was nearly at the door, that the words made sense to her. Rachel's feet slowed and stopped, and even knowing that she should not, she stood quite still, listening.

'You've done the best you could.' Zelda's voice came from inside, as loud as before. 'You always do your best, Will.'

Will said something low in reply, but Rachel could not make out his words.

'I think you're making a mistake,' Zelda retorted. 'If she loves you then it won't matter to her, will it?'

Will said something more, and now his voice was angry.

Zelda laughed sharply. 'Oh don't worry, I won't tell her, not if you don't want me to!' Then, thoughtfully, 'She's very young, Will. Maybe you'd have done better with an older woman, someone like Hannah. Someone with more experience of life.'

Rachel straightened, pushing back her hair. She shouldn't stay here, listening to their private conversation. And yet her heart was thudding in her breast, making her breathless—the same feeling she had had as a child, seeing monsters where there were only shadows. It's nothing, she told herself. I'm imagining something out of nothing. Later, I'll ask Will and he'll tell me and we'll laugh.

She came to the door, and they all looked up. Zelda appeared almost defiant, Benny guilty, and Will was smiling with his mouth while his eyes were cool and distant. 'I thought you might want to come and wash,' Rachel managed cheerfully. 'Before we eat.'

Will agreed. 'I'm finished here anyway,' he added. He closed up the shop, and walked ahead of them. Benny looked at Rachel, his eyes twinkling. 'You'll have to forgive us taking up Will's time. We've a lot to catch up on.'

Zelda glanced at her sideways. 'We're friends from long ago,' she said. 'The good old days, Benny calls 'em,' and her mouth twisted. 'But men always think like that, don't they?'

Rachel straightened her back. 'Will doesn't,' she replied rather sharply.

Zelda eyed her for a moment. 'Doesn't he?' she mocked. And changed the subject.

Rachel decided that what made her really angry was her sense that they knew Will better than she, and that she was being excluded. Suddenly, it seemed to her as if there were two Wills, one for her and their life together in Greengage, and another who belonged to Zelda and Benny and the bad dreams. And the second Will was a frightening stranger.

They'll be gone tomorrow, she reminded herself tensely. And then things can get back to normal again. During the meal, Benny made them all laugh. Even Rachel found herself beginning to relax and enjoy herself.

'I'll make you a carriage,' he told Will. 'With your

names on the side in curly gold writing. You can ride about Greengage in it.'

Rachel laughed. 'Everyone would be green with envy.'

Zelda snorted. 'You'd be locked up!'

Later, when Zelda and Benny were leaving to spend the night at the inn, Zelda remembered she had left her shawl and Rachel went to fetch it. It was a ruse, she realised afterwards, so that Zelda could have a last word alone with Will. But the window was still open to the fresh air, and her voice carried. And Rachel heard.

'She's not right for you, Will. There's something about her.'

'It's nothin' to do with you,' he retorted, impatience barely held in check. 'Understand that, Zelda. You can't come between me and my wife.'

'I don't intend to,' Zelda said sharply. 'I'm just warning you, she's too young. You need someone older, someone more forgiving. Rachel seems sweet enough, but underneath it she's as hard as rock. She'll make you bleed, Will.'

He laughed angrily. 'It was Rachel made me want to live again. Before her, life wasn't even worth fightin' for. And now every morning's a miracle, because she's there.'

Rachel felt love for him overwhelm her. She knew then that she wouldn't question him about Zelda and Benny. She would say nothing, trusting him and loving him as he did her. And perhaps one day, when he felt able to, he would tell her what this was all about. Taking a deep breath, the shawl clasped firmly in her hands, Rachel went outside to take her leave of Will's friends.

Later, alone in the darkness, he made love to her with slow and exquisite tenderness. And nothing mattered then, not his past or hers, only that they were together in the present.

For a time, things between Will and Rachel were perfect. Zelda's words were forgotten, and Will had no bad dreams. Rachel felt as if nothing could touch them. Sarah said she was besotted, and it was the truth. Will hadn't touched a drop of liquor since he asked her to marry him. It was like a fairy story come true. So perfect. And yet Rachel's sense of foreboding remained. There was something dark, waiting below the surface. Just waiting.

George and Suzy were getting married. 'George thinks I'm only doing it so's I can be free,' Suzy had told Rachel, after the banns were read—George having served his sentence and been pardoned, was now a free man. When Suzy married him, she would also be assigned to him, and as near to free as it was possible to be without the actual document to prove it.

'He thinks I mean to go back to Hobart Town and leave him here,' Suzy went on, and smiled to herself. 'Not that I couldn't if I wanted to!'

'Poor George,' Sarah put in. 'You'd break his heart.'

Suzy smiled again, pleased with the notion of wielding such power. 'I could, couldn't I?'

'But you won't,' Rachel retorted.

Suzy's smile faded. 'No,' she muttered crossly. 'How can I? I love the silly fool.'

Suzy looked voluptuous in a her wedding dress, but then Suzy would have looked voluptuous in a sack. A great deal of her bosom showed over the top, and her golden hair curled down her back. The Reverend Jones eyed her with misgivings, and somewhat reluctantly pronounced them man and wife. George promptly caught Suzy up and gave her a great, smacking kiss.

After the service, the guests mingled. Captain Potter came to have a word with Will, and Rachel went to wish Suzy luck.

'The Captain says we can live at Down Farm, in the cottage up the back,' Suzy told Rachel, looking smug. 'It suits us. George wants to stay for a time. Then maybe in a year or so we can go off and do something on our own.'

'What does George do, exactly?' Rachel asked curiously. 'Does he have a trade, I mean.'

Suzy twirled a lock of hair in her finger. 'A bit o' everything, that's George.'

Sarah, who had been listening in silence, suddenly looked up with shining eyes. 'I've just thought. What'll you call your first son, Suzy? We already 'ave Old George and Young George.'

Suzy sniffed. 'I'll call him Freddy, so there.'

George, overhearing, scowled at her. 'It'll be George, and you know it,' he told her firmly. And, with Suzy pretending to be meek and submissive, the bridegroom led her away.

Will and Captain Potter had their heads bent close. Martha had not attended; she was ill again. Her bouts of illness were growing more frequent and more severe. She rarely left her room these days. The illness may well be genuine, thought Rachel, but she still couldn't help but wonder whether Martha was making herself sick, a form of escape from a life she detested.

The two men looked up as she approached. 'Rachel,' Captain Potter smiled, and seemed to throw off his serious mood. 'I've a plough I want Will to take a look at.'

"I'll be up in the morning,' Will promised. After Captain Potter made his farewells and left them, Will's frown remained. 'Poor Frank. Not a happy situation. I wonder if Martha ever intends to forgive him for not sellin' up the farm and going to Hobarton.'

'Do you think that's what's wrong?'

Will shrugged. 'She was at him about it when she came back from her sister. Drove him mad with her nagging. In the end he had to tell her he'd no intention of sellin' the farm unless it was to buy more land. Frank's not comfortable in a town of more than ten people!'

Rachel sighed. 'I feel sorry for him, but I feel sorry for her too. She's very unhappy, Will. I think, if she cared less for what people thought, she would leave him and the children. Go back to the life she really loves.'

Will shook his head in disgust. 'So she's made herself unhappy and everyone else too. If she wasn't so selfish, maybe she'd see that leavin' would be less painful than stayin'.' So easy for Will, Rachel thought indulgently. Will was the sort of person who saw almost everything in terms of black or white.

Will linked his arm through hers. 'Time to go home now, darlin'?' he asked her softly.

His smile held the promise of a long, pleasurable afternoon. 'Oh yes,' she whispered, 'let's go home.'

CHAPTER 9

OUTSIDE, THE SUN BURNED HOT and bright, but as usual Will was working inside. Rachel broke off her own tasks, and carried a mug of tea down to him during the afternoon. Despite the heat of the fire, which had him stripped down to his trousers, sweat dripping off his skin, Will managed a smile. He wiped his face and arms on the towel Rachel handed him, rubbing it across his chest. And then he stretched his back and shoulders, flexing, as he allowed his big body to relax.

Rachel went still, watching him. It was always the same. She wanted to touch him, run her hands up his strong arms to his broad shoulders, press her lips to the warm, salty skin at the hollow of his throat. She wanted him to hold her, and make her feel small and protected, as she had felt as a little child in Pa's arms. And she wanted him to kiss her and make love to her, and remind her of the passionate woman she had become.

Rachel became aware, suddenly, how long the silence had lasted. She looked up into Will's eyes and realised that he was watching her, reading her mind.

'Later, darlin',' he teased softly, and winked. 'That's a promise.'

Rachel felt the colour flood her face. She opened her mouth to make a retort, but Will had stopped listening. He was looking beyond her, to the door-way, and something in his face made her turn.

There was a figure beyond the door, dark against the light. Rachel frowned and then her face cleared. 'Mrs Roadknight!' she gasped. In delight, she turned back to her husband and felt her blood freeze. He had a look on his face she had never seen before, a combination of resignation and despair that took her breath. She half raised her hand, as though to reach for him. Behind her, Mrs Road-knight called, 'Rachel? Rachel?' and came blinking into the gloom. Her pie-round face was split with a smile. 'Rachel?'

Rachel swallowed, trying to find her voice. 'Mrs Roadknight. I'm so pleased to see you. I never expected . . . I . . .'

Mrs Roadknight beamed, and clasped Rachel's hands. 'I thought of you a lot, dearie, after your visit. And I decided it was time I took a little holi-day from myself. You did ask,' with lifted eyebrows.

Rachel hastened to reassure her. 'Of course! I'm so glad you're here.'

Will turned his back and picked up the hammer, tapping at the cooling shoe he had been working on. Rachel could see by the way his shoulders were hunched how tense he was. Puzzled and annoyed with him, she said, 'Will, this is Mrs Roadknight. Will is my husband.'

Mrs Roadknight came forward, still beaming,

as Will turned to face her. Something flickered in her eyes, and a little crease appeared between her brows. 'Will,' she repeated. 'Do I know you sir?'

Will looked away. 'Why should you know me, Mrs Roadknight?'

The anxiety in Rachel was increasing, and yet she didn't know why. What was wrong? Will looked like he was waiting for an axe to drop.

'I do remember you,' Mrs Roadknight whispered, and Rachel spun back to her. A shiver ran down her spine; her throat went dry. Mrs Roadknight had such a look on her face, as though Will had turned into the devil himself. While Will. . . Will just stood and waited.

'This man is your 'usband?' Mrs Roadknight gasped.

'Rachel,' said Will, and his voice was quiet and gentle, 'go up to the cottage. Go up now. I'll come presently.'

'But Will,' Rachel cried, her voice high and anxious, like a child who senses something is wrong but doesn't understand what. 'What's the matter? Mrs Roadknight?' And she held her hands out, as if pleading to be given illumination.

Mrs Roadknight looked at Rachel at last, and her round face was flushed and hard, her brown eyes hot with a hatred that made Rachel tremble deep inside. 'I can't stay 'ere!' she burst out. 'You know what you've wed, don't you, Rachel? This,' and spittal sprayed out with the intensity of the word, as she pointed at Will. 'This is Will Moody. Oh, he's famous, is your 'usband! I've seen him in Hobarton. I've watched him ride in, and I've watched him sit up in the court, and I've cursed him to hell where he belongs. He's a paid killer, Rachel, a bounty hunter. The best the police in Vandemon ever had. That's what Will Moody 'ere is.'

Rachel opened her mouth and shut it again. A mistake, she thought. Mrs Roadknight has made a terrible mistake. Her eyes flew from the old woman to Will, pleading, seeking a way out. . . but Will said nothing, and there was a look on his face that struck her to the heart.

'Scum,' Mrs Roadknight spat, her old face alive with hatred. 'Twenty five good men died, because of you, Will Moody. Twenty five,' and hot tears shone in her eyes. 'I hope you remember their faces well, because one day you'll answer to them in a higher court, so you will!'

Shock and horror clouded Rachel's vision. The room went dark, and it was only when she felt Will's arm about her waist that she realised she had almost fainted. Before her, Mrs Roadknight's face came back into sharp focus. She was watching Will, fastening greedily onto the despair and loss she saw in his expression, and her eyes were full of satisfied malice as she let the axe fall.

'What would your Pa say, Rachel,' she asked softly, 'if he saw you now?'

Rachel pulled out of Will's arms and fled. Out of the smithy and up the path to the cottage. Tears burned her eyes, but she bit her lip to hold them back.

Inside the cottage, the air was still and cool. Everything was as it had been when she left, only moments before. She could not believe nothing here had changed, when her whole world was devastation. Rachel sank down at the table and put her head into her arms. Her heart was beating wildly, her mind felt numb. The words played over, an echo in her head: A paid killer, a bounty hunter. She put her hands over her ears, but her thoughts whirled on. Will, a bounty hunter? Will? No . . . and yet he had had such a look on his face, such a look . . .

The step at the door made her start, but she didn't turn around. She heard him come in, pausing as he saw her sitting with her back to him, and then move to pour himself some water from the jug.

'I could do with a real drink,' he muttered.

Rachel turned her head sharply then, to look at him. But he met her eyes levelly enough, though his smile was grim. 'Oh, don't worry. The likes of Mrs Roadknight isn't going to send me back to the grog.'

'Mrs Roadknight?' Rachel whispered the question.

'She's gone to stay at the inn,' he replied evenly. 'She's catchin' the first coach back to Hobart Town. She won't stay under the same roof as me, she says.'

'Who are you?' she breathed.

His gaze didn't waver. 'You know who I am, Rachel.'

Rachel put her hands to her head with a groan. 'Will, I need to know. Don't you see? I need to know. I've pretended that there's nothing wrong, but now it's time for you to tell me the truth.'

For a moment he didn't reply, and then he sighed. It was a sigh from deep inside, a sigh of surrender. The chair creaked opposite her, as he sat down. And then suddenly he reached out and grasped her wrists, pulling her hands away from her face. He searched her eyes, and whatever he saw there convinced him he had no choice—she meant what she said.

'All right. If that's what you want. The truth.' He bent his head, and his hair flopped forward over his eyes. Rachel watched him turning the mug of water around and around, as though collecting his thoughts. And then at last, he started to speak, his voice even and utterly emotionless.

'Five years ago I began a new life. I put aside my past and made myself a future. At least, that was how it was meant to be.' He looked up again, his grey eyes wry. 'The night I met you, by the river in Richmond, I was comin' here, to start that new life. But it's not easy to turn your back on all you've known, and there were doubts. . . and memories. Lots of memories. I felt at odds that night, and very alone. But you made me see that I wasn't alone after all. You were like a spark in the darkness, Rachel. A fire to warm my hands by.' He smiled, but she couldn't respond, and he looked away again. 'So I came to Greengage and I met Hannah and married her, and everything was going so well. Will Moody was dead and buried, just as I'd wanted him to be. But then there was the accident and . . .' he shrugged. 'You know the rest. Until then I'd always known what I had done in the past was right, but suddenly, I started to doubt. I started to wonder if Hannah and our child's death were some sort of punishment, some sort of retribution on me for lives I'd taken. It became a torment. Then the dreams came, like ghosts to haunt me, night after night. And I just let go. I started drinkin' to stop the dreams and the memories. . . and the grief. Everything good slipped away. That's how I was, when you came along; that's the sorry man I saw reflected in your eyes.'

'I know this,' Rachel prompted, softly, impatiently. 'I need to know about before you came to Greengage. I need to know if what Mrs Roadknight said is . . . Will, please, please, I need to know the truth!'

Will nodded grimly. 'Do you, darlin'? It seems like it all happened to someone else now, you see. Not me, Will Trigg. Maybe . . .' he paused, 'if I tell you once, then you'll know and we can both forget.' But he didn't sound convinced, and there was something in his eyes that frightened her. As though she had opened the lid on Pandora's Box and must now take the consequences.

'Tell me,' she whispered.

Will nodded, slowly, and then looked down at his hands. His voice was so soft, it was as if he were speaking to himself.

'I came to Vandemon when I was a little lad, with my parents. From Devizes that was. My dad was a blacksmith and a farrier, better than I'll ever be. My Ma kept him on the straight and narrow, he used to say. She was half his size, but she ruled our house.' He smiled at the memory. 'When she set her mind to a thing there was no stoppin' her. I suppose I'm like that—stubborn. I began to learn my father's trade when the time came. I was their only child and well-loved. I thought. . . I expected to take over from my father one day, but that seemed so far in the future I hardly thought of it. As a family we were close, and happy. My parents were travelling to New Norfolk to visit some friends. They were held up on the road by a band of bushrangers . . . bandits, whatever you like to call 'em. The country was rife with such filth in those days—convicts bolting or men just gone bad. They used to ride around, preying on lonely homesteads and travellers—oh, they were brave and bold men,' he jeered, watching her. 'But you know all this, don't you, Rachel?'

She couldn't answer.

'Well,' he went on, 'this particular band held up my Dad and my Ma. I've gone over it in my mind so many times . . . I think I know what must have happened. I suppose my Ma told them what she thought of them—she had a cutting tongue when it suited her. Then Dad would have had to protect her. Once those kind of men get the scent of blood there's no stoppin' them.' His voice fell away briefly, and then he cleared his throat. 'I can't say they died quick and clean. When they'd been robbed and raped, their throats were cut, and what remained was left for the birds and the beasts.'

Rachel knew her face was white. 'Oh no, oh Will—'

'No defence?' he mocked. 'I thought they were all brave gentlemen who robbed the rich to feed the poor?' He shook his head in disgust. 'Some men are animals, Rachel. They don't think the same as you and me—our rules mean nothing to them. They see something they want, an' they take it. And sometimes they kill for it.'

'These men,' she managed. 'The ones who murdered your parents. What happened to them, Will?'

'I went after them myself,' he said quietly. 'I was

a good bushman. Better than them,' with scorn. 'I was nineteen then, but man enough to do the job. And I brought the three of them back and saw them hanged.' He shook his head angrily. 'But it wasn't enough, and there were plenty more where they came from. I could never go back to my father's smithy, to the cottage we'd all shared. That life had died with them. I was persuaded— although I admit it wasn't very difficult to do—that I would be doing the community a service if I continued to rid Vandemon of vermin. And I was being paid for it, although I wasn't doing it for the money. Every time I got another bandit I thought: Well that's one for you, Ma and Dad. And do you know, Rachel, I found out somethin' about myself. I found out that I could be as cold and ruthless as the men I was hunting. The job suited me. I was good at it.' He looked up and smiled straight into her eyes. 'I was the best.'

A shiver ran down to her very toes. 'You mean you really were a bounty hunter . . . a paid killer?' cried Rachel, the bushranger's daughter.

He nodded slowly. 'I went after thieves and murderers with a price on 'em, if that's what you mean. Sometimes,' and his hands tightened around the mug, 'I brought them in alive and sometimes they were dead. Usually they were better dead— less trouble. The choice was theirs. But I didn't kill them deliberately,' softly, as if he sensed Rachel's withdrawal. 'Not in cold blood.'

Rachel's stomach twisted. Her world was falling apart around her, and she couldn't lift a hand to stop it. Will, her gentle, loving husband, had killed for a living, he had ridden the wild country of Vandemon and hunted down the bandits and bushrangers—Mrs Roadknight's 'boys'! He was that thing she had abhorred all her life, the bounty hunter. A man like the one killed Pa . . . Her eyes flew to his. 'Pa . . . ?' she gasped.

He shook his head. 'Before my time, Rachel. At least that much is spared me.'

And yet it could so easily have been Will, she thought bitterly.

'That was my profession,' he went on at last. 'But it's a lonely, isolated life. For much of the time it's just you and the bush, and the man you're followin'. Even though I knew I was right to do what I did, the knowledge wasn't much company. And all the time, there's an edge to it. Because you know you might be the one to die this time, not him. So you don't make mistakes; your mind goes over and over every possibility, workin' out what he'll do and what you'll do . . . It's like a game, and the best player wins. I got used to seeing it in their eyes, when I cornered them at last—the hatred and the fear. And I got to like it, Rachel—I got to look forward to it. The right and wrong of it no longer mattered—there was no law. I was the law. That's when I realised I had to stop, before it was too late.'

Rachel spoke with difficulty. 'I don't understand.'

He smiled, amused perhaps by her naivety. 'Oh Rachel, I began to enjoy it. I don't mean a sense of achievement! I mean I began to enjoy the hunt and, sometimes the kill. And that was bad. I knew that soon there'd be no difference between me and the men I was hunting. So I stopped; I put my past and the man I'd been behind me—Benny and Zelda help me there. They were friends of my parents, from my early days, and knew the truth. I changed my name, and I became the blacksmith my father had taught me to be. And Will Moody died.'

Only he didn't die, Rachel thought in despair. He continued to exist in Will's dreams, that chilling voice he used, the scenes he reenacted. Will Moody was still there, even though Will Trigg had locked him away.

'When you came back into my life I fought hard, Rachel.' He shook his head. 'There's irony. The woman I loved was the one woman I knew I couldn't have— because of your past as well as mine. But in the end I was too weak—I looked into your eyes and saw the possibility of all the things that were denied me with Hannah. And I couldn't resist. That's why I never really believed our luck would last. There was always that chance . . . and today our luck ran out.'

Rachel had begged for the truth, and now she wished he would stop. Her heart was broken, and she wanted to be alone with her pain and misery. Guiltily, she wished he would just go away.

'It was just a dream after all, wasn't it, Rachel?' he asked her softly, sadly. The grey eyes pleaded with her, but she couldn't look into them any more. Rachel stumbled to her feet, and fled to the bedroom, shutting the door after her. She leaned against it, squeezing her eyes closed.

It was all so terrible, so dreadful . . . Rachel shivered uncontrollably. She had married a murderer, she had loved a killer. It was beyond her comprehension. What had Mrs Roadknight said? 'What would your Pa say'. . . ? Pa, oh Pa! Will Trigg—or, she thought hysterically, was it Moody?—was a lie, and she had believed in it. She felt like screaming and smashing something, but she stood as still as stone.

There was a knock on the door, and Will's voice, so close she knew he was leaning his head against the panel. 'Rachel?' Rachel jerked away, staring at the wood in horrified fascination.

'Go away,' she whispered.

'Rachel, let me in.'

Silently, she turned away, hugging herself with her arms, and after a moment the door opened. Will said nothing for a time, gazing at the straight, uncompromising line of her back. He felt as though his life were ending.

'I knew,' he said softly, and there was no anger in his voice, no rancour, just quiet acceptance. 'That's why I didn't tell you. It was different with Hannah, she felt as I did. But you . . . how could I ever tell you? You loved your Pa, I understand that. And that stupid old woman who ran the inn. She came to all the trials, you know. Hating me. I could feel her eyes making holes in my back.'

Rachel moved angrily. 'That was why you tried to turn me against her, wasn't it? Because she knew who you were.' Then, swallowing the anger, 'It was dishonest of you. You should have told me from the first, Will.'

'Would you have married me then?' he asked her, and her silence was his answer.

'I don't know,' she hedged at last. 'I can't say. It's too late anyway. I did marry you, didn't I?'

He put out his hand and touched her shoulder, and she flinched away, trying to disguise it by walking quickly to the window.

'I don't know you any more,' she said shakily.

'I'm no different.'

Rachel gripped the window sill until her fingers ached. 'No?'

'Of course not,' sadly now. 'Look at me. Rachel?'

She took a breath and turned. He was in the shadows by the door. And despite the pleading in his grey eyes, he seemed frightening and overpowering. She could not go to him. Something had happened to her, so that she felt as if she no longer even loved him. He was a man she had met for the first time today—Will Moody. And until she was able to think clearly again, to decide what was right and what was wrong, to sort through her emotions, she could not go to him, dared not. She had loved a man who did not exist. Will Trigg was a ghost after all.

He saw the rejection in her eyes and bowed his head. 'All right. Let's leave it for now. I'll go back and finish my work.'

Rachel moved as if to call to him, but did not . . . could not. She was frightened of what she might say. She felt cold and hard, just like the rock Zelda had said she was. Will is bleeding, she thought bitterly, but so am I. Oh God, so am I!

That night was the longest she had ever spent. He did not come to bed, and after a time she lay down alone and closed her eyes. But there were so many memories, so many pictures in the darkness of her mind. It was as if she had been there, riding with Will. She saw him, the young man, embittered by his parents' murder, his quiet, neat life thrown into chaos. Will would have kept his grief to himself, letting it fester inside him. Hunting down his parents' killers had given him some purpose, some sense of resolution. But to keep on doing it! Rachel could picture him, hunting through the silent bush, alone, needing no-one. That would be Will Moody—self-contained, believing completely in himself and what he was doing. No doubts for Will Moody. Famous, Mrs Roadknight had said. A famous bounty hunter. 'The best'. And then, realising he was looking forward to the hunting, the cornering, the fear and the killing. That must have rattled him. And he had stopped. Just stopped. He would be able to do that. Will was so strong, so sure. How he must have suffered when Hannah died and the doubts crept in; a man like Will rarely had to contend with self doubt.

Rachel pressed her cheek into the pillow. Memories of the night by the river in Richmond flooded her, taunting her. Will, her hero! The man she had loved and longed for, the Will she had married. All a lie. Nothing was real anymore. A dream, as Will had said. A long, sweet dream. But all dreams must end with awakening.

And this was reality.

At last the morning came, Rachel felt cold, as though her feelings as well as her flesh were numbed. And Will still wasn't there. She wondered suddenly if he had gone to the inn and got drunk, but even that could not touch her.

But when she rose and dressed and went outside, she could see the light in the smithy, and knew he had spent the night there rather than come back to the cottage. Without thinking, Rachel made him some breakfast and put it on a tray to carry down.

Will was bending over, mending the wheel from a dray. When he looked up she saw how tired and drawn his face was. The weariness in his eyes warmed when he saw the tray. 'Rachel . . .'

'I feel I should cry,' she burst out. 'If I could cry, perhaps I'd be able to feel something again, but I can't even do that.'

He looked away, wiping his hands on a cloth. 'What do you want to do about it?'

The tray was suddenly very heavy. She put it down and straightened, smoothing her apron over her skirt. 'I don't know. Do we have to do anything? I need time, Will. You must give me time to . . . I need time, that's all.'

He nodded slowly. 'All right. I'll give you time, Rachel.' He met her eyes again, and his smile was lop-sided, 'Zelda said you were too young for me.'

'I know."

'When you get older, like me, you'll see that life is too short. Sometimes you have to compromise, Rachel. Accept the things you can't change, and change those you can. Accept people for what they are now, rather than what they have been.' Then, softly, 'I can't live with you, you know, if you can't do that.'

She nodded miserably.

'I love you very much, Rachel.'

She turned and fled. Once back at the cottage she stood, trembling, swallowing down her feelings of betrayal and revulsion, and others she hadn't even sorted out yet. She would never have imagined her beloved Will could cause such dark turmoil within her. These emotions were all beyond her experience and her ability to cope.

'I wish I'd never found out,' Rachel said miserably. 'If only I'd never found out!' And at last, the tears slipped down her cheeks and she sobbed, grieving desperately for the husband she had lost.

Outwardly, life went on as before. But inwardly, it was drastically altered. She could not bear for Will to touch her, and she could hardly look at him. Will came and went as though he were a stranger. And as the days passed, it became harder and harder for Rachel to imagine life ever returning to what it had been before.

One night she dreamed that she and Will were galloping through the night, and it was wonderful . . . until she realised they were pursuing another man. And that man was Rachel's father.

Another night, she dreamed Will was holding her and kissing her, and she was kissing him back. His hands slipped up to cup the fullness of her breasts, and she moaned softly, arching towards his caresses. His body slid into hers and she clung to him, feeling the muscles of his back tightening with each thrust. She cried out in ecstasy, and then froze. Her eyes opened wide.

He was gazing back at her, his face a dark shadow

above her. For a long moment neither of them spoke, and then she turned her face away and he rolled off her, and lay on his back with his arm across his face. 'At least your body doesn't reject me, Rachel.'

'That isn't fair,' she whispered.

'Can't we start again?' he asked her softly, and his voice was full of longing. She felt that longing, a mirror image of her own and felt too, his pain and loss. But she could not, dared not, let it sway her.

'I keep thinking,' she replied shakily, 'of what you've done. It's as if what we had between us is all spoiled. I don't know if I can ever start again, Will. I need time to sort it out. I need more time.' Her voice broke and she bit her lip.

He said nothing. She moved as if to touch him, to reassure him, but could not even do that. He sat up, his arms loosely clasped around his knees, and stared into space for a long moment. They were only inches apart in the bed, and yet Rachel knew that they may as well have been in different rooms. 'All right,' he said expressionlessly. 'I'll give you time, Rachel. When Benny was here, he asked me to go and see him in Hobart Town. Look at the business, offer him some ideas. I'll leave in the morning. There's nothin' in the shop that can't wait a week or two.'

There was a silence. Was he waiting for her to protest? To beg him not to go? All she said was, 'Yes, all right.'

'We'll talk again, when I come back,' he went on matter of factly.

Rachel nodded, and closed her eyes. He was going away, she thought. I should be upset, I should be weeping, but all she felt was a vast relief.

At first the days went swiftly enough. Rachel was glad to be alone, it gave her time to put together the pieces that had been Rachel Trigg. She had loved Will so much, could it have died so quickly? Surely there was something . . . some spark left? It was as if he had betrayed her with another woman, only worse. She felt a terrible sense of being betrayed, and a terrible aching hurt. At least, she told herself wryly, the numbness was gone.

The days turned into a week, and then the week into two weeks, and still Will did not come back. He's only giving me the time I asked for, she told herself. He knows we need time. Even if, eventually, she could forgive him, and accept him as he asked, Rachel doubted it would ever be as it was. She had been so innocent and open in her love of him, almost worshipping him, and he had revelled in it. But now, she told herself bitterly, she saw him as he really was. The Will she had loved was no more. This man had lied to her, and fooled her into thinking he was something he was not. She had not forgiven him, she honestly wondered if she ever would.

It was very dark one night when she heard the horse halt outside the cottage. Rachel stood up, holding her breath. Will, was it Will? Her heart beat fast, and nervously she wiped her palms on her skirt. The tap on the door made her jump—

not Will then—and slowly she went to open it. Captain Potter nodded a greeting, but his mouth and eyes were grave. Rachel stared at him, puzzled and suddenly afraid. 'Sir? I . . . it's very late to be out visiting.'

Captain Potter stepped forward into the light. He looked very tired, she thought suddenly. 'I'm sorry to intrude at this time of the evening, Rachel. I couldn't come earlier, and this isn't a task I could pass on to someone else.'

She stared back at him, her dark eyes enormous in her white face. 'Is Will dead?' she whispered.

'No!' He caught her hand and squeezed it firmly. 'No, Rachel, that's not my news. I'm sorry if I've given you a fright.'

She half laughed, putting a hand to her eyes. 'I don't know why I thought . . . you looked so serious and I thought . . .' She made a dismissive movement. 'Come and sit down by the fire, Captain Potter. It's so chilly these autumn nights.'

He came and sat by the fire, but refused the hot drink she offered. 'There's no easy way to say this, my dear,' he murmured at last. 'And I think you'd prefer me to be direct with you.' The blue eyes met hers, 'Will isn't coming back. He wrote asking me to tell you, and to pass on a letter he's written to you.'

Rachel looked blindly down at the communication he pulled from inside his jacket, and automatically took it from him. Slowly she opened out the thick paper, spreading the sheet in front of her, her hands smoothing and smoothing the creases.

'Where is he now?' she whispered.

Frank shook his head. 'He didn't tell me exactly. Looking for new opportunities, was all he said. He sounded confident enough, cheerful even.'

Rachel nodded. Her eyes fixed on the letter, and after a moment she forced herself to read what she was afraid to read. Will's goodbye.

'Darling Rachel.' he wrote. Tears stung her eyes, for suddenly it was as if she could hear his soft, slow voice speaking to her.

'Darling Rachel. I have made arrangements for Frank to sell the smithy in Greengage and for you to have the money to do as you will. Benny and Zelda would be glad to offer you a home in Hobart Town, until you decide upon your future. Or you can remain in Greengage. It is up to you.

I won't be coming back. I loved you and I still love you, but I know that what we had is over. And I can't face staying on, watching our marriage turn sour. Better to go now. I can start again. I did before. I want to thank you for what you did for me. Without you, I probably would never have had a reason to give up the drink. You told me once that you could put me back together again, and so you did. Believe me, I wish you good luck in your life, Rachel.

All my love, Will.'

Frank Potter stared into the fire, waiting. He heard her refolding the letter, as if each crease must be followed precisely. 'So he's left me,' she said bitterly. 'I'd almost rather he was dead. At least then I could mourn him.'

'Rachel,' he began, and put out his hand towards her. But she stood up abruptly, knocking over her chair and, without even glancing at it, went to the window. Pain was raging in her heart. She had rejected him for what he had been, and he did not believe she would ever reach out to him again, so he was leaving. He could do that; he was so strong. He would put it behind him just as he had put Will Moody behind him. Rachel wondered, bitterly, whether he would ever dream of her. 'I asked him for time,' she said. 'Time to sort out my feelings. But he didn't give me enough. He didn't believe in me, just as I didn't believe in him.'

'Will felt he'd dealt your marriage a mortal blow,' Frank replied gently.

'You knew all about it, didn't you? About his past, about what he was.'

Frank nodded. 'I knew. Rachel, I think I told you once that Will was a good and decent man. I stand by that. He did what he thought was right and when he began to doubt his motives he stopped, and moved on. He deserved happiness, and I think he found it with you.'

Did he? Rachel asked herself. Memories flooded her and she gritted her teeth as they pummeled her like so many fists: Will's struggles to resist his feelings for her, and Will giving in at last, Will's smiles and his kisses. Once, she had felt he was a part of herself—perhaps he still was, and that was why she felt so empty without him.

'Can I write to him?' Rachel whispered at last.

'I don't know where he is. Perhaps he will write to you.'

'He should have told me what he meant to do!'

she cried, folding her arms hard about herself, as if to hold in the pain. 'He should have said, that last night, that it was my last chance. Why did he have to cut the bond between us so utterly? It's too much . . . too much . . .'

Frank sighed, watching her. What could he say? If Will had come to him, he may have tried to dissuade him. But it seemed that Will had already made his decision, and like most of Will's decisions, it was swift and final.

CHAPTER 10

IN THE END, RACHEL'S FUTURE was simple. Captain Potter wanted her to come back to Down Farm with him, and resume the position she had left some seven months before—had it been so short a time, her great happiness?

The 'dragon' as Sarah called her, had given her notice and was only awaiting a replacement to be on her way. It was so easy for Rachel to slip back into her old life, easier than trying to cope on her own. Particularly now. For Rachel had discovered Will had left her something besides memories after all. He'd left her his child. And if she'd been thinking clearly, she would have realised it two months before.

At first she was stunned. But as the days passed, Rachel began to feel a quiet joy. Whereas she had felt guilt for her love for Will, there was no such burden with the child. It was innocent, and she knew she could love it wholeheartedly.

When she told Captain Potter, a flash of pity darkened his face, and then he smiled. 'Well that's a good thing, isn't it?'

'Yes.' And Rachel smiled too.

It was so comfortable at Down Farm. She could forget all the uncomfortable things she had been feeling. No-one mentioned Will. No one asked what had gone wrong. Whatever Captain Potter had said to them had been enough to lock their tongues. Rachel was glad of it in one way—it saved her the pain of answering—but in another it began to seem as if Will had never even existed.

Except for the baby.

Rachel had already begun sewing tiny clothes, and dreaming. When she had time! Frank and Matty and Victoria were glad to have her back, but it took a deal of effort to reassert her authority, and to teach them to trust her again. At first Frank was so naughty. He played tricks on her, and screamed at her, and ran away. One day, when she found him with a cut on his finger, he shouted, 'What do you care? You'll go off and leave us again!' And Rachel realised that somehow her leaving to marry Will, and Martha's illness and the coming of the 'dragon' were mixed up in his mind, and he thought he was being punished.

She bent down, close to him, and put her hands on his narrow shoulders. 'Frank, I do care. I promise, I do. And I'll not go away again, not until you really don't need me any more.'

He shrugged, pretending indifference, but later, she saw him watching her, considering her. And after that, he was never quite so naughty.

Matty too, was difficult. She burst into tears at the smallest things, sobbing as though her heart would break. And then, in the blink of an eye, she would be laughing and chattering as if nothing had happened. 'Should be on the stage,' Sarah told Rachel morosely. 'Likes to make a pumpkin out of a pimple, just like her mother.'

Baby Victoria was the easiest of them all to care for. Nothing bothered her, apart from her next meal. She slept well now that her teeth were through, and was placid and smiling most of the time. Rachel could only hope her own baby would be so undemanding.

As her body grew with the child, she naturally thought about it more and more. Imagining what it would be like. And inevitably, she thought of Will. Sometimes in the night she woke, with his image so clearly in her mind she thought he must be there, beside her. Of course, he never was. *Wishing him home*, she called it to herself, but if he heard her thoughts, he never responded. Will was gone, and gone with him were her tangled emotions of anger and sadness, and the sense of loss that she knew would never leave her. Their relationship was unresolved, and to be properly laid aside and forgotten it must have a proper ending.

At least Suzy and George were happy. Suzy wore a smug smile on her pink mouth and George had put on weight. They lived in the cottage at the back of the house, and although Sarah claimed that Suzy never did a scrap of housework, George didn't seem to mind.

Once, when Rachel came face to face with George in the yard, he looked at her growing belly and said, 'I reckon you've got another blacksmith in there.'

Rachel was startled into a laugh. George had smiled back at her, and something in his eyes warmed her. It seemed that he was her friend, just as he had been Will's.

Then there was Martha.

Martha had changed so much from the Martha Potter Rachel had known that she was shocked. She had heard for Sarah about Martha's decline, but she had never imagined just how drastic it was. The farm had never really interested her, and now she didn't even pretend. She spent most of her time in her room, complaining that her head hurt. 'Laudanum,' Suzy muttered. 'Drinks it like water.'

'She must be in dreadful pain,' Rachel began, but Suzy would have none of it.

'I reckon the problem is the laudanum more than anything in her head. She's like a drunk, craving a nip of gin.' Suzy stopped, and bit her lip, remembering Will.

Captain Potter had changed, too, in his attitude to his wife. Everyone felt it. He had slipped from the tolerant and almost affectionate indifference he had displayed when Rachel was last at Down Farm, to just plain indifference. And there was a certain resentment, too, as though Martha were a ball and chain about his neck, holding him back from his ambitions.

'He wants to take up land on the mainland,' Suzy informed her knowledgeably. 'George says Captain Potter is worried that he's makin' less and less every year from Down Farm, and soon it'll be too late to sell up. No one'll want it.'

Suzy knew a lot of things Rachel didn't. Obviously she and George discussed these matters— Captain Potter confided in George more than anyone else in his employ. Except maybe Rachel.

He had some maps of the Port Phillip District, and he looked over them in the evenings. Sometimes, if Rachel was passing the open door of his study, he would call her in and point out various details to her. The names were meaningless to her, but she nodded and listened. Captain Potter was full of enthusiasm. 'I feel our future lies there,' he said to her one evening, and Rachel wondered exactly who 'our' referred to. Martha certainly didn't see her future lying in anywhere other than Down Farm, unless it was in Hobart Town.

As if realising Rachel wasn't really listening, Captain Potter asked in a gentler voice, 'How are you feeling, Rachel? Everything all right?'

She smiled. 'Everything is all right, yes. Thank you.'

'How long have you got to go now?'

'The doctor thinks another four weeks, sir.'

'Have you heard from Will?'

Startled, she looked up and met his eyes. Perhaps he sensed her unwillingness to talk, for he shrugged.

'I wondered, that's all. I haven't heard either, Rachel. I rather think Will is like my brother Israel —he does not feel he has to explain his actions to anyone.'

'Yes,' she whispered.

'You've never written to those friends of his in Hobarton? It's possible they could pass on a message.'

Rachel shook her head. Benny had been friendly, but Zelda had disliked her—she sensed Zelda was glad Will had left. The woman had obviously believed that Will could do better than Rachel.

'What use is a letter?' she asked harshly. 'Even if it was passed on? It couldn't make things as they were.' Rachel had been telling the children a story about a beast who turned into a handsome prince. Will had done the opposite, turned from her handsome prince into a bloody monster she could not even bear to contemplate. And yet her heart ached.

The stairs seemed steeper than ever, as she climbed them to bed. She felt so weary and so heavy—were there really still four weeks to go? Sometimes she felt so alone, despite the children and Sarah.

'Oh, Will,' she whispered, and stopped, shocked at her own voice and the words she had spoken. Will was not here, and he would never be here again. Will had gone and left her to her fate. Or had she sent him away? Well, it was for the best.

Her little room was particularly quiet tonight. She sat in the chair by the window and stared into the darkness. And Will was back again, slipping into her mind no matter how she tried to lock him out. Perhaps he'd already found somebody else to share his life with. Did he ever look at her face, when he opened his watch? Did memories come to him, as they did her, sometimes so suddenly and vividly it was frightening. A word could do it, or a certain scent, and Will was there. And the sense of loss crushed her all over again, until it was replaced by the anger and the bitterness, and the horror.

Rachel had been sitting at the window a long time. Her feet were chilled, and she had half fallen asleep, when the pain jerked her awake.

She sat up, startled, wondering what the matter was. And then it happened again. A cramping pain, low in her belly. Her breath hissed in and she stood up, toppling over the chair behind her. 'Sarah!'

Sarah was there in an instant, her nightcap askew, her blue eyes blinking like a possum in the light.

'Fetch the doctor.' Rachel's own eyes were like saucers with fear and excitement. 'I think I'm having my baby.'

Sarah opened her mouth, shut it again, and bolted down the stairs. A moment later the house was awake, lamps being lit, voices out in the yard. A horse galloped off down the track to Richmond, but Rachel didn't hear any of it. The pains were coming quickly now, and although Sarah was there, she wasn't too sure what to do, and neither was Rachel.

By the time the doctor arrived, Rachel was well into labour. In fact, minutes after he rushed up the stairs, he was delivering Rachel's baby—'A girl, Mrs Trigg!'—and presenting her with the dark haired bundle.

A daughter. Rachel, weary but happy, gazed down at her daughter's wrinkled little face. Will's daughter. But she wouldn't let herself feel sad, not tonight. Suddenly Rachel realised she was no longer alone. She had another person to love, and to love her.

Sarah peered down at the baby, holding it carefully in her arms while Rachel bent to pull on Matty's shoes. 'Why did you call her Bella?' she asked.

'Because,' she retorted, 'she's so beautiful.'

Sarah wrinkled her nose. 'Sounds foreign to me.'

'It is,' Rachel answered.

Sarah held the tiny hand in her own. 'She's got her daddy's eyes,' she murmured at last, 'but she's got her ma's hair.'

'She also has a powerful pair of lungs,' Rachel complained. Bella had kept her up half the night, until she settled at last to Rachel's breast and fell asleep. It was ironic, she thought, when she had hoped for a placid child. Instead she had one who already showed all the signs of being strong willed and stubborn—like Will.

At first, Rachel had looked obsessively for indications of Will or herself in her daughter. Now, some months later, Rachel saw Bella as an individual in her own right. How could she not, when Bella was constantly reminding her mother of it? She was soon trying to crawl, doggedly following the other children, while Rachel attempted to rescue her from the more dangerous situations. And when she found she couldn't do exactly as she wanted, her little face would pucker in frustrated anger. At other times, Bella would watch her mother, her grey eyes following her silently—Will's eyes.

It was a year since Will had left Greengage, and Rachel realised that, apart from Bella, he might never have existed. No-one mentioned him, and Rachel had slipped back into her old life at Down Farm with scarcely a ripple. She was content, but others did not feel the same. The Potters may be married, but they no longer acted as if they were. Martha had grown to hate her husband with a vicious, sly hatred that worried Rachel. And Captain Potter looked more miserable every day.

One evening, when she was listening to Captain Potter discuss the merits of land along the Murray River—his determination to move to the Port Phillip District had not diminished—Martha called from upstairs. 'Rachel!' her voice was shrill and demanding.

Captain Potter's mouth tightened, but he said nothing as Rachel murmured an excuse, and hurried away.

When she reached Martha's room, she found her sitting up against her pillows, her hair loose about her, glaring at Matty at the end of the bed. 'Matty should not be here, Rachel. Please take her back to her room.'

Rachel sighed. Evidently, Matty had crept in to see her mother, despite Rachel's warnings that 'Mamma was sleeping'. She reached for Matty's hand, seeing the hurt in her blue eyes. 'Come on now, Matty. Back to bed.' But Matty had had enough. She burst into tears and fled.

Martha groaned and covered her face. 'Is it so difficult for you to control them?' she asked heavily. 'My head aches so. I can't bear to have them near me at the moment. When I'm well perhaps . . .' her voice trailed off.

At that moment, whatever sympathy Rachel had felt for Martha evaporated. Perhaps Martha knew it, for her manner changed to whining self pity. 'I know you all want to be rid of me.'

Rachel blinked. 'Mrs Potter, I don't—'

Martha made a dismissive gesture. 'Oh, I know. The way you look at me. And Frank. Frank is just waiting for me to die, and then he'll be off to fresher fields. You see if I'm wrong. You see.'

'You're not dying,' Rachel replied impatiently.

'No?' she cried, her voice trembling. 'I may as well be dead. There's nothing for me here, nothing! I wish I was dead.'

After a moment Rachel said softly, 'You should go back to Hobart Town, Mrs Potter. I am sure your husband would allow that. You need to stay with your sister a while, take walks in the garden, see all your friends again.'

Martha's eyes narrowed. 'He won't let me. He says my home is here.'

'But surely—'

'Anyway, if I go to Hobart Town, he'll say I'm well enough to go to New South Wales.' Suddenly her expression was pure malice. 'He's had a letter from his brother, did you know? There'll be nothing stopping him now. Apart from me. Even Frank can't sell Down Farm with his sick wife still in it!'

Rachel took a breath, 'Mrs Potter—'

Martha turned her face away. 'Oh, stop. I know you want me dead too, so that you can marry Frank and give your brat a father.'

Rachel was too shocked for a moment to speak. 'My child has a father,' she breathed at last. 'You know that. My husband—'

'Oh, your husband! Well, I warned you about marrying the likes of him. Now he's gone. Just as Frank wishes I was gone.'

Rachel took a deep breath, trying to steady herself. 'I'm sure you're wrong, Mrs Potter. Your husband is very concerned about you.'

Weary now, Martha shook her head and closed

her eyes. 'Don't talk lies to me. Go away, Rachel, you make my head ache.'

The conversation was upsetting. Rachel stood a moment on the landing, wondering why it had hurt her so. Only the cruel ramblings of a sick woman, she told herself. They should not affect her. Slowly, she retraced her steps to Captain Potter's study and knocked on the open door. He looked up, his face warming at the sight of her.

Rachel saw, as she drew closer, that he had another map laid out on the table. He smiled, and the drawn face was almost young again, the tired blue eyes sparkling with new life. 'I meant to tell you,' he said eagerly. 'I've had a letter from my brother. He's taken up land in the Port Phillip District, and he's asked me to join him in the venture. He needs capital, you see, to buy stock and begin clearing. Just having the land is not enough. You have to make use of it.'

Rachel's brow crinkled in a frown. Martha had been right in that, at least. 'I see,' she began slowly. 'But that would mean leaving Down Farm, wouldn't it?'

'I know, I know,' his eyes shifted away from hers. 'Look here!' he went on, and gestured her over to the map, pointing out the area of which his brother had written. 'The land is here. My brother bought it from another chap. Israel had money then; it seems he owned some blocks of land in Collins Street, when the site for Melbourne was first being carved up. It was like a big juicy pie in those days, a speculator's paradise.' And Captain Potter's eyes narrowed at the thought of opportunities lost. 'Well,' he went on with a sigh, 'he sold those blocks, within a couple of years of buying them, for a great deal. He fancied the life of a squatter, you see . . . or he thought he did. He bought a run to the north. Unfortunately, however, he returned to Melbourne all too soon. He says the run looked to be in good hands, and he wanted to enjoy himself. Young fool lived too high, and by the time he realised those 'good hands' had made a hash of things, he had no money left to put matters right.'

'So he needs yours,' Rachel said, stirring herself and trying to take an interest.

Captain Potter's eyes twinkled with anticipation. 'He does indeed.'

'And that would mean leaving Down Farm,' 'Rachel repeated.

They fell silent, their thoughts turning to Martha. The fire in the hearth crackled, and Rachel looked to it, suddenly uneasy. 'Sir, there is a matter I would like to speak to you about.'

Something in her voice drew his attention. He looked up reluctantly, his hand still resting on the map as if he couldn't bear to break the connection.

Rachel cleared her throat. 'It is about your wife, Captain Potter. She . . . I think she might benefit from another stay with her sister. In Hobart Town.'

An expression of annoyance flicked across his face, and he bent to peer more closely at the map. 'My wife is too ill to travel.' Then, frowning, 'Has she told you she wants to go?'

'No,' Rachel said, suddenly uneasy at his change of manner. 'She says she will not go. But I think—'

A muscle flickered in Frank Potter's cheek. 'No, she will not go. What else did she say, Rachel?'

Rachel crossed her arms, avoiding his eyes. 'She

is very unhappy, sir. She thinks you mean to leave her or sell the farm from under her. She thinks you and I—'

His eyes were still fixed on her—she felt them even though she was too embarrassed to lift her own. 'You must not take account of what a sick woman says,' he told her at last, and his voice was quiet and gentle, the voice she trusted. 'You are Will Trigg's wife and I would never betray his trust, even if I did not value you for yourself.'

Relief washed over her. 'I'm sorry, sir . . .'

'No, it is I who am sorry, Rachel. My wife's quarrel is with me, not you. She is only trying to hurt me through you.' She did look at him now, and there was something in his eyes, something of the same pain and longing she often felt in herself. 'Go up to bed, Rachel,' he said wearily.

Gratefully, she went.

She undressed, checked on Bella, and climbed into bed. The light from her candle wavered on the ceiling, making strange shapes and patterns. Like ocean waves. *On and on to the sea.* The words came back to her with a jolt. She almost heard his voice. Almost. Could she have forgotten the sound of it? There were times when she tried very hard to forget. And his face, had she forgotten that too? Rachel moved uneasily in her bed. I'm happy the way things are, she told herself firmly. No need to go stirring up the past again. No need to . . .

Suddenly, there was a knock on her door. Rachel half sat up, thinking one of the children must have awoken. 'Frank?' a tremulous voice whispered. 'Frank?'

Rachel froze.

'Frank,' the voice moaned, and hands clawed at the panels, slipping down. There was silence. Rachel strained her ears above the thudding of her heart. She knew she should open the door and speak to Martha, but the fear of what Martha would say — an extension of her bitter fantasies of earlier—held her back. The next moment Rachel was glad she hadn't acted, for she heard Martha pulling herself to her feet, and her steps stumbling away.

But Rachel's sigh of relief was short lived. There came a thud, as though someone had dropped something heavy. And then more sounds, as whatever it was tumbled over and over. And afterwards silence.

Rachel didn't remember moving, but suddenly she was, her breath coming in quick, frightened gasps. She wrenched open the door. The corridor was empty, but Martha's bedroom door was wide open. She peered in, and saw the bed empty and rumpled. On the landing, the lamp wavered in a draft, throwing odd shadows up the walls. Rachel stepped forward and looked down.

Martha lay on her back at the bottom of the stairs. Her nightgown was tangled about her legs, one bare foot sprawled across the bottom step. Her hair fanned out about her head, not quite hiding the pool of blood collecting beneath it. Strangely, her face was unmarked, and her eyes, wide open, gazed with surprise up into the shadows.

Rachel could only stand, frozen. The door to the study opened. Captain Potter stepped out and stood, unmoving, staring at his young wife. He knelt over her, lifting her gently in his arms. Martha's head lolled and her sightless eyes gazed into his. For a long moment he was still before, as if sensing someone watching, he looked up. Rachel could only think it was like looking at a mask. His face was yellow under the tan, his mouth a hard line, and his blue eyes full of anguish—or could it be relief?

'Is she all right?' Rachel breathed, even knowing she was not—could not possibly be all right.

'I fear . . . I very much fear . . .' But he couldn't go on, and bowed his head. Behind him, Sarah appeared from the kitchen, and let out a smothered shriek.

Rachel began to descend the stairs, but realised her legs wouldn't hold her and sat down on the second step. Suddenly there seemed to be so many people. George was there, pulling on his shirt as he came, and Suzy, eyes agog. Sarah was sobbing, and somewhere a child was wailing. Rachel knew she had to get up and help, had to do something. With an effort she rose, barely conscious of her nightgown, gripping the bannister with cold, clammy fingers as she made her way to the bottom of the stairs.

Captain Potter was still holding his wife. George gently disengaged his arms. Someone had ridden for the doctor, and Sarah, shaking, had gone to make tea. Suzy, whom Rachel had always felt was so level-headed, had gone home, totally useless when it came to this tragedy.

'She fell down the stairs,' Captain Potter said quietly. He looked up, and met Rachel's eyes, and it was as though he were asking her something. Some question. Frightened, she remembered Martha's slurred voice at her door. Even as she opened her mouth to mention it, he had turned away, walking like an old man back into his study, and George closed the door.

Rachel had seen death before, at the Orphanage. After George had carried the body into the parlour, it was Rachel who straightened it, smoothing back Martha's tawny hair and closing her wide eyes. The smell of laudanum was strong, so strong . . . The poor woman. She had obviously been wandering about, confused after her draught, her mind full of nightmares. 'I'm sorry,' she whispered. 'I'm so sorry.' Rachel shuddered; only hours before Martha had been accusing Frank and Rachel of wanting her dead. Now she *was* dead.

Behind her the door opened, and Sarah spoke. 'The children are awake, Rachel. What'll I tell 'em?'

Rachel leaned against the back of the sofa and took a breath. 'You can tell them a story, Sarah, and put them back to bed.'

'But—'

Rachel turned and looked at her. 'No use in upsetting them now. It'll be time enough, in the morning.' Then, before she could stop herself, 'She was knocking on my door. She thought Captain Potter was there.'

Sarah's mouth dropped open. 'He wasn't, was he?'

Rachel shook her head, suddenly too weary to be indignant. 'No, of course not. But I should have spoken to her. I should have gone out and put her back to bed.'

Sarah patted her shoulder. 'Don't blame yourself for this, Rachel. She had a nasty tongue sometimes. So, you didn't want to be on the receivin' end of it! You didn't know she was going to fall down the stairs right afterwards.'

Rachel looked at Martha's body. 'I know, I know. It was an accident.'

The doctor thought the same. He examined Martha, and pronounced life extinct—'Broken neck.'

'It'll be quiet without Martha shouting out to us all day long,' Sarah murmured.

And it was quiet. Down Farm was hung in black mourning. Visitors came to offer the Captain their condolences, and he gave every sign of being the grieving husband, whatever the truth of what he felt in his heart. It was just as it should be. And yet, Rachel could not help but remember Martha, whispering at her door, and the guilt remained with her.

'What's this about, anyway?' Sarah asked, jerking her head towards the door.

Rachel pursed her lips as she knelt to help Matty with her shoes. 'You mean why Captain Potter wants to see us all in the yard? You'll know soon enough.'

'I thought *you* might know,' and Sarah's eyes were sly. 'He's got a soft spot for you, Rachel, and you know it.'

Rachel frowned, glancing at Matty to see if she was listening. 'That's nonsense,' she whispered. 'It's only that Will was his friend.'

Sarah hesitated. 'What really happened between

you and Will? Captain Potter told us when you first came back that it was none of our business, and that if he ever heard anyone talkin' of it, he'd have words of his own to say.'

Rachel pulled a face.

'Suzy says he took up drinkin' again. Did he?'

'No.'

'Then what?'

She shook her head. She couldn't talk about it. Even after all this time, the pain was still too sharp, like a needle in her heart.

Outside, the employees of Down Farm were gathered in the yard. For a moment Rachel felt as if she had been here before, and realised she was thinking of Martha's funeral, some months previous. It had been a painful affair, as had the questions that followed, but nothing had come of them. Martha had fallen down the stairs, while in a state of delirium after taking her medicine. An accident. Sometimes, she wondered what would have happened if Martha hadn't died. What would have become of Frank's dreams? But it was best not to think such thoughts, and best not to remember the look in his eyes, as he stared up at her from the bottom of the stairs.

Captain Potter faced them now from the verandah. He moved restlessly, with an air of suppressed excitement. Rachel watched, as he began to speak, but she already knew what he would say. He had told her the evening before. He was selling Down Farm, and travelling to the Port Phillip District. And he was taking the children, and Rachel, with him.

'See if you can persuade Sarah to come too,' he'd

told her, with a smile. 'You'll need help. And I'll speak to George. I want a good, trustworthy man, and later there'll be opportunities he'd never have if he stayed here.'

Now, Rachel let his voice roll over her. She turned, looking out across the paddocks to the Greengage Road. Vandemon. It had been home for her entire life and it would be a wrench to leave. Everything she had ever known was here. All the memories, good and bad, that went to make up the woman she was.

But she was young and she had her daughter to think of. It was best to go with Captain Potter; he offered her security and there would be little of that with him gone.

And what was there, after all, to keep her?

Maybe Will will come looking for you, a voice inside her head teased. What would he think, to find her gone? She had loved him, she didn't try to pretend otherwise. Rachel sighed, perhaps time would heal the hurt inside her. She could only hope so. She must believe that Will was gone forever and would not come back. It was the only way in which she could survive and move forward to make a new life for herself, and her daughter.

But there was a little kernel, deep inside her, that resisted all her efforts to set Will aside. A little hard diamond that insisted, whatever she told it, that someday, somewhere, she would find Will again. Or he would find her.

RACHEL
&
ISRAEL

1842

CHAPTER II

PORT PHILLIP BAY WAS AN enormous stretch of water surrounded almost entirely by coast-line—like a giant inland lake. Or, thought Rachel with a smile, an enormous teacup, with mountains and sand dunes on the rim instead of gilt, and grey-green rippling saltwater instead of tea.

Bass Strait, notorious for bad crossings, had been quite calm—they had waited until January, when the easterlies made the journey much safer. Not calm enough, however, to ease poor Sarah's stomach. She had spent her time in the cabin, lying green-faced, wishing she were dead. Captain Potter had had little sympathy for her. He was more concerned with the four pure bred Leicester rams, cared for by George during the voyage. There was no need to bring ewes—Israel had written to say that the price of sheep had dropped so low now in the Port Phillip District it was cheaper to buy them upon arrival than, as had been the case in the early days, ship them over from Van Diemen's Land.

Port Phillip was in the grip of a depression, and it was getting worse. Rachel didn't think of that. In fact, Rachel had rather enjoyed the voyage. It was exciting, standing at the railings, while the salt wind blew her black curls into tangles and the white sails slapped above her head. Behind them, the water bubbled and surged—a white track in the green—while the seagulls swooped and screeched. She remembered, wryly, the day she had left the Orphanage, longing to see 'life', longing for adventure. Well, she had it now, in full measure!

Once through the Rip—that dangerous narrow stretch of tidal water which was the only entrance into Port Phillip Bay—Rachel looked about her. Although she found Port Phillip Bay vast beyond belief, she could not say she found it endearing. It was too big, too intimidating to one used to the creek in Greengage. Away to the right stretched long, sandy ridges, like blank weathered faces, topped with hair of withered, sun-dried scrub. To the left, a lighthouse and cottages stood atop high, rugged cliffs, while surging waves lapped curved, pristine beaches. Seagulls dived into the bay, occasionally surfacing with fish in their beaks. Far ahead, across the forty miles of water they must travel to reach Hobson's Bay and Melbourne, was a hot, hazy view of mountains, smoking with bushfires and wavering in the heat. It hadn't rained properly in Port Phillip for some time, and the country was beginning to show the effects of drought.

The breeze from the water was some compensation, but Rachel felt the sweat trickling down her back, and longed for a bowl of fresh water and a sponge, to clean herself. It seemed a long time since she had had a proper bath. The shipboard conditions had been primitive to say the least. There were a large number of people travelling from Vandemon to Port Phillip, quite apart from the little group from Greengage. Many of them were ex-convicts, looking for work and a new start.

Sarah had been eager to come. 'I'd 'ave to be reassigned if I stayed,' she grimaced. 'My next master mightn't be such a gentleman as Captain Potter.'

Suzy had persuaded George to come, too. 'Captain Potter needs my George,' she told Rachel smugly. 'He admitted it 'imself. And later, well we can look around, maybe find land for ourselves, or a little business.' The hazel eyes narrowed, turning over possibilities.

And, of course, there were the children, Martha's three as well as Rachel's daughter. Thankfully, by the time Captain Potter had sold Down Farm and made arrangements to leave, some months had passed. It was summer, and Bella had grown into a plump, inquisitive toddler, no longer the baby she had been. And Rachel's private and terrible fear, that Bella may not survive the journey to her new home, began to recede.

Captain Potter had come to join Rachel, as she stood at the rail, gazing into the depths of the bay.

'I don't know what to expect,' he said. 'I've read everything I can about Port Phillip, but seeing it will be different.'

He had already explained to her that vast tracks of land had been taken up beyond Melbourne, mostly by Vandemon squatters with their own money behind them, or overlanders from Sydney, bringing their sheep or cattle with them. Few brought their wives or families. The land was still wild, still inhabited by savages, still too dangerous.

'Not like Greengage,' he teased her, blue eyes

twinkling. 'Vandemon is green and pleasant, Rachel, full of towns and people. This place is vast and deserted.'

'Except for the savages,' Rachel murmured, her heart thumping unpleasantly. Before she left, she had read in the newspaper of an attack north of Melbourne. A squatter had been speared and one of his men killed, sheep had been stolen, and the people of the Port Phillip District outraged. Retribution was hinted at, if the 'proper authorities' did not take appropriate action.

'Superintendent La Trobe supposedly runs the Port Phillip District, but really everything he does must be approved by the governor. And Governor Gipps is in Sydney, and Sydney is a long way away,' Captain Potter said, as if reading her mind. 'Besides, us Vandemonians resent being governed by Sydney, we're independent and don't take kindly to someone six hundred miles away telling us what to do. My brother writes that men here feel like kings and do as they please.'

Was Israel a king? Rachel wondered. Of course, his brother had already told her how Israel's speculation on some blocks of land in Collins Street had made him a great deal of money. Determined to be a squatter, he had bought a run to the north. Rachel couldn't blame him for such an ambition. Captain Potter had explained how, in those days, the squatters strode the streets of Melbourne like kings indeed. With their blue serge suits and cabbage tree hats, faces covered in whiskers, and pistols dangling from their belts as spurs jingled from their boots, the squatters were looked on as a breed apart. But she could find fault with Israel for his careless attitude in leaving his sheep run in other hands so that he could return to the pleasures of Melbourne. That seemed, to Rachel, to suggest a want of common sense. However, Captain Potter had not blamed Israel particularly for it. Perhaps he looked upon it more as a lesson to his brother that there was more to being a squatter than socialising in Melbourne.

'He tried to borrow money,' Frank Potter had told her, 'but no-one wanted to lend. The depression was being felt by then. When the early Vandemonians came to Port Phillip, they had their own capital behind them and no need to borrow. Later men didn't have their own capital, but the banks were bursting with British speculators' money and eager to lend to anyone. Unfortunately as soon as the depression set in and sheep prices began to fall, the banks called in their debts.'

'So your brother turned to you,' Rachel reiterated.

Frank nodded. 'I'm going to join him in partnership. Israel says he has learned his lesson, and that may well be so, but I want to be there to keep an eye on him. And I want to be a part of it.'

'How big is this sheep run?'

'About 50 square miles,' Frank Potter told her, 'and there's another run he's got his eye on even further to the north. Unclaimed land as yet. We'd have to move quickly if we want it.'

Rachel's eyes widened at the thought of so much land.

Frank smiled wryly at her expression. 'The land is nothing without capital. You need money to improve it, in other words, building yards and sheds, buying more ewes and setting up the new run if we get it. It's one thing to have the land, Rachel, another to actually make a profit from it. And profit from running sheep is a long, hard business. The initial outlay is enormous compared to the return. Fortunes aren't made overnight—not any more. Israel must learn that lesson, too, if he hasn't already.'

'How did your brother get his name?' Rachel asked suddenly, a question she had often pondered on.

Frank glanced at her and smiled wryly. 'We were very poor at the time Israel was born. My father decided the only way to impress our only wealthy relative was to flatter him by naming the new son after him. So, Israel it was. And it worked, too. He died and left us his money.'

Israel Potter sounded like an interesting person, and as they drew closer to their destination, she grew more and more impatient to meet him.

Williamstown was a little village in its own right. There were cottages and huts, and lighters plying back and forth across the bay. Melbourne was eight miles away, inland up the Yarra Yarra River, too shallow for larger ships unloading their goods—food, probably, for the population was growing so quickly it found it impossible to feed itself—as well as ships like themselves from Van-demon or Sydney, and an immigrant ship just in from England. The passengers were flooding to the deck, impatient for the signal to disembark. Voices were raised in excitement and impatience, muffled on the hot air, while the ships rocked on the swell, their spas and riggings seeming to entwine. People milled about on the beach, awaiting their transport into Melbourne—small steamers which plied the Yarra Yarra River, or carts travelling the rough track from nearby Liardet's Beach.

Captain Potter opted for the steamer, and their luggage was loaded aboard. His precious rams would, for the time being, be penned at Williamstown. George stayed with them, looking sullen and resentful. He had not really wanted to come; Suzy had pushed him into it. Like a stolid, dependable pony, George preferred to trot over the same ground day after day. Change worried him. However, there were a number of hotels in Williamstown, and Rachel felt sure he would make himself familiar with them as soon as his job was done.

The Yarra Yarra was a pretty little river, the water clear and clean. Overhanging trees made cool, dark shadows, giving relief from the burning sun. Wattles, ti-trees and other native shrubs grew to the very edge of the water, so that Suzy, reaching out an idle hand, could break off a twig and use it to swish at the flies. There were flowers everywhere, and Rachel breathed in the sweetness, while the birds squabbled, drunk from the nectar.

Until Raleigh's Wharf was built, the year before, the steamers had tied up to stumps along the river bank. It was to the wharf now that the steamer brought its passengers, and they stood at last on

Melbourne soil. The settlement had only been thought of seven years before, and was still in many ways a frontier town. The streets had been carefully laid out; so what if some of them still had tree stumps in the middle, or there were so many pigs and goats and dogs about it was like a farmyard. Rain had caused gullies to form in some of those streets, over which citizens on foot carefully picked their way and those on horseback jumped. The Yarra Yarra dissected Melbourne, but there were as yet no bridges—although the Governor had promised—and the river had to be crossed by punt.

The buildings, thought Rachel, were a strange mixture. There appeared to be few buildings laws in Port Phillip and everyone built to their own taste and pocket, so that wooden huts and cottages of wattle and daub were constructed beside substantial brick and stone edifices. On top of Flagstaff Hill, various pennants were fluttering, signalling which ships had just arrived in Hobson's Bay. The residents were well aware which colours signified which country or colony, and looked forward eagerly to news, as well as anything else the vessels brought with them.

There were plenty of shops, boldly avowing that the goods sold within were as good as, or better, than those found anywhere else in the Australian colonies. Rival tradesmen had set up, keen to lure customers away from each other. Bullock yards and milking sheds rubbed shoulders with hotels and grog shops, doing a roaring trade. And for the wealthier squatters and 'gentlemen' the Melbourne Club had opened its doors a couple of years before.

There was even a Turf Club, as well as various banks, churches, numerous newspapers and a post office. And Melbourne had not even been officially declared a town yet! It was new and brash, compared to Hobart Town. Rachel, looking around, felt a throb of excitement.

Israel Potter, who was supposed to meet them, was nowhere in sight. They waited at the wharf, in front of the new Customs House. The children were tired, grizzling for this and that. Young Frank teased his sister, and Sarah lifted up Victoria— nearly three now but still called 'Baby'. Bella, in Rachel's arms, slept on, totally indifferent to her new surroundings. Suzy looked bored, but as she nearly always looked like that, one couldn't be sure what was really going on in her head.

'If he doesn't show up within the next half hour, I'll take you to a hotel.' Frank Potter met Rachel's dark eyes and tried to smile reassuringly, but worry only made the lines in his face seem deeper. 'The sun's hot enough to cook eggs in.'

'Bella doesn't seem to notice,' Rachel replied wryly, glancing at her daughter.

Frank Potter's face softened as he looked down at the sleeping baby. At fifteen months, Bella was already a beauty, like her mother, with dark, curling hair and a smiling mouth. It was only when she lifted those long lashes that Will's grey eyes stared back at him, making him uncomfortable, accusing him of betrayal in thought if not in deed.

A voice shouted out his name, and Captain Potter's head jerked up.

There was a man bearing down on them at a run. Rachel watched him, surprised, for he was younger than she had imagined, some fifteen years younger than his brother Frank, though he had a look of Captain Potter about him. Israel, for there was no doubt this was Israel, had tawny hair and a beard of the same colour covering his handsome, sunbrowned face. He reached them with a breathless laugh, and the two men grasped hands. Rachel noticed then that his eyes were blue, a brilliant, striking blue.

'I'm sorry,' he was saying. 'I was late into town yesterday—my horse went lame—and then I overslept this morning.' But the apology was said in such a careless, laughing voice, that Rachel could tell he didn't think it necessary. People would always wait for Israel Potter, and if they didn't. . . well, he would consider it their loss.

Frank Potter was indicating the rest of the group. Israel's blue eyes widened, and then he laughed out loud. 'You don't do things by halves, do you brother! Have you brought the house as well?'

Frank looked annoyed. 'I couldn't leave my children,' he retorted. 'And Rachel is their nursemaid, and Sarah her helper. Suzy and George are wed—I left George with the rams. They're all prepared to pull their weight, Israel.'

Israel looked dubious. 'Nerinbilly is very primitive,' he warned. 'It's frontier country, Frank. Usually the women and children wait behind until there're better conditions.'

Rachel watched Frank Potter's stubborn face grow more stubborn. Martha's sister had wanted the children after Martha died, but he had refused her request. 'How can you take them out among savages and wild animals?' she had written to him, when she found out what he intended. 'For Martha's sake, let me care for them.' But Frank had not wanted his children to go to Martha's sister. He loved them, and Rachel had not realised just how much until then.

'They'd be strangers to me,' he had explained to Rachel. 'I can't let them go. They're part of the reason I'm doing this. It's their future I'm building.'

And so the children had come this far, but now it seemed that Israel would be another obstacle.

'Surely there's a hut on the property?' Rachel put in quietly. 'I'm sure we could manage, until a cottage was built.'

Israel looked at her for a moment, his mouth smiling, but his eyes were hard. He began to explain with exaggerated care. 'I don't think you realise just how things are out there. We have a hut, yes, but the floor is dirt and the roof leaks, and I share it with four other men. Three of them are old lags who are determined to drink themselves to death at my expense; the other is a New Chum, only in Port Phillip a month, who complains all the time and seems to think he was made for better than to be a shepherd. A lot of men only stick the life for a short time unless they're half mad. The isolation gets to them. Hardly the sort of place for women and children, is it?'

Rachel felt the colour come into her face. He was speaking to her as if she were a child, or a fool. Did he think she was some dainty miss who didn't know what hardship was? Her mouth tightened angrily, and she bent over Bella. He would learn.

Frank Potter frowned at his brother. 'Surely there are other settlers about? Other women? I refuse to believe not one man to the north of the range is married!'

Israel took his time in answering. 'Some are, but most of them leave their wives at home here, in Melbourne, or Sydney or Vandemon. Oh, there are a few hardy souls. Some of the squatters employ married shepherds and the wife becomes the hut-keeper, but. . .'

Frank Potter lifted an eyebrow. 'Well then?'

Israel hesitated and then laughed, abruptly shaking off his mood. Enthusiastically, he threw his arm about his brother's shoulders. 'Never mind that now. We'll settle it later. I'd better go and fetch a cart, to get you all over to our lodgings. I didn't think I'd need one.' He turned his head and his smile encompassed them all, but as his eyes met hers, Rachel felt a warning shiver pass over her skin. As if he had marked her out.

Israel Potter had leased a cottage in a place called Newtown, one of the little areas of civilisation beginning to grow around the centre of Melbourne. Reasonably priced accommodation was difficult to find. Israel assured them that Newtown, though separated from Melbourne by half a mile or so of untouched bush, was perfect.

'Newtown is higher up,' he announced, 'cleaner, healthier . . . You'll like it there.'

Newtown, Rachel saw, was a mixture of houses large and small, sometimes two built on the one block of land, one facing the street and one backing on to it. 'It's the depression,' Israel answered his brother's question. 'More money to be made by leasing out as many houses as you can fit on your block, or else dividing it again and again and selling each bit.' He shrugged, 'There don't seem to be any housing laws in Melbourne, or if there are no one takes any notice of them.'

Richmond, next to Newtown, was where many of the wealthier settlers were congregating. 'Heidelberg, too. Plenty of good land there, and along the Merri Creek, for growing crops to feed the hungry mouths.' The grander houses, Rachel noted, were built on rises—the better ground—while the poorer cottages appeared more often in hollows or on marshy ground. And all about the grey bush made a backdrop, as if to remind the white settlers that Melbourne was only a speck in a vast unknown.

The cottage was reasonable, if rather cramped and, once they were all inside, airless.

'We might as well be back aboard ship,' Sarah whispered crossly, her face red and damp from the heat.

Built of slabs, and divided into two rooms with some sort of lean-to at the back, their accommodation had floors that were planks, laid straight onto the ground, buckling a little from the damp, and walls of plain plaster. A couple of windows opened onto the front verandah, letting in the flies and the heat during the day and the cool breeze and mosquitoes at night. A fireplace would do duty for cooking their meals, and there was a food safe in one corner for keeping provisions in and flies and mice out. The backyard was large and bare, fenced with stringybark palings.

'Settle in. This is your home for now,' Israel told them, moving restlessly around the room. There was so much life about him—Rachel felt as if it sparked from his skin and would burn her if she got too close. The bright blue eyes flickered over her, his grin radiating confidence. He was only of medium height, but had the assurance of a much bigger man. Rachel had been looking forward to meeting Israel, but she had never imagined she would feel so physically attracted to him. Indeed, it was a long time since she'd felt attracted to any man.

Young Frank and Matty began to run around the cottage, while Bella struggled to join in, tottering after them. Victoria sat down on the floor amid the mayhem and pulled off her shoes.

The men had soon gone again, to see about getting the rams looked after until they were taken north, and to enquire about various provisions. 'I know where we can get good ewes for a couple of shillings each,' Israel had said. 'Prices are dropping all the time. Everyone is starting to feel queasy. But things have got to lift again. If we can only get a start and hold on, Frank, we'll do all right.'

Rachel took off her bonnet with a sigh, and began to sort out the children's trunk. Suzy wandered to the window, humming to herself, and looked out. She didn't seem to think it was her place to do anything much. She was George's wife, and that was it. Outside, Matty yelled while Young Frank terrorized his two sisters by pretending to be a lion—an animal he had only ever seen in picture books. At last Rachel went to fetch them all in. They were tired now, too tired even to complain when she settled them as best she could on the makeshift beds, stripping them down to their underthings so that they could be cool. It was so close and hot, with no noticeable breeze from the bay, eight miles away.

'What do you think of him then?' Suzy asked lazily, turning narrowed hazel eyes on the others.

Sarah and Rachel looked at each other. 'Think about who?'

'Israel. His lordship,' Suzy laughed. 'Thinks he's God's gift, don't he?'

'He seems all right,' Sarah muttered, glancing at Rachel for a lead.

'What do *you* think?' Suzy asked at last, impatient, as Rachel failed to answer.

Rachel shrugged.

Suzy laughed softly, as though she sensed Rachel's unease. 'Well, he's a man all right.' And she smiled her secret smile.

Sarah made a disgusted noise. 'Don't let George hear you sayin' that.'

Suzy shrugged impatiently. 'George's got nothing to do with it.'

Rachel closed her eyes, listening to their half argument. Sometimes, she wondered whether it would have been better to have returned to Mrs Finn at the Orphanage. Mrs Finn would have taken her in, and Bella too, and given her work to do, but somehow it had been easier to remain with the Potters. She felt as if she belonged to them, now, and she had no desire to strike out on her own.

Rachel straightened her arm, easing Bella's weight carefully as the baby drifted to sleep. Once, all she had dreamed of was a man to love her and a home to make with him; life had seemed to offer nothing else and besides, she had wanted nothing else. Did she still see things so simply? Or had she changed? If Will walked into her life today, would she love him as fiercely and believe in him so utterly, asking no questions? If another man were to want her, and she were to want him, would she act in the same way she had before? Or was the part of her that had loved and trusted so unconditionally damaged forever?

The trouble was she didn't know, or wouldn't know until someone else came along. The thought upset Rachel, and she moved restlessly, making Bella squeak. The distraction was a relief. I'm so glad I have Bella, she told herself. Bella and I will make a life together. What need have we for anyone else?

The men returned at last, bringing George with them—grinning tipsily—and the women prepared the meal. The children, refreshed from their sleep, wanted to play and talk. Young Frank was full of questions. Bella tried to eat a candle, and Rachel swooped her up with a laugh, only to find Israel's eyes on her. For some reason she blushed.

The evening was cool. The sun, leaving streaks of brilliant red and orange behind it, promised another hot day. The men went out onto the verandah to have a smoke. Inside, the women, clearing up after the meal, could hear their voices. Suzy was yawning at the window, but her glance was on George, asleep in the corner. 'George should be in charge,' she murmured. 'Overseer, you know.'

Sarah looked at her sideways. 'You going to tell them that?'

Suzy tossed her head. 'I will, if I 'ave to.'

She would too, Rachel thought to herself. She would push and pull George as far as he could go, no matter how much he hated it. Because she loved him, or because she was ambitious and he was the only way she could fulfil that ambition? A bit of both, perhaps.

Outside, Young Frank asked something, and his father reproved him in a low voice. Israel laughed. 'No, no, Frank. The boy has to learn. He's been listening to frightened women's talk, eh?' There was a note of scorn in his voice which irritated Rachel. 'Some men will say that the savages in this country are of a lower form than us, boy. That we're of British stock, and we British have a right to go where we will and bring our ways with us.'

Frank Potter made a sound that could have meant anything.

Israel laughed again. 'Come now, Frank, isn't that what we all think? Deep in our hearts? That we have a right to this place, a right through superior numbers and superior minds, and no black savages are going to stop us.' He paused, and when he spoke again his voice was different, softer. 'Do you know how Melbourne came about, Young Frank? A Vandemonian, named John Batman came here and stepped ashore and liked the look of the place so much, he decided it was the very spot for a village. And he gathered the natives together and they signed a treaty. He gave them some blankets and tobacco and knives, and in return, for a yearly payment, he was given all the land he wanted. It was a good deal, wasn't it? Always assuming the poor bastards knew what it was about—'

'Israel!'

'Sorry, sorry, Frank. I forgot myself for a moment. Been with those rascals at Nerinbilly for too long.

It brings a man back to earth, eating and sleeping with his inferiors, I can tell you. Makes you realise you're all one under the skin, after all.'

There was silence. Rachel stared into the darkness beyond the window, listening. His voice enthralled her despite herself, weaving a spell. She waited, breath held, for it to continue.

'Batman's dead now, of course,' Israel went on softly. 'Died in poverty, drank himself to death they say. But we all know better. It was the syphillis got him in the end.'

'Israel. . .'

'Though I don't suppose that'll stop me, brother. And Young Frank here will have his share of pretty ladybirds, too, when he grows a bit. We Potters just can't help ourselves, can we? Even if some of us don't always choose wisely.'

'I think it's time for bed, Frank,' his father said firmly.

Israel laughed. 'I suppose it is. I didn't mention Johnny Fawkner,' he added thoughtfully. 'He's set himself up as Batman's rival to the founding of Melbourne—he runs one of the newspapers here now, and has his fingers in a dozen other pies. Although he was never one for the truth, not Johnny.'

Young Frank came inside, his face brightening when he saw Rachel. She pulled him close, stroking his fair hair. At six years he was still a little boy, she told herself. Israel Potter had no right to speak to him about things he could not understand.

'Come on, my dear,' she murmured. 'Your sisters are already asleep. I'll sing you a little song if you like. Would you like that?'

He hesitated. 'I'm really too big to be sung to,'

he told her kindly. And then, glancing up, 'Well, all right, Rachel.'

She hugged him again, laughing, and led him into the other room.

Outside, the two men smoked in silence, listening to Rachel singing. She had a low, smooth voice; like honey in the darkness. Israel liked the sound of it. She was a lovely woman, and when he had a little more time . . . Israel smiled to himself.

Frank watched his brother's profile against the stars. Israel, he thought, had changed very little. He was still as confident as ever, still exuded that warm, friendly air which won him so many friends and admirers. But beneath it was the shifting ground . . . the uncertainty, the puzzle. He had never understood his brother, not really. Was he the enthusiastic, no nonsense man he liked to portray, or was he the self-obsessed man, who didn't give a damn for anyone but himself? He's so different from me, Frank thought. That's the problem. I'm not complicated myself, and therefore I cannot understand complication in my brother.

'Where is Rachel's husband?' Israel's voice came out of the stillness, sounding deceptively bland. 'Or doesn't she have one?'

Frank tapped his pipe out on the arm of the chair.

'Don't cast your eye in that direction,' he said softly. 'Rachel has a husband and a child. She is a respectable woman and doesn't look at other men.'

Israel laughed. 'What, is she your exclusive property? Or did Martha take away your eyesight as well?'

Anger shone in Frank's eyes, but the darkness hid it and his voice was calm enough. 'Her husband was a good friend of mine. And she is my employee. That's all.'

Israel laughed as though he didn't believe it. 'Where is her husband?' he repeated.

Frank hesitated. 'No-one knows.'

'Ah,' said Israel.

CHAPTER 12

FRANK POTTER, ISRAEL AND GEORGE had left for Nerinbilly. With them had gone what Rachel thought an enormous amount of stock and provisions—a flock of 300 ewes, a few head of cattle, extra horses, a bullock dray and driver, loaded with provisions, and several men— all expirees from Vandemon—hired to help get the sheep north, as well as build yards when they got there. When she exclaimed at the size of the expedition, Israel was dismissive. 'Enough for a start,' he informed her, his blue eyes meeting hers. 'There are about another 500 sheep for sale on the McCrae's Castle run. We'll pick them up on the way north.'

'How long will you be away?' Young Frank's eyes were big with a mixture of excitement and disappointment.

Israel grinned. 'We'll be back before you know it. Don't worry about your father, I'll make sure he doesn't get into trouble.'

Young Frank chuckled, but Rachel felt his hand slipping into hers and squeezed it tightly.

'You're needed here,' Israel went on. 'These

women,' with a grimace, 'need a man to take care of them. Can you manage that?'

The boy nodded, his eyes even larger at the thought of such responsibility. Suzy rolled her own eyes at George. 'I reckon us "women" could run rings around the lot of you,' she said loudly.

But Israel had already turned away.

'Things are too dangerous for you just yet,' Frank Potter explained to his children. 'Next time, you'll all be coming with us. I promise.' His smile wavered. 'Israel is right, you know. You are grow-ing up Frank. I'm going to need to think about a school soon, or at least a tutor.' His eyes met Rachel's over the boy's head, and his son was for-gotten. 'You'll be all right?'

She smiled and nodded. 'Yes, we'll be all right. You will take care, sir?'

He touched her shoulder briefly, and then bent to embrace his children. Bella squalled, lifting up her plump little arms, and with a laugh he hugged her too. Israel, waiting by the horses, looked on with barely contained impatience.

And so, they had gone.

The cottage in Newtown seemed quiet. Suzy sulked at being left behind, and worried about George without her there to make sure he wasn't being passed over. Rachel and Sarah ignored her complaints, until at last Suzy flounced outside and plopped down onto a verandah chair, fanning her-self in the heat.

Because of the heat, they needed to buy their food almost every day. Rachel began to enjoy strolling out into the melee every morning, peering into the shops, and examining what was on offer.

It seemed to her that, despite the depression, there were plenty of new buildings going up, and plenty of people like herself looking to buy. Water was something else they needed every day, and there was a water wagon on the corner near the cottage, at which the local residents filled their buckets. On one such expedition, Frank made friends with a skinny little dog that followed them home.

At first they shooed it away despite Frank's pleas, but when Rachel caught Sarah secretly feeding it scraps, things came to a head.

'It smells,' Suzy said, holding her nose. 'And I'm sure it 'as fleas.'

'The poor thing's starving,' Sarah retorted. The dog, knowing who was its friend, looked piteously up at her with its big, brown eyes. 'We can't turn it away.'

'Oh no?' Suzy retorted. The two women turned and looked at Rachel. She realised with some unease that they were waiting for her decision. Ever since the men had gone, they had begun to treat her as if she were in charge. Rachel was at first startled, and then flattered that they should think so. But being in command was not all pleasure, and problems, such as the little dog, constantly beset her. Whatever she said, one of the other women would be put out. So, rather than try and please everyone, she would do what she always did, and follow her own instincts.

'Perhaps we'll let him stay for the moment,' Rachel said. 'Until the men get back.' And she escaped out into the yard, leaving Sarah smiling and Suzy scowling after her.

Frank and Sarah set to and washed the little dog,

and afterwards he looked more respectable. 'Always wanted a dog myself,' Sarah said gruffly to no one in particular. 'A child should 'ave a dog.'

'Why don't you go up to the native camp,' Suzy retorted. 'They've got plenty to spare.'

The local natives, dispossessed of their land, had moved to the bush around Melbourne, and there they lived on white man's food and drink. They expected to be fed, Rachel had heard. They were confident that the 'White Queen across the water' would look after them. At first the black, shiny bodies, wrapped in possum skins, had frightened the women, but now, like the rest of Melbourne, they paid them little heed.

Frank Potter had given Rachel money to buy any extra clothing and provisions that may be needed for the women and children, when they finally came north. Rachel had decided that they would all need lighter clothing, if they were to cope with the summer heat. She planned to buy some cloth and cut and sew what was required while she had time.

'There are plenty of shops,' she told Sarah. 'No doubt we'll be able to buy what's necessary.'

So, she and Sarah set out with the children, making their way along the well-used track through the bush and into Melbourne's rough and busy streets. As always, Rachel was surprised at the number of people about. She had heard that in earlier years

Port Phillip had cried out for labour, had even considered allowing convict ships to unload their miserable cargoes on its shores. Now there were so many men and so little work for them, that wages had been halved.

The women made their way to one of the larger establishments—a sort of barn, Sarah said—and stood looking in at the endless shelves of merchandise, pipes mingling with bonnets, boots with handkerchiefs. The shop smelled of spices, and the darkness was cool and soothing after the glaring heat of the streets. Another customer—a stocky gentleman—browsed amongst some boots, examining each one with close attention. The attendant, who had been standing patiently beside him, moved towards Rachel.

'Can I assist you, madam?'

'Indeed, I hope so,' and Rachel smiled, and told him her problem.

He listened with flattering attention. 'Of course, of course. I know just what you will need,' And he gestured for Rachel to be seated, ignoring Sarah whom he seemed to think was her maid, and bustled away further into the gloom.

'Don't know how you do it,' Sarah muttered, pulling Victoria away from some carefully stacked leather buckets. 'One flutter of your eyelashes and he's buzzing about all over the place like a bee gone mad.'

Rachel pulled a face. 'He thinks I've lots of money to spend.'

Bella climbed on her knee, and Rachel tucked an unruly strand of hair behind one little ear.

'Ma'am?'

The voice was quiet and polite. Rachel looked up, thinking the assistant had returned, and saw instead that it was the stocky gentleman who had been examining the boots. He was standing in front of her, watching her with uncertain eyes.

'I couldn't help but overhear you just now. You're going into the wild country to the north? You and your children?'

He, too, thought her the mistress rather than the servant, and the mother of all these children! Rachel smiled to herself, about to disabuse him of his error, but he didn't give her the chance.

'I hope you don't think me rude, but I've just travelled through that country. I would not have thought it the place for women and children.'

He meant well, Rachel supposed. He looked a pleasant enough young man, with a square, plain face topped with a crop of short, spiky brown hair, and brown eyes surrounded by long, dark lashes. 'It'll never be the place for women and children,' Rachel told him gently, 'until some of us make it so.'

He smiled uncertainly, inclining his head. 'You are a woman of determination.'

'I hope so.'

Suddenly his smile broadened, and he held out his hand. 'Thomas Dart.' Then, ruefully, 'I am seeking work, ma'am. Is it possible your husband is look-ing for a good, honest man? I am used to keeping books and counting figures. I have been employed in that capacity in Sydney, and, until recently, here in Melbourne. I read and write extremely well. I have no wife, no encumbrances, and am willing to travel almost. . . almost anywhere.'

He stopped, embarrassed. Rachel felt sorry for him. Obviously, this man was not used to pushing himself forward, and obviously he must be desperate to do so. She realised, looking at him more closely, that his jacket was worn and shiny at the cuffs and elbows, and his boots were so old that, despite numerous mendings, they were on the verge of coming to pieces. Thomas Dart had fallen on hard times.

And she had allowed him to assume she was something she was not. Guiltily, Rachel put him right. 'I'm so sorry, sir. I should have corrected you sooner. I'm an employee of Captain Potter of Nerinbilly. His wife is, sadly . . .' she bit her lip, glancing at the children.

The brown eyes narrowed slightly, and there was a flash of dejection. And then he sighed, a sigh from the heart. 'No harm done,' he murmured ruefully. 'As I said, I overheard, and I hoped—'

But the assistant had returned, and Thomas Dart shifted out of the way. The next half hour was taken up in deciding which materials were best, and then purchasing the lengths and the cottons and various other items Rachel felt she would need, including some sturdy boots. Sarah, standing by the door, kept glancing out into the street, and was no help at all. Finally, Rachel had finished. She arranged for their order to be delivered, and they made their way back into the relentless sunshine.

Sarah's mouth was turned down. 'Poor young man,' she muttered. 'He needs a good square meal, that one. Not even a wife to see to him. Did you see his jacket? A button off, and the elbows nearly worn through.'

Rachel lifted her eyebrows. 'What could I do? I can hardly hire men in Israel Potter's name, can I? What would he say to me?' She had a fair idea of what he would say!

'You know,' Sarah went on after a moment, 'I was thinkin' about what he said. How he could read and write, and everything. And how Young Frank here is old enough to have a tutor. Martha was always going on about tutors and the like. You can't expect the children to go to school when we go north. Doesn't sound like there's much of anything up there but sheep and savages. What if we were to ask Mr Dart to be the tutor?'

Rachel opened her mouth to disagree, and closed it again. Sarah was right. It was a good idea. Always assuming Thomas Dart would do it, and that he was suitable in other ways. You could not hire someone off the street without checking up on their credentials.

Sarah saw her wavering, and grinned. 'I saw him go in the 'Fox and Hounds' there. I'll run after him.' And she was gone, skirts flying, down the dusty street. Rachel stood and watched her. What would Captain Potter say? And worse still, what would Israel say? Rachel shuddered at the thought, but put her doubts aside. For the moment, she was in charge, and she had followed her instincts and made her decision.

'I can't promise,' Rachel said firmly, as she faced

Thomas Dart across the trunk that doubled as a table in the front room of the cottage. 'You see my problem?'

Thomas nodded. 'I understand that. I have references, and I'm willing to try.' He looked dubiously at the children as they crowded around him, watching, as if sensing his unease.

Rachel hid a smile.

Sarah was hovering, pouring tea, and nodding at him encouragingly. When she had brought him back to the cottage, he had seemed a little bemused by his good luck, and Rachel wondered what the other girl had been saying to him. But he was willing to give the job a go, and eager to do his best. He had no choice perhaps, with work so scarce and wages so poor.

'I am from Sydney,' he said suddenly, looking up with uneasy eyes.

Rachel blinked. 'I beg your pardon?'

Suzy snorted. 'Sydneysiders and Vandemonians are sworn enemies here in Port Phillip,' she explained to Rachel. 'Mr Dart thinks he's in the enemy camp.'

Rachel laughed. 'I'm sure that will have no bearing on Captain Potter's decision. He's a very reasonable man.'

'To some perhaps,' Suzy murmured, narrowing her eyes.

Thomas Dart shifted uneasily in his chair. Noticing it, Suzy smiled and smoothed her skirts over her thighs with a slow, sensual movement. Thomas blinked, and the colour stained his thin cheeks. Suzy laughed softly, enjoying the effect she was having on him.

Sarah glared at her, before turning protectively to the man. 'Perhaps if you could make a start, before Captain Potter comes back?' she suggested breathlessly. 'Then they can see that you're serious and . . . and if you don't like it, you'll know that too.'

Rachel nodded. 'What a good idea! Would you be willing to have a trial, Mr Dart?'

He set down the cup with a rattle. 'I. . . yes, all right.' But his enthusiasm seemed a little lacking, and again he glanced nervously at the children, trying to smile. Bella gazed up at him, her thumb in her mouth, solemn as judge. They arranged for him to return in the morning. As he went out, Thomas tripped over the dog, and nearly stood in the water bucket. Suzy laughed until the tears rolled down her cheeks. 'What a walking disaster,' she said at last. 'Where'd you find him, Sarah?'

Sarah glared at her. 'He needs work, and he's a nice person. You wouldn't know about that.'

Suzy lifted one eyebrow. 'Are you sure he's not just another starvin' mongrel you've picked up?'

'Suzy!' Rachel cried, and stood between them. 'There's no need to talk like that.'

But Suzy, from the heat or boredom or both, was in the mood for a fight. *'There's no need to talk like that,'* she mocked savagely. 'What would you know? You couldn't even hold on to the man you 'ad. What 'appened to Will Trigg? What'd you do to make him take off like that? Or was it somethin' you didn't do?'

Anger and misery swamped Rachel. Her pale skin flushed a vivid red. 'He left me,' she whispered. 'We couldn't live together any more. Not after. . . not after. . .'

Sarah's arm was warm about her shoulders. 'It doesn't matter,' she murmured, glaring at Suzy. 'Don't talk. You don't 'ave to.'

But Rachel had had enough silence. Suzy had lanced the boil, and must now take the consequences. 'You were right, Suzy,' she said bitterly. 'He wasn't who I thought. He was a stranger, with Will's face and Will's voice. His name wasn't even "Trigg" and he'd done things I couldn't forgive. If I'd known in the beginning, I'd never have married him. I couldn't have.'

Their eyes were wide with shock and amazement. Suddenly Rachel couldn't bear it, and turned her back. Beyond the window, the light was harsh, hurting her eyes. Even the constant, irritating flies had retired into the shade.

'When he left,' she murmured almost to herself, 'I was glad. I was glad! He was right to go. We would have ended up hating each other.'

'Poor old Rachel,' Suzy muttered, half mocking and half ashamed. 'Well,' with a return to usual bravado, 'these things 'appen. You just got to pick yourself up and get on with it.'

Thomas Dart came the next day, tentative, uncertain. But as day followed day, he grew more confident, and the children, less critical than Suzy, liked him. Perhaps for the very reasons she didn't—his simplicity and his honesty. It came to be understood that after the lesson, he would stay to take tea with the three women, and they all began to look forward to the interruption in the ritual of their day.

Suzy made eyes at him, of course. Smiling her lazy smile as Sarah collected the cups, crashing them together in a way that made Rachel grit her teeth.

'She's a tart,' Sarah muttered to Rachel, under cover of the children's chatter. 'If George found out, he'd kill her with his bare hands.'

'It's a game with her,' Rachel soothed. 'She's bored. Don't let it bother you.'

'It don't bother me,' Sarah said furiously. 'Who said it bothered me?'

Rachel sighed. Thomas Dart was pleasant, but there was nothing about him that really caught at her, as Will had done. Obviously Sarah saw him differently, and it was unfair of Suzy to spoil it for her.

When Thomas Dart took his farewell of them, Sarah stepped out with him onto the verandah, and Rachel heard their low voices as they walked slowly to the gate. 'You shouldn't do that,' she said quietly to Suzy. 'She's fond of him.'

Suzy snorted in disgust. 'He's not even a man! You can say what you like about George, but he's a man.'

'Sarah doesn't want someone like George.'

'Well if that's the best she can do, she's welcome to him,' Suzy snapped. 'I always think you should test the water a bit, before you jump into the bath.' Then, the hazel eyes narrowing slyly, 'What do you think Israel Potter'll say when he comes back and finds you've hired 'im?'

Rachel's expression was her answer.

'You don't like 'im, do you?' Suzy asked her softly. 'Israel, I mean.'

Rachel thought for a moment. 'I don't know what I feel. He's not like his brother. He's not like anyone I've ever known.'

Suzy smoothed her skirts, slowly, and said, 'But you haven't known many men, Rachel, now have you?'

Rachel bristled. 'Well, what do you think of him?'

'I think he's dangerous,' Suzy said softly, smiling her secret smile. 'But sometimes danger is excitin', isn't it, Rachel?'

And there was something knowing in her eyes that made Rachel shift uncomfortably.

The heat continued. Rachel and Sarah decorated the cottage with their bits and pieces, trying to give it a homey air, and the children helped. It was Frank who would sometimes look beyond the window and ask after his father. He, the eldest, understood better than his sisters that his father was gone into the 'wilderness' in Sarah's words.

'I thought I might drop by this evening.' Thomas Dart murmured. Suzy rolled her eyes at such transparency—Thomas was always 'dropping by'—but Rachel smiled and asked him to join them for supper. He accepted with alacrity.

Rachel hesitated, 'Have you no family?'

He shook his head. 'No. My mother was an

invalid after I was born, and has been dead many years now. My father. . .' with a grimace, 'he went back to England, to his wife and children.'

Silence greeted this disclosure. Thomas's face was very red. Rachel saw Sarah slip her hand into his.

Afterwards, when he was leaving, Rachel walked with him to the corner, where the water wagon was drawn up. Thomas eyed her warily. 'Do you mind if I come for supper?'

'Of course not.'

'I wondered,' he began after a moment, 'about Sarah. She says she's assigned to your employer. I . . . that is, I am fond of her. Do you think she would . . . that is, if I were to ask her to . . . I realise it is far too soon, but if one doesn't grab at the things one wants, they are apt to slip out of your grasp. I've learned that much, at least!'

Rachel smiled and touched his arm. 'You must ask her yourself,' she told him gently. 'But I feel sure Sarah won't disappoint you.'

He looked relieved, and then he was gone, his step light as he vanished around the corner on the way to his lodgings.

Victoria's birthday was an excuse for celebrations and excitement. The children made themselves sick on cake and sweets, and Suzy got drunk on beer— Melbourne had its own breweries. When she had been put to bed, with the children, Sarah and Rachel sat together in the stillness.

'You still miss him, don't you?' Sarah asked her softly.

Rachel, startled, looked back into the clear blue eyes of her friend. 'Yes, I miss him.' And it was an admission to herself as well as Sarah.

'Maybe he misses you too.'

Rachel wondered if he did. If he felt that sense of loss, of incompleteness she herself often felt. 'I'll never forget him,' she said at last. 'How can I, when I have Bella? But I wish I could.'

'You're young yet. There'll be someone else.' Sarah spoke with the certainty of one in love herself.

Rachel smiled. 'Maybe.'

Maybe, she told herself, she should do as Suzy said, and test the water a bit before she jumped into the bath again. But, truthfully, she shrank from a casual encounter of that type. She was too straight-laced for such a notion not to repel her. Perhaps she was fated to remain alone.

Newtown brought together the rich and poor of Melbourne in a jumble. The Newtown residents often complained about the way in which the streets were left unattended by the police at night. Under cover of darkness, crimes of all types were carried out and fights were common. There had been petitions to Superintendent La Trobe, but nothing much had come of it. It was at one of the well-attended meetings of the Newtown residents that Rachel discovered the extent of ill-feeling by the New Chums towards her birthplace.

'It's the Vandemonians who are to blame,' someone behind them muttered sourly. 'They bring their convict ways with 'em. We don't want 'em here. Thieves and murderers the lot!'

Sarah's eyes popped with fright, and she clutched onto Rachel's arm.

'Not everyone from Vandemon is a ruffian,' Thomas Dart said loudly, though his face paled at his temerity.

A large woman with grey hair glared at him. 'I've never met one that ain't,' she retorted, as if there were no more to be said.

He glanced apologetically at Sarah, but she was so proud of him she didn't notice. He had stood up for her, he loved her, and she would never forget it.

The petition was duly signed, but once again nothing came of it. The fights went on, the grog shops continued to trade. There were still parts of Newtown where Rachel did not venture, wynds where all sorts of villains congregated. It was like a part of London or Sydney or Hobart, transported to Port Phillip intact, where the more villainous inhabitants felt comfortable.

Suzy had only just recovered from her hangover when she visited the nearest grog shop and took to her bed yet again. 'Where's George?' she sobbed. 'I want George in me arms once more.'

Thomas Dart was embarrassed by Suzy's behaviour, but for once Sarah stood up for her. 'She's all right,' she said, borrowing one of Suzy's own phrases. 'Just because she acts tough, don't mean she doesn't feel sad and lonely like the rest of us.'

When it was time to leave, Sarah walked with Thomas to the gate and they were there a long time in the darkness, murmuring in soft voices.

Inside, Rachel turned down the lamp and tucked in the children. Sarah and Thomas were weaving their future out there in the darkness while she, Rachel, was in limbo. Soon it would be two years since Will had left her. Time to put the past to rest, she thought suddenly. She had been grieving, whether she admitted it or not. After all, the Will she had loved had died, in spirit if not in fact.

It was 1842, and she was resident in a new land. Rachel pushed back her hair, feeling it hot and heavy in the still, humid night. She was no longer a girl but a woman with a child. And she was lonely. I'm still young, she cried out silently. I want to be held again, and loved again. I want to give love in return. Surely, that's not too much to ask? Even Will would not begrudge her finding some happiness in the next twenty . . . thirty years of her life. For tonight they stretched out before her like a dark, desolate plain.

CHAPTER 13

THE MEN HAD RETURNED.

Young Frank came running inside, shouting and pulling at Rachel's hand. Before she could make sense of what he was saying, the crunch of boots on the hard ground had her head up and her eyes wide.

Frank Potter stood in the doorway, looking tired and drained, only his blue eyes as bright as ever. The beard he had grown over the last eight weeks made him almost a stranger. His son ran to him and he caught the boy up and, when Matty crept closer, hugged her in his other arm. Victoria came running and Bella, never backward, was there too for her kiss and hug. He was laughing, and the laugh caught at Rachel. It was somehow dear, just as his face was dear—she wished she too were a child again, and could run to him and be hugged and kissed and comforted.

'I'm so glad you're back again, and safe,' she said instead, with a broad smile.

He returned her smile, putting the children down at last. 'I missed you all,' he replied, and she could see he meant it. 'Everything has been well?'

She nodded, reassuring him. Her smile just wouldn't go away. So good, so *good* to have him back. And then her eyes slid past. Israel was slapping his hat on his leg, amid billowing dust. He too looked tired, but whereas Frank Potter had seemed to come alive when he saw his family, Israel barely spared them a glance apart from a grin thrown to his nephew and a brief touch on the head for each of the girls. He wanted no more. He was already striding restlessly about the cottage, making it seem so much smaller.

'Where's George?' Suzy, in the doorway, was trying to look unconcerned, but Rachel saw the fear in her hazel eyes.

'We left him at Nerinbilly,' Captain Potter's voice was reassuring. 'He's well, don't worry. You'll see him soon. But we needed him to stay there and keep an eye on things.'

Rachel watched Suzy struggling between relief and misery. She had missed George more than she had ever said, except for the times she was drunk. Rachel thought she missed Vandemon, too.

Israel sank down at last, stretching out legs in grubby trousers and dusty boots. His gaze went to Rachel, and there was a challenge in it. 'I need a drink.' After a moment, unwillingly, she fetched him some water. He took the mug and drank deep. And then he smiled at her over the rim, his blue eyes brilliant as the sky. 'Thank you, Rachel,' he said.

And it was as if there were no-one in the room apart from Israel and her.

That evening, Frank Potter told them about Nerinbilly, and the new run they had claimed to the north of it. 'We'll get our lease made official with the Commissioner of Lands while we're here,' he added. 'The land looks like it'll support 2,000 sheep, maybe more. We left three men there to build a hut and some yards, ready for when we move some of the sheep up there. The feed at Nerinbilly's getting scarce.'

The heat and lack of rain was starting to affect the countryside. The further north they went, the drier and deader and hotter it became. After a dry summer and now a dry autumn, the creeks and rivers were disappearing, turning into strings of water holes or, in some cases, gullies of dust. At least their own creek, at Nerinbilly, was still running.

'It's so hot,' Israel said, 'the birds drop from the sky dead at your feet.' No-one knew whether to laugh or not; no-one knew whether he was joking or not. But looking at Frank Potter's serious face it seemed he was telling the truth. 'It's not the country to take women and children into,' Israel added bluntly.

'My brother is right, I'm afraid,' Frank put in regretfully. 'The place is not yet fit.' And, when his son began to cry out with disappointment, 'No, wait! We've worked something out. There's a station to the south of us, only a good day's ride away from Nerinbilly, leased by a Mrs McCrae, a widow. She's a Vandemonian, too. Her husband died in a fall from his horse, and she stayed on to look after the station. And I must say it's well run. You'll be looked after there better than I could possibly look after you at Nerinbilly. And Mrs McCrae'll be willing to take you all in—with board of course—until we can build a proper homestead. She expects some work in return, but nothing you wouldn't be doing at Nerinbilly anyway—it'll be good practise! Believe me it's the only way.'

Of course his son pleaded and the girls joined in, until Rachel felt bound to say, 'Surely if this Mrs McCrae can manage living rough, we can?'

Israel, twitching with impatience, snapped, 'Don't talk rubbish, girl. You know nothing of it. McCrae's Castle is a palace compared to Nerinbilly.'

Rachel felt her face burn with humiliation. Why had she thought she liked Israel? The man was insufferable! 'It's best,' Frank Potter added gently, coming to her rescue.

After a moment, Young Frank broke the uncomfortable silence. 'Did you see any savages, father?' he whispered, his eyes wide.

His father smiled. 'A few. They didn't harm us. You must understand, Frank, that each tribe has its own territory . . . that is, own land. And the tribe around Nerinbilly is friendly enough. It's the ones to the west, on the Campaspe and the Goulburn Rivers you have to watch. They're wild men, all right. Sometimes a few of them come over, looking to steal sheep, all done up in their war paint. But they don't come near us. Uncle Israel,' with a nod of his head towards his younger brother, 'has a big gun.'

Young Frank looked to Israel, half in excitement and half in fright. 'Do you shoot them?'

'I would if I had to,' Israel replied evenly. 'And I know others who have. But if they leave me alone, I'll leave them alone.'

Bella came and crawled onto Rachel's lap, pushing at Victoria who was already there. Frank Potter lifted his little daughter onto his own knee, laughing delightedly when she reached out tentatively to touch his beard. Israel sat back and watched his brother with tolerant mockery.

'When are you planning to return?' Rachel asked.

'We need more sheep.' It was Israel who answered her. 'Some of the ewes left on Nerinbilly are scabby, and we've had to separate them from the rest. We can move them up to the new land, but they're really only good for boiling down into tallow.' He smiled. 'If it wasn't for the demand for tallow and skins, half of Port Phillip would be bankrupt.' Then, with a lift of his eyebrows, 'Is there some problem? Can't you manage the journey?'

He was taunting her, throwing her off-balance. Rachel put up her chin. 'Of course I can.'

After a moment he smiled, something like approval flickering in his eyes.

Sarah came with a mug of beer for Israel—he seemed to be as fond of the stuff as Suzy—and her eyes met Rachel's and slid away. And then Rachel remembered. Thomas Dart. She had to confess what she had done. With sudden cowardice, she thought that perhaps she could leave it for the morning, and then she knew she wouldn't sleep all night from thinking and worrying about it. Better to speak now, better to get it over with.

'Captain Potter,' she began tentatively, and he looked up inquiringly. 'You spoke of getting a tutor for the children . . . for Frank and Matty?' And, when he nodded, her voice rushed on, 'Well, we've found just the man. He's been coming here every day, for a trial, and the children like him. We thought. . . we hoped . . .'

Israel pulled a face. 'You haven't promised him anything, have you?' With a glance at his brother, 'There are plenty of villains around. Probably found this lot easy pickings!'

The anger showed on Rachel's face. 'He's perfectly respectable,' she managed at last. 'We're not fools, Mr Potter, even if we are *only* women.'

'I will certainly take a look at him,' Frank Potter put in swiftly. 'And if he is as you say, Rachel. . .' He glanced at Israel sternly, 'Rachel is an excellent judge of character.'

'Except perhaps when it came to her husband,' Israel retorted lazily.

There was a silence. Rachel felt the colour drain from her face, leaving it white. She stood up. 'How dare you!'

But Frank Potter was before her, his own face mirroring Rachel's outrage. 'Israel, that was quite uncalled for. You know nothing of the matter. I think you should apologise to Rachel.'

The blue eyes shone with a mixture of stubbornness and scorn. Rachel stood, stiff as a board, and waited. And, at last, he smiled slowly, eyeing her up and down, and said, 'I beg your pardon, Mrs Trigg.'

It wasn't a real apology, but it was all she would get. Rachel nodded her head, still rigid with fury.

'Now,' and Israel stood up to stretch and yawn, 'I'm tired, and I think I'll turn in.' He brushed against her as he passed, deliberately she was sure.

And then he grinned, and strode off, whistling, to the lean-to where he and his brother slept.

Over his shoulder, Suzy's eyes met Rachel's, and she winked. Rachel turned crossly away, accepting Captain Potter's apologies, shrugging off the insult. It didn't matter, she told him. No, really, it didn't matter . . . Only it did matter, it mattered very much!

Thomas Dart surprised Israel after all, and Frank Potter was pleased with him, and his references. It was decided to employ him as Frank and Matty's tutor for the time being at least. Of course, Sarah was ecstatic. She had been afraid that they would decide Thomas was unsuitable and leave him behind.

'I'd have stayed with him,' Sarah said emphatically. 'I would!'

Evidently, Thomas had not yet mentioned marriage, but Rachel was sure that was his intention. Despite the differences in background, Thomas and Sarah seemed ideally suited to each other. Sarah was strong, while Thomas was timid; Thomas needed someone to look after him, and Sarah needed to mother her man; Thomas was kind and honest, and so was Sarah. Rachel was glad for her friend. Suzy, too, was glad . . . if a little jealous. She still missed George more than she would admit. Sometimes, Rachel smelt beer on her breath, and occasionally she would slip out to one of the grog shops and come back unsteady on her feet. It was for the company more than anything, she said, when Rachel asked her.

'I like men,' she admitted boldly. 'I get tired o' a house full o' women.'

'She'll be all right once she's with George again,' Rachel told Sarah, when Suzy lay snoring on her bed. 'She misses him.'

'I wonder if George misses her,' Sarah retorted. 'Probably glad of the peace and quiet.'

Frank Potter took the children and Rachel out to Sandridge—Liardet's Beach as it was called locally.

They went by wagon, crossing the Yarra Yarra by punt.

The children loved running on the sand, and the view of the bay, with the ships at anchor, was delightful after being in the stuffy cottage. There were two inns to cater for townsfolk and travellers, but Frank Potter had asked Rachel to prepare them a picnic lunch, and they sat eating in companionable silence.

Afterwards, Frank Potter lay back and had a snooze, while Rachel ran with Frank and Matty, as if she were a child again herself, and built up sand-castles for Victoria and Bella to knock down. But eventually even she tired, and sat down beside Frank Potter, leaving the play to the children.

Rachel found her eyes straying to her employer. The beard flattered him, she thought, and the sun had burned his skin even browner than before. The life here in Port Phillip suited him; he was happy.

As if aware of her gaze, Frank Potter half sat up. He moved his hand in the sand, letting the grit slide slowly between his fingers. 'Rachel,' he murmured.

She smiled, waiting.

'Do you remember when Martha died?'

Slowly her smile faded; he felt the tension in her.

'I wished her dead, you know. I wished for her to be removed from my path. You know that, don't you?'

She looked away. After a moment she whispered, 'Yes.'

'When I came out of the study and found her, lying there at the bottom of the stairs, I was shocked. I was also relieved.'

The past flashed back. Rachel was there again, the night he looked up at her from the bottom of the stairs. She had seen the guilt in his face— guilt for wishing Martha dead.

He met her dark eyes and smiled wryly. 'I have been sorry for it ever since. And yet, if she had lived, would we be here now?'

'Martha would have hated it,' Rachel said simply. 'Captain Potter, I never told you before . . . Martha knocked on my door that night. She thought you were there. I should have gone out to her, but I was afraid. I didn't want her to accuse me of . . . of . . .'

He touched her shoulder. 'Don't you see?' she whispered urgently. 'Martha might still be alive if I had gone to her.'

He shook his head. 'I think you should know what the doctor, and I, suspected happened, Rachel.

It's quite possible that Martha meant to fall down the stairs. That, in fact, she threw herself.'

Rachel swallowed. 'You mean it wasn't an accident?'

Frank grimaced. 'We said nothing at the time. It seemed unnecessary to make things more unpleasant than they already were. So don't blame yourself.'

Slowly, the taut set of her shoulders relaxed. The guilt eased.

Seeing it, Frank sighed. There was more he wanted to tell her, other secrets he'd kept to himself, but he knew she didn't want to hear them. What point was there in declaring his love for her, of baring his soul? If she had been free, if Will wasn't his friend, it might have been different. But some things were just not meant to be. Abruptly, he stood up, and held out his hand. 'Come on. It's time we went home. Let's go and round up our children.'

Rachel's eyes searched his apprehensively, as if she knew what was in his mind, and then she gave him her hand with a grateful smile.

'Rachel, are you awake?'

It was dark in the back room. Rachel turned her head on the bed, peering into the blackness beside her. 'Sarah?' Sarah's white-blonde hair was a pale blur. Outside, the clouds that had been gathering for hours covered the moon and stars, broken only briefly by a flicker of lightening.

'I wanted to tell you first,' Sarah's voice was even more breathy than usual. 'Thomas has asked me to marry him.'

'I'm so pleased!' Rachel's voice rose and she bit her lip to stop it. She found Sarah in the darkness and hugged her. A crack of thunder close by startled them both, and they laughed nervously.

'I love him,' Sarah said shyly. 'He's too good for me, oh, I know that. He's educated and clever and—'

'That's not true—'

'Maybe,' and her voice held a smile. 'But it's what people'll say.'

'He needs someone like you, Sarah.'

'I think so, too. We're getting wed before we go north. It's best.' Ministers of religion were scarce beyond Melbourne, and churches non-existent.

'I'm so glad.'

The thunder crackled again. Rachel lay and gazed up at the ceiling. She was glad Sarah and Thomas had found each other. It was right they should marry. Lightning split the darkness, and for a moment the room was brilliant. Bella began to cry beside her, and Rachel gathered the child in her arms. The little body trembled against her own before relaxing once more into sleep.

Outside, Frank's dog began to howl, frightened by the storm. Suzy groaned and covered her head with her arms, and Sarah scrambled up to fetch it in before Israel Potter threw his boot at it. No mention had been made of the dog yet, but Rachel was waiting. She had seen Israel looking at it with narrowed eyes, as though trying to work out exactly what breed it was.

Sarah returned, the frightened animal with her. 'If I find one flea tomorrow, I'll murder that mongrel,' Suzy announced with gritted teeth.

'Don't be cross,' Young Frank's voice piped up, full of suppressed excitement. 'Sarah's getting married.'

There was a silence. 'Is she?' Suzy asked laconically. 'Congratulations. Now can we get some sleep?'

Rachel walked slowly along the street. She rarely had time to herself, and it was pleasant to be alone with her thoughts. The sun was hot on her back and shoulders, though her bonnet shaded her face. This might be one of her last journeys to the shops, Rachel thought to herself. She had enjoyed her stay in Melbourne, but the men had almost finished their business here, and shortly they would all be setting out to the north. Rachel gave a fleeting thought to Mrs McCrae and her station, then put it aside. There was no point in worrying about the future; she must just face it when she came to it.

The step at Rachel's side startled her. She turned sharply and looked into Israel Potter's lively blue eyes. 'You're walking my way, Rachel. Do you mind?' And he smiled as if it never entered his head that she might.

Rachel shook her head. 'No, I don't mind. I needed some thread. The shop is just up ahead.'

He said nothing for a moment, matching his steps

to hers. 'My brother regards you highly.' The tone of voice was not as complimentary as the words.

'I'm glad.'

Israel met her dark eyes, trying to read them. He saw pride there, and wariness, but no coquetry, nothing of the flirtatiousness he usually found in women's eyes. This one is different, some voice inside him taunted. Respectable, just as Frank had said. And yet something lurked in the curve of her mouth, the sweep of her lashes. Passion? Calculation? Perhaps . . .

'It was a pity about Martha.'

She said nothing, but he thought her shoulders stiffened. He smiled to himself. There *was* something, then. He'd known she couldn't be as perfect as she seemed.

'It's a shame your own husband isn't dead,' he went on smoothly. 'Then you and my brother could marry. That's what you want, isn't it?'

She turned and looked at him, and the anger leapt into her eyes like hot flames. 'Martha's death was an accident,' she whispered furiously. 'And I think your brother is a fine man, but I wouldn't marry him, even if I could. I would no more marry him than . . . than you!'

He laughed.

Furiously, she took a step towards him, but he only laughed louder. He had been baiting her, she realised. Trying to get a reaction from her. And he had succeeded. Furious, now, because she hadn't kept her calm in tact, Rachel turned and walked swiftly away. But he came after her.

'Rachel. . .'

She tightened her lips and kept walking.

'I only wanted to know if you were really what you seemed . . . ' his voice trailed off, and he looked at her almost apologetically.

Rachel stopped and frowned. 'And am I what I seem?'

He put his hand on her shoulder and rested it there, warm and heavy. His eyes had lost their laughter. 'I'm very much afraid that you are.'

What was she supposed to make of that? Rachel asked herself later. Israel was a puzzle. She was drawn to him, and yet at the same time she felt he was a threat to her peace of mind. Like a quickening breeze rippling the smooth waters of the Yarra Yarra.

During the evening meal, she found her eyes drawn to him again and again. There was vitality about him, as if the very air crackled around him. It disturbed her, excited her. Different to Will, who had always impressed her with his stillness, his solidness. Will had encircled her with love, like soft, endless rain; Israel was like summer lightning, threatening to strike.

'Can we take my dog, father, please?'

Young Frank's pleading voice interrupted her thoughts. The children had gathered around Frank Potter, and he was half stern, half laughing at their entreaties. 'Oh very well!' he said at last, looking up at Rachel with a wry smile. 'Though what Mrs McCrae will say I can't imagine!'

'If it touches her sheep she'll shoot it,' Israel's impatient tones cut through the merriment.

Rachel came forward to put a comforting hand on the boy's shoulder. 'Then we'll have to keep him tied up, won't we, Frank?'

Frank nodded jerkily.

'Come now, it's bed time, children . . .'

They went with relief, or so it seemed to Rachel. How could two brothers be so dissimilar? Even now, Frank Potter was rising to follow his children and kiss them goodnight. Behind him, Israel made a sound of impatience, and went out into the darkness of the verandah. Rachel nodded at Sarah to take her place, and followed him out.

For a moment she stood in the doorway, enjoying the cool breeze. The glow of Israel lighting his pipe drew her eyes to the side, and she came closer. Her skirts swished angrily.

'Frank is only six, Mr Potter. Must you be so hard on him?'

He looked at her, his pipe halfway to his mouth. 'I don't believe in treating children leniently,' he said evenly. 'They have a tough time ahead of them—best prepare them for it.'

'They've lost their mother. I think they deserve a little gentleness.'

'Tell my brother that, or Mrs McCrae. Not me.' He puffed on his pipe, indifferent.

Rachel clenched her fists. 'I grew up in an orphanage, Mr Potter—'

Israel turned to face her. 'I grew up on the land, Mrs Trigg, and we were poor. We pretended we were a cut above the villagers, but in truth we were even poorer than them. It was all pretence with us, all show. Later, things were better . . . my father inherited money we never expected to have. But I never forgot those early years. If you want something, you take it. And if someone tries to take it from you, you fight. There's no room in this life for gentleness or pity . . . no room for the softness in your eyes, Rachel.'

She said nothing. He was watching her. And suddenly it was as if the mood between them had shifted. 'There's always room for kindness, Mr Potter,' she whispered, 'and love.'

'Love?' he mocked softly. Israel's hand reached out, dark against the starry sky, and touched her cheek. 'By God, you frighten me, woman,' he said suddenly, harshly.

'Why?' Her breath was coming fast, as if she were running.

'Because you make me weak, Rachel. You're that thing that frightens the life out of me—a *good* woman! It'd be so easy to lay my head on your shoulder and give myself up to you.'

Rachel floundered, trying to understand his meaning. Was he attracted to her? Was that it? She gazed back at him, her dark eyes shining. *She* was attracted to *him,* there was no denying it. He could be arrogant and impatient, and sometimes he made her angry, but his confidence and energy were to be admired. Israel knew what he wanted and where he was going, and the combination drew Rachel irresistibly.

'I'm frightened, too,' she admitted, and licked her lips.

His eyes followed the movement. 'Why?'

'Because . . . because I fear you could hurt me, Israel Potter, if you wanted to.'

'Rachel. . .' He was close now, close enough to kiss her.

The scrape of a boot behind them startled them, and sent them spinning around. Frank Potter said nothing, though his eyes were watchful. And then he moved purposefully to the edge of the verandah, scanning the vault of the sky, as though he had noticed nothing out of the ordinary.

'No rain in sight?' His voice was quiet.

Israel joined him. 'We need it, that's for sure,' Rachel heard him say, as she slipped away. 'We can't start burning off until we're sure of a good shower or two to get the new stuff growing . . .'

'All right?'

Sarah glanced up, as Rachel peeped into the doorway of the bedroom, and smiled and nodded. 'They were tired.' Rachel looked pale and drawn, she thought, her dark eyes glittering almost wildly. Something had upset her, but Sarah didn't have time to contemplate that. She had Thomas to think of, and her wedding on Saturday. Rachel had been helping her sew her dress, and they were nearly finished.

As if she read Sarah's thoughts, Rachel whispered, 'You'll look beautiful.' There were tears in her eyes. Suddenly Sarah knew she was thinking of Will and remembering her own wedding. Rachel hardly ever spoke of Will, but Sarah was certain she thought of him—that had been love on a grand scale.

Suzy said once that it was better not to love so hotly, that it burned you up in its fire, and destroyed you from ever loving again.

Poor Rachel.

But Sarah's sadness could not last. She was just too happy.

The church was in Russell Street, a wooden structure built by public donation. Sarah looked a picture, Rachel thought, and Thomas Dart was the proud groom. I'm happy for them, Rachel told herself. But the sadness grew, threatening to swallow her up, as the service went on and the children waited impatiently with their handfuls of rice.

Just as the tears pricking her eyes began to fall, Frank Potter bent towards her. 'Israel says we'll be leaving next week,' he murmured softly. 'No more time for weddings.'

Rachel glanced up at him, blinking. 'Good!'

He laughed. 'That's the spirit.'

And suddenly Rachel felt much better.

CHAPTER 14

THE DRAY JOLTED TO ONE side, the tarpaulin covered contents moving slightly beneath the tightly knotted ropes. The bullocks tossed their heads in temper, pulling hard as the wheels came up on the rise and over, one of the many rises they had climbed since they left Melbourne.

As they moved further and further out from the main centre of settlement, Rachel became increasingly aware of the isolation of the countryside. At first, there were cottages and slab huts on bush covered acreages, or farms with crops planted and animals grazing, food to feed the new town. And there were inns, like wretched animals, skulking in the bush, chimneys steaming. Their rooms were full of men, drinking or sleeping still wearing their spurs and hats. This was a man's country, it seemed, and women were viewed almost as intruders. If Rachel had not realised it before, she certainly did now.

Most of the early labour in Port Phillip had consisted of expirees or assigned servants from Van Diemen's Land or New South Wales. They had

made the country their own, revelling in their freedom to do much as they pleased. Which usually
amounted to drinking themselves into a stupor.
Most of the 'old hands' clung together from a sense
of loyalty, and their leaders were usually those
whose crimes were the most dire. Women were
so few and far between, the men had little to do
with them, unless they could find a black woman
to barter for. And when a squatter employed an
unmarried female cook or servant, she'd best find
a protector as fast as she could, or the men considered her everyone's. Out in the lonely, sheep-filled
country of Port Phillip, the law was in the hands
of the lawless.

The bullocks were so slow. The party travelled
much more slowly than it would have done with
horses pulling the wagon, but horses soon grew
tried pulling heavy vehicles through this country,
and besides there was little feed for horses. Bullocks, Israel told them, could find their own food,
and live on the promise of water.

Frank Potter and his brother rode horses though,
often galloping ahead to take a look at the country
to come. Thomas Dart had been offered a mount
but had preferred to ride in the cart with the
women—much to Israel's silent derision. Rachel
would have preferred a horse—Will had taught
her to ride at Greengage—but no-one had offered
one to her.

The bullock driver was a surly chap from Vandemon, who hardly said two words at a time. Sarah
poked her tongue out at his back, and even Suzy's
charms couldn't move him to do more than spit on
the ground. His name was Crow, because he had a

voice like one, and as with so many 'old hands' that was all they knew about him—because that was all he wanted them to know.

The further they travelled the less there was to show of white man's habitation. Sometimes they came upon a shepherd's hut along the track to the north—hardly even a track, just the marks of other wagon wheels to follow—where they could pause for a moment. One night they slept in relative comfort with a roof over their heads. But mostly there was just the track they were travelling, and the bush, and sleeping beneath their wagon.

At first, Rachel found the bush almost threatening, so silent apart from the cries of the birds, and the occasional glimpse of kangaroo or wallaby. It was not like Vandemon, with its almost English style of village and town life—apart from the rugged mountains to the west where Rachel had never been. Rachel was filled with a sort of wonder and a sort of fear, as they moved further and further away from all she had known.

'Mrs McCrae is the nearest thing we have to a neighbour,' Israel had told them. 'Most of the other runs bordering on to Nerinbilly are managed by overseers and shepherds. A couple of owners are in Sydney, and a couple are in England, and one is a speculator who lives in Melbourne. There is Redcliffe's, I suppose. That run borders the McCrae place and Nerinbilly.' He shrugged expressively. 'Redcliffe is as mad as a dog in a thunderstorm, and his wife . . . no-one ever sees her. You'll get little company from them.'

'Sounds bloody awful,' muttered Suzy.

Behind them, Rachel could hear the sheep. It

had been difficult finding feed and water for them. Much of the time they were reliant upon the good graces of the shepherds and overseers of the land they were crossing. At night the men set up nets around saplings hammered into the ground, making a sort of pen. And there was always someone on watch for wild dogs or natives or other hazards of the bush.

Rachel had soon got used to frying lamb chops over the camp fire, and drinking black tea. Crow, the bullock driver, took his meals to the edge of the firelight, but the others ate companionably around the fire. The men smoked and spoke of their plans, while the children's eyes grew heavy, and soon it was time to turn in, ready for an early start and another long, hot, dusty day.

One night, when Israel was on watch, Rachel had to fetch some water for one of the children. His eyes followed her and whereas with any other man she would have spoken or smiled, somehow with him she didn't dare.

'Pour one for me, while you're there,' he'd said evenly.

Rachel had brought the water to him, waiting while he drank. When she stooped to take the mug back from him his hand closed over hers, holding her. 'You're supposed to be watching the sheep,' she whispered, and her voice was husky.

'The sheep can wait,' he retorted. His mouth was warm against her neck, and for a moment he buried his face against her, just as he'd told her he longed to do. Rachel closed her eyes, feeling a rush of something she hardly remembered. Desire? Love? She had pulled away, stepping back and staring into his eyes like a frightened animal.

His eyelids came down; his voice mocked her. 'Better get some sleep, Rachel. Another big day tomorrow.'

Her hands were trembling when she lay down again, but the next morning she was able to act quite naturally with him. Outwardly as least. Inside was a different matter. It was as if the darkness had stripped away all pretence and laid bare the truth. She was drawn to him; she liked the set of his shoulders and his brisk stride; she liked his confident grin and brilliant eyes. She liked him, she liked him very much. The problem was, was liking Israel a good thing for Rachel?

They had been travelling on McCrae land for some time. Israel had pointed out the boundaries—the line of a creek and arrows emblazoned on the trunks of trees. It was hilly country, with jagged lines of rock erupting from the ground. Gullies were thick with timber and wild life, and behind it all rose the gloomy bulk of a mountain. Mount Alexander, said Israel, a landmark for squatters travelling into the empty north.

They passed one out-station—a primitive slab hut with a bark roof. The two shepherds were away with their flock, and only a dog greeted them, barking hysterically. Emus ran, chased by Israel's own dogs, their long, powerful legs throwing odd shadows as the dusk lengthened.

It was almost dark when they reached McCrae's Castle. Castle? thought Rachel. It was indeed a castle! Far better than the other places she'd seen, and a sense of relief filled her. The wooden structure was etched against the skyline, set as it was on

a rise. Lamplight shone through the drawn curtains, and a tall gum tree sheltered it with loving
arms. All around were the usual sheds and huts and
yards, as well as what looked like a couple of paddocks of cultivated land and one of pasture. As the
party straggled to a halt, the place came alive. Men
ran from everywhere to help. Thomas Dart gave
Rachel his hand, as she climbed stiffly down. She
felt as if every bone in her body had been jarred to
pieces. The other two women followed her wearily, and stood, silent with exhaustion.

The Castle's sheep were already secured for
the night, locked up in some of the yards, while
next door fat lambs were being readied for market. There were horses running free in a paddock,
while others were enclosed, ready for tomorrow's
work. Rachel watched Frank Potter helping to
persuade his sheep into an empty yard, dogs running and men calling, while Crow began to water
his bullocks. 'Women and children come after livestock,' Suzy muttered sarcastically.

Then at last, Israel Potter was striding towards
them. Behind him, like a big ship in full sail, came
a woman holding a lantern.

'Mrs McCrae, this is my brother's entourage,'
Israel said, and the smoke from his pipe stung
Rachel's eyes.

Mrs McCrae was even bigger close up. A tall,
heavily built woman, with hair that was once black
streaking to steely grey. The lines on her face were
deep, but her smile, in the light of the lantern,
warmed Rachel to the very bottom of her heart.

'Come in, come in,' she cried, her accent educated Scots. 'I've plenty of food for you all, and the

little ones can sleep a while, if they've a mind to it.'

Gratefully, they went with her. Frank Potter looked up as they passed, stretching his back. It had been a long, slow ride—Israel had hated every moment of it, impatient to get on. But then, that was Israel. Frank sighed. This country would need hard work and effort to make it pay. The climate was the main problem. Fickle. Too little rain and there was a drought, the long kangaroo grass dying back to baking earth; too much rain and there was a flood, the bare soil washing away down creeks and gullies. One battled against the elements constantly, and never really knew whether or not a venture would succeed. And then there was the added burden of the financial depression.

His eyes focussed on the home station, and the lamplight spilling from the doorway as Mrs McCrae led her little 'flock' inside. She was a good hearted woman. He trusted her with his children . . . and Rachel. The Castle was a haven of luxury and sophistication compared to some of the stations he'd seen. With another sigh, he began to move back towards the wagon to help the men ready things for the night. They would go on in the morning, on to Nerinbilly. There was no point in staying with so much to be done on their own run. And if he felt empty at the thought of leaving his family behind he'd best not let Israel see it.

Mrs McCrae made them all comfortable. The home station consisted of a central sitting room, where all meals were taken, and four other rooms opening on to it. A verandah ran around the building, protecting it from the hot sun in the summer and driving rain in the winter.

The 'sitting room' was large, with an enormous fireplace, flanked incongruously by a red damask sofa and a wooden stump, still 'in situ' and covered with a white cloth. The walls were decorated with stockwhips and various other pieces of station paraphernalia. There was a long table, with an equally long bench on one side and ill-matching chairs on the other; a couple of stools completed the picture. A book shelf was filled to bursting with, among other things, novels by Walter Scott and poetry by Burns, a glass fronted cupboard held Mrs McCrae's better pieces of crockery, while, finally, in pride of place, the piano, rather battered from the journey across sea and land, but polished to a soft glow by loving hands.

Rachel later learned that the kitchen was reached by a covered walkway from the back door, and a large room adjoining it was used as the station store, where flour, sugar, tea, rum etc were kept secure, as well as clothing and boots and various other bush necessities, which could be purchased by the station hands. There was a one room cottage beside the kitchen, once used by the cook who, Mrs McCrae informed them, had decamped some weeks ago after an argument. Mrs McCrae and a girl named Alice had been doing the cooking and cleaning for the home station—the station hands had their own cook and quarters. The one room cottage at the back would do for Thomas and Sarah. 'Hazelwood's been using it, but he can move back to the men's quarters. He's my foreman,' she explained.

'We don't want to put anyone out of their home,' Thomas began, but Mrs McCrae flapped her hand at him dismissively.

'I'm glad of the company!' And Rachel, after her long journey, understood why.

The foreman, Hazelwood, was a big dour man, who nodded brusquely when they were introduced, but Rachel noticed him wink at the children. If he resented losing his cottage he didn't say. Mrs McCrae had no children. She and her husband had owned land in Vandemon, and sold up when they heard of the fortunes to be made in the Port Phillip District. They'd relied on their own capital rather than borrowing from the banks, and so had done well, surviving comfortably when others went to the wall.

'We were already in our forties when we arrived from Vandemon,' Mrs McCrae said. 'Old, compared to most of the squatters. Boys! In their teens, some of them. You'd walk through the streets of Melbourne, and not see one person over thirty years of age—or one woman. And here I was, both woman and middle aged. I turned some heads, I can tell you!'

'How long have you been here?' Rachel asked curiously, and took a hungry spoonful of mutton stew.

'Since '36,' Mrs McCrae told her. 'We came with the first rush for land. Some of the original squatters are still here, but others have sold out or gone under.' Her hostess chuckled. 'You should have seen the Castle before we built the home station. A dirt-floor shack with a bark roof that leaked. And there was I, used to spending my days sending the servants about their business, and calling on my friends!'

The three women stared at her in wonder. Had Mrs McCrae really been such a person? It was hard to believe, as she bent to ladle out some more stew for the men who had come in for their meal. She seemed so at ease in her surroundings.

Frank Potter glanced at Rachel, giving her an encouraging smile as he took his plate. Israel flung himself down near the hearth, stretching his legs and appearing to be perfectly at home.

Hazelwood grunted. 'You're not tired, young fella?' he said laconically.

Israel smiled. 'I could get up and ride fifty mile, if I had to.'

'My brother has embraced the squatter's life,' Frank said wryly.

Israel shrugged. 'I love it. I couldn't imagine living any other.'

There was a silence. Rachel thought he might be embarrassed to have admitted such a thing, but Israel continued to smile to himself, totally at ease. He had simply stated a fact.

Rachel was giving Bella her night feed, holding the warm little body against her own as the child sucked herself into blissful contentment. She knew she should wean the child but it was difficult to let these intimate moments go.

'Rachel?' Rachel turned at the whisper, and found Suzy standing close behind her. Sarah and Thomas had retired to their cottage, and the Potter brothers had also retired to their guest room. Rachel and Suzy and the children were to share another of the rooms—the smallest one. But after all, Rachel reasoned with a sigh, they were to be hired labour. Servants. And servants shouldn't expect too much.

'What is it?'

Suzy sank down beside her, corn coloured hair falling over her shoulders. She was unhappy. Rachel had sensed it during the journey, but there had been neither the time nor the opportunity to speak to her.

'Rachel, I'm to go with 'em in the morning.'

Rachel frowned. 'To Nerinbilly? I thought it wasn't fit for women?'

Suzy shrugged. 'Seems I don't count. They need a woman to help with the cooking, a "hut-keeper" they call it. They want me 'cause George and I are married—safer amongst all those men.' She scowled. 'You know what that Israel said to me when he told me? "No whoring neither" he said. Bloody cheek! I'm a respectable married woman now.'

Rachel said nothing, biting her lip.

'At least I'll be with George . . .' her voice trailed off miserably.

'He must be missing you.'

Suzy said nothing. Her unhappiness could no longer be contained. 'I don't think I like this country,' she whispered. 'I'm sorry now I ever left Greengage. If it weren't for George I might turn round and go back, whatever Cap'n Potter said.'

'Suzy,' Rachel murmured, 'give it a try. Once you see George you'll change your mind.'

But Suzy turned her head, and didn't reply, her long hair hiding her face.

The men set off early the following morning. Rachel stood, her shawl about her shoulders, and watched them go. Frank Potter's hand was warm on her arm. 'I'll get back as often as I can.'

'Soon we'll have a home of our own,' Matty informed Rachel in her serious voice. 'Father is building one, you know.'

'And it will need to be a very big one indeed,' Frank told his daughter, hiding his smile. 'But first we must see to the sheep, because they are what will make us our fortune.'

'Perhaps we can come and visit Nerinbilly?' Young Frank asked anxiously.

'Perhaps.' Captain Potter's eyes met Rachel's. 'Take care of them. And yourself.'

She nodded, feeling she'd had this conversation before, and then he was striding towards his horse.

Suzy was by the wagon. Rachel hugged her, feeling the tremble in the other woman's arms, but Suzy's face was blank when she pulled away.

'Give our love to George,' Sarah whispered, wiping tears. 'And look after yourself.'

Suzy tossed her head. 'O' course.'

She climbed into the wagon, and Rachel heard her mutter, 'Get on with it then!' to Crow. The wagon moved slowly out onto the track. Suzy looked back suddenly, as though she couldn't help it, and then her white face was enveloped in dust.

Israel had mounted, and was about to follow the bullock dray and sheep. Rachel caught his eye. She remembered suddenly the warmth of his lips against her neck, and wondered if he was remembering, too. Then he was gone, and only the trail of dust remained to show where they had all been.

And the memory of Suzy's white face.

CHAPTER 15

L IFE AT MCCRAE'S CASTLE WAS certainly not the dull, lonely life Rachel had expected. The station ran to a routine, everyone knowing their own tasks. And if they didn't, Hazelwood was there to tell them. The Castle had two outstations, where shepherds lived for months at a time, watching over the sheep and only seeing others from the home station at two week intervals, when fresh supplies were brought. The home station ran its own flocks, the shepherds moving them from place to place as the grass became scarce. They were fattening lambs for the Melbourne market, but feed was hard to come by now, because of the heat and lack of rain. Every morning, Hazelwood and Mrs McCrae peered at the sky ... hoping.

Of course, there weren't only sheep at the Castle. There was a small herd of cattle, and numerous horses, as well as the big garden, the wheat—Mrs McCrae hoped one day to be able to grind her own flour—an orchard, and a small vineyard.

Rachel and Sarah were mostly concerned with the children and the kitchen. Alice, the other servant, was a sullen, dark haired woman married to one of the shepherds. Her cooking was well enough, if basic. Most of the meals served on the stations were basic, consisting of lamb, mutton, damper and hot tea. The Castle was fortunate to have its own vegetables and fruit, to vary the monotony.

Thomas Dart began teaching Frank and Matty and, very soon, had four of Alice's children as well. Sarah whispered to Rachel that she was learning to read and write, too. Sometimes the children sat out in the yard, the little ones playing while the older ones read or wrote on slates.

A month after Rachel arrived at the Castle, a group of natives camped down in the gully near the creek. Mrs McCrae didn't seem perturbed. 'They come and go,' she shrugged. 'While they're here we'll make use of them about the place. They work for food, and tobacco. Probably not much game around for them at the moment. Soon, they'll move on. They never stay long. Got the wanderlust in them.'

The local tribe were called the Djadjawurrung. Tall, strong people, they wore possum skins and, sometimes, a feather or two in their hair. They were peaceful enough, traders rather than warmakers. Occasionally, as Mrs McCrae said, they worked on the station, but they never stayed for long. They weren't driven by the same concerns as the whites, and they were as puzzled by station life as the whites were puzzled by them. 'Sometimes they steal some sheep,' Mrs McCrae explained. 'And we have to give them a fright to stop it. They know they can come and do a bit of work at the Castle and I'll feed them. It's the other tribes we have trouble with, those to the north. They're warriors, always making raids, stealing each other's women and children. Usually they're too busy fighting each other to worry much about us.'

The government had set up a number of Mission Stations or Protectorates. Here, Protectors were employed to care for the natives who came to make their home there. They were fed and clothed, and attempts were made to educate and 'civilise' them, but they wouldn't stay there very long. The white man's ways were so alien to them, and besides, why stay on a few miserable acres when for generations your people had owned plenty of land to hunt and fish on, even though white men now claimed it as their own?

'Good money spent on the murdering savages,' Hazelwood muttered around his pipe. 'Government gives 'em blankets and feeds 'em up, so they can go out and spear our shepherds.'

There were always reports coming in of sheep or cattle or horses being killed or stolen, empty huts being pilfered, and shepherds speared, sometimes fatally. It was a constant war waged between black and white. And yet Mrs McCrae was not blind to the underlying problems.

'You can't blame all the blacks for what a few do,' she retorted. 'And if some of the squatters or their men would give the blacks food instead of shooting them, their sheep would be a lot safer!'

'I suppose it'd please you to see me with a spear in me back,' Hazelwood snarled. 'If you want me, I'll be out checking me traps.' And he slammed the door behind him—Hazelwood trapped possums in his spare time, and although Mrs McCrae refused to eat them, the station hands looked forward to the change in diet.

Mrs McCrae shrugged, glancing at Rachel. 'The tribes are dying anyway—though not quick enough for Hazelwood's liking. There's sickness among them—I believe influenza wiped out hundreds last year. I fear the race is doomed, and I can't help but feel it a pity.'

One afternoon, Rachel met the Assistant Protector of Aborigines for Mrs McCrae's area, when he rode up from the Jim Crow Mission Station. A dynamic but harassed little man by the name of Bedford. He spoke to Mrs McCrae for some time, asking her how many natives she had seen of late and their condition.

They seemed of a like mind, both concerned and sympathetic to the well being of the original inhabitants of Port Phillip—although Rachel sensed that McCrae's Castle was Mrs McCrae's main passion.

'Have you seen Big Mary?' Mr Bedford asked her, eyes narrowed.

Mrs McCrae shook her head slowly. 'Not since the spring. Has she had her child?'

He nodded. 'A little girl. The father,' with a delicate pause, 'was white.'

Mrs McCrae shook her head gloomily. 'Then the little mite may be dead. Mary, too.'

He sighed, and rose to his feet. 'You must let me

know, ma'am, if you see her or hear of her. I rely on you,' and he gripped her hand.

When he had gone, Rachel curious, asked about Big Mary.

Mrs McCrae answered readily enough. 'Poor Mr Bedford had high hopes of Big Mary. She was eager to learn, and stayed almost six months on his mission. But her husband wasn't happy and she left with him. They were seen about for a time. Unfortunately,' with a glance at Rachel, 'some of the shepherds bribe the tribes with tobacco . . . sugar . . . alcohol, for the use of the women. Big Mary's child is half white.' Then, impatiently, seeing Rachel's blank look, 'The tribe will probably kill it. Even the mothers sometimes kill such children. There is no place for them, you see, in either world. They think they are doing what is best.'

Rachel's mouth was dry. 'How dreadful,' she gasped. 'Is that why Mr Bedford wanted to know if you had seen her and the child? But what can he do?'

The other woman shook her head. 'He may take the child back with him, care for it himself. It is half white, after all. Big Mary is at risk, too. If she was raped, her husband may consider her unclean and drive her away . . . or kill her. It's possible, however, he bartered her willingly. Her feelings in the matter would be unimportant.'

Such a thing appalled Rachel. She looked at Bella, and the other children, and felt her stomach knot in sick revulsion. She thought of Big Mary used so carelessly, so cruelly, raped or else bartered for food and drink. Rachel's life suddenly seemed blissful by comparison.

Mrs McCrae, watching the girl curiously, read the emotions flitting across her mobile face. Here was one with a heart. For what good it would do her!

They had another visitor, this time a mounted trooper from the Mount Macedon Police Post, or the Border Police, as they were known. The troopers stationed there were often called upon to investigate incidents between blacks and whites, and to 'disperse' black warriors. They were also called upon to apprehend escaped assignees or other so-called 'dangerous persons', and generally dispense justice in their own designated area of Port Phillip. The trooper was on his way north, and only stayed overnight at McCrae's Castle. There had been trouble on the stations up there, he said, with several spearings and retaliatory shootings, and the Murray River Police Post needed reinforcements to cope with all the extra work. He set off the next morning, soon vanishing along the track into the dry, grey bush.

One day, Mrs McCrae took Rachel, with two of her men as escort, over to Redcliffe's run. She brought some of her precious vegetables with her, saying, 'Redcliffe is too mean to have a proper garden. He feeds his men on as little as possible. As you can imagine, they never stay long!'

The day was cool and cloudy, pleasant for a journey. At times the trees grew thick, and then they would thin out until it was almost like travelling through gentle, rolling parkland. Redcliffe's was a three hour ride from McCrae's Castle, but Mrs McCrae seemed to think that was nothing. 'Had a stockman who walked to Melbourne regularly,' she said. 'You get used to being a long way from everything. The Castle is a world of its own.'

They reached Redcliffe's at last. As the little group came upon the wooden hut and outbuildings, a sort of stillness fell over them. Rachel saw that, as usual, the walls of the hut were made of uneven slabs, with a roof of bark. A drift of grey smoke wafted up from the makeshift chimney, and a dog ran out, barking wildly. A couple of horses, penned in a grassless little paddock, looked up listlessly. But there was no sign of human life. Obviously, the two shepherds Redcliffe employed were out with their sheep, but where was Redcliffe and his wife?

Mrs McCrae halted her horse, and glanced at one of her men. He dismounted and walked towards the hut, kicking at the dog, which avoided his boot from long practise. As he reached the door, it was flung opened and a man stood there glaring at them.

'Redcliffe,' murmured Mrs McCrae with distaste.

The squat figure looked as if it hadn't washed in months. 'What do you want?' he shouted, his face almost covered with a wild dark beard, while long, lank hair fell over his shoulders.

Mrs McCrae began to dismount. 'I've brought some fresh food for you, Mr Redcliffe,' she said in a hearty voice. 'Where's Greta?'

Narrowed eyes slid over her. 'Food?' he muttered and hesitated, plainly wanting to tell her to clear off but wanting the food, too. The food won. 'Come in then,' The attempt at geniality was piti- fully unsuccessful.

Mrs McCrae lifted her eyebrows at Rachel, as the two women walked towards the hut.

The hut reeked of old mutton fat and human sweat and other less discernible, but equally unspeakable substances. At the doorway Rachel stiffened, feeling the bile rise to her throat. She watched in admiration as Mrs McCrae marched straight in. Trying not to breathe, Rachel followed.

The earth floor was littered with scraps, obvi- ously thrown for the dog. Against one wall, was a dirty unmade bed. A chest doubled as a table, with a grubby towel thrown over it. There was what looked like a sheep's skull on the mantelpiece, along with a row of old, broken pipes. Below, on the hearth, a dog growled, lifting its battered head from its paws; Rachel eyed it uneasily.

Mrs McCrae set down the food, talking as she did so, asking how Redcliffe had been, and if he had seen any natives about. Close up, Rachel thought, he was even worse than at a distance. And his eyes, little darting eyes, made her think of the rat Alice had caught in the storeroom.

'Saw Big Mary,' he offered at last, grudgingly.

Mrs McCrae lifted a bottle from the basket. Redcliffe fixed it with an unblinking gaze, but she held back, her eyes hard. 'Yes?'

With an effort he spoke. 'I saw her yesterday. By herself. Beggin' for food. I had none. Told her to go over to the Castle. She was whinin' and carryin' on. I picked up the gun in the end, to get rid o' her.'

Slowly, Mrs McCrae put the bottle down, and

Redcliffe snatched it with a grunt.

'Did she have a child with her?' she asked quickly.

He shook his head. He'd obviously lost interest.

'Where's Greta?' she asked again, looking about as if expecting to see Redcliffe's wife.

He shrugged indifferently. 'Never about when you want her. Out in the scrub somewhere. Thinks she's one o' the blackfellas, that girl. A red-headed gin.'

He grunted again. And then, as if he couldn't wait any longer, opened the bottle, upending it into his mouth. The liquor ran into his beard. Sickened, the two women went outside.

'It happens to some men,' Mrs McCrae murmured. 'The drink takes them over. I suppose in some cases it's an escape from the loneliness. The curse of the colonies, the grog.'

'I know,' Rachel whispered. 'My husband used to drink.' She felt the other woman's sharp eyes on her, but kept her own straight ahead.

'Is he dead?'

Rachel shook her head, hoping she would not ask more questions. Perhaps sensing Rachel's reluctance, she didn't. They stood a moment looking about. Mrs McCrae called a number of times for Greta.

'I can't blame her for preferring the bush to him,' she said at last. 'She's a wild little thing. Not that she's a fool. I think the only reason she stays is the land. This run is as much hers as his. More—she does the managing of it. And she knows that if she leaves he'd never let her back.'

Greta's situation was far from happy then, thought Rachel, but what choice had a woman in such a place? If she left, she would have neither status nor money. And if she stayed . . . Rachel looked about, at the mean hut and silent trees . . . and blinked.

The woman appeared abruptly from the bush, so abruptly that Rachel was sure she had been observing them for some time. Mrs McCrae let out a long, relieved breath.

'Greta.'

Greta was tall and skinny, with dark auburn hair and a pale, freckled, narrow face. She came forward, her eyes lowered, her steps slow and reluctant.

'You'll come in for a cup of tea, Mrs McCrae,' she said, as though visitors were an everyday event, and led the way back to the filthy hut.

Redcliffe was sprawled on a chair by the hearth, gulping from the bottle. He stopped to watch his wife as she stepped lightly over the dog and set the kettle on to boil. 'So there you are,' he grunted, and reached out a hand as if to touch her. Greta looked at him, that was all, just looked. Rachel saw Redcliffe's eyes flicker, and then he dropped his hand. He laughed, as though she amused him, but it was something else in his uneasy eyes.

'I was asking your husband about Big Mary,' Mrs McCrae said into the silence. 'Did you see a child with her when she was here?'

Greta seemed to hesitate, and then shrugged. 'Didn't see her. I was busy.' She glanced at her husband, and her eyes gleamed with malice. 'Big Mary was Redcliffe's business, not mine.'

Mrs McCrae frowned but said nothing. Greta set out some grubby looking mugs for the tea.

It was her indifference that struck Rachel most forcibly. The hut was filthy, but she said nothing . . .

no apologies, no shame. Greta just didn't care.

'This is Rachel, by the by,' Mrs McCrae went on after a moment, refusing to be defeated.

Greta looked up, green eyes narrowed on the other woman. Briefly, interest sparked in their depths, but then, when Mrs McCrae added, 'She works for me,' the interest died. Greta turned away, indifferent once more.

The tea was drinkable. Mrs McCrae made a few more attempts at conversation, which Greta answered in monosyllables. Redcliffe slumped in his chair, getting more and more sullen, his little eyes hating. It was a dreadful place, and Rachel was glad when they headed back to McCrae's Castle.

For a long time they rode in silence, Mrs McCrae deep in thought. And then she spoke. 'You mustn't think ill of Greta. She's had a harder time than most. Her parents near enough to sold her to Redcliffe, straight off the boat. They needed money to get a start in Melbourne, and Redcliffe offered a good price.'

Shocked, Rachel said nothing.

'She was sixteen, I believe. It would have been the end for some girls, but not Greta. I know Redcliffe beats her—I've seen the marks. But he's as frightened of her as she is of him. . . maybe more. She's strong, that one.'

She would have to be strong, Rachel thought. Either that, or as mad as her husband.

When they reached the Castle, they found Sarah, pale-faced, waiting for them on the verandah. 'Mrs McCrae,' she whispered, 'there's someone to see you.' And her eyes were like saucers.

Inside, sat a tall, majestic black woman, quite at

home on Mrs McCrae's sofa despite the fact she wore only a possum skin about her hips and the raised, white scars of tribal initiation across her shoulders and breasts. In her arms was a baby with curling brown hair and a warm brown face, out of which gazed blue eyes.

'Big Mary,' whispered Mrs McCrae, and went at once to the other woman. 'Mr Bedford was looking for you. He wants you to come back to the mission, you and your piccaninny.'

Big Mary turned sorrowful eyes on her. Her voice was low and sad, the words running into each other so that Rachel found it difficult to understand her 'I no go back. I bring my baby to you. You look after her. They want to kill her. No more children, they say. What use children when we have no land no more? White man take everything. We all tumble down soon, all gone.' The words were as mournful as Big Mary's eyes, and Rachel felt the other woman's grief as if it were her own.

But the baby was delightful. Mrs McCrae took it in her arms, handing it carefully over to Rachel.

'What about you?' she asked. 'Will you stay here? Or let me write to Mr Bedford? He would come and take you back with him.'

Big Mary shook her head. 'My baby's father, he want to shoot me. White men no good. I go back to my people now.'

Mrs McCrae and Rachel exchanged glances, remembering what Greta had said. 'Redcliffe?' Mrs McCrae cried. 'Was the father of your baby Redcliffe?'

Big Mary's eyes dropped, and her mouth closed stubbornly.

'Mary, please! You must tell me what happened! Did he force you, hurt you? Mr Bedford can have him punished.'

But Mary shook her head and was silent.

Mrs McCrae sighed. 'My dear, if only—'

Big Mary stood up in a single, fluid movement, her body beautifully firm and well muscled. 'Goodbye, Missus. You look after my baby. I know you a good woman.' She looked at the baby, and her hand went out to brush the soft cheek, and then she turned and walked away.

'How can she do that?' Rachel whispered. 'How can she just walk off?'

Mrs McCrae grimaced. 'She has no choice.'

'Redcliffe,' shuddered Rachel. 'Can you do something about him?'

Mrs McCrae rubbed a hand across her weary eyes. 'If Big Mary refuses to speak to me about it, I can do nothing. Redcliffe would just say she came willingly, with her husband's full knowledge. You must realise, Rachel, that Big Mary has two very serious handicaps when it comes to justice in Port Phillip. She is black, and she's a woman.'

Israel Potter, when he came with Frank on one of his Sunday visits, was amused to hear about Big Mary's child.

'You're running a home for waifs and strays!' he told Hazelwood, who scowled at him.

Mrs McCrae gave Israel a hard look. 'I hope you

realise how serious a matter cohabitating with the native women is, Israel Potter.'

Israel's smile hardened. 'I can't watch my men every moment of the day. If the blacks want to lend their women, I can't stop them. Besides, they get well paid for it.'

How could he say such things? fumed Rachel. As if there were no question of right or wrong. He made her angry—as he often made her angry—and she wondered how she could possibly be attracted to him. And then, next moment he was laughing at something, full of good humour, and her heart softened towards him once more. She reminded herself that she should not expect him to think as she did. Israel Potter was a man who lived by his own rules.

Frank Potter spoke with Rachel later, as they watched the children playing in the yard with Young Frank's dog and a baby emu Mrs McCrae had reared and which now seemed to think it was part of the family. 'You don't understand how it is, Rachel. The shepherds get so bored and so lonely. I'm not saying it's right, and yes, there are some men who are brutal, but when the women are willing—'

Rachel shook her head angrily. 'They have no choice. I think Mrs McCrae is quite right—it's appalling.'

'Maybe,' he went on doggedly. 'But we're all here now, Rachel, and we're not likely to pack up and go home where we came from. If we did, likely the French would come and do the same as we're doing. These people are so primitive, they were destined to be conquered by someone; it just happened to be us. And now that it's happened, we'll all just have to live together the best way we can.'

'Mrs McCrae says there are less of the tribes every year,' Rachel said softly. 'They die from our diseases, in the most miserable conditions. We should care more than we do, instead of just wishing they would all die quicker, so that we wouldn't have to worry about them any more.'

He took her hand firmly in his and she stopped, blinking, as he bent closer. 'Rachel, Rachel, please. I've been looking forward to seeing you so much. I don't need a lecture on the native issue!'

Chastened, she bit her lip. He was right. He could do little about it, he was no different to everyone else. Even the Government in Sydney didn't particularly care. Oh, they paid lip-service to caring, but when it came to sending cash and food to the Protectorate Stations so that the Aborigines could be fed and looked after properly, they said they could not afford it. And the squatters, with their powerful lobby in Sydney and Melbourne, were good at persuading others that the money spent on the natives was wasted. Of course, there were those, like Mrs McCrae, who did care. And then there were the others, like Israel, who were totally indifferent to the whole matter.

'We've made a garden,' Frank was saying. 'Now all we need is some rain, so that we can grow something in it! And we've laid the foundations for the new home station. It won't be quite as grand as the Castle, I'm afraid.'

She smiled. 'The children don't care about things like that. They miss you very much.'

'Do they?' He looked at them sadly, as they ran

and squealed. They didn't look as if they missed him. But it would be good to have them all at Ner-inbilly, just as he had dreamed it would be. Israel was the problem. Israel didn't want his station clut-tered up with women and children. Women, to him, were all right for brief liaisons but certainly nothing permanent. Well, Israel would just have to put up with it.

'How's Suzy?' Rachel shaded her eyes against the sun.

Frank grimaced. 'That's another reason I want you up there, Rachel. We'll starve to death at this rate.'

Rachel laughed, the sound rich and sweet. He watched her, feeling his heart turn over. Such a beautiful woman; her warm and generous heart reached out to him. How he wished . . . She had bowed her head, gazing fixedly at her hands folded neatly in her lap. A faint colour stained her cheeks. For a moment he thought she had read his feelings in his eyes, and then he heard footsteps, and real-ised that Israel was approaching.

Anger filled him, but he forced it back. What was the use? He had no right to be angry or to con-demn. Rachel was not his, but a grown woman who would not thank him for interfering in her life. And Israel was attractive to women—he drew them like flies to sugar. If only Will were here, he thought, and then berated himself for his own stupidity. If Will were here, Rachel would never have noticed Israel. But it was over two years now since Will had left and Rachel was a healthy young woman. And probably a lonely young woman. Could he blame her for looking elsewhere?

Rachel hardly heard Frank Potter make his excuses and leave. She was aware only of Israel, as he sat down in the empty chair beside her. So close that the heat of his body reached out to hers, and her breath caught in her throat. Why did he have this ridiculous affect on her? She, who had always prided herself on being so level headed, so sensible?

'We're staying overnight,' he said quietly. 'My brother's decided he needs to see his children to bed.'

There was mockery in his voice, but it was tolerant mockery. Rachel turned to look at him, and found he was looking at her. He was a handsome man, she thought dispassionately, not classically handsome perhaps, but with even features and a wide, smiling mouth. And his eyes, so bright and full of restless life . . . she loved his eyes, and the way they looked so directly into hers.

'I'm glad,' she murmured, before she could stop herself. 'Glad you're staying, I mean.'

Rachel watched those eyes narrow, and his smile soften. 'Oh, Rachel. What am I going to do about you?'

The colour deepened in her cheeks, but she refused to look away. 'Why do you have to do anything?'

'If things were different, if you were different, I'd pick you up now and carry you into my room and . . .' He shrugged, turning to watch the children play, as her face turned even redder. 'I'm not the sort of man to stick to one woman, Rachel. I'm not the sort to settle down. That's Frank, not me. I'm a free spirit, you see.'

Rachel's heart was thudding. 'How do you know I'm not like you,' she whispered. 'A free spirit, too?'

He shook his head very slowly, smiling at her again. 'Oh, Rachel . . . We both know better than that. You have that look in your eyes that says you want to chain a man down. You'd be darning my socks and cooking my supper before I knew what had hit me. And God help me, I might even start to like it.'

Rachel said nothing for a time. Perhaps he was right. Hadn't she always thought herself that she was that kind of woman? Domestic? Respectable? How daunting he must find that, how boring! And yet there was something between them, like a vibration in the air, whenever he was close to her.

'What can I do then?' Her voice was soft and sad.

Israel smiled. He reached out, his finger brushing her cheek. 'You'll have to decide,' he murmured. 'If you come to me, you do so on my terms. No promises. And you put aside your respectability, Rachel; it has no place between you and me.' Her eyes gazed into his; she felt mesmerised. And didn't protest when he leaned forward and kissed her on the lips. Rachel shivered, and closed her eyes. The kiss deepened, and an excitement such as she had never felt before gripped her. I don't care, I don't care, she thought wildly. I'll do whatever he says. But just as she reached to draw him closer, he pulled back.

'Remember Rachel,' Israel murmured. 'No promises.' And he walked away.

Rachel stared after him, at first shocked, then angry with him . . . and then with herself.

Why did she feel like this? He was always saying

things that infuriated her, and yet she longed for
him as a thirsty man craves water. He made her
blood run hot, her hands tremble . . . did she love
him? Or had loneliness tricked her into thinking
lust was love? Rachel remembered how she had
held Will at a distance, making him wait until they
were wed. Was she now supposed to treat Israel differently? Give herself to him without any promise
of permanency? Was this a test he was setting her?
A test of the strength of her love?

    Take me as I am, he was telling her, or else forget
me. And Rachel felt as if she was caught, like one
of Hazelwood's possums, in a trap.

CHAPTER 16

SPRING BROUGHT RAIN. THE EARTH, like a dry, parched throat, drank in the water thankfully. The nights were still cool, but the air had an awakening feel to it. Sometimes the wind blew so hard in the gum tree beside the home station, it was like the roar of ocean waves. Rachel lay in the darkness, unable to sleep, listening to the sound and thinking of Israel.

It was as if he had somehow got into her mind, and now occupied a permanent place there. He had become an obsession with her. No promises, he had said, but she was sure, if only she could say the right thing, do the right thing, he would realise she was the woman for him. Oh, she knew he had said he was not a man to settle to one woman, but surely that was just because he had not yet met the right woman? And Rachel knew in her heart that she was that woman.

'I could win him over,' she whispered to herself. She was still attractive, her skin clear, her body firm. She knew by the way other men turned to look that they thought so, and if she'd wanted to, she could have her pick . . . But they didn't approach her. She was a respectable woman. The fact, Rachel thought bitterly, must be written large on her brow. 'Respectable, do not touch.' Only she wanted Israel to touch her; she wanted it very much.

Lambing at the Castle had begun and the station was a hive of activity. Rachel felt sorry for the bedraggled little creatures, but when the golden spring sun shone and they kicked their long legs, she laughed as delightedly as the children. This was what places like the Castle and Nerinbilly made their living on. Everything depended on the sheep, and Mrs McCrae spent long hours in the storeroom where she kept her books, tallying figures.

'A good station needs well-kept books,' she told Rachel, rubbing her tired eyes. 'Those squatters who over-spend . . . they've never learned to add and subtract. If the money isn't there, how can you spend it?'

After the lambing came the shearing. Mrs McCrae hired some extra men, and they set to work in the open sided shearing shed. A good shearer could shear from sixty to a hundred sheep a day.

'The Vandemonians are a little slower, but they're the best,' Mrs McCrae announced with a smug smile, as if she were not biased. 'The Sydneysiders may be faster, but they're careless.'

The Vandemonians were distinguished by their kangaroo skin bags and tall hats; the Sydneysiders by their rolled swags and the quart pots they carried to boil their tea in.

Before the shearing, the sheep had to be washed in the creek, so that their fleece was reasonably clean. Clean wool was better priced in Melbourne, and Mrs McCrae was canny enough to get the best possible price for her wool. Nerinbilly, too, had done reasonably well from their first shearing. They wouldn't, Frank Potter said, make a profit, but profits were never made in the first year. And things were starting to look up in the colony in general. The depression was beginning to turn around.

Young Frank was growing up. He went about McCrae's Castle, watching what went on and was eager to help. Hazelwood began teaching him what life on a sheep station entailed, and once or twice Frank Potter took him back to Nerinbilly. Matty was more withdrawn, but she was clever. Thomas Dart was pleased with her progress, whereas Young Frank was a constant frustration to him. Victoria was still placid, nothing much worried her, and she ate as much as Matty twice over. She had turned into a plump and pretty little girl. And, despite the fact that she was the elder, it was Victoria who gave in to Bella.

Bella was different. Solemn and watchful, she had to have her way, always. She had already learned to wheedle things from Young Frank, and Matty adored her. And then there was Big Mary's baby. Mrs McCrae had, as she promised, kept the baby at the Castle. They called her Maggie, because, for wont of another, that was Mrs McCrae's name. With her soft brown curls and big blue eyes, everyone loved Maggie. She was a beautiful child, and Bella adored her, often sitting beside her, just watching her.

One afternoon, Rachel was out in the yard supervising an over-boisterous game of ball. Victoria had fallen into a mud puddle, left from a recent shower, and Rachel was splattered too. Matty was laughing, a rarity for her, and at first they failed to hear the sound of horses and the rumble of a cart. And then Frank shouted, pointing, and Rachel turned to see a procession bearing down upon them.

They stood staring.

There were men on horseback, and a horse drawn cart, and—the strangest thing she had ever seen—a carriage painted red and gold, carrying two ladies holding parasols.

As Rachel stood dumb-founded, the carriage drew in to the yard, scattering children and chooks. The women's gowns were extremely fashionable, if rather drab, in the modest, earthy colours preferred by Queen Victoria. The bodices were in the latest tight-fitting style, while a great many stiffened petticoats held out the skirts. Their glossy curls peeped out from beneath their bonnets, as they gazed down their noses at their surroundings, and gradually lowered their parasols.

They might have appeared very well in Sydney or Melbourne or Hobart, but here at the Castle, Rachel thought they looked utterly ridiculous.

'Girl!' one of them called. Rachel hesitated, but an imperious finger beckoned. 'Yes, you girl!'

Hesitantly, Rachel came forward, wiping her face and smearing mud over her cheek.

'Girl, fetch your mistress,' the older woman

instructed. When Rachel continued to look bemused, she turned to her companion. 'What do you say to these natives, Delia? So primitive, really! I don't suppose she speaks a word of English.'

Delia tittered into her gloved palm.

'Go and get your mistress, girl!' the woman tried again, only louder, and Rachel realised at last that with her dark hair and eyes, and her sun browned skin, she had been confused with an Aboriginal servant girl. Behind her, the men were dismounting, and Hazelwood was coming from the direction of the stable, his eyes popping and his pipe puffing at the sight before him. Rachel heard Mrs McCrae's step crossing the verandah, and moved aside with relief.

Mrs McCrae was offering the women the hospitality of her home, and they swept into the Castle, holding their great skirts well above the ground. There they stood for a moment, surveying the cluttered interior, and in particular the piano. And then the elder, who seemed to do most of the talking, sighed. 'Well, it will just have to do!'

Behind their backs, Mrs McCrae lifted an eyebrow at Rachel. 'Who are they?' Rachel mouthed.

'The Turners,' Mrs McCrae whispered. 'Come to take up residence at their station, Wattle Bank.'

Wattle Bank? Rachel knew it vaguely. A large station far to the north. Until now, it had been under the management of an overseer, while the Turners resided in Sydney.

The women's enormous skirts filled the room, and Rachel gritted her teeth every time they turned around. She had never seen anyone quite so fashionable. Lace dripped from their wrists and bows adorned their gowns, even the parasol had little bows around the scalloped edges. I should feel envious, she told herself. These are clothes I will never wear, no matter how long I live. Instead she was amused. The Turners were like beautiful, fragile cage birds, totally unsuited to life in the wild—and Wattle Bank was definitely in the wild.

'My husband is already at Wattle Bank,' Mrs Turner explained. 'He came overland from Sydney with the sheep. It was a very long, rough trip.'

Delia shuddered slightly.

'Such a journey would be quite out of the question for a lady. We came by ship to Melbourne.'

'And your . . . your equipage?' Mrs McCrae managed.

'Oh, we brought the carriage on board,' Mrs Turner replied grandly. 'Indeed, how could we leave it behind?'

Hazelwood, gritting his teeth around the pipe stem, turned his back abruptly.

'I imagine it will be very primitive,' Mrs Turner went on, lifting her chin. 'But we shall just have to be very brave.'

Delia's lips trembled.

'My guess is they've hit on hard times,' Hazelwood said the following day, when the Turners, and their equipage, had gone. 'They've nowhere else to go.'

He laughed again, remembering their arrival, and, although Rachel felt sorry for them, she couldn't help but join in.

After a moment Hazelwood drew breath and said, 'I've heard Wattle Bank is a shambles. The hut's filthy, and the men they hired to look after the place are desperadoes. Wouldn't surprise me, either, if half their sheep are missing.'

Rachel, who had seen the state of a number of shepherd's huts, felt sorry for them again. 'How will they get on, out there alone?'

He grinned. 'They'll find life a lot different to Sydney Town, that's for sure. A few weeks on mutton stew and damper, and they won't be so hoity-toity!'

Israel was staying overnight at the Castle, on his way through to Melbourne. The sight of him had given Rachel such a jolt, she hardly knew what she was doing. She longed to speak to him alone, but with Mrs McCrae and Hazelwood there, it was impossible. Rachel returned to the kitchen, clashing pots, drawing Alice's curious looks. There were vegetable scraps to take out to the chicken coop and Rachel carried them out in the bucket, as the afternoon shadows lengthened. She tossed them with a will, watching as the hens scratched and pecked at the peelings, squawking over the choicest bits.

'Rachel?'

He made her jump. Rachel looked over her shoulder in disbelief, wondering if her hair was neat, her apron clean. And then suddenly those things didn't matter, as she looked into his eyes.

They stood a moment in silence, watching the hens. Say something, Rachel told herself. For

Heaven's sake, say something!

'How's Suzy?' she asked breathlessly.

Israel grimaced. 'She's not cut out to be a hut-keeper, but she'll do until the home station is finished.'

'Poor Suzy. What about George?'

Israel shrugged. 'Suzy isn't happy, and I don't think George is either. He doesn't like life as a shepherd. He'd go back to Melbourne, if he could. Said he was interested in starting up some sort of business. But Suzy says they need more money, so he'll have to stay. Don't know how long they'll stick it out after their year comes up. To be frank with you, Rachel, I'll be asking them to go if they don't go themselves.'

She nodded. Israel could hardly be expected to keep on workers for sentiment's sake—he was not the sentimental kind.

'What about you?' he asked her. 'Are you sorry you came up here? Do you want to go home to Vandemon?'

She shook her head, not looking at him, gripping the bucket tightly in her hands. 'No, I'm not sorry, though sometimes I'm lonely.'

His hand caught her chin, turning it with a jerk so that her eyes met his. 'If you're lonely,' he retorted softly, 'you've got no-one to blame but yourself.'

She couldn't pretend she didn't know what he meant. He was looking straight into her eyes, into her mind. 'I'm still married.' Her voice was shaking.

He snorted, dropping her chin. 'To a man who left you and who you haven't seen for years! You're no more bound to him than I am. Look, I'm not asking you to be my wife or whatever you want to call it. I'm asking you to be with me, for a day or a year, for however long it lasts.'

She nodded as if she understood, but she didn't. Love wasn't like that for Rachel. How could he say he might leave her in a day or a year? She felt him move as if to go, and panic struck her. She flung her arms about his chest, almost knocking him backwards. He laughed, surprised and pleased, and put his own arms about her. It felt nice, she decided. As if she belonged there. Couldn't he feel that too?

'I just want to feel loved again,' she breathed. 'Do you understand what I mean?'

He bent, and kissed her temple. 'I understand what you mean, Rachel. The trouble is, there's no such thing as love—only desire.' So said Israel, who'd never loved anyone in his life but himself, and maybe his brother Frank.

'You're wrong.'

He laughed, 'Am I?' and bending, caught her lips with his, kissing her with passion as the sun sank lower, and the shadows grew longer. Rachel trembled, pressing closer. But he held her away, watching her with narrowed eyes. Beautiful Rachel, he thought. If he wanted, he knew he could have her in his arms tonight. Or could he? Beneath her need of him, he still sensed an intriguing resistance. Better to wait a little longer . . . let her sweat, wondering if he'd lose interest in her. That always worked with the difficult ones.

What it came down to, really, was the thrill of the chase. The woman evaded and he pursued. It would be the same with Rachel. He would have her, eventually. And then? Well, she was a beauti-

ful woman; he didn't expect the affair to pale too
soon. It was when the woman became possessive,
cloying, that was when the chill set in.

'I'll give you time to think,' Israel said, touching
the tip of her nose lightly, affectionately. 'I'll see
you when I come back from Melbourne, Rachel.'

Her face coloured, but she nodded her head.
Israel turned to go, and then as if he couldn't help
himself, caught her to him and kissed her again.
And then he was gone, his steps fading, leaving
her to her thoughts. His kiss sent a tingle through
her such as she hadn't felt in a long time. She had
wanted him to go on kissing her, holding her close.
It was strange, but even though every moment of
every day of her life seemed filled to bursting, and
there were always people around her, she was alone.

'I need him,' she told herself. 'I ache for him. Is
that so wrong? And he cares for me, I know he
does.'

Israel strode across the yard, whistling. Nearly got
her, he thought to himself. It was funny really. He
prided himself on his honesty. He always told them
it wouldn't last, that he didn't believe in love and
marriage. But they never listened. Alice looked up
from setting the supper table, and gave him a knowing smile. Israel considered her offer—he'd taken
her up before—and rejected it. Too risky. Rachel
would hear. He couldn't chance losing her when
he was so close to having her. Israel hadn't lied
when he'd said Rachel frightened him. She was
different to any other woman he'd ever seduced;
she was, as Frank had once told him, a fine person.
No, he couldn't upset Rachel by taking Alice to
his bed. Anyway, there were plenty of women in

Melbourne.

The day after Israel left, Rachel was with the children in the yard. Frank was playing with his dog, and Bella was by the verandah, sitting as usual beside Baby Maggie. Rachel was day-dreaming, hardly noticing what was happening. She was dreaming of Israel, remembering the feel of his lips, the taste of his kiss. Was it wrong to want him like this? 'I don't care if it is wrong,' she muttered to herself. 'I don't care.'

The shrill scream shattered the peace. For a moment Rachel was stunned, unable to move, and then she spun around. Bella had jumped up, rigid, screaming again and again.

And then Rachel saw it.

The brown, gleaming body of the snake, as it twisted through the dirt towards the verandah . . . and the baby. In terror, she ran, shouting and waving her arms. But Bella ran too, and stood directly in the path of the reptile, directly in front of the baby. The child's face was white, her grey eyes enormous, but she stood her ground.

The dog bumped against Rachel as it shot past, almost knocking her over. It twisted, like a whirl-wind, leaping and barking, drawing the attention of the snake. The wicked brown head lifted, tongue flicking. But the dog kept up its dance, jumping, nipping, as the snake tried to get away to safety.

Rachel reached her daughter, and snatched her

up before grabbing the baby to her breast. Mrs McCrae appeared in the doorway, the gun in her hands. 'Get out of the way!' she shouted. Rachel backed away, dry-mouthed and shaking. Mrs McCrae lifted the gun, aimed, and fired. The snake jerked, and was still. The dog, barking hysterically, made little runs at the now limp brown body, but when it found there was no longer any fun to be had, it turned and trotted away. Frank ran to hug his pet warmly. 'Brave boy,' he whispered, 'brave boy!'

Rachel's face was white. Back inside, Mrs McCrae made her sit down and drink some brandy. 'You've had a shock,' she said kindly.

'It was going towards the baby,' Rachel whispered. 'And Bella stood there in front of her. Oh, my little girl my brave little girl,' and she put her head in her hands.

'It was probably going under the verandah, into the cool,' Mrs McCrae said gently. 'Maggie and Bella just happened to be in the way.'

The children were playing again, as though nothing had happened. Even Bella had recovered swiftly enough from the shock. It was Rachel who was shaken. She could hardly bear for her daughter to be out of her sight. What would happen if she were to lose Bella? There would be nothing and nobody. The thought pierced her to the heart. And then she remembered.

Israel. There was Israel.

I will agree to what he asks, she told herself firmly. It doesn't matter if it lasts for a day or a year. I need him.

The rain set in, a constant, light drizzle from a grey, miserable sky. Everything seemed to drip with moisture, and the home station was full of people who were longing to get out. The children grumbled, and the adults snapped. Frank Potter had visited, and taken his son back to Nerinbilly with him. Rachel had watched them go, heads bowed against the rain beneath their broad-brimmed hats. At seven years, Young Frank already rode well, and often went out with Hazelwood to check on the flocks. He would make an excellent squatter, Rachel thought with a smile.

It was dark when Israel pounded on the door. He came in, dripping and cursing. Mrs McCrae took away his jacket to dry, and Rachel settled him by the fire, while Hazelwood poured him a large swig of rum, saying, 'It'll warm the cockles of your heart, young fella!'

Israel sank back, bright blue eyes squinting in the light of the lantern, the water steaming from his clothes and hair. 'You should have stayed overnight at the inn,' Mrs McCrae scolded. 'Such a dirty night it is.'

Israel grinned. 'I had reasons to keep going.'

He means me, Rachel thought, and a shiver slid over her flesh as though he had actually touched her.

'Mama?'

The little voice in the doorway brought their heads up, and Rachel smiled at her daughter. 'You should be asleep, darling. Have you had a bad dream?'

Bella twisted one leg around each other, screwing up her face in the affirmative.

'Come here then,' and Rachel held out her arms. Bella curled against her, pressing close, looking for the comfort only Rachel could give her. Rachel could hear Mrs McCrae behind her, telling Israel about the snake. 'I'll take you back to bed,' she whispered, and carried her daughter through to the other room.

'Frank?' Bella asked, her eyes beginning to close.

'You know where Frank is, he's with his father at Nerinbilly.'

Matty sat up, her clever eyes curious. 'Where's Bella's father, Rachel?'

The question startled her. None of them had ever asked such a thing before, just accepting that Captain Potter was Frank and Matty and Victoria's father, and Rachel was Bella's mother. Sometimes Rachel had wondered whether Bella thought Captain Potter was her father, too—perhaps she even hoped she did.

'Is he dead, like our mother?' the little voice went on.

Rachel sighed. When Matty wanted to know something, she would not be fobbed off. Should she say Will was dead? And yet the lie sat uneasily on her conscience, as though she were in fact wishing him dead. Perhaps he *was* dead! The idea stilled her heart. And then she shook her head angrily. What did it matter? He had lied to her, and left her, and she would never see him again.

'Bella's father's gone somewhere else to live,' she managed at last, her throat tight. 'Far, far away. Now go to sleep, Matty. And you too, Bella . . .'

But Bella was already asleep. Rachel looked down at her daughter. The dark lashes lay on faintly flushed cheeks, the dark curls spread over the pillow. She's my daughter, she told herself firmly, not Will's. It was I who brought her up, and fed her and loved her, not Will. He has no right to her, whether he's alive or dead.

Out in the other room, Israel was half asleep by the hearth. Mrs McCrae had retired and Hazelwood was yawning. When Rachel appeared he stood up, saying he would be going now, as he had to be up at dawn to ride to one of the outstations. The door closed on him, and there was silence apart from the crackling of the fire and the tumbling rain on the roof.

Israel held out his hand. 'Come here, Rachel,' he murmured. She went to him, pressing close, just as Bella had done to her, for warmth and comfort and love. 'I missed you,' he said, and sounded surprised.

Rachel smiled, her cheek to his rough shirt. She felt his hand touching her hair, smoothing the soft curls.

'Frank has warned me off you, you know.'

Rachel lifted her head, frowning at him.

'He thinks I will hurt you,' Israel said. 'Do you think I'll hurt you?'

Rachel shook her head.

He sighed, and slid his arms about her waist. 'I probably will, Rachel.'

She didn't believe him, and leaned closer as he kissed her, his lips playing softly with hers. The kiss deepened. Gently, Israel pulled her to her feet and, lighting a candle, led her into his room, closing the door. The cool silence swept in on them. Israel pulled his shirt over his head, and she saw the muscles and hollows of his chest and stomach, coloured gold by the candlelight. 'Your turn now,' he whispered, and began to unbutton her bodice with deft fingers. His warm hand slipped inside the cloth and molded her breast. Shock and desire made her head spin, and she gasped as he bent to kiss her again.

'You didn't ask me what I'd decided?' she managed.

'I don't have to,' and he smiled against her mouth. 'I saw the answer in your eyes.'

She let her hand slide over his chest, let her lips follow. Her heart was beating so hard it filled her ears, and her body ached for his. So long, she thought, so long since a man has held me and kissed me and loved me like this. She had almost forgotten what it was like, as Israel caressed her, undressing her inch by inch, touching her body. Rachel lost herself in sensation, and when he was poised above her, lifted her hips with a groan to draw him inside her.

It was the same, wasn't it? she asked herself feverishly. The rocking bodies, the rub of flesh on flesh, the hot murmurs and small sighs. It was the same?

And then the passion began to build and she no longer cared. Her body took over, craving his, greedy for the sensations she had not felt for such a long time, eager for whatever Israel could give her.

When she regained her senses, it was to find she was lying beside him, her naked flesh hot and damp against his. Israel smiled into her eyes, running a lazy finger over her breasts. 'You've been starving yourself, Rachel,' he mocked softly. 'How long has it been?'

The extent of her abandonment came back to her, making her self-conscious. 'I don't know,' she lied.

He nuzzled his mouth against her throat. 'You're a beauty, Rachel. You were made for this.'

Was she? She had thought, with Will, it was something special, but perhaps she was wrong. Perhaps it had been nothing out of the ordinary after all. Perhaps all men were the same, and all women, too.

The thought depressed her.

Israel was leaning over, kissing her again. His hands and mouth were growing more persistent. Rachel kissed him back, allowing him to pull her on top of him, holding her against him so that every inch of their flesh was touching. 'Do you love me, Israel?' she breathed, feeling him grow hard against her thighs. 'Do you?' She didn't know why she wanted to hear it, only that the words were suddenly very important to her.

'I love you,' he gasped, in angry surprise, and rolled her over, making her forget everything once more.

She said goodbye to him the next morning. The rain had cleared, and a weak beam of sunlight struggled through the clouds. She was tired. It had been many hours before she found her own bed, and then she hadn't slept. Even though she kept telling herself there was no need now to worry. She had taken Israel as her man, and she was his woman. They loved each other.

He couldn't kiss her, or say anything much, with others present, but Rachel thought the expression in his eyes was enough. Besides, he had told her all she needed to know last night with his kisses and his body.

'When will the home station be finished?' she had asked him, cuddling against him as the rain fell outside.

'Be patient, Rachel,' he'd teased.

'If I was at Nerinbilly, we could see each other every day,' she whispered.

'You mean every night.'

Already she missed him, Rachel told herself, as Israel mounted his horse, ready to go. Hurry back, her eyes told him. And he grinned, and then was gone. The pounding hooves turned to silence. The loneliness that Rachel had thought banished by Israel's arms swooped down upon her again, bringing hot tears to her eyes.

CHAPTER 17

DURING THE NEXT MONTHS, ISRAEL seemed always to be there. Once, he rode over in a summer storm, dodging the lightning, he said, and laughed when Mrs McCrae called him a young fool. And if they knew why he was there, they didn't say anything. Their world seemed to be turning on a different axis from Rachel and Israel—they had their own world, and it revolved around the night, which was the only time they could be together. Properly together.

He said things to her that she treasured during the cold light of day, repeating them over and over to herself. *I love him,* she told herself. I really love him. And I know he loves me. As soon as the home station is built I'll be up there at Nerinbilly, with him all the time. We can live as if we're married—others do it. What's it matter if it's a lie? In our hearts we're married already.

In the darkness of her room, while the children slept, she longed for him with a physical ache. She made plans, and weaved dreams. She had it all worked out. She didn't have to speak to him about the future; Rachel was quite sure his plans and his dreams tallied exactly with her own.

Sarah knew, of course. But Sarah said nothing, only eyeing her uneasily when Rachel sometimes smiled for no reason. Happiness had made her even more lovely, giving a shine to her dark eyes and a glow to her cheeks. Frank Potter tried to pretend he didn't notice, and Rachel was hardly aware of the reticent note in his voice these days. Nothing mattered, did it, except Israel? His love and care for her were like a bolster between her and any misgivings.

And then the doubts crept in, like clouds across the sun.

At first she laughed and ignored them, because she was so supremely confident, so certain of their love. When Israel didn't come for a week, and then another, she began to wonder. She felt a little sick.

'Greta Redcliffe,' Sarah murmured in her ear. 'Some Nerinbilly sheep strayed onto Redcliffe land, and Israel went over to claim 'em. Greta was there.'

Greta Redcliffe? Rachel asked herself. That thin, silent woman? And now they were saying that Israel, after one meeting, was smitten with her? How could that be, when he loved Rachel Trigg? How could that be, after all he had said to her?

She wouldn't believe it. She loved him, and that meant trusting him. She would wait until she next saw him, and then he would explain. It would be nothing. Just a misunderstanding. And Rachel lifted her chin high, and blinked back the tears, and pretended that nothing had changed.

'In all, for new station owners, we've not done too badly,' Frank Potter said with a self-satisfied smile.

Rachel nodded, and tried to be pleased for him, but she felt as if she could hardly sit still. Israel was around somewhere with Hazelwood. He hadn't spoken to her yet, but she'd seen him. She was so tense with fear and longing, her hands were shaking and her stomach was churning.

The two brothers had arrived only an hour ago, and Frank had been quick to discover Rachel's whereabouts, greeting her with his usual pleasure. But not Israel. Rachel's stomach lurched again, queasily, and she went very still. She had vomited this morning—nerves, she told herself. That's all it was. Her longing for Israel was making her ill. She sat, pretending to be pleased, as Frank spoke of their success and hard work. And all the time, she hardly heard a word.

It wasn't until supper that he came near her. The children had eaten early, as always, so Rachel had no excuse to hover about the sitting room. But she could hear his voice, and his laughter, and the longing gripped her, like a hawk, in strong, hurting talons.

If she were Mrs Turner or even Greta Redcliffe, she thought bitterly, she would be allowed to join Mrs McCrae's supper table. But she was just a servant, and servants were there to serve. For the first time in her life, Rachel felt a chasm between herself and another human being. Israel was there, so close, and yet quite beyond her reach.

At last, supper was finished, and Frank Potter came to kiss his children. He and Israel were leaving in the morning, he said, and they meant to retire early. 'I wanted a word with your brother,' Rachel burst out, and couldn't meet his eyes. 'Is he still up, sir?'

After a moment, Frank said quietly, 'He's outside having a smoke. I'm sure you can speak with him if you wish, Rachel.'

She nodded, and was gone, leaving him standing looking sadly after her.

The darkness was almost complete—no moon tonight, but there were plenty of stars. Rachel picked out the glow of Israel's pipe and relief flooded her. But where once she would have run to him without hesitation, now she paused, her hand gripping the verandah post. A whirl of emotions flooded her, doubt and fear and anger, but she swept them aside, telling herself she was being foolish. She loved Israel; she knew him better than anyone. With a shake of her head, Rachel ran lightly across the verandah towards him.

His head came up, startled, and then slowly he rose to his feet. 'Rachel,' he said, his voice the same. Everything the same. And yet somehow not the same. 'What are you doing out here?'

She laughed in what was meant to be a light hearted manner, but sounded instead slightly desperate. 'I wanted to see you, of course. I've missed you.'

She put her arms about him, pressing against him. His body was the same, hard and warm, and she nuzzled into his wiry beard. There was a brief moment before he returned her embrace, when she thought, in sheer terror, that he would not. And then his arms came around her, holding her, and he was bending to kiss her lips with his warm, tobacco scented mouth.

'My brother is sharing my room tonight,' he said softly. 'I can't let you come to me, Rachel.'

She shook her head. She'd already made her plans. 'We can go down to the creek,' she whispered. She'd come a long way from the respectable Mrs Trigg.

There was a silence.

'Israel?'

'Of course,' he murmured, 'why didn't I think of that?' And yet there was something in his soft laughter that flicked her with contempt.

'You don't mind?'

She was gazing up at him, her dark eyes like hollows in her white face, while her hands clung. Israel wanted to push her away, he wanted to tear at her clutching, grasping fingers. Why? he asked himself in silent anguish. Why couldn't this one have remained immune to him? The so-respectable, so-fine, so-lovely Mrs Trigg . . . He kissed her as his answer, being brutal about it, but she suffered the little cruelty in silence, not pushing him away. And that made him even sadder.

He was gone again in the morning, and she was missing him. But he had loved her as hotly as ever, and if there was something missing she had not noticed it. Greta? she asked herself with scorn. How could he care for Greta? It was all lies, made up by jealous tongues. Israel loved Rachel, and she loved him. And soon they would be together every day. And every night.

Mrs McCrae had organised a kangaroo hunt. This was a popular event among the squatters and their men, and it was always followed by a feast and dancing, often until dawn when it was time to go home again—mainly because the home stations had no room to spare for visitors who wanted to lie down and sleep.

'And I certainly don't expect anyone to be sleeping at McCrae's Castle!' she told Rachel, when she came upon her in the kitchen.

Rachel tried to smile, glancing down into the soup she was stirring. The now familiar queasiness assailed her. Her face paled, and beads of perspiration broke out all over her skin.

Mrs McCrae had noticed. 'Rachel? Are you all right?'

Rachel forced herself to straighten, forced herself to smile again. 'Of course,' she said. She refused to believe that the ominous signs meant anything; Rachel had never been ill with Bella.

'I've invited the Redcliffe's,' she told Rachel, 'and the Turners. Though whether they will come is anybody's guess! And, of course, Captain Potter and his brother.' There were others from Melbourne, whom Rachel did not know. In all it would be a large party, and Mrs McCrae was looking forward to it. 'A little splash of excitement in our dull lives,' she said with a smile.

Rachel heard only one name in the list of many. Israel Potter would be coming. She hadn't been alone with him since that night by the creek, although in her mind she had spoken to him, been with him, thought of him a thousand times. She never stopped thinking of him.

'When will the home station be built?' she had asked over and over again, becoming almost as bad as Young Frank. But there were always delays or reasons why it had to be postponed.

'We're doing our best, Rachel,' Frank Potter had told her at last, rather testily.

She was sorry, then, that she had caused him to lose his temper. But she had wanted so much to lie in Israel's arms in the darkness, for him to take away her growing fears, and to love him and be loved by him. Did he feel the same about her? She knew he must. And yet, the doubt remained.

Surely there would be a chance to be together at the kangaroo hunt? Rachel waited feverishly for the day to arrive.

And at last the day dawned, fine and cool. 'Perfect weather for it!' Hazelwood declared. The women had been baking and making preparations for days, and Mrs McCrae had been practising her piano, laughing at her mistakes and sighing over past memories. 'Reminds me of my husband,' she murmured. 'I still miss him. Sometimes I think it gets worse as time goes on, not better.' Her eyes narrowed, watching Rachel keenly. 'What about you?'

'Me?'

'Do you miss your husband, Rachel?'

Rachel hesitated. 'Yes,' she said at last, and her

voice trembled.

Mrs McCrae nodded, as if her ideas had been confirmed, and went away. Rachel stood uneasily, wondering why she felt so strange. As though for a moment a door she had kept closed for years, had suddenly opened. And behind it had been pain— pain she had held back all this time. No! her mind screamed. I love Israel now! But the ache remained, taunting her, as she followed Mrs McCrae to the kitchen.

The guests began to arrive. The Turners first, looking spick and span and yet, Rachel thought to herself, thinner and browner than they had been. The older Mrs Turner's hands were quite rough when she stripped off her gloves. 'How the mighty are fallen!' whispered Sarah in passing.

Surprisingly, disturbingly, Redcliffe and his wife turned up. Redcliffe looked clean, although his hair still hung lank around his head and he wiped the back of his hand across his mouth, as if he had a thirst he couldn't quench. Greta wore an old but clean pink dress, matched incongruously with heavy work boots. She presented an odd and pathetic picture. Looking at her, Rachel's fears were again soothed regarding Israel. Surely Greta was not the type of woman to attract a man like him?

'I'm so glad you could come,' Mrs McCrae took her hands. 'I've been worried about you, Greta.'

Greta smiled faintly. 'I can take care of myself,' she said softly.

'Well, today, we will take care of you!' Mrs McCrae retorted. 'Fetch Mrs Redcliffe a cool drink, Rachel.'

Greta's eyes didn't quite meet Rachel's. 'That would be lovely,' she murmured.

Israel was impatient to be off on the hunt, striding about amongst the others, slapping his hat against his thigh. Rachel watched him, dark eyes full of longing. Once, he turned and grinned at her, as if he knew quite well she was watching him, and it amused him.

Embarrassed, Rachel didn't look again.

The men rode off at last, whooping and shouting through the bush, and Mrs McCrae shooed her women guests inside to drink tea and exchange gossip. Not that Greta had much to say. She sat, head bent, listening, a faint smile curving her pink lips. They tried to draw her out, but Greta just shook her head or answered in monosyllables, until they gave up.

'What do you think of her?' Sarah whispered, in between serving cups of tea.

Rachel shook her head. 'Strange. But then who wouldn't be, married to that awful man?'

'I've heard a few things about her,' Sarah added, and hesitated. 'Her husband half killed one of his station hands over her. Seems she and he were . . . you know.' It was difficult to believe, looking at Greta, that she was capable of committing adultery. But then, as Rachel well knew, loneliness sometimes forced people to make choices they may not otherwise have made.

Unlike Greta, Mrs Turner was willing to talk, and did so at length. The Turners were actually too far away to have attended in ordinary circumstances, but they were on their way through to Melbourne, so the invitation had suited them. She declared she was horrified by the conditions at Wattle Bank, and they were presently building a homestead of stone, quarried on the property. 'We've had some trouble with the natives,' she added, 'but my husband frightens any troublemakers away with a few well aimed shots.'

The younger Mrs Turner shuddered expressively.

'There was a shepherd killed last month on the Goulburn River,' Greta said in a clear voice.

There was a silence, as much from surprise that she had spoken as from pity for the dead man. Mrs McCrae cleared her throat. 'So I believe, my dear. The troopers were there, sorting things out as they so delicately put it.' There was no mistaking the derision in her voice, which even politeness couldn't quite disguise.

Mrs Turner narrowed her eyes. 'You don't mean you sympathise with these savages?' she declared. 'We cannot allow them to kill our menfolk!'

Mrs McCrae sighed. 'No, we cannot. I know that. I agree that such acts of aggression must be punished. It is just the way in which we go about things that horrifies me. We turn these people off their land, and then expect them to survive without stealing our sheep. We say we will look after them, and then can't. Their way of life is being changed before their eyes. How can we expect them not to be desperate and vengeful?'

Mrs Turner made a dismissive gesture. 'Really, the feelings of savages are beyond my comprehension, Mrs McCrae. Have they any? I very much doubt it.'

Sarah waylaid Rachel in the other room, on her way to fetch more food for the ladies. 'Mrs

McCrae is going to explode soon. Her face was puce a moment ago.'

Rachel smiled. 'I'm sure it won't come to that. A slight difference of opinion, that's all. Are the men back yet?'

Sarah shook her head, her blue eyes compassionate, but Rachel slipped away before she could say anything— she didn't want lectures from Sarah. Lately, Rachel had been avoiding the other women, especially in the mornings. Even to herself, she would not admit why.

The men returned at last. Israel had bagged a big grey kangaroo, and his voice rose above the others in laughter and self-congratulation. The women came to gather around and admire. Beside Rachel, Greta stood quietly watching. Once, when Rachel turned to her to make some comment, she saw her eyes on Israel. And the fixity of her expression startled Rachel, and made her uneasy.

But she soon forgot about it in the excitement of the feast, and the laughter and joviality that followed. In the crush of people, she was able to find her way to him.

'Will I see you later?' she whispered, dark eyes anxious.

He smiled politely down at her, as if she had just asked him to pass the salt. 'Of course, Rachel. I'm looking forward to it.'

And that was all she had to hold on to, as the evening slipped by. Mrs McCrae was soon persuaded to play upon her piano, and all the furniture was moved aside so that they could dance. Sometimes, the sound of stomping feet and clapping hands was so loud, no one could hear the music. Rachel was afraid that the building would fall down around their ears.

During one dance, Frank Potter twirled her around and around, his face alight with drink and merriment. Rachel's dark hair swung out, loose from its pins, and she laughed, happy for a moment. Until she caught sight of Israel standing beside Greta Redcliffe—her husband had vanished outside, probably to get drunk. Greta's lips were moving, she was speaking to him, but not looking at him, and her hands were clasped tightly at her waist. Rachel watched Israel frown, and watched him smile. He was standing so close to her, too close. Jealousy ate at Rachel, making her feel wretched and ill.

The children, one by one, were led off to bed. And still the night was alive with noise and laughter. Mrs McCrae sang a song, and Hazelwood accompanied her in a loud, rasping voice. Israel stood and laughed, a drink in his hand. The light of the lantern flickered over his face, making it into that of a stranger. And Rachel's fear grew.

In the end it was Rachel who asked Israel to dance, shrugging off her pride, telling herself pride did not matter when they were in love. He would not care, so why should she? He took her in his arms, and she longed to press closer, longed to rest her forehead against his chest and just stand in his silence among the melee. She knew in her heart that he would look after her, he would soothe all her fears.

'I've missed you so,' she whispered. 'I need to see you alone.'

He laughed. Something in his eyes shifted, and

suddenly Rachel stilled.

'Israel?' she breathed.

'I'm afraid that won't be possible,' he told her in a hearty voice. 'You're starting to treat this thing too seriously, Rachel. It was never meant to be taken seriously.'

Rachel swallowed. For some reason her tongue had grown too big for her mouth. 'I thought you said,' she began with difficulty, but he cut her off.

'Oh, I said!' he mocked. 'A man will say anything if it gets him what he wants, Rachel. Are you so naive you don't know that by now?' And then, the coupe de grace, 'By God, I'm not surprised you married a blackguard. You are far too trusting.'

His voice was harsh, and he couldn't meet her eyes. Rachel didn't notice that. She heard only the tolerant mockery, as if he were amused, and a little scornful of her. She had been naive, she had believed in him, and now he derided her for it. She had been honest, and he was not. Rachel felt as if she had turned to stone.

The dance finished, and he bowed over her hand before releasing it and turning away. But her face remained in his mind, perfectly white, mortally wounded. He had never felt more disgusted with himself, and yet . . . it had had to be done.

Behind her, Greta's soft voice murmured in her ear. 'I think Mr Potter has fallen out of love with you, Rachel.'

Rachel spun around and stared at her, uncomprehending. 'How can *you* know that?' she gasped.

Greta smiled her pussycat smile. 'How can *you* not?'

The children were asleep.

Rachel stood, staring at them. The room was cold, and she put her arms around herself but couldn't seem to get warm. The gravity of her situation had sucked every ounce of warmth from her body. Greta was right and she had been a fool. She had believed him . . . no, she had wanted to believe him. She had wanted to love him and for him to love her. She had made a fine mansion out of a shepherd's hut, and had only herself to blame.

'I wanted him to be Will,' she whispered to herself. The tears fell, hot and salty, down her cheeks. She licked them off her lips with her tongue, but they kept falling. Will, oh Will, where are you? a voice inside her cried. And she didn't try to still it, as she had tried so many times before. I don't care, she cried to herself. What you did no longer matters. Nothing matters. I want you back.

Of course, there was no answer. Only in the dawn light, when she slept curled beside Bella, did she find an answer of sorts. She dreamed she was alone on a windswept hill, and there was a man riding a horse, and he was riding towards her. And as he drew closer she saw it was Will. He looked just the same as he had looked the night he left. And she was so happy, so very happy. She cried out, and held out her arms, sure that he would stop, that he had come back to her at last. But as he rode closer and closer, he still didn't look at her. Just kept staring straight ahead. And then he was past her, and she dropped her arms and watched him go, not quite believing, until he was out of sight.

CHAPTER 18

T HE SUN SHONE, DAY AFTER day, golden in the blue sky. That was wrong, thought Rachel. It should have been grey and raining, to match her mood.

The building of Nerinbilly home station had had to be postponed again. Frank Potter said that, sadly, they had neither the time nor the money to complete it at present. They were fully occupied with the new run to the north. 'But you're happy here, aren't you, Rachel?'

'Yes, I'm happy here,' she replied quietly.

He looked at her sideways. She had changed, he thought. She was thinner, paler, but it was more than that. She had lost her open frankness, her vivacity, and he was sad, because he thought he knew what was wrong. Israel had hurt her. He wanted to say: I warned you!—but he knew she wouldn't want to hear it. She had learned her lesson, for what good it had done her. Now only time could heal.

Israel had been visiting the Redcliffe place more frequently than was necessary. 'Redcliffe will shoot you,' Frank had said, 'he's done it to others.' Israel laughed.

'He's too drunk to shoot anyone,' he retorted, not quite meeting his brother's eyes. 'Besides, it's only neighbourly to call when I'm passing.'

But he seemed to be passing rather often, and Frank Potter's heart ached for Rachel. She glanced up, and caught his eyes on her, full of sympathy, and suddenly there were tears on her cheeks, and she was sobbing.

'Rachel, Rachel! Come now, it can't be so bad. Rachel!'

She tried to stop, and then found enough breath to gasp, 'Oh, it is so bad, it is! I'm having a baby, and it's Israel's!'

Shock froze him, and then a rage so hot and molten filled him he could hardly breathe. 'He will be punished for this,' he whispered hoarsely. 'I'll whip him, Rachel. Believe me, I'll—'

Rachel shook her head, putting up a hand to silence him. 'I don't care about that. I was mad to let him . . . I was lonely.' She pulled a face. 'And what can he do? Marry me?' There was a savage bitterness in her voice, and in the hard line of her mouth.

'No, he can never do that,' said Frank.

'Mrs McCrae will throw me out,' she whispered, her voice shaking again. 'Where will we go, Bella and I? Where will we go?'

He held her shoulders, forcing her to face him. 'That will not happen. I will speak to Mrs McCrae myself. She is a sensible woman. She will understand. Believe me, Rachel, she will! If I do not condemn you for what has happened, why should she? It is my brother who should be condemned.'

But they both knew he wouldn't be. It was the woman in such situations who was punished. She had done wrong in allowing herself to fall pregnant. It was not the man's fault. It was his right.

Rachel stayed outside, while Frank went in to speak to Mrs McCrae. He was away a long time, and when at last she heard the step on the verandah, she didn't turn, too afraid of what she might see. And then a warm hand rested on her shoulder, and Mrs McCrae murmured:

'You poor, foolish girl. I thought you had more sense, Rachel, than to fall for a scoundrel like Israel Potter. But I suppose loneliness makes us all weak, sometimes.' Her hand gripped harder. 'Well,' with a quick breath, 'you must stay of course. Though it will not be easy for you. There will be talk.'

Rachel sighed, and allowed herself at last to relax. She could cope with the talk; she would have to. The main thing was that she and Bella were safe.

The wind was cold today. Rachel held her arms about herself, feeling the chill of it striking her flesh through her clothes. Beyond the yard, in the perimeters of bush, a group of about ten natives sat together beneath their possum skins. Some wore European style clothes, while others were half naked. A couple of them looked thin and sickly, and Mrs McCrae had rummaged through her medicine chest for something appropriate. The rest of them had come for food, and when Mrs McCrae had given them what she could, they had moved to the edge of the bush, made a fire, and camped.

Big Mary was among them.

As Rachel watched, the woman rose to her full regal height and walked towards the building. She wore a possum skin about her shoulders, but otherwise her dress was European. She looked thinner than she had last time Rachel had seen her, but her eyes were the same.

'Where's my baby?' she asked.

Rachel tried to smile. 'Inside. Do you want to see her?'

Big Mary nodded, and waited. Rachel went in to fetch Maggie. The baby was growing fast. She was now at the crawling stage, getting under everyone's feet and into trouble. She made grabs at Rachel's hair, as Rachel carried her out onto the verandah.

Mary looked solemnly at her child, and Maggie looked at her, gurgling and chortling. 'I heard your girl saved her from old brown snake,' Mary said at last.

Rachel smiled. 'Bella. Yes. Little Maggie here was very lucky.'

Mary nodded to herself. And then she sighed. 'I seen her now,' she said.

'Don't you want to hold her?' Rachel asked softly.

But Mary shook her head, glancing over her shoulder. Rachel wondered if one of the men sitting around the fire was her husband, and if he knew Redcliffe was the father of her child. Big Mary didn't give her time to ask. 'She's the Missus' baby now,' she said. And turned away before Rachel could see the tears in her eyes.

The months slipped by. Rachel felt her own baby growing inside her and, from a sense of shock and outrage, she grew to acceptance and even anticipation. It would be nice to have a sister or brother for Bella. And it would be *her* baby, despite Israel's part in it.

She had seen him several times since that terrible night of the kangaroo hunt. He avoided her eyes, or else mocked her with his smile. She felt she was an embarrassment to him. She had heard there was a woman in Melbourne he visited whenever he was down there, and that he had been calling at Redcliffe's, and no doubt telling Greta the same lies as he had told Rachel.

Mrs McCrae shook her head. 'He's not to be trusted that one. I told Greta so. She just laughed and said that as she didn't trust him, I needn't worry about her.'

Rachel remembered how Martha Potter had called Israel names so long ago. She had been right, after all. For once she had seen true, rather than through her own petty jealousies. Israel was untrustworthy and a scoundrel, although Rachel had to admit, with her sometimes irritating sense of fair play, that in many ways he was an admirable man. He worked hard, with a single mindedness others' envied, and he was generally well liked.

I love you, he had said, but he hadn't. He knew nothing about love, except of himself. And she had been so desperately blind to anything but her need of him, that she had believed what he said. Perhaps, in the final analysis, they had both been selfish.

Autumn brought beautiful warm days, with cool, frosty nights. Still, calm weather—the best Port Phillip had to offer. Rachel was five months pregnant, her figure beginning to swell through the thick folds of her skirts. The truth could no longer be hidden, and everyone at the Castle seemed to be looking at her with censorious eyes. Rachel ignored them, going about her usual tasks. Alice treated her with scorn.

'You shoulda' got rid of it,' she sneered. 'I coulda' helped you. Now it's too late.'

The idea hadn't even occurred to Rachel, though she didn't tell Alice that. Later she repeated the words to Sarah, and she rolled her eyes. 'Good way to get yourself killed,' she said. 'I've known a few who died tryin' to get rid of their troubles. You have to be sure of what you're doing, and I wouldn't trust Alice within a mile of me.'

Rachel sighed. 'It would have solved a lot of problems.'

'Things'll get worse before they get better,' Sarah warned her, and patted her hand to take the sting from her words.

This would be a spring baby. Soon, Rachel took out Bella's baby clothes, carefully folded and stored with sprigs of lavender and southernwood. They looked so tiny now that Bella had grown so big, for the little girl was two and a half years old. Rachel touched the soft cloth and delicate stitchery. No, she could not have gone to Alice, even if she had thought of it.

Frank Potter sought Rachel out on his next visit, with what he thought was good news. 'The home station at Nerinbilly is nearly completed. You and the children will be able to move up there at last.'

Rachel said nothing for a moment. 'I don't think I want to move to Nerinbilly,' she told him gently. 'It'd be too awkward . . . for everybody. I'm sure Israel doesn't want me there, and I certainly don't want to be near him. You see that, don't you?'

He nodded, sadly. 'I see it. If only—' but he turned away. 'I told him what I thought of him, Rachel. But Israel lives by his own rules. I promise you, if you did move to Nerinbilly, he wouldn't upset you in any way.'

'I think it would be best for everyone if I stayed here, at least for the time being,' Rachel replied softly. 'Mrs McCrae says she doesn't mind. And you'll have Sarah to help at Nerinbilly, as well as Suzy.'

I'd rather have you, Captain Potter thought. Israel had ruined all his plans, and yet Israel couldn't see that. When Frank ranted and raved at him, he just shrugged and said it was Rachel's fault as much as his, and that she had practically begged him for it. Which Frank knew was untrue. Somehow, Israel had wheedled his way around her, and this was the result.

And what about Will? His heart failed him whenever he thought of Will and imagined Will seeing Rachel carrying another man's child. But if Rachel was Frank's wife, wouldn't he want to know? Whatever pain the knowledge might cost him?

He had been putting it off for weeks, but now he knew he could leave it no longer. Slowly, reluctantly, Frank set about composing the letter.

It was a very still night. The silence hung over them, suffocatingly, so that when the dogs began to whine and bark, straining against their ropes, the noise woke them at once. Next came a hammering on the door and Sarah's voice shouting to be let in. Mrs McCrae jumped from her bed, snatching up the gun as she reached the door. The others crowded behind her, peering into the darkness as she inched it open.

Sarah bolted in, Thomas behind her, his eyes wild. 'Someone's out there!' he gasped. 'Someone was scratching on our window, but when we went out whoever it was ran away.'

'Can't see a thing,' Mrs McCrae whispered, looking out. 'There's no moon.'

'Perhaps it was an animal,' Sarah breathed. 'Or blacks . . .' The word struck terror into their hearts. No one wanted to be speared to death.

Then, out in the trees, a white shape flickered past them, setting the dogs off again, barking and tugging at their ties.

'Oh my God, a ghost!' cried Sarah, and clamped her hand over her mouth.

'I don't believe in ghosts,' Mrs McCrae said

sharply.

By the window, Hazelwood loaded a gun, finding one of the auger holes cut into the walls, from which he could fire safely into the yard. Rachel blinked. Hazelwood? Where had he come from? And wearing only his trousers? Her eyes slid from Hazelwood to Mrs McCrae and back again, as an idea blossomed in her brain. 'Loneliness makes us all weak,' Mrs McCrae had said. Did she include herself in that statement?

Rachel had no time to consider it further. The white shape flickered past them again, weaving through the scrub. The dogs went into another barking frenzy. Hazelwood swore, 'I've had enough of this!' and suddenly he was outside, crouching low as he ran across the yard to the cover of the trees. Mrs McCrae made a move to stop him and then stood still. They held their breaths waiting. There was a scuffle, followed by a scream, loud and shrill. It made the hairs on the back of Rachel's neck rise, and one of the children in the other room started to cry. Outside they could hear a crashing of bushes and snapping of branches, and then Hazelwood was returning, holding something white in his arms which kicked and squirmed and shrieked.

The lamplight wavered in the draft from the door. Hazelwood heaved his catch into the room, and dumped her on the floor. The 'ghost' was a girl. She curled into a ball, sobbing into her hands. Her white nightgown was torn and dirty and bloody, and her auburn hair tangled over her shoulders like a cloak.

Some of the men from the workers' quarters were beginning to arrive, but Mrs McCrae closed the door on their interested faces. She bent to the girl. 'Greta . . . ?'

'Put up a devil of a fight,' Hazelwood muttered. 'Damn near bit me finger off.'

Mrs McCrae gently removed the girl's hands from her face, brushing aside strands of auburn hair. Her face was pale and puffy with crying, her eyes swollen, one of them black and bruised. There was blood on her hands and her nightgown, and her feet were scratched and torn.

'Greta, what has happened? Greta!'

Green eyes opened wide, staring up at Mrs McCrae in horror. Rachel could see Greta's throat working, as though she were fighting for air. 'Redcliffe,' she gasped. 'He's dead. The blacks . . . he's dead!'

The room went very still. Rachel shuddered, drawing her shawl closer about her as if for protection. Hazelwood was already out of the door, yelling for horses to be saddled. Mrs McCrae bent closer, her arm around the younger woman's shoulders— for indeed Greta suddenly looked very young to Rachel.

'How many of them were there, my dear? Can you tell us what happened, Greta?'

Greta gulped, putting up a hand to push back her hair. Her fingers shook so much, Mrs McCrae had to help her. 'I don't know,' she said, her voice wavering up and down. 'I was asleep. I heard noises, and then he was shouting. I . . . he told me to run. So I climbed out of the window at the back, I . . . he was dead . . .' her voice rose to a wail on the last word, and she began to sob, her whole frame shuddering.

Mrs McCrae whispered a prayer under her breath, holding the girl tightly in her strong arms. 'Come,' she murmured at last. 'Come and sit by the fire. Rachel! Heat some water. We'd best see how hurt the poor girl is.'

Greta was not, after all, badly hurt. Her feet had been damaged from her run through the bush—she'd ridden most of the way but the horse had thrown her five miles short of her destination—and she had scratches on her hands and arms, and on her cheek where a branch had whipped back into her face. The black eye was disfiguring rather than serious, and most of the blood on her white nightgown was not hers.

Mrs McCrae poured her a brandy, and held her shaking hands while she sipped. After that she was better, and seemed to regain something of her usual quiet calm. Rachel found Greta another nightgown—one of her own, Rachel being nearer her size—and they helped her to change. She didn't speak again, her face blank, her eyes looking inward.

They made her up a bed in the guest room, and tucked her in like a child, and she fell asleep, her tangled hair shining like firelight against the bed-clothes. It was dawn when the men returned, grim faced, to report that Greta's story was indeed true. 'He's dead all right,' Hazelwood muttered. 'A spear through his chest. The usual way the blacks deal with things.' He shrugged. 'Couldn't tell if anything was missing. The dogs were still chained up and still barking. The two shepherds 'ave been out with the flock all night. Didn't know anything about it until we called in on them.'

Mrs McCrae nodded, her face drawn and pale. She looked old this morning while Greta, still sleeping, looked young and innocent, despite the discoloured eye.

'We'll have to send down to the Border Police, at Mount Macedon,' Hazelwood went on. 'They'll need to be told. And,' quietly, 'we'll need to warn the shepherds at the outstations, and put a watch on here, in case we're next.'

Mrs McCrae met his eyes and it was as if something invisible passed between them. 'Rachel, the children mustn't go beyond the yard. At least not until the troopers have come to see to matters. Do you understand me?'

Rachel understood.

'That's the trouble with the blacks,' Hazelwood muttered sourly. 'They can be your best mates one minute, and cuttin' your throat the next.'

'You're sure it was the blacks then,' Mrs McCrae asked. 'There's no mistake?'

Hazelwood shook his head. 'There's no mistake.' And he snapped his teeth around his pipe stem, effectively closing the conversation.

A soft footstep behind Rachel made her glance over her shoulder. Greta had woken up and was standing in the shadows, listening. Green eyes, brilliant in her white face, met Rachel's. And, just for that instant, Rachel was sure she was smiling.

A man was sent south, to the Mount Macedon Police Post, and McCrae's Castle waited under the warm sun. Hazelwood had ridden back to Redcliffe's, but although he and his men scoured the run, he could find no sign of any blacks. 'Probably gone back to where they came from,' he said, and puffed furiously on his pipe.

'It couldn't be the local tribe,' Mrs McCrae murmured anxiously.

Hazelwood gave her a hard look. 'Have you thought that this might have something to do with Big Mary's baby?'

It was clear she hadn't. 'You mean her husband might have revenged himself on Redcliffe? Oh no . . .' But even as she said it, Rachel could see she was wavering.

They had brought Redcliffe's body back to the Castle, but they didn't dare bury it until the troopers arrived. Word came from the outstations that they were prepared for attack, but had seen nothing as yet. Hazelwood had sent a man north, to warn Nerinbilly.

The day dragged on. Rachel felt tired and frightened. Her body weighed her down, and it was an effort to be calm, while Greta sat silently beside her. The girl disturbed her peace of mind. Bella clutched a fold of Rachel's skirt with one hand and sucked the thumb of the other.

At last, outside, came the confused sounds of horses and men. Voices shouting and then softer, drawing closer. Rachel straightened to face the door, pulling her daughter against her. There would probably be hot food to prepare and serve, drinks to pour . . . 'Looks like they're here at last,' Mrs McCrae's voice held relief, as she peered out of the window. The door swung open, and Hazelwood came in, talking back over his shoulder, the inevitable pipe between his teeth.

'—in the chest. Nothing taken as far as we could tell. Of course his wife might know more, when she's up to it.'

'We'll have to wait until tomorrow now anyway.' The trooper followed, stooping under the lintel. He was tall, and he looked tired, the weary lines on his face a testimony to his long journey north. His grey eyes narrowed as he darted a quick glance around the room.

It was Will.

CHAPTER 19

IT WAS WILL, IT WAS! Rachel's head felt as light as air, and yet she saw everything very sharply, very clearly. The way in which the lamplight caught the polished leather of his gun belt, and the shine of his buttons. His uniform was dusty and stained from the hard ride, his boots mud-splattered, and there was a thin line of sweat and grime about his neck, at the collar. His head was bent slightly to listen to Hazelwood—a habit he'd adopted, being taller than nearly everyone else. He nodded, pushing his hair back off his forehead, the gesture so familiar, so precious, it caught at Rachel's heart like a jagged blade.

Hazelwood was introducing him to Mrs McCrae and he held out his hand, his smile more from polite necessity than pleasure. He looked serious; a serious man about serious business.

Bella squeaked, and Rachel realised she had been gripping the child's arm too tightly. Her daughter shot her a resentful look and trotted away towards Matty, who was perched on the sofa with Greta, playing with her doll.

'Greta?' Mrs McCrae was smiling at the girl, but her eyes were anxious. 'This is Sergeant Moody from the Border Police. He'd like to ask you about last night?'

Greta glanced briefly upwards and then back to the hands folded in her lap. She nodded.

Will came towards her. As he did so his gaze swept over the room, and over Rachel. For a brief moment, she was looking into the grey eyes she remembered so well. Had once loved so well. Something in them flickered, and then they had passed on, indifferently, to Greta. Will turned his back.

Rachel stood, her hands icy, staring at his broad shoulders. He had seen her, she knew that he had seen her, and he had turned away. He was speaking to Greta, but Rachel hardly heard what he said. The quiet, gentle tone—guaranteed to win over a grief-stricken widow—was a blur to her. Was she so changed? So unrecognisable as the girl he had married? Or had the memory of her been lost among the twists and turns of his new life?

The thought was like a rush of dark water, engulfing her, choking her. It was as if her nightmare had come true. Will had ridden past her without a single glance, as if she didn't exist.

'Rachel?' With a start, Rachel realised that Mrs McCrae had been standing beside her, murmuring her name. The older woman frowned at her curiously, and Rachel looked away. She felt a trickle of cold perspiration on her brow. 'Rachel, would you see about some food for Sergeant Moody? And a tot of Hazelwood's rum, to warm him after the long ride.'

'He doesn't drink,' she blurted out, and then closed her eyes in dismay. 'I mean, I don't believe he—'

Mrs McCrae stared at her. 'Rachel, whatever is the matter?'

Rachel shook her head. Will's back mocked her, and her emotions were threatening to overwhelm her; in another moment she would lose her tenuous control. With her head bowed and her hands clenched at her sides, Rachel slipped around the sofa and vanished down the dark coverway towards the kitchen.

Sarah was there, with her sleeves bunched up, rolling a pie crust for tomorrow. She looked up with a smile, and stopped. Rachel was as white as the flour on Sarah's arms, and her dark eyes were enormous.

'What is it?' Sarah's words racked with fear—Sarah and Thomas had not got over Greta scratching at their window.

'It's Will,' Rachel whispered, her voice thin and strange. 'Will's here. Will's the trooper come up from Mount Macedon.'

Sarah gasped, and then set to coughing, her eyes streaming, so that Rachel had to come and pound her on the back. 'Will Trigg,' she managed at last. 'Oh Rachel but that's wonderful!' Then, the reddened eyes narrowing, as she mopped her nose with her handkerchief, 'Isn't it?'

'He calls himself Will Moody,' Rachel whispered, still as white and rigid as Matty's doll. 'That's his real name. And he doesn't remember me, Sarah. He looked right through me as if I weren't there. No, it was worse than that. As if I were a stranger!'

Rachel's voice rose.

'Hush.' Sarah caught her arm, leaving a white floury handprint. And then her eyes looked down to Rachel's waist and she sighed. 'You're in deep trouble. Even a blindman can see you're carrying, and Will knows for certain it can't be his.'

She had forgotten. Somehow, she had forgotten. In the moments when she recognised Will, and waited for him to recognise her, she had forgotten about Israel's baby. His presence had filled her heart and mind with a wonderful golden joy and excitement. But now . . . the reality of the baby and all it meant rushed over her, swamping her again. Was that why his eyes had passed over her as if she were nothing? Was that why he had turned his back? Rachel dropped her head into her hands.

'He can't say anything against you,' Sarah was saying, her words tumbling over each other in an attempt to offer comfort. 'He left you, didn't he? Lord knows what he's been up to, all these years. He can't come swanning in here now and act as if you're not good enough. And if he tries, I'll be the first to tell him just what I think of him!'

Rachel hardly heard her. Suddenly she hated her unborn child with a venom that shocked her. If it wasn't for that, Will would have smiled at her, if it wasn't for this blatant sign of her betrayal, he might have looked at her once more with love.

Stupid, she told herself. For all she knew, Will had stopped loving her long ago. He had moved on from Rachel. He had made the break the day he left her and, Will being Will, he would have put her out of his mind from that moment.

'Sarah! Rachel!'

They spun around, pale and guilty. Mrs McCrae stood in the doorway behind them. 'I'm waiting for the food I asked you to fetch,' she said sharply. 'What on earth are you doing?'

Sarah began to answer, but Rachel cut in with, 'I'm sorry, Mrs McCrae. I'll bring it now.'

Mrs McCrae looked at her a moment more, as though she might ask further questions, then shook her head irritably and went out. They listened to her steps fading towards the house.

'Why didn't you tell her?' Sarah asked quietly.

Rachel shook her head. 'Tell her what? No, if Will wants to pretend he doesn't know me then I can do the same.' Suddenly a glorious surge of anger spurted into her veins. She marched over to the stove and began to fill a plate with the inevitable mutton stew, cutting a large slice of damper to soak it up. The kettle was still hot, and she made him black tea, ignoring Hazelwood's rum on the shelf in the corner. If he had taken up drinking again, she didn't want to know, and she certainly wasn't going to abet him.

Her anger wavered. It was Will, wasn't it? Could she have made a mistake, imagined it? Had she been longing for him so much that she had turned a stranger into him, just as she had tried to turn Israel into him? But no. She could never be mistaken about Will. I would know him, she told herself bleakly, even in the dark.

Sarah was watching her face. 'He can't hurt you,' she said firmly. 'He left you. Remember that.'

Rachel picked up the plate in one hand and the mug in the other. 'I'm not frightened of him,' she replied desperately.

The journey had never been so long, and as she approached the sitting room, the lantern seemed to illuminate the people within as if they were on a stage, and she were the audience. Greta sat on the sofa, with Mrs McCrae beside her, a comforting arm about her shoulders. Bella was playing with Maggie, and Victoria hugged a grubby rag doll, while Matty kept a maternal eye on them all. Will—and oh yes, it really was Will—was seated at the table, with Hazelwood beside him puffing clouds of nauseating smoke.

She stopped at the door, wondering suddenly whether she really could go on. Will was leaning forward over his interlocked fingers, concentrating on what Hazelwood said. There was a carbine resting against the wall behind them. Young Frank, close beside Hazelwood, was gazing at it with wide, delighted eyes.

Rachel made to speak out, but even as she opened her mouth, Will had noticed the boy's interest. With a brief shake of his head, he moved the weapon away. 'These things are my tools of trade, I'm afraid,' he said to Hazelwood, as if in apology.

She should have known he would go back to being the hunter. He had told her, that terrible day she discovered the truth, that he was good at his job . . . that he was the best. Of course he would go back to doing what he did best. And where better to do it, than in the employ of the mounted police?

'Uncle Israel has a bigger gun than that,' Frank announced loudly 'He says he'll teach me to use it, when I'm older. He says the blacks don't come near Nerinbilly, because they're frightened of him.'

The childish voice was proud and boasting, but Hazelwood only laughed, ruffling the boy's hair. 'Bloody Israel Potter,' he muttered, his yellow teeth clenched on the pipe stem. 'His gun's not the only thing he's been shooting around here.' And he leaned closer to Will and spoke in a hoarse whisper before ending with a loud snigger.

Something inside Rachel shrivelled up into a cold, tight little ball. She watched Will's face go hard, the muscles of his jaw bunching. He looked up, as if suddenly aware of her presence, straight into her eyes. Rachel felt his glance like a blow. She had never witnessed such cold fury in his face before— as though he would like to kill her with his bare hands. And then, before she could even flinch, the expression was gone, shut down into the indifference he had previously shown her, and he turned back to Hazelwood.

'Rachel?' Mrs McCrae had seen her and was coming towards her. 'Bring the food in, it'll be cold!' She shot Rachel an impatient look, and took the plate from her, leaving Rachel to carry the mug of tea. 'And I thought I told you to bring some of Hazelwood's rum,' she added irritably, as she set down the meal. 'Sergeant Moody must be in need of a restorative.'

But Will was shaking his head with a wry smile. 'I don't drink, Mrs McCrae. Must be the only trooper in the colony who doesn't. Tea'll be fine.'

Mrs McCrae's eyes narrowed at Rachel, but all she said was, 'Would you sit with Greta? She's rather upset.'

Rachel would have preferred to have returned to the haven of the kitchen, but she nodded and went over to the sofa. Greta sat in her usual self-contained manner, but there was something tense in the angle of her head, and the way her hands clenched and unclenched in her lap. Rachel could understand grief—although in Redcliffe's case, this was a little extreme—but there was more to Greta's demeanour than that. It was almost as if she were afraid.

'You're quite safe here you know,' she said impulsively, placing her hand over Greta's.

The girl stiffened, and then forced herself to relax, nodding briefly. 'Yes,' she said. Then, slyly, glancing up, 'Do you think Mr Potter will come tomorrow?'

Israel. Of course. With all his visits to Redcliffe's, with all his attentions, Greta had fallen in love with him.

'I don't know. Maybe.' She withdrew her hand, suddenly feeling distaste for the girl.

Greta's green eyes mocked her. 'He'll come,' she said.

Rachel's head was aching, and the soft hum of voices in the room magnified, so that she put a hand to her eyes to rub them wearily. Perhaps this was a bad dream, just like the one she had had the other night.

A warm little hand slipped into hers, tugging, and Rachel lifted her head with a smile. Bella. She had forgotten Bella. What would Will say when he knew about her? The curve of the plump little cheek seemed suddenly so vulnerable, and the stubborn bottom lip wrenched at her heart. Bella meant nothing to Will, how could she? He did not even know her. He had given up that chance when he left Rachel.

The sound of a chair scraping on the wooden floor brought Rachel's eyes around. Will had finished his meal, and Hazelwood was standing up, speaking with Mrs McCrae. Frank, yawning, had come to lean against the sofa beside Greta. It was past the children's bedtime.

Carefully avoiding looking in Will's direction, Rachel pushed herself up. Calling the children together, and lifting baby Maggie into her arms, she moved towards the bedroom. They were all tired, and made no protest as she undressed them and put them to bed. Even Bella, who usually complained at bedtime, closed her eyes obediently and curled into a ball with her thumb in her mouth. It was only then that Rachel realised Frank wasn't there.

Her head was aching worse than ever, and she was tempted to leave him to make his own way to bed. But his welfare was her responsibility, so with a sigh, Rachel made her way back to the other room.

The front door was open. Outside, the darkness was like a curtain, but as Rachel moved closer to it she saw Will and Hazelwood standing on the verandah, talking. Greta and Mrs McCrae were no where to be seen. But Frank was there, leaning nonchalantly on the verandah rail, pretending to be part of the scene. 'Frank, it's bed time,' she hissed.

The men heard her and turned. Frank stomped crossly off to bed, and Hazelwood gave a snort of laughter. He touched Will's arm. 'I'll show you where you're to sleep,' he said, and slouched off across the yard. Will moved to follow him, and then hesitated. He looked back at Rachel, his face lit oddly by the lantern inside the door. Weariness had made dark hollows under his eyes and drawn new lines. There was nothing of warmth or welcoming in his expression, and Rachel held her breath.

'I've a job to do here. That's the only reason I came. And as soon as the job's done, I'll be gone.'

She said nothing.

'Oh, don't worry,' and he looked at her quickly, dismissively. 'I've no right to interfere in your life any more. Just as you're nothin' to do with mine.'

Was he asking her a question? 'Yes,' she whispered.

As if satisfied with that answer, he turned away and his long strides soon brought him up with Hazelwood. The door to the men's quarters opened—a burst of light and noise—and the pair of them vanished inside.

The night seemed endless. Rachel tossed and turned, trying not to wake the others, but her mind would not be still. She felt bereft, and then angry, and then so empty she could have sobbed into her pillow. Memories flooded her—the first time she saw Will by the dark river, and their wild ride. And then later, at the smithy, the broken man. There had been a bond between them from the first moment, she was still positive of that. Something had joined *them* together in defiance of all of the other men and women they might have loved, and that something was raw and unrelenting and almost mystical in its intensity.

The day Mrs Roadknight came to Greengage was etched deep in her mind; she even remembered the expression on the old woman's face. As well as the satisfaction in her smile when she destroyed their happiness. It had been such a shock! And it had taken Rachel a long time to come to terms with the truth. The years away from him had brought her a new maturity and tolerance. Even now she could not fully understand or forgive what he had done—but she could accept it. And with that acceptance came the realisation that because they had been unable to bridge the rift Mrs Roadknight had made, she and Will had been broken asunder.

If only he had stayed and waited, she told herself. But could any man wait so long, be so patient? Will had seen the situation as hopeless, and perhaps it had been. If he had stayed, they would probably have torn themselves apart anyway with her stony inability to forgive, and his bitterness because she could not accept him for what he was. Maybe they had had no choice but to separate and preserve what was left to them.

The memories.

But of what use are memories? Rachel cried out in silent agony. I want the man. I want Will! The desperate, passionate need left her shaking. And the futility of her want left her stricken. Will had made it quite clear to her tonight he was here to do his job, that was all, and she no longer had any place in his life.

Rachel fell asleep at last, tired and drained, and

when she awoke the troopers and Hazelwood had gone to the Redcliffe run. Her body felt heavier, as though Israel's baby were determined to make its presence felt. Her head still ached, and she knew her face was pale and drawn. What did Will see when he looked at her? A haggard woman, shabbily dressed and swollen with child. No wonder he had dismissed her so easily. What was there to attract him? The young and pretty girl was gone. 'As fresh as a daisy,' George had called her once. Well, she did not feel like a daisy this morning.

Rachel laughed bitterly. What was the use in worrying over what she had been? The past was past, and she could not change what had happened. Israel's baby would be born, whatever the consequences, and life would go on around it. With an impatient, fatalistic shrug of her shoulders, she went out to face the day.

As if conjured up like a bad genie, Israel Potter arrived during the morning, He was on his way south to Melbourne, he said. Immediately, Greta clung to his arm, and Rachel watched him respond by bending solicitously over her.

Captain Potter was still at Nerinbilly, but sent his condolences to the young widow. As if, thought Rachel, Redcliffe would be a loss to Port Phillip. And yet she would not have wished such a brutal death on anyone, even Redcliffe.

They had a small burial service—apparently Will had viewed the body—and Redcliffe was laid to rest in the little cemetery at the Castle, along with three other poor souls. 'My husband is buried here,' Mrs McCrae murmured. 'As well as two shepherds. He will be in good company, my dear.'

Greta smiled and nodded, as if taking comfort, but Rachel noticed she did not remove her hand from Israel's arm. Mrs McCrae read the service with suitable solemnity. 'We'll have a minister say a few words,' she added, 'next time we have one call in.'

Afterwards, Sarah waylaid Rachel in the dairy, blue eyes popping with excitement. 'What did you say to Will?' she wanted to know. 'I saw him this morning, and . . . I just stared, Rachel. He must have thought me empty-headed.'

'He told me he's here to do his job. He's not interested in me.'

Sarah was silent, thinking that over. It all seemed very strange to her. Sad too, when she remembered how they had been at Greengage. She had discussed it with Thomas—and sworn him to secrecy of course!—and he had listened carefully, and then told her that people change. Sometimes they change so much, and grow so far apart, they can no longer be friends, let alone be married. It was just the way of the world.

'I hope that never happens to us!' Sarah had cried, gripping his arm.

'We won't let it,' he retorted, and hugged her. Sarah was everything he was not, and he relied on her just as she relied on him.

'I just feel so sorry for Rachel,' she went on after a moment. 'There must have been a chance they'd get together again, but what husband would take her now, with another man's child in her belly? Men don't like being made fools of.'

Thomas didn't reply. He had seen Sergeant Moody for himself, and had not thought him the sort of man to forgive easily. Rachel was a lovely woman and it was a shame she had involved herself with a smooth scoundrel like Israel Potter.

The men returned at midday. Rachel watched from the window as they rode into the yard, each face as drawn and tired as the others. There were five troopers in Will's charge and they lounged about, very much at ease, while they waited for their orders. Will and Hazelwood stood, deep in conversation, until at last Will turned and spoke to his men and they wandered off with the horses while he followed Hazelwood towards the house.

Greta and Israel came from the direction of the garden, and Rachel held her breath as Hazelwood paused to introduce the two men. Will bent his head to listen to Israel, and Rachel saw him nod and then smile. Israel laughed, and slipped his pipe out of his coat pocket, tapping it on the palm of his hand to empty it, before filling it with fresh tobacco.

Slowly, they began to make their way towards the home station. Rachel turned and fled out to the kitchen, heart thumping. Mrs McCrae was at her desk in the store. As Rachel passed, she looked up from her ledgers with tired eyes.

'Rachel? Are they back yet?'

She nodded unwillingly. 'Yes, they're back. They're talking with Israel Potter in the yard.'

Mrs McCrae rose and stretched her back wearily. 'Israel . . . yes. Well, I'd best hear what they have to say. And Rachel?' with a grimace. 'I know it's difficult for you to have Israel Potter here. Believe me, I sympathise with your situation, but other than to support you in your troubles, I can do little. Do you understand?'

She meant she would give Rachel a home, but she would not punish Israel by sending him off. He was the owner of Nerinbilly, and an important man. Mrs McCrae was too clever a businesswoman to alienate Israel.

'I understand,' Rachel said, with hardly a trace of bitterness. It was the way of the world. The woman paid the price, while the man went on his way. Especially if the man were a squatter and the woman a servant.

'Oh, by the by,' Mrs McCrae went on, turning back at the door. 'Sergeant Moody mentioned he would like to speak to everyone who was here the night Mr Redcliffe died. He will send for you later this afternoon.'

'I'll look forward to it,' Rachel murmured, and walked away on wobbly legs.

Her afternoon was full of the usual chores. There was mending to be done, and the children needed their hair washed. It was something she and Sarah usually tackled once a week, bathing them and washing their hair in the tub in front of the kitchen fire. They were halfway through the chore—children sitting about in various stages of undress, while Rachel and Sarah knelt with sleeves rolled up— when one of the troopers appeared in the doorway.

It was the moment Rachel had been dreading. 'Mrs Trigg?' The man eyed the two women insolently. He was middle-aged, with the rough, weathered face of someone who had lived hard. The troopers tended to be ex-convicts and were often so dissolute no one else would employ them.

It was little wonder, she thought, that someone honest and intelligent and diligent, like Will, had risen so far in so short a time.

'Yes,' Rachel replied quietly, 'I'm Mrs Trigg.'

'Sergeant wants to 'ave a word with you.'

He leaned against the door jamb while Rachel pulled herself to her feet, straightened her skirts and smoothed down her sleeves.

'Treat you well does he, the Sergeant?' Sarah asked, with a jerk of her head.

The man grinned. 'Well enough. A bit of a stickler for the book. But he'll look after you in a tight spot.' His grin broadened. 'The Captain likes 'im. Fact is, this ain't the sort of job our Sergeant usually comes out on. He asked partic'larly.'

'He asked to come,' Rachel repeated. Something was pounding in her head, the headache back again, thumping and banging in her skull. Will had asked to come here to Mrs McCrae's Castle. Why was that?

Silently, she followed the trooper towards the guest room Will was using as his office, and waited while he knocked, grinned at her sideways, and opened the door.

Will sat with his back to her, his pen scratching on the paper spread before him. He was so big, he made the room seem tiny and airless. Rachel swallowed an urge to bolt as the trooper closed the door behind her.

'You asked to see me?'

He nodded, still writing, and indicated a chair to the side. After moment, he said, as if in explanation, 'I like to get the statements down as soon as possible.' The grey eyes slid to her and away again. 'It's procedure.'

He finished writing and placed the pen carefully in its holder. Briefly, he glanced over what he had written then, seemingly satisfied, leaned back in his chair. It creaked dangerously under his weight, and Rachel bit her lip as he stretched out booted legs beneath the desk. How could she have forgotten his size? The strength of his arms and shoulders, and the way the cloth stretched across his chest. She had forgotten, too, how his dark hair lay straight against his nape, and fell across his brow. How often had she smoothed it back, laughing into his face, kissing him? He looked as tired as he had last night, his eyes narrowed with weariness, and he was frowning as if he had a headache. Had he, too, lain awake most of the night? If only he had! Then at least Rachel could believe he still cared. But she feared, she very much feared, he didn't give a damn.

He was watching her.

Nervously, Rachel looked away, but she felt his eyes on her cheek, like warm fingers, touching, and the colour stole slowly into her face. Did he see changes in her? Was she old and ugly to him now? She felt the baby inside her move, and her heart stilled. You're a fool, Rachel told herself scornfully. He isn't interested in you. How could he be? He wants answers to his questions, that's all. Give him what he wants and be done with it. Perhaps then he will go away.

She turned and faced him, her eyes brilliant and her voice harsh. 'You wanted to ask me something, Sergeant Moody?'

Slowly he nodded. 'Tell me about the night Mrs

Redcliffe came.'

She told him, brisk and unemotional. There was little to tell, really, and it was soon done. He made a few notes with his pen, silent until she finished.

'Mrs Redcliffe's very young.'

'Yes.'

'Her husband was quite a brutal man, I'm told.'

'And a drunk.'

He turned and gave her a long, cool look. Rachel dropped her eyes.

'I think he hit her,' she added, pleating her skirt with shaking fingers. 'Mrs McCrae said Greta spent most of her time in the bush, hiding.'

'Why didn't she leave him?'

Her head was aching again, making his words seem muffled. 'I . . .' her voice broke, and she tried again. 'I think it was because she thought the land was as much hers as his, and if she left she'd lose it.'

He nodded as if she had confirmed something for him, and wrote again. The silence dragged on. Let me go, she pleaded. Please, let me go.

'Mrs McCrae has told me about a black girl called Big Mary. Do you think Redcliffe fathered her child?'

Rachel put a finger to her temple, pressing the ache. 'I don't know. He was a horrible man.'

'Do you think Big Mary's husband was agreeable to the situation?'

Rachel swallowed. 'I can't believe any husband would be agreeable to such a situation.'

He was silent, and his silence was worse than his words. An accusation.

'What about Israel Potter?'

Rachel froze, thinking he meant her and Israel.

The colour drained out of her face. And then she realised he was speaking of Greta, and was able to breathe again. Somehow she managed to make her voice sound normal. 'I heard he often visited her. They're neighbours. Frank . . . Captain Potter would know.'

'Israel Potter's here now,' he went on quietly. 'Has he come to visit her, or you?'

She shook her head. Perspiration made beads on her forehead, and she felt her dress sticking hotly to her back. Please, please, just let me go . . .

'Am I right in thinkin' that he's the father of your child?' he continued, cold, efficient and unfeeling.

Her voice was a croak. 'You're the father of my child—'

His hand clenched on the pen—she saw his knuckles turn white. 'I'm talkin' about your unborn child, Mrs Trigg. Is Israel Potter the father of your unborn child?'

'Yes.'

'But he didn't come to see you today?' the pen hadn't moved, but he was staring at the paper, so still, so still . . .

'No,' she breathed. The room was jumping before her eyes, lights flickering strangely. Her head felt peculiar, twice its usual size, and her feet were so far away.

'Why is that, Mrs Trigg?'

She opened her mouth but nothing came out. At last he turned and looked at her, and his eyes were blazing just as they had been last night.

'Why is that?'

And suddenly something burst inside her, a great flashing explosion of dammed-up emotion and she screamed back at him in a voice she didn't recognise, 'Because I mean nothing to him! Nothing! He used me, and when he'd had what he wanted he didn't want it anymore! Is that what you want to hear? Is it?'

He was on his feet, gripping her arms, his fingers biting into her flesh. His face was suddenly so close to hers, she felt his breath on her lips. And felt the power of his anger even though he held it in, and that made it even more frightening. 'I don't enjoy this any more than you do,' he said in a low, grating voice. 'Do you think I want to know what he's done to you?' And then he let her go, abruptly, as if he didn't like touching her.

Rachel rubbed her arms. Strangely, the ache in her head was gone, as if her outburst had released it. Now she just felt very weary. 'I think I've answered enough of your questions,' she said.

But he appeared unconcerned. 'I'll need you to sign a statement.' His voice was quiet again, emotionless. 'When I've written out what you've told me, I'll send it over to you to sign.' The grey eyes held hers. 'You don't need to come back here again.'

Did he see the relief in her face?

'You can go now, Mrs Trigg.' He said at last the words she had wanted to hear. His anger, or whatever it had been, was gone, and so was any interest he may have had in her. He didn't even look up as Rachel left the room.

CHAPTER 20

WITH THE CHILDREN IN THE care of Thomas and Sarah, Rachel was able to finish some sewing she had been doing for her baby. Each stitch was a chore, but she forced herself to take them, tiny and delicate, concentrating on her work, and gradually her calm began to return. She had always been an accomplished needlewoman, and now the discipline helped her to settle her thoughts. The interview with Will had upset her, but it was over now. There was no need to see him again.

Surely he didn't need to stay any longer at the Castle? He had seen everything he needed to see and asked all the questions he needed to ask. It was so simple—Redcliffe had been speared in the chest by natives. There was the question of Big Mary's husband—who had conveniently disappeared, according to Hazelwood— but that shouldn't worry Will. He need only report back to his superiors and await their instructions.

So why was he still here?

The previous evening, he had taken his meal out

with his men. Israel had made a joke of it, saying that Mrs McCrae had confused him by laying too many forks on the table, and laughing in that hearty way of his.

'I thought he was an expert bushman,' he went on, a sneer creeping into his voice. 'The way his men talk about him he should have had those murderers hung, drawn and quartered by now.'

Greta flinched. Mrs McCrae smiled thinly, her eyes flicking to Hazelwood and back. 'I'm sure Sergeant Moody knows what he's about. He seems a capable sort of chap.'

But Israel had snorted in disbelief. He appeared to have taken a dislike to Will, thought Rachel, as she served the meal. She wondered, with a sort of forced detachment, what Will thought of him.

And then, this morning, Israel left for Melbourne, and soon after the troopers had ridden off in the direction of Redcliffe's again. Greta had stood in the yard and watched them go, her face lifted to the bright, cool day. She turned at last, moving slowly back towards the house, and Rachel, sweeping the front verandah, had asked her if she were all right. Greta pushed by her in silence, not even bothering to answer.

Rachel took another careful stitch, surveying her work. The baby was due in September. And then? She had not let herself think beyond the birth. To think further frightened her too much. Of course, she could stay here, but already she felt Mrs McCrae cooling towards her. The older woman thought her a fool to have fallen for Israel Potter, and Rachel had the feeling she would be more comfortable if she could persuade Rachel to leave. Going to live at Nerinbilly was the obvious step, apart from the fact Israel was there. Could she face that? Rachel cringed at the thought. Better to strike out on her own, but that, too, was full of uncertainties . . .

A step at the door, and Sarah interrupted her thoughts. 'Rachel. . .' Rachel's smile died when she saw Sarah's uneasy eyes. 'Rachel, I think you should come and see this.'

Slowly, Rachel followed the other woman out onto the verandah. At first she didn't know what she was supposed to look at. The children were playing, Frank's dog barking with excitement. The troopers were back, and some of them were lazing against the barn wall, smoking or dozing in the sun. A few dapper black and white magpies strutted in the yard— the children had been feeding them—and Frank's dog ran at them, trying to chase them away. But they just flew up onto the barn roof, heads cocked to the side, watching with their beady eyes.

Frowning, Rachel turned to Sarah. 'There!' she hissed, jerking her chin. Rachel followed the general direction, and froze.

Bella and Victoria were sitting on the step of Thomas and Sarah's cottage, and on his haunches beside them, head bent, was Will. Even as Rachel took in the scene, she heard Victoria giggle, holding up her grubby doll for Will to inspect. He took it cautiously, turning it over in his hands. Victoria giggled again. And all the time Bella watched him, her serious little face secretive, her small booted feet placed exactly side by side on the hard bare ground. 'He knows about Bella then,' Sarah said in her ear. 'Did you tell him?'

Rachel shook her head. She felt like running across the yard and snatching her daughter up. Was he trying to steal her child from her? And then Sarah's words sank in, and she turned and stared wildly at her. 'Someone must have told him! Did you?'

Sarah jumped back, peering at her in amazement. 'Don't be a goose.'

Slowly, Rachel released her breath. 'No, of course you didn't.' Sarah hadn't told him, Rachel had herself, yesterday afternoon—easy enough for him to find out which child was Rachel's.

Confused, Rachel looked back into the yard. Bella was nodding her head slowly and importantly, darting Will a look from clear grey eyes. And then, to Rachel's relief, he stood up. He straightened his jacket, doing up the top buttons, glancing about as he did so.

'Let's go,' Sarah muttered, backing away, as he caught sight of them.

'Yes,' Rachel breathed.

But neither of them need have worried, for he had turned away, back towards his men. Rachel's shoulders slumped with relief. For a moment she gazed blindly at the troopers, thinking what a disreputable lot they were. Ex-convicts, if what she heard was right, and the worst of that breed rather than the best. Brutal drunkards, swaggering in uniforms. Mrs Roadknight had always felt such men were traitors to their kind. Did it please Will to be in charge of them? Was this what he wanted from his life now?

The freshening breeze teased wisps of her hair

from its pins. Rachel put up a hand to smooth it back, and found it was shaking.

'Come on,' Sarah said gently behind her. 'I'll make us both a cup of tea.'

The thud of the horse's hooves caught Rachel's ear as she turned to go, and she glanced quickly over her shoulder. A rider, crouched low over his horse, was coming hell-for-leather down the track. As she watched, the horse stumbled and only by a miracle managed to regain its footing. The rider's hat had come off, and his hair was gritty with dust. She saw the grimace on his dirty, sweaty face as he tried to draw his mount to a brutal halt in the yard. But he was going too fast, and the horse had difficulty in stopping. Hooves skidded, and it ended up only inches from the verandah. The rider saw Rachel as he jumped down, and it was only then that she recognised one of Israel's men.

'Captain Potter,' he gasped, his voice hoarse. 'He's been speared. Can someone come?'

The man had doubled over, catching his breath, while beside him the horse staggered. Rachel ran towards the steps, and somehow missed the first one as she came down. She fell forward, and for a terrible moment her hands clutched at empty air. And then she came up hard against a solid wall of warm flesh and muscle; Will. Briefly, they were pressed together, his hands gripping her arms, one of his buttons scratching her cheek as, winded,

Rachel tried to catch her breath. And then he had thrust her away, his grey eyes searching hers.

'Will!' she gasped. 'This is a Nerinbilly man. He says Frank's been speared.'

One moment he was there, and then he was not. She heard him shouting to his men, and the yard was alive with horses and troopers, and suddenly they were gone, only the dust, slowly settling, to show they had ever been.

Mrs McCrae was informed, and was soon gathering together her medicines. 'I'll leave first thing in the morning,' she announced. 'It's too late now—it'd be dark before I reached Nerinbilly. Too dangerous.'

'I'll come with you,' Rachel said quietly, and moved to help pack the basket.

Mrs McCrae looked at her narrowly. 'Rachel, I don't think that's a good idea in your condition.'

Rachel waved her hand. 'Captain Potter needs me,' she replied firmly. 'And besides, "women in my condition" can, and do, travel hundreds of miles by cart and on horseback. I'm coming.'

Mrs McCrae said no more, other than to suggest Rachel pack herself some clothing and have a good night's sleep. 'Who knows what we'll find when we get there,' she said grimly.

The cart rattled and rumbled over the rough track, the horses straining. They had been travelling for hours. Rachel sat, tense and still, gazing ahead as if that would somehow hasten the journey. Beside her, Mrs McCrae shook the reins, muttering under her breath for all the world like Hazelwood. She had brought with her everything she thought she would need, as well as bedding and a canvas tent for herself and Rachel, as they didn't yet know what state Nerinbilly was in.

The man who had brought the news—when he was somewhat recovered—had been able to tell what happened. Only the day before they had seen a tribe they knew—Captain Potter had given them food— and they had not expected to see more so soon. The blacks who attacked were different, strangers, and they had come seeking trouble. Captain Potter had been alone at the hut, and for some reason had ignored his own orders, and gone out to the yards without his gun. Of the four men who usually remained at the home station, one had headed to the outstation with supplies, and the rest were away looking for some missing sheep, and it was only sheer luck that they were on their way home when they heard Captain Potter's shouts. They rode back without delay and found him struggling with one black man while another rifled the hut. As soon as the horses appeared, the blacks had run off. One of the station hands had pursued, and shot one of them dead, but he was sure there were a couple more.

'How bad is he?' Mrs McCrae asked quietly.

The man looked grim. 'A spear in his leg and one in his side, ma'am. Didn't look too bright when I saw him last.'

Poor Frank, Rachel thought. Don't let him die, not like this. It isn't fair. Why didn't life have some justice in it? The children had been so upset when they heard. Their mother dead, and now Frank . . . Rachel had tried to reassure them, but her words had sounded hollow. She knew that the only way in which she could repay him for all his kindnesses to her was to go with Mrs McCrae.

Rachel had never seen Nerinbilly before, and hardly had eyes for it now. The hut and, beside it, the half finished home station, were etched against a chill blue, windy sky. There were the usual out-buildings, stock yards and horses in a fenced paddock. The land was softly undulating, well timbered and grassed. Ordinarily, Rachel would have viewed it with delight, but just now it meant nothing.

They drew the cart to a halt, and, ignoring the stares of the three men on guard, Rachel followed Mrs McCrae towards the hut. No sign of the troopers, some part of her mind noted, but she had no time for Will, either. She was already at the doorway, her eyes adjusting to the gloom, frightened of what she would see.

Frank Potter was lying on a makeshift bunk. He was stripped down to his breeches, one of the legs slit, and there was a bandage around his thigh and one around his chest. Kneeling beside him, bathing his face and throat, was a thin woman in a grubby dress, with matted fair hair hanging about her face. At the sound from the door, she looked up with startled eyes. Hazel eyes, the shadows beneath making them look bruised from fear and exhaustion.

'Suzy,' Rachel whispered, and felt the tears sting. Suzy had never been so thin! The girl stood unsteadily, and suddenly threw herself at Rachel, almost knocking her over. Rachel, hugging her, felt her ribs through the dress, where once there had been opulent flesh.

'He's that sick,' she burst out. 'I don't know what to do. Them black buggers! They should be shot, the whole lot of 'em!'

Rachel hugged her tighter, watching over her shoulder as Mrs McCrae took Suzy's place by the sick man and set about feeling his brow and checking his wounds. Captain Potter had not moved a muscle, only the shallow rise of his chest hinting at life, but Mrs McCrae appeared unperturbed. She glanced up at Rachel.

'Take the girl outside,' she said authoritatively. 'She needs a break. We'll have some tea and something to eat presently. I'll do what has to be done here.'

Outside, Suzy took a deep breath and wiped her cheeks with the backs of her hands, like a child, leaving dirty smears. Rachel shook her head and, finding her handkerchief, proceeded to gently clean her friend's face.

'You weren't here when it happened?' she asked at last.

Suzy shook her head, shuddering. 'George and I was at the outstation. We only 'eard yesterday afternoon. Came in straight off. George 'as gone out with the troopers.' A thought occurred to her, and she swung her reddened eyes onto Rachel. 'Did you know—' she whispered.

Rachel nodded bleakly. 'I knew.'

Suzy swallowed and took another breath. 'Like old times, hey?' She seemed to be regaining something of her old laconic self. 'They've gone over towards the Campaspe. Will seemed to think that was the way the blacks were headed. He said they might be out for days.'

Will was in his element, Rachel thought with a flash of bitterness. Hunting down men.

'I'm going back to Melbourne.' Suzy's voice interrupted her thoughts. 'I've 'ad enough.'

Rachel didn't blame her. She really did look as though she had had enough. 'What about George?'

'Him too. We reckon we can get work. And anything's better 'an dyin' out 'ere. I'm frightened o' this country, Rachel, and frightened of the blacks. They can 'ave it, far as I'm concerned. It's theirs, isn't it? Give it back, I say. Melbourne is more my place. I'm used to towns, I want to live in towns.' She stopped, biting her lip. The tears threatened again, but she held them back. 'I 'ope he don't die,' she whispered, glancing at Rachel. 'He's a good man, is Cap'n Potter, and them sort are few and far between.'

'Mrs McCrae will do everything she can,' Rachel spoke the conventional words. While inside she was praying: Make him better, please make him better. Rachel and Suzy made tea and heated some mutton broth. They helped to lift Frank Potter's head, so that he could drink, and though he didn't wake up fully, he swallowed a little water and some of the broth. Mrs McCrae eyed the thin greasy stuff with disgust, and after a few spoonfuls herself, took the pot outside and heaved the lot onto the ground.

Suzy, pink with anger, opened her mouth on some choice words but one look from Mrs McCrae stopped her. 'Rachel,' the older woman said sternly, 'make some more broth please, and this time make it properly. You,' to Suzy, 'I have a marigold and yarrow salve to apply to the wounds. That should stop any more bleeding and help clean healing. Come and lift him, so that I can unwind the bandages.'

Suzy turned paler than ever beneath her dirt. 'Can't Rachel do that?' she muttered.

Mrs McCrae raised her grey eyebrows. 'Rachel is in no condition to be lifting a heavy man. Or are you blind as well?'

Suzy frowned, and looked at Rachel. 'Oh,' she said.

The wounds were inspected and new bandages applied, and by then Rachel had the broth simmering over the coals. Mrs McCrae had brought food of their own, and they sat and ate it. Then the older woman settled into a rugged looking chair and closed her eyes. Suzy wriggled herself over closer to Rachel and jerked her head at Rachel's stomach.

'It's true then?' she whispered loudly. 'I didn't believe it when I first 'eard. And then Cap'n Potter was shoutin' and makin' a fuss, threatenin' to whip Israel half to death . . . Israel, he just laughed.'

'I made a mistake,' Rachel replied stiffly.

Suzy snorted. 'Mistake all right! I thought I told you to watch out for him? He's a bad one, is Israel. He's like a dingo after lambs, sneakin' around, pretendin' he's harmless, and then pouncing. Only it's women with this dingo. Got women all around the place.'

Rachel's eyes widened at Suzy, but Suzy shook her head in disgust.

'Not me. I'm not interested in that sort. Seen enough of 'em in me time. I'm not sayin' he didn't try,' with an unconscious note of pride. 'But I told him straight: George is the one for me, and I know it now more 'an ever.' Suddenly another thought occurred to her, and she jabbed Rachel with a sharp elbow. 'What does Will say about all this? Must be pleased.'

'Will and I are not living together,' Rachel told her grudgingly, wishing she'd be quiet. 'He's here to do a job, and then he'll be going. It's just a coincidence.'

'Well, I'd say it was bad luck,' Suzy retorted, and laughed loudly.

Mrs McCrae opened an eye and glared, and after that everything was very quiet.

Frank Potter awoke at dusk, his blue eyes bright and unfocused with fever. His gaze slipped past Mrs McCrae, unrecognising, and moved on. 'Rachel?' he whispered, and there was such pleasure in his drawn face, she felt like weeping as she came forward to kneel beside him and take his hand in hers.

'We're here now,' Rachel's voice shook. 'Don't you worry about anything.'

The blue eyes warmed and then closed, but the smile remained, as if he had put his trust in her.

Mrs McCrae nodded to herself. 'It's always good when they wake up. Look, he's sleeping more normally now! I think we'll win this one back from the Lord, girls.'

Suzy choked on laughter.

However it seemed that Mrs McCrae was right. Throughout the night they kept the fever down by sponging him with tepid water, and although the canvas tent was set up outside, only Suzy slept. The broth was kept warm for Frank Potter to sip whenever he woke, to give him strength. By morning the fever had gone, and he was sleeping quite peacefully, still white and drawn, but mending.

Mrs McCrae announced she was exhausted and would take a nap, and tottered out into the dawn. Suzy yawned and snuggled closer to the hearth, cradling her head on her hand. If this was her idea of housekeeping, Rachel thought wryly, no wonder the place was in a mess.

'Rachel?'

Frank Potter's blue eyes were open again, and he was staring at her. She came and gave him her hand, squeezing it gently 'How are you feeling?'

'Odd,' he whispered. 'My head's stuffed with straw, like Victoria's doll.'

Rachel smiled. 'The children were so worried. You must come back with us to the Castle when you're well enough, so that we can look after you properly.'

He hesitated, as if debating whether or not to say something. 'Was I dreaming,' he asked at last, 'or was Will here yesterday?'

'You weren't dreaming.'

He searched her taut face. 'I wrote to him,' he said, and it was almost an apology. 'His friends, in Hobarton, knew where he was. I had his address.' His mouth twisted. 'He was only sixty or so miles from you, Rachel. I was afraid he would ride up one day and see . . . I felt responsible: Israel's my brother. I didn't want Will to find out like that.'

What about me? she thought angrily. Didn't my feelings matter? 'He's not the Will I married,' she said stonily. 'He's Will Moody.'

His hand tightened on hers. 'Forgive me?' he breathed, and he sounded so weak and strained, her heart melted.

'Of course.'

His eyes closed. Rachel sat there for a long time, his hand still in hers, gazing at his face without seeing it. Sixty miles from her, all this time. If only she had known, perhaps things might have been different. Or would they? She had been so set against him, so determined to shut out his memory. Perhaps only a hurt like the one Israel had dealt her could have made her realise the truth—and ironically, now she knew it, it was too late. But the fact remained, Will was the one she loved, and had loved all along. Her love for him had been there, even when she denied it. Indeed, it was so strong and unyielding, it took no account of Will's past. Rachel could not just snuff it out like a candle, it endured and had endured for the past three years, and before that, since the night by the river in Richmond when she first met him.

Mrs McCrae woke Suzy with a push of her boot, and when Suzy rose, grumbling, to make breakfast, Rachel staggered to the tent and collapsed on the bed. She was asleep instantly, neither the sunlight glinting through the flap, nor the sounds of the men and the animals about their daily business, making any impression. It was not until the shadow fell over her, blocking the low gleam of the late afternoon sun, that she woke. And even then she didn't open her eyes.

'She's sleeping.' Suzy's voice, half defiant, half frightened. 'What do you want with her anyhow?'

'She looked so still,' Will said in his soft drawl.

'She's bloody exhausted, that's all. It's no mean feat to come rattlin' up here when you're five months gone!'

Rachel flinched inside, imaging the look on Will's face. The silence drew on.

'Why are you back anyway?' Suzy went on, pushing her advantage.

Will sighed. 'We caught the two blacks. We were goin' to take them to the Police Post on the Goulburn, but we met up with a trooper from there doing his rounds, and I sent them back with him and two of my men. I wanted to see how Frank was.'

So he'd caught them. He was still the best, after all, thought Rachel. And then felt ashamed—Frank could have died. Will only wanted to see justice done, and in this case Rachel could not fault him.

'He's on the mend,' Suzy said proudly, as if she had done it all herself. 'The old biddy's in there with 'im.'

'Mrs McCrae?' he asked, amusement warming his voice. 'Don't let her hear you say that.'

'I'm not frightened o' her,' Suzy announced, and then spoilt it, when Mrs McCrae called out to her from the hut, by scuttling quickly away.

Will made a sound that could have been laughter. And then he looked at his wife again, where she lay just inside the canvas tent. She was so still, her breast hardly moving with each breath. The dark hair had come loose, tangled about her face. He remembered touching that hair, he remembered kissing the silken strands, and kissing that mouth and feeling the heat of her, as she cried out his name . . .

Will turned abruptly and walked away. Such memories were best forgotten. He had learnt that much. At first, he had been sure she would write to him through Benny and Zelda, that she would realise what her stubbornness had cost her. He had been prepared to wait, she meant that much to him. Leaving her had been like tearing himself in two, but it had been the only way. If he'd stayed they would have grown to hate each other, and he couldn't bear that. But as the months went on, and then the years, he had come to realise—and to accept—that she would never forgive him.

Perhaps it was just as well. He had moved onto a new life, a life he felt at ease in. And he was good at what he did, he was appreciated. In no time at all, he'd been promoted to sergeant. His commanders saw his honesty and determination, while his fellow troopers saw his toughness. After the first argument, they didn't dispute his right to give them orders. Will Moody, the word went around, meant what he said, but if you tried your best to please him, he'd treat you well. If you didn't . . . he could be a cold, mean bastard.

So, Will had concentrated on his job, putting away emotion, like childhood toys in a closed trunk. His life became a routine of rising, doing what was required of him, and sleeping, usually from sheer exhaustion. His quarters were bare apart from the essentials—they told nothing of Will, the man. Everything was just as he wanted it. He felt nothing, he thought of nothing, but his job. Will being Will, he didn't allow himself to.

Until Frank's letter.

Feeling had returned in an instant, negating all his effort, all his hard work. Rachel, his wife, was no more than a day's ride from him! And he wanted to make that ride, desperately. He ached with the need to go, instantly. And then he'd read on . . . It he been like a shot from his carbine, lodged in his chest. The bullet was still there, burning him, hurting him. Rachel had betrayed him for Israel Potter—a man he had despised on sight. And not only that, she was carrying his child. The feeling that knowledge gave him was indescribable. He'd still gone to McCrae's Castle when the chance came his way. He couldn't help it. However he went not as a husband seeking a beloved wife, but rather as a betrayed husband, full of rancor. And when he finally saw her, he could hardly bear to look at her, in case he might lose control and strike out with the bitter words building inside him. He wanted to hurt her. He wanted to take her white throat between his hands and twist until her dark eyes clouded over. That was why he had turned his back on her in the sitting room at McCrae's Castle, because the thought of losing his iron control shocked him. He hadn't realised he could hate her so much; that love could turn so dark.

And now, seeing her lying there, seeing his

Rachel, his wife . . . All the pain returned. The invisible bullet in his chest twisted again, excruciatingly. His wife . . . Only she wasn't his. She would never be his again. 'I'll never forgive her,' he said quietly to himself. 'Never.'

CHAPTER 21

FRANK POTTER WAS PROPPED UP for his supper, when Will came in to see him. Frank's blue eyes widened with pleased surprise, and then he was smiling broadly.

'Will!'

Will came to clasp his hand in his two big ones, frowning down at him. 'You look bloody bad, Frank.'

Frank laughed and then grimaced when it hurt his side. 'I'm better than I was, believe me,' he said with feeling.

Mrs McCrae smiled smugly. 'He'll mend.'

Will sat down beside the bed. At the hearth, Suzy and Rachel were preparing the meal, making the best of the supplies to feed the extra mouths.

Someone outside was playing a tin whistle, the sound competing with voices laughing and talking. It was another world from McCrae's Castle, more primitive by far. Rachel could suddenly understand Suzy's unhappiness—she must have felt like she was all alone in the world.

'You caught the men responsible?' Mrs McCrae

demanded.

Will nodded. 'I did. They were warriors from the Campaspe Paver tribe, different to the Aborigines around here. We've 'ad trouble like this before. A few of them decide they'll make a raid on Djadjawurrung territory, for whatever reason, and travel fast, strike their mark, and go home. The Djadjawurrung get blamed.'

'Do you think Mr Redcliffe's murderers were the same men?'

'No.'

'Then you believe it was Big Mary's husband?'

Will paused. Mrs McCrae beckoned Rachel over to continue feeding Frank Potter. She came reluctantly to join their little group, in time to hear Will's quiet answer.

'There's a problem.'

A frown crinkled Frank's brow. 'What sort of problem?'

'I've found no signs of blacks on Redcliffe's run. I don't think there were any.'

Rachel searched Will's profile, wondering if he was serious, wondering what he meant. Mrs McCrae was more direct. 'He could hardly have speared himself!' she cried, and made as if to laugh.

Will glanced at her, and the smile died. 'There haven't been any blacks on Redcliffe's run in the last two weeks. The shepherds said they hadn't seen any for at least that long, and then it was a tribe they knew well, passing through to new hunting grounds.'

'But he was speared,' Mrs McCrae retorted. 'Who could have done it?'

Will rubbed his fingers across his eyes, as though

he were too tired to think straight. Rachel took up the broth and, with a strained smile at Frank Potter, began to feed him.

'I've wondered that myself,' Will said at last. 'The shepherds, I thought—but they were out on the run at the time. I suppose they could be lying, but I have a nose for liars, and I believe them. They said that Mrs Redcliffe sent them out. Plainly, it was Mrs Redcliffe who ran the place—her husband was only interested in drinkin' grog.'

'Someone passing through?' murmured Frank.

Will nodded. 'It happens. They might have thought Redcliffe had somethin' to steal. But why use a spear? Why not a gun or a knife? More likely. A spear makes you think of blacks. And I'm beginnin' to believe we were meant to think of blacks.'

'Greta?' Mrs McCrae asked with a narrowed look. 'Is that who you think it was? We only have her word that Redcliffe told her to run away. Only her word for everything.'

He hesitated, and now his eyes shifted to Frank, who was listening avidly to the conversation. Suddenly Rachel understood. Shock held her hand frozen over the bowl, and she drew in her breath with a soft, sharp hiss. Will looked up quickly and met her eyes. What did he see there? Horror at the thought of Israel murdering Redcliffe? For that was what Will was thinking. Rachel knew it and, knowing, could not hide her sick revulsion.

He shook his head ever so slightly, warning her not to speak. 'It'd be wrong of me to accuse Greta Redcliffe or anyone else, without proof,' he said coolly, but he was still looking at Rachel. 'I've no clear evidence. I've nothing. All I can do is write my report.'

Mrs McCrae looked unhappy, but Rachel couldn't decide whether this was because she didn't agree with him, or she did. Forcing her hand to steady, she continued to feed Frank, ignoring Will getting to his feet, ignoring Suzy stomping resentfully out into the night with the food for the men. She was only amazed she could be so calm about it. *Which only goes to show,* she told herself evenly, *how little you ever loved Israel Potter.*

Frank was still very weak; even the act of eating exhausted him. He soon slipped into sleep again. Gradually the rest of the camp settled down to sleep, too. Mrs McCrae said she would watch the sick man for an hour or two, and then Rachel could take over. 'I don't think we'll have any problems, but best to be on the safe side.'

Rachel agreed, and leaving Suzy curled in the same spot by the hearth, stepped out into the fresh air. It was sharp and cool after the stuffy warmth of the hut. Rachel stretched to relieve the ache in her back, lifting her face to the black sky—a vast dome of stars—and gazed up in wonder. How could people do such base things in such a beautiful place? They belittled it by their actions. Suddenly she understood something about Will she had never really understood before. It must be very satisfying to bring such people to justice.

'Rachel?'

She spun around, peering towards the group of men by the fire a few yards away. One of them was scrambling to his feet—a stocky, bearded man in canvas trousers and a check shirt. For a moment Rachel failed to recognise him, and then something about his smile and his eyes clicked in her mind. Her face split into a broad smile as George gripped her hands.

'George!' she cried, and then laughed when he bent and kissed her cheek. He too was thinner, with a beard covering half his face.

'We're goin' back to Melbourne, Suzy and me. This has been the last straw for us.'

'I know.'

He hesitated, and then burst out with, 'Come with us! We'd welcome you, Rachel. This isn't the life for a woman.'

Rachel wondered whether Suzy would welcome her as eagerly as George seemed to think. Briefly, she allowed herself the luxury of imagining life back in Melbourne, busy in the busy town, among people again. She could leave Mrs McCrae, who was beginning to find her presence an embarrassment, and she would never have to face Israel again . . . Or Will. She could leave him behind and make a new life with Bella and the baby 'I'll think about it,' she replied, and reached out to squeeze his arm. 'It's so good to see you, George.'

His teeth shone white through the beard.

She hesitated, and then asked stiffly, 'Did you see where Will went?'

He nodded towards the yards, and peering into the darkness Rachel saw a man silhouetted against the rails. 'Will's not one to say much,' George murmured. 'Never was. But he's hurtin', Rachel.'

She didn't want to hear that. Will's pain was beyond her ability to heal. 'He's not the same,' she said expressionlessly.

'He's the same,' George retorted. 'It's you that's

different.'

There was nothing more to say. George turned back to the fire, finding his place among the circle of men.

Slowly, Rachel made her way down the slope towards Will. The ground was rough, and she picked her way carefully. A nightbird cried out in the valley below, but otherwise the trees were still and silent. The land at Nerinbilly was different to the Castle, with rounded rolling hills and valleys, and less rocky outcrops and less water. But at night, under the stars, it was just as vast and beautiful.

Will must have heard her, but he didn't turn. He didn't seem to need to. He was leaning against the yard rails, arms folded on top of one of the posts, gazing out over the dark land. Was George right? Was he the same? Rachel shook her head. How could he be? They had both changed. Time and experience had altered them in so many ways. Will was Sergeant Moody now, and she was the less-than-respectable Mrs Trigg. George was just trying to play matchmaker again, and not doing a very good job of it.

Will spoke quietly as she hesitated a few steps behind him. 'The whites are afraid of the dark. They think the blacks are out there, waitin' to spear them. And sometimes they are. But usually the blacks are just as afraid of the dark as the whites. Too many spirits.' His voice dropped even lower, and for a moment Rachel was back by the river at Richmond. 'I like the dark. It suits me. It wraps around me; I'm safe in it.'

'Safe?' she whispered. From what? Oh, Will, Will.
. .

'The darkness strips a man down,' he said at last. 'Until all that's left is the core of him. The hunter . . . the savage. The killer.'

'You're no killer,' Rachel breathed, but her skin was tingling.

He turned and looked at her, his face a shadow, unreadable. 'No?' Who did he mock? Her or himself? 'What do you want, Rachel?'

She had forgotten what she had come for. And then the voices up at the campfire intruded, bringing the present back into sharp focus. Rachel forced her mind to concentrate, pushing the words out.

'You think it was Israel, don't you?'

He didn't deny it. 'I've no proof.'

'But you think it was.'

He said nothing, and she dared to step closer, gripping the railing beside him. She looked sideways at his profile, set dark against the stars, and tried to read his mind. It was impossible, just as it had always been.

'I have no reason to like Israel,' Rachel said quietly. 'But I think you're wrong. He's weak, yes, and sometimes cruel. But I can't see him killing Redcliffe, even if he and Greta are lovers. No woman would be worth risking his freedom for.'

Will was silent. Condemning me, Rachel thought angrily, because I won't blame Israel for a crime I'm sure he didn't commit. I just can't do it, no matter how much I hate him. 'Why don't you arrest him?' her voice was sharp.

He looked at her now, and she saw the gleam of his eyes. 'I'll tell you what I have. I have hearsay, talk, rumour . . .' He shrugged. 'There was a station hand workin' for Redcliffe a few months ago. Redcliffe tried to kill him, because Greta and the man were lovers. And then I hear that Greta asked this man a favour. "Kill my husband", she said. But Greta says that's a lie, and where's the man anyway? Long gone. Still I can't help but wonder if she didn't say the same to Israel Potter, and unlike the station hand, Israel agreed. But I've no proof, and if I tried to make a case, Israel'd claim I was biased against him for reasons I don't need to explain to you.'

There was no answer to that. Rachel knew such a thing must grate on him, and make him hate her more than ever. She wished Israel was guilty, she really did! Instead her sense of fairness would not allow her emotions to rule her.

Will went on with cool logic. 'Redcliffe's murder wasn't a spur of the moment thing—it's just meant to look like that. Blame the blacks—why not? No one cares enough to look further than the spear and all that it means to us whites. Send the troopers out to shoot a few blacks, and we're even again.'

'Are you sure it wasn't Big Mary's husband?' Rachel managed, clearing her throat. 'Are you sure you're not biased?'

He was quiet a long time, and she was glad of the darkness which hid her face, but it had had to be said.

'I'm not sure of anythin',' Will said at last. 'Except that I don't want Frank worried. He's got enough to go on with at the moment.'

He looked at her sharply, and she nodded.

Then, when he didn't seem about to speak again, 'You'll be leaving now I suppose?'

'Yes.' He paused. 'Do you mind if I see Bella

on the way through?' It was said in a rush, as if he expected her to refuse. A sudden fear gripped Rachel, and then she told herself not to be foolish. He had a right to see his daughter, and it was likely he would never see her again. She could say yes, she could be generous.

'All right. But . . . she doesn't know you're her father. I think sometimes she's so used to being with the Potter children, she almost believes Frank is her father. Leave it that way.'

'Of course,' he said coldly. And again, he looked out at the dark trees, as if his thoughts were far away, beyond her reach. Suddenly, she knew that George was right. Will was hurting. But he would never admit it, and he would not let Rachel help him, not this time.

There was nothing more to say. It really was the end. Rachel nodded again, although he wasn't looking at her. 'Goodnight, Will.' She managed to sound calm—he could not tell she was crying.

'Goodnight.' It was dismissal.

Rachel made her way back up the slope. Her feet stumbled once on the rough ground, the tears blinding her. Long ago she had run across the grass, turning to stare at a tall man on a dark horse. She had promised herself then that she would meet him again, that she would find him no matter what. Well she had found him, for a time. But he was lost to her again now, and the way ahead was darker than ever. She could not see her path any-more, and her heart was aching just as that young girl's had ached.

When Rachel rose at midnight and went to take her turn at watching Frank Potter, she received another shock.

Israel was there, lounging against the hearth, while Suzy eyed him resentfully, and Mrs McCrae sipped tea from a mug. His eyes raked over Rachel's body, a glint in them she recognised. Israel was bent on mischief. Rachel straightened her spine instinctively, and moved to look down at Frank. He was asleep, but some of the colour had returned to his cheeks and he was breathing deep and slow.

'He's been asleep all the time,' Mrs McCrae said, breaking the awkward silence. 'I've some broth warm on the side of the hearth there, if he wakes.' She put down her mug and stood up stiffly. 'Well, I think I'll take my rest now, Rachel.' She nodded at Israel, and closed the door behind her.

Rachel sat down carefully in the spot Mrs McCrae had vacated. Israel was still watching her; she felt it but she wouldn't say anything. She never spoke to him these days unless she had to, and now she had even more reason not to speak. He knew she hated him, and sometimes it amused him to bring the colour flooding to her face. At others it pleased him just as much to ignore her.

'Want some tea, Rachel?' Suzy asked, giving Israel a dark look.

'Thank you.' She took the mug gratefully, sipping the hot black liquid.

Israel watched her drink. She looked tired, and her hair was uncombed, tangling untidily about her face. He'd caught himself, sometimes, thinking of her, wondering about her, but mostly his time was taken up with Greta. Greta was a puzzle to him. Just when he thought he had conquered her completely, she would suddenly change, become all soft and loving, or hard as flint. He was being tested as he had never been tested before, and he was beginning to wonder if in Greta he had at last found his match.

'Suzy here tells me the good sergeant is known to you, Rachel.'

Rachel's head lifted sharply at the sound of his voice. Israel's eyes were very blue, watching her, mocking her with his knowledge. Rachel shot an accusing look at Suzy, who pretended not to notice.

'Very well known to you, in fact,' he added, smiling. 'She seems to think I'd better watch my step as she put it so quaintly, or he might teach me a lesson. Was that it, Suzy?'

Suzy screwed up her face.

'Just as well you and the surly George are leaving, Suzy. Otherwise, I might have to throw you out.'

'There's one thing we won't miss round here, that's for sure,' Suzy muttered.

Israel only laughed. Rachel finished her tea, her eyes fixed on Frank Potter. She could feel Israel still watching her, biding his time, and her heart beat uncomfortably fast. 'How's my son, Rachel?' he asked and reached out a hand, as if to touch her. She slapped his hand away, her eyes blazing. He laughed again; he was enjoying himself. 'Oh Rachel,' he mocked softly, 'you weren't always so fierce. There are times I could remind you of, if I

KAYE DOBBIE

weren't a gentleman, when you wanted my hands on you. When you said you loved me. Have you forgotten?'

'Israel!'

Frank's voice was husky from sleep, but there was no mistaking the note in it. He glared at his brother, his eyes bright with anger.

At once Israel was contrite, shrugging apologetically before Frank's accusing look. 'How are you feeling?' he asked, moving closer. 'Hazelwood sent a messenger after me, and I came as soon as I could. The black bastards. I'll show them a thing or two, don't worry about that!'

Frank moved his head slightly. 'Will's already caught the men who did it. They're on their way to the Goulburn Police Post.'

But Israel flicked his hand in a dismissive movement. 'What'll that teach them? That we're soft. That we're too frightened to show them who's boss. One of the men tells me you gave some of the blacks food that morning, and that they headed west. I'll ride after them at dawn.'

Frank watched him a moment, as though gauging his mood. He felt so weak, too weak to get up and shake his brother as he used to when Israel was a child. Brute force was the only thing that had ever had any effect on Israel, anything else he treated as a joke.

'The tribe I gave food to were friendly,' he tried again, wearily. 'They were old men, women and children, Israel, not warriors. They gave us no trouble.'

'They're all in it,' Israel snapped impatiently. 'Hazelwood reckons the blacks all know what's going on. They could have warned you, if they'd wanted to. Instead they just crept away and left you to be killed—or so they hoped! I've been too kind for too long. It's time I showed them who's boss in this country.'

'If you really feel that way,' Frank whispered, 'tell Will. . . write to La Trobe . . . get them to take some action.'

Israel shook his head stubbornly. 'I don't need anyone else to do my job for me. I'm king here, Frank, remember?'

'Israel,' Frank muttered in a fading voice, but his eyelids were fluttering. Rachel watched, appalled, as they finally closed.

'Shoot one for me,' Suzy said savagely, curling up with her back to them.

Rachel reached out and touched Frank's brow. It was cool. She should have fed him some broth, she thought guiltily, instead of sitting here, listening to them argue.

'Frank tells me you won't be coming to Nerinbilly after all,' Israel went on, his voice lowered so that Suzy couldn't hear. 'It's probably best, Rachel. Things could get awkward. What if I took a wife? She might not want my past mistakes staring her in the face.'

Her eyes flared, and he watched appreciatively as anger took hold. 'Past mistakes?' Rachel whispered furiously. 'If anyone made a mistake it was me when I thought I could trust you.'

'Be fair now, Rachel. I warned you, remember? But you didn't take any notice.'

'You lied to me!'

'Did I? Well, maybe, but it was what you wanted

to hear.'

She was too angry to answer. Suddenly she wondered if Will was right, and she was wrong, and Israel had killed Redcliffe. He seemed to have no morals, none of the inbuilt limits of ordinary men. He did what he wanted to do, and thought he was above punishment—Israel truly believed he was king in his own country.

'Will won't let you go after those people,' she said, anger overriding better judgement. 'They had nothing to do with the attack on Frank. He'll stop you— Will's dealt with worse than you.'

Israel's blue eyes fixed on her, and although she held them, her heart gave a frightened thump. 'No-one tells me what to do on Nerinbilly. Not even the good sergeant,' he said softly, amiably. But there was something in his gaze, a glitter of fury, that was at odds with his voice. He smiled, gently, but his eyes remained hard. 'I expected a little more loyalty from you, after all we meant to each other. You won't tell him now, will you Rachel? I don't like hurting women. Women were made for loving, not hurting . . .'

Slowly she shook her head. Her gaze was pinned to his, and she understood a little of how Bella must have felt when the brown snake slithered towards her. Terrified, and yet mesmerized. He looked away, and her shoulders slumped. A few deep breaths seemed to help, but she didn't make the mistake of looking his way again.

'You don't have to worry,' she said in a husky voice. 'I don't want any more trouble. I have enough already.'

He laughed. 'I'll give you something towards the

baby,' he told her offhandedly. 'I always meant to. But you see, Rachel, I can't show you any favouritism, now can I?'

She shivered, her eyes fixed on Frank's peaceful face. Did he believe what he was saying? Did he expect her to? 'So not a word to Sergeant Moody, eh?' His finger brushed her arm, making her jump, and then he rose to his feet. 'Goodnight, Rachel.' The door closed softly behind him.

Suzy's voice drifted over from the hearth. 'That man's a shit.'

Rachel was dozing when Mrs McCrae returned to the hut. 'Go to bed, Rachel!' she commanded, and shooed her out into the still darkness. The smell of smoke hung in the air, stinging her nostrils. The men were sleeping in their blankets around the smouldering remains of the fire—apart from the one on watch. He turned silently to look at her, before resuming his boring assignment. Rachel hesitated and then slowly, picking her way, crossed to him. 'Please,' she whispered, 'where is Sergeant Moody?' The man looked at her consideringly, his glance moving pointedly over her figure. He hesitated, about to tell her to take herself to bed, and then changed his mind. There wasn't much a woman in her condition could get up to, was there? And who knew with Will Moody—he might want to see the girl. There had been talk that this one was known to him, though no-one had dared ask.

The watch pointed her towards the barn further down the slope. 'The Sergeant likes his own company,' he said, a sly edge to his voice. 'Better call out your name at the door,' he added, 'or you're like to have a bullet through your pretty head.'

Rachel nodded and moved away towards her tent. Her steps slowed again, until eventually she stopped. It was no use. How could she let Israel ride off at dawn tomorrow, knowing what he was going to do? How could she not do something to stop him, despite his threats? He had said Rachel owed him loyalty—Rachel knew she owed him nothing. Women and children, Frank had said. How would she feel, if one of those children was Bella?

Hesitating, longing for someone to tell her what to do, Rachel glanced behind her, towards the watch, and found he had disappeared. Probably gone to relieve himself or to have a smoke. No help there then.

She looked towards the barn.

The bulk of it loomed dark against the stars. The moon had risen while she was in the hut and now hung, a suspended crescent, over the bark roof. All was silent, apart from the occasional bleating of a sheep, or wicker of a horse and, further away in the valley, the howl of a wild dog. The choice was hers alone, and Rachel knew that she had already made it.

As Rachel walked towards the barn, she tried to think of what she would say. Her mind was blank. She was tired, that was all. When she returned to the Castle, she would crawl into bed and sleep and sleep . . . She drew a deep breath. Will would know what to do. That was one thing about Will, he always did. She was almost there and suddenly the shadow of the barn wall fell over her, dark where the moonlight did not reach. There was a damp chill here and she put her arms around herself, shivering. Some sixth sense warned her, shrieking silently in her head. Her steps slowed again, hesitating, and she half turned.

He came at her so quickly she had no defence. One arm snaked around her waist, the other about her head. His hand closed over her mouth and nose, cutting off all chance of screaming . . . and breathing. She knew him before he spoke, and her body went rigid with terror.

'You bitch! I trusted you.'

Israel's voice was low and furious; he *had* trusted her. Rachel had never lied to him. . . until now. Now, when she'd made a choice between Israel and Will Moody. His grip was so hard Rachel couldn't breathe. She struggled, trying to free the arms he held pinned to her sides, but he was too strong. There was a roaring in her ears, like the flapping of a thousand wings. Rachel twisted her head, trying to bite him, and managed to get her teeth into the soft flesh between his finger and thumb. Blood flooded into her mouth, but some of it was her own, where he had mashed her lips against her teeth.

Israel's breath hissed, and he swung her closer in against the barn, into the thicker darkness. Her shoe struck the wall with a faint thud. And then he threw her down to the ground. She drew an agonised breath, but before she could move, he was on top of her, pressing down with all his weight. Her head was spinning. She felt the baby moving—perhaps sensing her own terror, or perhaps crushed by Israel's weight.

Her body was soft and warm, just as always. Suddenly Israel wanted her; the need flooded him in a great, black, mindless tide.

'You won't tell him, will you, Rachel,' he hissed into her ear.

The hand he had been using to hold her arms moved up, closing over her breast. She opened her mouth to scream, but instantly his mouth was on hers, cutting off any sound in a suffocating kiss.

Rachel fought to free her own hands. Scratching at him. She felt the flesh on his arm tear, and he yelped, slackening his grip. 'Let me go,' she moaned, trying to roll him off. They grappled together. He was so strong. His weight was crushing her. She couldn't breathe! The wings were back, flapping all around her, brushing her cheeks, her eyelids. Angel's wings, she thought light headedly, come to take her to heaven. One shoe had come off and she felt the damp earth between her stockinged toes. A cold, chill damp that seemed to soak into her very bones. 'You know you want me,' he whispered, his mouth hot on her neck, his hands pressing and probing. 'How long has it been, Rachel? How long?'

'No!' and she lifted her fists to strike him, only to have him grasp her wrists and stretch her arms above her head. Like a sacrifice. He bent towards her, enjoying her struggles, and she felt her strength ebbing. And then in the instant she knew he had won, she sensed that there was someone else standing over them. A strong hand fastened on Israel's shoulder. 'Let her go,' Will said in a voice as cold as winter rain.

Israel froze and then snarled, 'Get your hands off me.'

Will gripped harder, dragging him to his feet, leaving Rachel free at last. She took a deep breath, trying to clear her head. The two men stood close together for a moment—Rachel saw that Will wore only his breeches—and then Israel pulled furiously away. 'Get back to your bed,' Will said it quietly, but it was an order.

'You're not in charge here!' Israel was angrier than Rachel had ever seen him. 'This is my place and what goes on here is none of your business!'

'Isn't it?' Will asked softly.

Israel opened his mouth to retort, and then suddenly understanding what Will meant, laughed. 'Well, if you don't want your wife looking elsewhere, you shouldn't go off and leave her on her own, should you? She wanted it and I was just obliging her. Go on, why don't you ask her?'

Rachel felt sickness curdling inside her, and swallowed hard.

'I intend to,' Will replied savagely

Israel laughed again, his teeth white in the darkness, enjoying the feelings he was stirring in the other man. 'You're jealous,' he sneered. 'That's what it is. You're jealous because she chose me over you. Because when she needed a man, I was it.' Will lunged at Israel and grabbed him by the front of his shirt. He lifted him up into the air, his feet dangling, and shook him hard. Rachel screamed, for it seemed as if Will meant to kill him. And then he simply dropped him, sprawling, onto the ground. Rachel heard the air go out of Israel's lungs, and the great gasp as he tried to draw a breath.

The thud of footsteps, and the watch reached them, alerted by Rachel's scream. The man gabbled out apologies and questions at the same time.

'Get your sergeant off me.' Israel had got his breath back, but his voice sounded thick and strange. He managed to stagger to his feet and stood, swaying slightly, clasping and unclasping his fists.

The watch eyed Will uneasily. 'Sir?'

'Tie him up and guard him,' Will said shortly.

'You've no right to do this!' Israel shouted. 'You're jealous—

But Will had had enough. He took a purposeful step towards Israel. Israel stumbled backwards, almost falling over in his haste. 'Shut your mouth,' Will said through gritted teeth.

Israel was breathing hard. Rachel could almost see his mind turning over, seeking the weak point. 'Or what?' he sneered.

Will had turned to the watch to give his orders.

'You should be thanking me,' Israel added, goading the other man, as though he sensed his power over him, as though he wanted to see how far he could push him. 'She's probably learned a few new tricks you'll enjoy—

Will swung around without a word. He struck Israel, a hard blow to the jaw, and then another. Israel's head jerked upward. Rachel saw the spurt of blood from his nose. And then Will caught him up in both hands, swinging him off the ground, and threw him against the barn wall with a resounding crash. Israel slid, as limp as a doll, to the ground and lay there, silent.

Rachel stared at him, feeling dazed and sick, and

then looked at Will. He was rubbing his knuckles. The watch gave him a half nervous, half admiring stare.

'Was that a good idea, sir?' he whispered.

'Probably not, but it felt bloody good.'

There were others coming now, drawn by the noise of the fight. Voices filled the darkness as the camp roused. Rachel saw lamplight spilling from the hut as the door was flung open. The watch had begun hauling Israel to his feet. Will turned to Rachel, and bent over her where she sat, his face close to hers. She gazed back into the dark hollows of his eyes.

'What was it about? Quick before they come.'

She told him, the words falling over each other, finishing with, 'He told me not to tell, but I was going to. I was coming to wake you. He must have been waiting—' Her breath sucked in, and for a moment she thought she would never get the final words out.

His hands closed, warm, either side of her face, giving her courage.

'I think he meant to rape me.'

His hands dropped away. In disgust? Rachel asked herself, forcing back tears. Surely he could not have believed what Israel said? And then they were surrounded, and Will was giving orders for Israel to be locked in the store and watched. He shook his head at the questions, telling the others to go back to bed, just as he intended to.

Embarrassed, Rachel tried to stand up, but her legs wouldn't hold her and she sat down again. Will made an impatient sound. Brushing aside the others, he caught her up in his arms. A moment later he was striding quickly towards the hut, where they could see Mrs McCrae and Suzy framed in the doorway.

'Are you all right?' he asked her.

She nodded, too nervous of him to speak. She felt awful, but she wasn't going to tell him that. He might have saved her questionable honour, but it meant nothing, was nothing more than he would have done for any other woman in distress. It was his job, after all. She remembered how he had spoken to Greta, in the same gentle way he had spoken to her. It meant nothing . . . less than nothing. Suddenly she felt very, very weary.

'I'm sorry,' she whispered.

Will looked down at her, and something in his eyes shifted. For the first time, as they drew close to the lamplight from the hut, he saw her properly. Her face was scratched and bruised, her cut lip already swelling. Will felt a great surge of anger.

'No,' he said, his voice flat. 'It's me who's sorry, darlin'. I should have broken his neck for you, while I had the chance.'

CHAPTER 22

MRS MCCRAE CLEANED AND DRESSED Rachel's wounds with tender care, and when she had finished Rachel didn't look quite as bad. Of course, her lip was still swollen, and there were the bruises and scratches. As for the baby, only time would tell. Rachel was shaking so badly she had to be helped to hold the mug of rum-laced tea Suzy brewed her.

Suzy was furious.

'That man's an animal,' she muttered, hazel eyes darting fire. 'I hope Will 'angs him.'

Mrs McCrae thought this was somewhat extreme and said so. 'I should think a reprimand from Sergeant Moody would be sufficient,' she added thoughtfully. 'Rachel would not wish to make a fuss about this, I'm sure. Embarrassing, Rachel, to have to go into court and explain to everyone what happened. The magistrate could be forgiven for believing it was just another case of a jealous husband . . .' and her eyebrows lifted slightly, mean-ingfully.

Rachel knew she was right. How could she tell a

magistrate and a court full of people about Will and Israel? They would never believe it was attempted rape, they would think she was lying, frightened of Will's anger. Will would look like a fool. She would rather just leave it. Frank would keep Israel in line now. He had roared like a bull when he saw Rachel and was told what his brother had done. And, if it hadn't been for Mrs McCrae holding him down, he would have gotten up then and there and given his brother a thrashing.

'Captain Potter will be well enough for us to leave in a day or two,' Mrs McCrae said—Frank had decided he would remain at Nerinbilly, despite the women's protestations. 'Someone has to keep an eye on my brother,' he said forbiddingly.

But all that meant nothing to Rachel. Because Will had gone. He had left at daybreak that morning, and she would probably never see him again.

He had spoken to her briefly, in the corner of the hut, while Mrs McCrae and Suzy moved away, and pretended not to hear.

'Frank'll take care of Israel,' he said quietly. 'You could bring charges if you wanted. You know I'd back you up.'

Rachel shook her head violently. Her face was so white that the marks on it stood out even redder and angrier. He didn't blame her for baulking at that. It was Israel's word against hers and he knew who would likely win. All the same, Will thought with grim satisfaction, Israel had been punished. His face was bruised and swollen, and he had a thundering headache. No, he wouldn't soon forget his lesson, and if he stepped out of line again, Will was quite happy to give him another.

'Well, it's up to you,' he went on aloud.

Rachel took a breath. 'Thank you . . . I mean, for what you did. For saving me.'

Will avoided her eyes. 'It's my job,' he replied stiffly. And then, visibly relaxing, 'I forgot to tell you. When I met up with the troopers from the Goulburn River they were talkin' about the Turners, over at Wattle Bank. You know them?'

Rachel nodded and looked up blankly, wondering at the change of subject.

His smile twisted. 'There's a woman stayin' there, a friend of Mrs Turner. From Sydney. Name of Mrs Hymbury. Mary Hymbury.'

Rachel just stared.

He went on matter-of-factly, giving her time to take it in. 'This woman's a widow, her husband was someone important they thought. They didn't know anything more . . . Oh, one thing else. She's a blonde, and a 'looka', according to one of the men, even if she is gettin' a bit long in the tooth.'

'It can't be her, can it?' Rachel breathed. 'Not after all this time?'

He shrugged, but he was watching her, the smile still playing around his mouth. 'Write to her,' he suggested. 'She no longer has a husband to tell her what to do. She might want to see you, Rachel.'

The idea of it was so overwhelming—her own mother!—that Rachel hardly dared believe it. Her eyes were shining as she looked up at him. At least, Will told himself, I've given her one worthwhile thing, out of all the bad. A goodbye present.

'I will write to her,' she told him. 'As soon as I get back to the Castle.'

He nodded. 'Good.' He had said everything now.

'I have to go.'

Disappointment stung her. What had she hoped for? Some word, some sign that he loved her still? After last night, when he called her "darling", she had thought . . . But, of course, she had forgotten all that lay between them. Will wouldn't forget, and Will would never forgive. Besides he had a new life and a new career to pursue. He may even have a new woman.

The idea hit on nerves already raw. Rachel looked at her hands. She and Will had come a long way since the days of Greengage. Too far. There was no going back. And now they seemed to have so little in common in their lives, so few threads to draw together to make a whole. Bella, perhaps? But Bella was a stranger to Will—he would not take on Rachel and her problems for one small girl. Why should he?

'Take care,' she whispered, and suddenly reached up, wrapping her arms around his neck in a brief, hard hug. It was only for an instant, and then she had turned her back and he straightened to his full height, and walked away.

She had heard him speak to Frank, but not what was said. The door closed. Outside, the troopers were all ready to go. She could hear the stamp of horses' hooves and voices murmuring. Someone laughed. And then they were off, pounding past the hut and down the sweep of the valley, towards the track to Melbourne.

Now, she thought, he's gone and I can cry, but the tears wouldn't come. She was so numb inside, she couldn't even cry. Had it taken her so long to realise the terrible mistake she'd made, that day she let him leave her in Greengage? She should have accepted him for what he was, but she had been young and full of the importance of her own opinions. And now she was older and, just as he had told her then, with time had come wisdom. Only she had left it too late, and Will would no longer welcome her love and acceptance. He didn't need her, that was the irony of it. She needed him and Will didn't need her.

A hand slipped into hers, and Rachel squeezed it gratefully. 'You have a rest,' Suzy said gruffly. 'No use thinkin' about it now.' And after a time, she slept.

The Castle was the same. Only Rachel was different. She hugged Bella's warm little body to her own, the sense of love and relief washing over her. She still had Bella, whatever else she had lost.

The other children were full of questions, and Matty burst into tears when she found her father wasn't with them. Rachel promised he would be coming to visit soon, and that he was well now, and thinking of them all. Sarah too was full of sympathetic questions, and her blue eyes seemed a little hurt at Rachel's evasiveness.

'Mrs McCrae said you've got to take things easy.'

'I'm all right.' The tiredness, and the weakness had persisted, but Rachel ignored them. They would pass with time. It was the memories she found difficult to ignore. They came in the night, keeping her from sleep, and when she did sleep it was to dream of the dark barn against the stars.

'Will came through on his way back to Mount Macedon,' Sarah was saying, moving closer. 'He took Bella up on his horse. She thought she was a princess, Rachel. You should have seen them!'

Rachel smiled mechanically.

'He said that next time he was passin' he'd drop in.'

He could put himself out for Bella, evidently, thought Rachel. And then was ashamed. Was she jealous? Of her own daughter?

'He's movin', did you know?' Sarah went on, her eyes sharp. 'The sergeant in charge of the Goulburn River Post is leavin' in a few weeks, and they've given the job to Will. It's a sort of step up, he said. Shows they think a lot of him, don't it?'

Rachel said nothing. She had been right then. Will's career meant everything to him now. And what did it matter, Mt Macedon or the Goulburn? Both may as well be the moon.

Greta was no longer at the Castle. She had moved back to Redcliffe's as soon as the troopers had gone. The two shepherds were still there, and as she had run the station before, no doubt she planned to again. Mrs McCrae seemed relieved she had gone. Later, Sarah heard that Israel was still a regular visitor to Redcliffe's, to the extent that it was suggested he was 'courting' her.

'Well, I don't envy her,' Sarah commented viciously.

Rachel had written to Mary Hymbury. A brief, anxious note, stating Rachel's name and the events of her birth, and asking whether Mary knew something of it. Once the letter had gone, she could only wait for a reply . . . if there was one. It was such a long time ago, and Mary, if she was Rachel's mother, may well prefer the scandal forgotten.

As the weeks dragged by, life returned to normal, but the joy had gone out of it for Rachel. If the affair with Israel had changed her, his assault and Will's coldness had completed the transformation. The bright eyed, open and eager girl, whose future Mrs Finn hoped would be so sunny, was no more. Life had hurt her badly. Something in Rachel was damaged almost beyond repair.

Suzy and George came through, with Frank Potter, and stayed at the Castle. He was a little stiff in his movements—his leg still ached he admitted—but otherwise well. The children ran for their hugs, and he swooped them up, laughing. 'I have some news,' he told Rachel. 'Israel's suddenly keen to have the home station finished. He's working like a demon. So the children can come to Nerinbilly!'

Sarah, behind him, grimaced at the thought of her fate, but the children were overjoyed.

It turned out that Israel was planning to marry Greta Redcliffe, although she hadn't accepted him yet. Once they were married, Israel could run Redcliffe's as another outstation from Nerinbilly.

Frank Potter had visited her and, typically, been charmed by her modesty. 'I know that Will suspected Greta may have been involved in her husband's death, but I can't accept that. Not now that I know her better,' he'd said. Rachel wondered how he could be so blind, but she comforted herself with the thought that, even if Israel did marry Greta, Sarah and Thomas would be there for the children. She sighed. They had been like a family for so long! It would be hard to see them go. Especially when she couldn't go with them—Frank Potter didn't even mention that possibility any more.

Suzy and George were determined on their Melbourne venture. Frank Potter had written them some letters of introduction to people he thought might help.

Sarah had been as shocked as Rachel by Suzy's altered appearance. Nerinbilly had destroyed what little pioneering spirit she had and she had no intention of ever going back. Since Suzy's arrival at the Castle, Sarah had insisted she have a bath and washed her hair, and constantly offered her food. Suzy didn't complain, soaking up such unaccustomed attention like a sponge.

'I can't believe it,' Suzy breathed now, sitting in the kitchen with Sarah and Rachel. 'Just like old times, isn't it?'

Sarah and Rachel exchanged a glance.

Suzy hesitated, looking at Rachel, and then burst out with, 'I've news, too. We'll be havin' an addition soon. A Young George for Young George!"

Sarah laughed. 'So it wasn't all hard work and misery?'

'Bloody Israel told me not to waste candles, and there was nothin' else to do at the outstation when the sun went down.'

'I'm so glad for you,' Rachel's smile was genuine enough, and yet ... She was different in a way Suzy couldn't pinpoint. Rachel, always so friendly and open, had withdrawn into herself—like a tortoise, Suzy thought wryly. And her shell was just as hard to crack!

Suzy leaned forward over the table, dropping her voice. 'Will wrote to Captain Potter when he arrived at the Goulburn Post. He mentioned someone. A woman called Maeve. She runs the inn there.'

The hurt was instantaneous, but Rachel didn't let them see it. 'It's nothing to do with me.'

Suzy made a sound of disgust. 'You're a bloody fool, that's what I think. You should go up there. Don't let 'im forget you so easy. You're his wife, aren't you?'

'Suzy,' Sarah hissed, but Suzy wouldn't be stopped.

'Tell this bitch to clear out, Rachel! He's married to you and nothin' is goin' to change that. Why are you givin' up? Fight for him!'

But Rachel shook her head listlessly. 'I won't force myself on him when he doesn't want me. I don't want . . . I . . . He's changed. He's made a new life. And besides . . .'

'And besides,' mocked Suzy, 'you're both too proud and stupid to forgive each other.'

There was a silence, and then Suzy waved a hand, half apologetic, though her eyes were still brilliant with anger. 'Oh, what do I know?''

'It's not so simple,' Sarah told Suzy, when Rachel had gone.

'The Rachel I knew in Greengage would've fought for her man. She's changed.'

Sarah nodded. 'Israel's knocked the stuffin' out of her. He hurt her bad, Suzy, but inside, where it doesn't show. Then Will, acting like she's a stranger. She's had all she can bear. She's just not game to take the chance.'

'I don't believe Will don't love her no more,' Suzy declared desperately, blinking back tears. 'That sort of love don't just die. He's holdin' it in. George says Will's like gun powder on a slow fuse, an' one day he'll go up.'

Sarah said nothing. There wasn't much she could say. If Will still loved Rachel, he obviously wasn't admitting it, even to himself. And Rachel. . . well, Rachel just wasn't the same anymore.

Rachel had all but given up hope of ever receiving a reply from Mary Hymbury. Surely she would have returned to Sydney by now? Would Rachel never know whether or not the woman staying at Wattle Bank was her mother? And then the letter came. Her hands shook as she broke open the crisp sheet.

It was brief.

'Dear Rachel, I must apologise for the delay in answering your letter. You must appreciate how surprised and dismayed I was to receive it. For a long time I thought I would not answer. I had thought that part of my life was over. It is only during the past weeks I have slowly come to realise that it would be a shame for us not to meet. Mrs Turner has kindly agreed to allow me to offer you the hospitality of Wattle Bank, if you wish to visit. Believe me, I will understand if you don't.

Yours in apology, Mary Hymbury.'

The writing was well formed, with flamboyant curls and curves to the letters. Rachel sat staring at it for a long time, feeling a terrible disappointment. She would refuse! she decided angrily. But when the anger faded, she knew she must not allow hurt feelings to force her into making a hasty decision. Mary had stretched out a hand to her, albeit in a rather half-hearted manner, and Rachel must take it. For her own sake, and Bella's.

'Are you well enough to travel?' Mrs McCrae asked her cautiously, when Rachel explained her intention.

Rachel dismissed her concern. 'I'm perfectly well again. There's no reason I shouldn't go. And if I don't go now, there may not be another chance.'

That was quite possible, Mrs McCrae thought with a frown. Rachel might be well and resilient, although it had taken her a few weeks to recover from the visit to Nerinbilly, and the hurts Israel Potter had inflicted upon her. She was a strong young woman, and her baby appeared to have taken no hurt. All the same, there were times when Mrs McCrae wondered if she really was fully recovered. The girl was quieter, more reserved— gone was that ready smile that made your own lips twitch in response. And, once or twice she'd sensed a cautiousness in Rachel, as if she no longer trusted the world around her enough to open up her warm heart to it.

'Anyway,' Rachel was saying, 'Bella is feeling lonely without the others. It'd be a good time to go on a visit.'

Frank Potter had taken his children to Nerinbilly with Sarah and Thomas. Greta had come to stay, to help them 'settle in', Frank said. 'Israel seems set on her,' he added. There was something uneasy in his expression—Embarrassment? Rachel wondered. Because of what Israel did to me? There would probably be a wedding in due course—perhaps next time a minister made his rounds through the district, performing baptisms and marriages and burials, often belatedly.

It had been a wrench for Rachel, to part with the Potter children. She had cared for Frank and Matty and Baby Victoria as she would have cared for her own. She comforted herself with the thought that at least Sarah was there, to watch over them, and they had a father who loved them dearly. Saying goodbye to Sarah, too, had been painful. Rachel missed her very much.

Suzy and George had sent word that they had leased themselves a little tobacco shop and were doing well. 'Visit us,' they said, 'next time you're down.' And sent their address. They, too, had moved on with their lives.

'At least,' Rachel told Mrs McCrae, 'I'll be *doing* something by going to Wattle Bank.'

Mrs McCrae sighed. 'I suppose this is the best time to go. The weather is fine and it's dry. You can take the small cart and two of the men. Hazelwood can go with you. He's been longing to see Wattle Bank and now he has his chance. It will be a rough journey, Rachel. Are you quite sure . . .'

But Rachel was sure and eager to go. She hadn't been lying; physically she felt better than she had for a long time—and nothing was going to stop her from meeting her long lost mother, certainly not Israel's baby! Her body was healthy; it was only her heart that was broken.

Wattle Bank was a huge station. Two rivers flowed through it—the run stretched along the Murray River on its northern most boundary and the Goulburn on its eastern boundary. The country was quite different to that at McCrae's Castle, being much flatter and drier, with great tufts of kangaroo grass which the wheels of the cart bumped over every time they turned. At first Bella had laughed at this, but as the hours passed, it became less of a joke.

They had crossed the Campaspe. The river was still low, not the dangerous, swirling torrent it could become after heavy rain. It was a simple matter to float the cart across, and swim the horses. They made camp by its banks among gum trees, and when night fell Rachel looked at the stars. The sky seemed enormous, stretching on and on above them. She was sure there were more stars here than there had been at McCrae's Castle. Hazelwood snorted when she told him so.

'The trip's got to you, woman,' he muttered. The familiar pipe was between his teeth, and he puffed on it, staring into the campfire. Rachel glanced at him surreptitiously.

He was not a handsome man, and probably never had been, but there was a rugged dependability about him. Perhaps that was what Mrs McCrae saw, because that they were lovers Rachel no longer doubted. She had seen Hazelwood slipping out of the homestead too many dawns. Why did they not marry? Rachel asked herself, but already knew the answer. Hazelwood was an expiree from Van Diemen's Land. He was not a member of Mrs McCrae's social class—she would be lowering herself a notch or three if she wed such as her foreman. So they resorted to subterfuge.

Hazelwood had wanted to call in at Nerinbilly on the way north, but Rachel had refused. He hadn't insisted, but she'd felt his gaze on her more than once since. He knew what had happened with Israel Potter—everyone must know by now—and that Will was her husband. Mrs McCrae knew, of course, but said nothing. It wasn't her business. And Rachel was grateful for her silence. She'd had enough 'helpful' interference from Suzy and Sarah.

'It was kind of Mrs McCrae to send an escort with me to Wattle Bank,' Rachel told him now, still gazing at the stars.

Hazelwood gave her with a tolerant smile. 'Kind? You're joking, aren't you girlie? Mrs McCrae has ideas of taking up more land out this way, but she wants to see what it's like first. That's all. You gave her the chance to do it without committing herself. She's sly like that; the Scots are a sly race.'

'You mean canny,' Rachel retorted, and smiled back. They had reached an understanding during this journey, Hazelwood and herself. They were as close to friends as two such persons could ever be.

They reached Wattle Bank two days later. As the cart creaked along the plain, they had a wonderful view of the home station. It was built of stone, and looked square and solid, constructed to last for ever. There was a sapling fence surrounding it, with the usual paraphernalia of outbuildings and yards. Smoke drifted from the chimneys, spiralling into a hazy blue sky.

As they drew closer, a man on a horse came to inspect them and ask their business. Then, satisfied with Hazelwood's answers, escorted them in.

Rachel's heart began to beat more quickly. She had been imagining this moment for so long— ever since that day in Mrs Roadknight's house, when she had learned that her mother—the 'angel' of Pa's story—was still alive. And now at last it was about to come true.

Bella, beside her, gazed around with bright eyes. The journey had been new to her—she didn't remember the one they had made from Greengage, or from Melbourne to the Castle. Sometimes, at night, she had been afraid, but her mother was always there to cuddle up to. They had slept under the cart, while Hazelwood and the two men slept a little way off, near the fire. The darkness frightened her, although she never said. As young as she was, Bella held her fears to herself. As they drew closer to the stone building, Bella sensed her mother's strangeness. Mama's face was white and set, and she sat with a straight, rigid back. Bella peered ahead, trying to see what it was frightening her mother. Some women had come outside, opening the gate in the fence. They wore long, rustling dresses like Mrs McCrae. One of the women had yellow hair, like Frank and Matty and Victoria, and Bella felt sad. She missed them. They were like her own brother and sisters, and until they had gone she had not realised they would ever go.

Rachel was leaning forward now and Hazelwood was drawing them to a halt and then he jumped down, coming to help. First, he caught Bella up in his sunbrowned arms, swinging her down, making her gasp—she was too reserved to shriek in front of the strangers. She stood primly, gazing up at the three new faces, but they weren't looking at her. They were watching Rachel as she awkwardly followed her daughter.

The lady with the fair hair had stepped forward. Her hair was long and curly, and although she had it pinned in a bun at her neck, the curls were dancing and waving around her face in the soft breeze. She made a sound like a laugh and came forward to hug Mama. Bella watched, uneasy again, as Rachel returned the hug. There were tears running down her face and Bella had never seen her mother cry.

The little girl moved closer to Hazelwood and the cart, out of reach, just in case one of those ladies decided she should be hugged, too.

CHAPTER 23

'**Y**OU LOOK LIKE YOUR FATHER,' Mary Hymbury said for the hundredth time.

The statement had lost none of the wonder it had held for Rachel the first time she said it.

'I'd forgotten what he looked like. Oh, he was handsome, yes. But until I saw you, Rachel, I had truly forgotten.'

'He spoke of you,' Rachel answered, feeling the tears welling again. She had wept often since her arrival and laughed, too. Rachel had never thought of herself as someone whose emotions soared up and down in the space of a moment, but that had changed at Wattle Bank.

None of it had been as Rachel expected from the tentative letter she had received at the Castle. What *had* she expected? A lukewarm reception, a woman who was willing to meet her daughter, but unwilling to feel anything for her. Instead, as soon as Rachel and her mother set eyes on each other, it was as if they had known each other all their lives.

Certainly, Mary was not as Rachel had imagined. A tiny, fragile woman with golden hair and blue eyes and the remnants of a beauty that must have been quite breathtaking in her younger years—she was still stunning. No wonder Pa had loved her. What man would not? But with the fragility came a timidity, a weakness. Mary would never stand up and demand her rights. Mary was a gentle, pliable straw which bent before opposition and which was crushed by a harsh word or a cruel laugh.

'My husband was very angry,' she whispered, when at last they were able to speak of Rachel's birth. 'He was away at the time I met your father, and when he returned I had hoped to keep our meeting a secret. Of course, that was impossible when I discovered I was to have a child. Then I thought . . . I thought . . .' she flushed, and pushed at her hair. 'Well, I thought I might pass you off as his child. But he knew I was lying—I was never very good at it, you see!—and he soon had the truth from me.' And she shuddered, remembering.

'So you gave me away.'

Mary stretched out a shaking hand to grasp Rachel's tightly. 'Oh my dear, no! Not so easily as you imagine! I wanted you of course I did. And yet how could I keep you? He threatened to kill you, to take you out into the bush and leave you to die. And then he decided it would be more amusing to give you back to your father. So he took you away and I never saw you again.'

There was no doubting the grief in her face. The young Rachel might have condemned Mary for her inability to withstand her strong husband, but the older and wiser Rachel sympathised.

'The irony of it was,' Mary went on, 'we never had any children of our own. You are my only child, Rachel.'

'And now your husband is dead,' Rachel murmured.

Mary sighed, dabbing at her eyes, genuinely sad. 'I miss him,' she admitted. 'He was my rock, you see. Without him I am floundering a little. That is why I am here, at Wattle Bank, with my dear friends. When they left Sydney I missed them dreadfully, and then I thought: I am a free woman now, I can do as I please. So I came to visit, and am still here. No doubt a dreadful nuisance!'

Rachel doubted that, but smiled dutifully.

'Tell me,' Mary murmured anxiously, 'did you hate me very much for what happened? Were you very unhappy with your father?'

'No, I loved him!' Rachel cried. 'He was a wonderful man, a fairytale father.' It was true, Rachel realised with a pang. She had had an idyllic, romantic childhood despite the hardships. Pa had made it so, and she had loved him for being himself. 'I stayed with Mrs Roadknight when he died,' she went on, 'and then the orphanage. They were hard years. But since then I've heard of other childhoods much worse than mine, so I think I must be a little grateful.'

Mary shook her head, her big blue eyes sparkling with tears. 'You are so strong, Rachel,' she whispered. 'Not like me at all.' She mopped her eyes again, with a droll laugh. 'And your daughter, little Bella, so sweet. So precocious!' Mary could not stop marvelling at Bella's cleverness. 'Your husband must be very proud.'

The silence drew on. Rachel swallowed. She had been dreading this moment, and yet there seemed no way around it. 'My husband and I don't live together any more,' she said at last.

Mary blinked, amazed at such a statement. For such as Mary Hymbury, a husband would come above all else, even a daughter. 'What did he do?' she demanded quietly. 'Rachel, don't tell me he was a brute to you!'

'No, no,' Rachel laughed unsteadily. 'Not a brute.' Again she paused, and then suddenly the story came gushing out of her. She hadn't told it in its entirety to anyone before this—all this time it had been her secret alone. Now it came out, every detail, while Mary sat spellbound, listening, her blue eyes wide. And when at last Rachel was finished, she felt drained, cleansed— and so relieved.

Mary tapped her fingers on the arm of her chair. A frown came and went on her still smooth brow. 'Dearest,' she said, her voice almost reprimanding. 'You have been very silly, you know. Your father would have been the first to agree that what he did wasn't very honest. And although he was a gentleman—never doubt that, Rachel!—there were others who were quite awful. He never liked their methods. I think,' and she smiled wryly, 'forgive me, Rachel, but I think Will and your dear father would have got on very well, if they'd ever met.'

Rachel sat, unable to move. What Mary said had a profound effect on her. She had already come to accept Will's past, but the idea that her Pa would have agreed with his views! That was new indeed. And, the more she thought of it, quite likely. It had been Mrs Roadknight, after all, who coloured Rachel's outlook on life, not Pa. It had been Mrs Roadknight who had been listening that day—

through Rachel—when Will sat and spoke softly about what he had been and what he had done. And Mrs Roadknight, who had felt his betrayal so bitterly that she ensured Rachel could no longer live with him as his wife.

After a moment, Rachel shook herself slightly, putting up a hand to shade her eyes. 'It doesn't matter now,' she said. 'It's too late anyway. He has someone else and I . . . this child isn't his, you know.'

Mary stared, and then her mouth twitched on a wicked little smile. 'Oh Rachel,' she whispered, 'perhaps you do take after me after all.'

Prepared for condemnation, Rachel began to laugh.

Hazelwood and his men had returned to McCrae's Castle, but Rachel and Bella stayed on at Wattle Bank. The week stretched into two and then three. Sometimes Rachel and Mary sat and talked of the past, sometimes they took the Turner's carriage—a little the worse for wear these days—down to the river. It was wide, the Murray, and the ground nearby was marshy and reed covered. Wild ducks and other water birds congregated here in their hundreds, so that there was always good shooting to be had for the men of the station. Once the Aborigines had hunted here, but the whites had ousted them from their traditional hunting grounds. There were a number of blacks about the station, employed by the Turners. And there were others who paused for a day or two, to work and be fed, before moving on.

Once, the Native Police Corps came by. They looked impressive in their green uniforms and their cavalry boots, scabbards flashing in the sun. They had come to sort out some trouble west along the river, and stayed only one night. Rachel had heard they were quite ruthless in their fulfilment of their duties, and had no scruples when it came to shooting 'wild' blacks, as they called them.

As the days passed, Rachel decided that Mary was wrong. They weren't much alike, not really. All the same, she would never have missed this meeting, not for anything. Everyone at the homestead was kind to Bella, they baked her treats and made a fuss, but the little girl still missed her playmates. Rachel, involved in getting to know her own mother, told herself Bella would eventually get used to the fact that Frank and Matty and Victoria were gone, and make new friends. Besides, Maggie was still at the Castle. And soon Bella would have a new brother or sister.

I really should think about going back, Rachel told herself, but no-one mentioned her leaving. Mary was spoiling her, that was the trouble. Every day there was some little gift. She fussed about Rachel, making her feel like a princess. Making up in her own way, perhaps, for the past. They were both enjoying their roles so much they hardly noticed anyone or anything else. Even Bella.

'I want Frank and Matty and Victoria, Mama!' Bella demanded in the belligerent voice she always used when she was worried about the answer.

Rachel shook her head impatiently. 'You know

that's not possible, Bella.'

'But I want them!'

'Well what you want is not important,' Rachel snapped.

Surprised, the little girl blinked the tears back from her eyes. Mama didn't usually answer so sharply. Bella stomped off, her lower lip stuck out. For a long time she sat under the big gum tree down in the back paddock, watching some men mending the fence. They were slow, Bella thought. She was sure, if Hazelwood were here, he'd soon show them how it was done. Once or twice the men looked up and saw the little figure with the red ribbon in her hair.

It was while she was sitting, watching, that Bella conceived her plan.

At first it was just a vague idea, but as she mulled it over, it began to grow and take shape. Her eyes followed the track by which she and Mama had come. When they were on their way to Wattle Bank, Hazelwood had pointed with his whip and said, teeth clenched around his pipe, 'Nerinbilly over that way, Bella my girl!' Mama had been cross with him for that, but Bella had remembered.

Nerinbilly meant the playmates she missed so much, although she reminded herself that they were with their father now, Captain Potter. When she was tiny she had thought he was her father, too, but she knew better now. A little smile played over her mouth and was gone. She knew who her father was. The man on the horse.

He had come to see her while Mama was at Nerinbilly. And he lifted her up onto his horse so that the ground was far, far below, but she wasn't frightened, because his arms were safe. When he left the Castle, Bella had given him a kiss on the cheek and, after a moment he'd laughed and given her one, too.

She'd waved until he was out of sight.

Sarah had been crying, but pretending she wasn't, wiping the tears surreptitiously away with her finger.

'Why are you sad the man is going?' Bella had asked her, puzzled.

'I'm sad for you, my dear,' Sarah had replied.

'Why are you sad for me?'

'Bless you,' Sarah had mumbled. 'He's your father.' And then she had clapped a hand over her mouth as though she'd bitten off her tongue. After that, Sarah made her promise never to tell Mama that she knew, because Mama would be very angry.

Although Bella had never told, she'd remembered. She had a father, just like Frank and Matty and Victoria. And he was more important than their father—he wore a uniform and had a big horse and a gun, and he chased bad men. And now that Mama was being so mean, Bella wanted him very much. She was sure he would be pleased to see her, and she knew where to go to find him. She'd overheard Sarah saying he was on the Goulburn River. Hazelwood had told her Wattle Bank finished at the Goulburn River, and if they travelled in that direction—to the east—they would come upon it. All she need do was follow that river until she came to her father.

It couldn't be very difficult. She would walk to the Goulburn because she was brave. Frank always said she was the bravest girl he knew, braver than either of his sisters. She would sleep under the stars and walk during the day. She knew where Mrs Turner kept her food. She could wrap some up in a towel, enough for the journey. She didn't eat much, Mama always said so, and she wouldn't run out.

The station hands had finished working. The sun, low on the horizon, was turning the sky a brilliant red and gold, with sweeping strokes of azure blue. One of the men happened to glance up, as he walked towards the yards, and noticed that the little girl with the red ribbon had gone.

The others didn't notice until supper time.

Rachel and Mary had been pouring over some pattern books Mary had brought from Sydney, looking at the dresses and hats that were available from the shops there. Some were so outrageous they laughed, covering their mouths like school-girls, although there were one or two that Mary thought would be perfect for Rachel, and spoke of having them made up.

She had been saying such things quite often, Rachel realised. And realised too, that Mary was beginning to believe that Rachel would be returning to Sydney with her. The idea was vaguely comforting. Mary had a house there—a large house if her comments were anything to go by—but she also had friends, and relatives of her husband. Rachel could well imagine what they would say when Mary turned up with a long lost daughter and grand daughter.

Still, it was nice to pretend.

'Is Bella here?' Mrs Turner peered around the door with a smile.

Mary glanced about indifferently and shook her head, turning back to the book. Rachel looked up in surprise. Foreboding, like the warning buzz of a wasp, brought her out of her pleasant dream.

'I haven't seen her all afternoon,' she said, and realised it for the first time. Mrs Turner's smile remained, but something in her eyes shifted. 'I'm sure she's about somewhere.'

Rachel followed her from the room, anxiety growing. You're being foolish, she told herself. It's nothing. Bella is playing somewhere, and will come in a moment.

Rachel went out of the back door and called, scanning the long shadows of the paddock and the garden. The land looked green and gold, soft as butter in the evening light. There was no sign of Bella's little figure, running to meet her.

After a moment Mrs Turner returned, and this time there was no hiding her concern. 'No-one seems to have seen her,' she said quietly. 'I'll have a word with the men. Maybe one of them noticed the child about. Now don't worry, Rachel! I'm sure it's nothing at all.'

Rachel *was* worried, she was very worried.

Eventually they found the man who had seen Bella sitting under the tree. He answered Rachel's questions, eyes shifting away and back. There was a note in his voice that frightened her. He hesitated and then burst out, 'If she's gone walkabout we've got to find her quickly, ma'am.'

He didn't say any more, but there was plenty of danger out there for a child. Wild natives, snakes, and animals. And if by luck she wasn't speared or bitten, there was the land itself. So vast, so dry and foreign. It scared him sometimes; the thought of a child wandering alone out there, frightened and thirsty, was unbearable.

They mounted a search immediately. The entire home station was turned upside down, they looked in every nook and cranny, praying that Bella was hiding somewhere, playing a trick on them.

But Bella was nowhere.

Next they searched the outbuildings. Rachel stood, frozen, in the yard and watched the men moving from place to place, thinking . . . this time they'll find her. This time.

But Bella wasn't to be found.

It was getting late now. There was still enough light to search the paddocks, calling, covering every inch. And, finally, with flaming torches, they made sweeps out from the home station, calling and calling and calling.

Rachel watched the flickering blobs of fire, bobbing in the fading light. Voices rose and fell. She stared after them, her eyes stinging from the strain. 'They'll find her,' Mary whispered beside her, over and over, as if trying to convince them both of the truth of it.

Eventually, the search had to stop. The darkness defeated them. They came back to the home station, tired and dejected, to wait for the dawn to light up the bush again. Rachel didn't sleep. The image of Bella, alone out there, wouldn't leave her. She could see the little girl, curled up tightly on the ground, her eyes wide and frightened. She would be hungry and thirsty. Was she hurt?

Rachel squeezed her hands into fists, forcing away the terrifying thought. She began to think of all the things she should have done and said. She thought of all the mistakes she had made. She had already lost a husband, was that not enough? She brokered deals with God and then was afraid he would punish her for her audacity. Rachel sat by the window, until at last she heard the first birdcalls and the rooster crowing. And then the men were out again, calling.

'We'll find her,' Mrs Turner said. 'We'll find her. She couldn't have gone far. She's only little.'

Rachel didn't answer. She dared not. If she spoke she would break down completely, and that would not help Bella. She's out there, Rachel told herself. In a moment one of the men will ride up to the house, and there she will be, tired and tearful, but safe. And I will hug her and scold her, and . . . but the thought died. No man rode up to the house. The search went on all day and still no Bella.

'Rachel.' It was Mary who bent close, grasping her cold hand. 'You must lie down and sleep. You must.'

She was right, Rachel knew she was, but she felt as if it were vital she stay awake. If she closed her eyes, if she slept, it would be as if she'd given up.

'Soon,' she whispered, to prevent Mary insisting. 'Soon, I'll —'

'Rachel!'

Mrs Turner, her face working strangely, as if she didn't know whether to laugh or cry. Rachel was on her feet, gripping Mary's arm so hard her mother winced. And then she heard the voices outside, and pushed past the other women out onto the verandah.

There were the men, tired and dusty, their smiles splitting their faces. Peter, the black tracker, in his over-sized trousers and check shirt, grinning at her with gleaming white teeth. He was carrying Bella, and when he saw Rachel he lifted the child up as if she were a trophy.

'This one hiding,' he announced with a chuckle. 'Like a little brown snake. But I find her. I best bloody tracker around.'

Bella looked dirty and exhausted, but her mouth was closed hard and her eyes were unrepentant. Rachel flung her arms around both child and Peter, relief making her feel faint. Bella's hands slipped about her neck, gripping hard. Rachel felt her child shudder, and then heard her whisper in a hoarse little voice:

'Not lost, Mama.'

They bathed her and put her in a clean white nightgown, brushing her tangled hair. There were cuts and grazes on her face and arms, and Rachel gently smoothed in some lotion that Mary had given her. At last Bella lay back in her bed, eyes flickering, held open only by Bella's iron will.

'Not lost, Mama,' she whispered. The same words again.

Rachel shook her head slowly. 'Where were you going, darling? Nerinbilly isn't that way. And besides, you know we can't live there now.'

'Not Nerinbilly,' and Bella's voice shook.

'Do you want to live with Grandmother, darling?' She has a lovely house in Sydney.' Rachel bit her lip, knowing that if that was what Bella wanted, she would fight everyone who stood in her way to bring it about.

But Bella shook her head. Her eyelids were closing. 'I want the man on the horse,' she breathed. 'I want my father.' And slept.

Rachel stared at her daughter, feeling the colour drain out of her face. 'You should have seen them,' Sarah had said. 'He took her up on his horse, and rode around. She was like a little princess!' Oh God, not Will! She would give Bella anything, *anything* she asked for, but how could she give her Will?

The little chest rose and fell, and Bella's lips parted slightly in sleep. Rachel sat and thought. She remembered her own childhood, and her Pa. At least she had had him, for a short while, and now she had her mother, too. Bella had always had Rachel, and Rachel had thought that was enough. Now she wondered. Could she deny Bella a father because she was too cowardly to admit her mistake? Too frightened to pit herself against Will's intractable personality.

It was a long time later that Rachel made her way to Mary's room. Mary blinked at her in the lamplight, and then smiled. 'Come and sit beside me, dearest,' she murmured in her soft, sweet voice.

Rachel sighed. 'I'm sorry,' she whispered. 'I'll have to leave as soon as Bella's well enough.'

Mary frowned. 'Where will you go? You don't mean you'd go to Nerinbilly?'

Rachel shook her head. A pulse was beating in her throat. 'I have to go to Will. Bella wants Will.' She closed her eyes.

The admission was difficult, but somehow even the mention of his name made her feel better. As though, at last, she was doing what she should have done a long time ago.

Mary's hand clasped warmly on her own. 'I think you're very wise,' she said firmly. 'Not that it will be easy, Rachel, if he's as stubborn as you say. But you're still his wife; in that respect nothing has changed.'

'Yes.'

'I will write to you,' Mary added. 'And if you ever wish to come to Sydney . . .'

Rachel smiled. 'Thank you.' It was inadequate. Mary returned her smile, but she could see Rachel was already slipping away. Well, after all, it was for the best. Mary was not foolish enough to imagine she could have withstood her husband's relations' displeasure when she introduced them to her illegitimate daughter. In fact, with a shudder, it hardly bore thinking of.

Rachel closed her eyes. I'm doing this for Bella, she told herself. Bella needs her father, and I must give her the chance to be with him. Except in her heart she knew she was doing it as much for herself as for Bella. Since Will left, she had let others run her life, following them blindly, not caring where they led her. The track had twisted on through grey bush and sunbaked plains, never quite certain where it was going. For a time she had struck out and followed Israel, but that track had ended suddenly, at a cliff edge, plunging down into a deep, dark gully. Now, because of Bella, she had taken her destiny into her own hands again. She was in control of her life, and she was back on the right track, she knew it. She felt stronger than she had felt in a long time. Frightened, yes, so frightened that her knees were shaking! But she wasn't going to be stopped, not this time.

I'm coming back, Will, Rachel thought, and then smiled for no reason. And kept smiling.

RACHEL

&

WILL

1843

CHAPTER 24

It was the first day of spring. A chill breeze brushed Rachel's cheek, stirring tendrils of her dark hair, while above, a pale sun played peek-a-boo behind the clouds. Spring may be an uncertain time of year in the Port Phillip District, bleak and rainy one moment, hot and steamy the next, but Rachel saw it as a time of renewal. Of new beginnings. And it was fitting that it was spring when she finally reached the Goulburn River Police Post.

They had tried to persuade her against it. Even Mary, who understood her need to go, had felt it would be better for her to stay at Wattle Bank until the baby was born. 'You don't know what you'll find there, dearest. It will probably be very primitive.' But Rachel had known that if she stayed, the powerful sense of determination that was forcing her onward would wither and die. She would begin to think of all the things that might go wrong. She had to leave at once, while her need was fierce enough to hold back her fears.

So they had let her go.

It had been a necessarily slow journey. The Turners had been very kind, sending Rachel off in the wagon with two trusted men and the younger Mr Turner—he was bound through to Melbourne to sort out some difficulties with the bank. He had treated her gently, though with rather puzzled glances. Rachel could almost hear him asking himself: Why would anyone turn down the chance to live in Sydney with Mary Hymbury for a life on a godforsaken Police Post on the Goulburn?

Mary had understood.

'I felt the same about your father,' she had whispered to Rachel. 'Only I wasn't strong enough to do anything about it. God bless you, dearest!'

So, Rachel had set off with her daughter, and a firm belief that she was doing the right thing. It was only as the wheels turned and the miles slipped by, that doubt began to creep in, and with it, a cold, merciless logic. Will had made a new life. There was someone called Maeve. How would he feel, to be suddenly confronted with a wife he had left years before and a daughter he hardly knew, not to mention another man's baby? She wouldn't blame him if he turned them around and sent them straight back to Wattle Bank.

'Well, I won't go,' she whispered to herself. 'He can't make me go. I'm his wife.'

The doubts slunk to the shadows, but they soon crept out again, teasing her, mocking her, until she began to wish she had never chosen this path. Bella had no such doubts. Her grey eyes shone and she wriggled impatiently in her seat. Rachel didn't know how she had discovered Will was her father, although she had a fair idea, but she prayed that Bella would not be disappointed. If Will were angry, if he were indifferent, Bella would feel betrayed. And although Rachel could face the possibility of rejection for herself, she couldn't bear to think of her daughter being hurt.

I should have written first, she thought, and then shook her head. That would have given him the chance to refuse to see her, or to put her off. She could see his reply clearly in her mind—so cool and logical, so unbending . . . No, writing was no use. She must come in person, and once she was there, she must make certain that somehow she found a way to stay. It would be more difficult to refuse to see her, when she was actually on the spot. And if she stayed long enough, perhaps he would get so used to her being around he wouldn't want her to leave. Maybe he would even grow to love her again, a little. She wasn't greedy. Just a little love would do.

When they had reached the small settlement on the Goulburn—a store, a smithy and an inn—Mr Turner asked for directions from the owner of McPherson's General Store. 'Keep going towards the river,' he'd said. 'Can't miss it.'

Mr Turner had wanted to escort her all the way and check that Will was in residence before he left her. Rachel had refused. 'I want to go alone,' she had insisted. 'Just me and Bella.' Then with a grateful smile, 'Thank you so much, for everything.'

He had argued, but she was firm. In the end he shrugged and went on his way, leaving Rachel and her daughter where the track divided, one part branching off towards Seymour and Melbourne, the other turning sharply left to the Police Post, just visible through the trees. The inn was built at the road junction. White-washed walls and smoke rising from the chimney gave the place a homely air. The sound of voices and laughter came from within, and there were horses confined in a small paddock at the back. Maeve's Inn, thought Rachel. The painted name board over the door—Dream of Erin—was enough to convince her. She turned her back to it and, with Bella holding one hand and her heavy bag in the other, made her way with firm steps up the road to Will.

The cool breeze stirred her hair again, and Rachel pulled her cloak more firmly about her shoulders. The little Police Post lay before her— it was in a clearing which had been hacked from the bush. Grass grew sparsely around the buildings, the rest had been tramped to dirt by horses' hooves and booted feet. Closest to Rachel was a slab constructed building with an overhanging verandah and an open door. This was obviously the place to bring her business, and Rachel eyed it warily. Beside it was the watch-house, a small boxlike structure with a heavy door, where prisoners were held pending punishment or transfer to Melbourne Gaol. A bell hung from one of the branches of a nearby tree—an emergency measure—while a Union Jack fluttered proudly from a white flagpole. The stables were adequate and there were yards beside them for horses or livestock. Three more huts completed the picture, one smaller than the rest. Several children of varying ages and sizes were engrossed in a game in front of one of the larger huts.

Bella was looking up at Rachel, no doubt wondering why she was standing so still, and impatient

to see her father again. But Rachel felt the familiar fears clammering, stifling what was left of her
courage and rooting her feet to the spot. What
if Will wasn't here? she asked herself desperately.
She had been foolish not to take up Mr Turner's
suggestion and allow him to make enquiries. Why
had she said no? Rachel knew why. She'd wanted
to face him herself, just her and Bella. Mr Turner
would have been a way out for Will, a way to refuse
her admittance to the Police Post and his life. Now
that Mr Turner had gone, sending her away would
mean leaving her with no means of support and
no means of travelling on to Melbourne or back to
Wattle Bank. 'Oh please,' she whispered, 'don't let
him be that heartless.'

'Mama?' Bella pointed.

There was a blue-jacketed constable approaching
them. He came from the open doorway of the slab
hut, eyeing her curiously. He was limping, Rachel
saw, but the twist of his leg made it look as if he
were skipping.

'You after something, ma'am?'

Rachel's voice didn't come out properly, sounding husky and breathless, but he understood her
well enough.

'Sergeant Moody?' he repeated, raising an eyebrow. 'For what reason would you be wantin' to
see him?'

'I'm his wife,' Rachel replied, and looked straight
into his eyes.

She saw the shock there, followed swiftly by disbelief. His eyes sank lower, confirming the fact that
she was heavily pregnant. A smile flickered around
his mouth.

'As Sergeant Moody's not married, ma'am, how can you be his wife?'

'I am his wife.'

'He's not married.'

He was laughing at her. There was no pity in his eyes, only a sort of smug cruelty. Rachel knew it was pointless to try and persuade such a man to change his mind. She had met enough like him. Instead, she stepped around him, heading across the dusty clearing towards the three huts, and pulling Bella with her.

'Which one is his?'

But he was in front of her again, blocking her way, and this time gripping her arm. 'Look, we both know you're lyin'—'

'I want my husband,' Rachel said, desperation creeping into her voice. 'If he finds out you sent me away without letting me see him, he'll be very angry!'

The constable's hand tightened on her arm. 'I don't give a —' he began, but a second voice interrupted him.

'What is it, Yelland?'

Constable Yelland turned and narrowed his eyes at the approaching gentleman. At least, Rachel thought, he dressed like a gentleman. A relatively clean jacket over breeches and long riding boots. He was bald on the crown of his head, though a thick band of curly hair above his ears, the colour of fox fur, made up for it. Brown eyes surveyed Rachel and Bella, before he raised an eyebrow at Constable Yelland, awaiting a reply.

Reluctantly Yelland gave it. 'Just some tart lookin' for someone to blame for her condition, Mr Quill.'

Mr Quill's mouth tightened, but whether at the constable's choice of words or his unprofessionalism Rachel couldn't guess. 'Your name, woman?'

Rachel, whose face had turned scarlet, searched for words of her own. 'Rachel Trigg, sir. I've come to see my husband, and so I told this man here, but he won't listen.'

Quill frowned. 'There's no man called Trigg stationed here.'

Yelland smiled, and winked at Quill. 'I'll put her out then, will I, sir?' And he jerked at Rachel's arm.

Mr Quill, squatter and appointed magistrate for the Goulburn River district, disliked Yelland. He certainly disliked being spoken to in such a manner by a member of the lower orders. For both those reasons he looked at Rachel again.

'Is there any more you can tell me about this man Trigg?' he demanded.

The woman appeared to be at the end of her tether, but he quashed his pity. If one felt sorry for every wreckage of humanity one saw in Port Phillip, one would never be able to get on with one's job.

Rachel took a breath. 'You know him as Will Moody, sir. Will Moody's my husband.'

Quill's mild brown eyes widened slightly. 'I was under the impression, madam, that Sergeant Moody was a single man. Is that not so, Yelland?'

Yelland pretended to consider it, and then nodded. 'Never 'eard him mention a wife, sir.' His eyes, fixed on Rachel, gleamed.

'Please,' she begged, ignoring Yelland. 'Just let me speak to him.'

Yelland could see that Quill was weakening. The

bitch was working on him, and he was caving in. Well, serve Will Moody right. Let him clean up his own mess.

'Very well,' Quill said. 'Go and fetch the Sergeant, Yelland. Mrs . . . Moody and I will be in the office.'

Yelland limped away towards the smallest and closest of the three huts. His smile was hidden in the tilt of his head, but his eyes still gleamed with malice. He didn't make any bones about the fact that he hated Sergeant Moody. From the moment Will had arrived and begun closing off all of Yelland's profitable little sidelines, he'd taken a violent dislike to him. It wasn't as if he'd been greedy. Just a shilling here and a shilling there, put aside for his own use. No-one was the wiser, no-one even cared. Certainly not Sergeant Wheeler, who was drunk most of the time anyway, but Will Moody had replaced Wheeler, and now Yelland was as poor as the next man.

However there was more to his hatred than simple financial inconvenience, although Yelland didn't admit it to himself very often. Something in the way Moody looked at him whenever they came face to face—the contempt in his eyes—made Yelland acutely aware of all his shortcomings. Every man had a vision of himself, and Yelland's was large and bold . . . except when he met Will Moody's eyes.

Mr Quill had led Rachel into the 'office', the slab hut Yelland had come from. Inside, it consisted of a room with a table and chairs, a desk, shelving holding papers and books, and a fire burning brightly in the hearth. A locked and bolted door led to a further room at the back.

Pulling out a chair for Rachel in front of the desk and seating himself behind it, in the position of authority, Quill asked if Rachel would like some water. She refused, contenting herself with sitting in silence. The window behind Quill looked out over the Post, and Rachel watched Yelland knocking on the door of the smallest hut. Quill, observing her, thought that she seemed very nervous, her fingers twisting around themselves. She was young, in her twenties he guessed, and pretty enough, despite the exhaustion which gave her face its white, drawn appearance.

'You're from Melbourne?' Quill asked her.

The hut door still hadn't opened. Rachel was relieved to break the tension. 'No, from Wattle Bank, up on the Murray.'

'Wattle Bank!' he exclaimed. 'You work for the Turners?'

She looked at him, her eyes gazing straight into his. Like an equal, he thought with a start.

'I was a guest of the Turners.' Her mouth lifted a little in a smile, as she read his thoughts accurately.

Through the window behind him, she saw the door open. Rachel went still, her face turning even paler. And then Will filled the doorway. He was wearing an undershirt, rolled up at the sleeves, his braces dangling limp over his white breeches. His hair was untidy, as though he'd been woken from sleep. Yelland was talking. As she watched, Will ran a hand back through his hair, and turned to look in the direction of the office. The hand stopped. His face was a blur, but Rachel could all too easily imagine his shock and dismay.

The viciously tight knot of anxiety within her

tightened still further. She was finding it difficult to breathe. Her back was aching and her legs, too, the ankles puffy above her boots. She was exhausted, and she knew it. The journey, slow though it had been, was long and rough, and she'd hardly slept a wink. She couldn't go any further.

Will and Yelland's conversation had come to an end. Will disappeared inside the hut and Rachel's ragged breathing stopped, but then he was back again, pulling on the jacket of his blue uniform. He and Yelland began the walk across the dusty grounds towards the office. Rachel's fingers tightened on Bella's cold little hand, tucked reassuringly into hers.

Footsteps sounded outside the door, and then the fitful sunlight was blocked out completely. Stiffly, feeling disembodied, Rachel turned and looked up as Will entered the room in front of Yelland. She saw at once that he was prepared for her. It was in his grey eyes, so cool and watchful, and his closed expression. No welcome there, no forgiveness. The candle of hope and determination, which she had sheltered and kept burning during her journey from Wattle Bank, flickered and died.

Bella slipped out of Rachel's suddenly lifeless arms. Ducking around the table, she ran. Will reached out instinctively, stopping her in her tracks when she would have cannoned into him. Heart thudding, Rachel watched. Don't disappoint her, Will, she begged him silently. Please don't disappoint her. Will's hands tightened on the child and he lifted her up, holding her so that their faces were level. Rachel saw the smile curling his mouth, even as her eyes blurred with tears.

'Hello there, darlin'', he said.

Slowly, Will put Bella down. Quill cleared his throat. 'Sergeant Moody, this woman claims to be your wife. What have you got to say?'

Will looked at him, ignoring Rachel. 'She is,' he said.

Quill raised an eyebrow. 'I was under the impression, Sergeant, that you were a single man?'

Will's face didn't change. 'My wife's been livin' at McCrae's Castle. She's been nursemaid to Captain Potter's children while the Captain was building the new home station at Nerinbilly. Now it's finished, the children have gone up there, and . . . and my wife has finished her term of employment.'

Rachel gazed at him in wonder.

Quill frowned. 'Your wife says she was at Wattle Bank.'

Will's eyes gleamed faintly, as if the other man's suspicion amused him. 'She was up at Wattle Bank stayin' with her mother, Mrs Hymbury.'

'Well,' Quill moved restlessly in his chair, 'perhaps you'll fill in the necessary paperwork, Sergeant?'

Will bent his head, assenting, and looked at Rachel. There was puzzlement in the grey eyes, but behind it, cold and dangerous as a glacier, lay anger. He reached out one hand and picked up the heavy bag.

'I'll deal with this now, Mr Quill,' he said. 'Come on, Rachel.'

She followed him outside, Bella skipping ahead. He was walking with long strides towards his hut, not looking back at her, just expecting her to follow. Slowly she did so, quickening her steps when he turned back to frown at her. She was puffing when she reached him and he stepped aside to allow her to proceed him into the hut.

It was tiny. A single room, which was used for sleeping, eating and working. There was a narrow bed against one wall, a table and chair, and a sort of cupboard, above which was a rack to hold his carbine and a couple of pistols. A window looked out over the back of the Police Post. Some children were playing there, at the edge of the cleared bush. A thick line of trees followed the snaking Goulburn, the only evidence of the river she could see from here.

But it was the inside of the hut that struck Rachel so forcibly. Oh, the necessities of life were here, but little more. Will had scaled things down to a bare minimum. There was nothing to show Will's past, his hopes and joys, his disappointments. No clues to Will, the man, beneath the trooper's uniform. It was clean and uncluttered and impersonal, and it froze Rachel's warm heart.

'Sit down.' His voice behind her was expressionless. 'I'll make some tea and you can tell me what you're doin' here. Then I'll take you down to the inn. It's comfortable and the food's good. You can stay there tonight.'

Rachel sat down. Bella went to peer out of the window, watching the children, who were skipping now. Will bent to the hearth to heat the kettle, glancing at Rachel as he did so.

He'd known she was at Wattle Bank, just as he knew most things that went on in his district, but he hadn't gone to see her, and he'd refused to allow himself to think of her too often. That was a useless exercise and Will did not believe in wasting time on things he couldn't change. Besides, there was nothing more he had to say to her. He'd said good-bye at Nerinbilly and he'd meant it.

So what was she doing here now?

The first thing he'd noticed, after the shock of her being here at all, was that she was so thin. Oh, she was carrying the child, of course. No one could fail to notice that. But her face was thin and drawn, and there were circles under her eyes. She looked older and more tired than she had at Nerinbilly. The smile he had always associated with her, the smile she could hardly contain, was missing. And the big bright eyes that, even while he was hating her at the Castle, she had used on him to such effect, were dulled and wary. This was Rachel, but not the Rachel he remembered. The knowledge made him feel uneasy and threatened.

Will made the tea and set the mug carefully before her. Rachel looked at it and slowly slid her fingers around the warmth of it. Outside, the children's voices grew louder. One pressed its face against the little window, grinning at Bella, and then, seeing Will, took fright and ran off.

Bella fixed Will with her solemn look. He found her an apple and handed it over, watching as she settled herself on the edge of the bed and began to eat it with meticulous care. After a couple of bites she paused.

'You're my father,' she told him accusingly.

Will blinked and glanced at Rachel. She said nothing, staring into her mug of tea.

'I'm your father,' he agreed, watching her, won-dering what she would ask next.

But Bella was happy with that and returned to

her apple.

'I thought you weren't goin' to tell her,' Will said quietly. 'I thought you wanted her to think Frank was her father.'

Rachel glanced up in surprise. There was a bitterness in his voice that even the coldness couldn't hide. Had she hurt him by saying that? She hadn't thought of hurting Will, only of sparing Bella more confusion and pain. Now Will gazed back to her, hard and unforgiving, and silently she sighed. Once, she had forced her way through those barricades he was so good at putting up, and found the loving and gentle man within. This time Will was ready for her, ready to repel any of her advances. She could not win.

He hadn't waited for an answer to his question, but threw another at her. 'Is Mrs Hymbury still at Wattle Bank?'

'She's returning to Sydney,' Rachel murmured.

'Then . . . how did you get here?'

Rachel shrugged.

'Rachel.' There was a warning in his voice, and she took a breath.

'Mr Turner brought us most of the way in the wagon. He was going on to Melbourne. He dropped us at the inn, and we walked here.'

A reluctant smile curved Will's mouth. Whatever he might think of her, he couldn't help but admire her courage and audacity. 'You don't do things by halves, do you, Rachel?'

She didn't answer, bending to sip her tea. She held the mug with both hands, he noticed, and her nails were dirty. He looked further. Her hair was unwashed and her clothes dusty and creased, the

white collar of her dress almost grey. He remembered how, at Greengage, Rachel was so fastidious,
she would have been ashamed to be seen with so
much as a spot on her apron. He thought dourly
that it must be difficult to be fastidious, travelling
in a wagon in the middle of nowhere. Or had she
changed so much that she no longer cared? Had
hardship worn her down?

His iron control shivered and he held his breath,
steadying himself. He wanted her gone. Even being
in the same room as her was testing him. Looking
down, he saw with relief that she'd finished her tea.

Will stood up, too quickly. 'Well,' he said, and his
voice was too loud. 'I'll get you that room at the
inn.'

She looked at him then, her eyes dark and
unblinking. She made him uneasy, staring like that.

'I'll get your bag,' he went on, and stooped to
pick it up, walking to the door. 'Come on then,
Rachel, Bella.'

Neither of them moved, just sat there, watching
him silently. Until, after a moment, an inkling of
an answer came to him. He felt as if he was sinking
in quicksand. Slowly, he put the bag down again.
'You're stayin', is that it?' And when she still didn't
answer him, went on in an angry voice, 'Don't pretend you've come back to me, Rachel. You're too
late!'

She stumbled up, gripping the edge of the table
with white knuckles. 'No, no,' she whispered. 'I
haven't . . . I'll go to the inn.' But when she went
to take a step, her legs gave way and she would
have fallen if he hadn't caught her. He pushed
her back into the chair, not ungently, grey gaze

examining her white face. She closed her eyes so that she wouldn't have to look at him. Perspiration stood out on her brow and she knew she was close to fainting. The journey and the worry had taken their toll. She was here with Will, but she was too weak now to do all the things she'd promised she would do, say all the clever things she had thought she would say.

'All right,' his voice was quiet, resigned. 'We'll talk about this later.' And then, impatiently, 'Take my hand, and come and lie down. You look done in.'

She looked up, surprised at his concern. He was holding out his hand towards her. Slowly, she gave him her own and felt his fingers close hard. He helped her up, his arm sliding naturally across her back, and walked her to the bed. Rachel sank down, realising again how tired she was. Her body swayed, crying out for sleep, but she couldn't let it win. Not yet, not yet. . . She was afraid he would find some way of getting them out of the hut while she was asleep.

'Bella,' she murmured.

'I'll take care of Bella,' Will retorted. 'Lie down, woman, before you fall down!'

Rachel lay her head back onto the pillow, and felt him lifting her feet up and pulling off her sturdy boots, and then he tucked the blanket over her. During the whole proceeding he wouldn't look her in the eye. Weariness hit her like a slap and her eyelids fluttered shut. Just before sleep claimed her, she heard Will and Bella cross to the door and go out, closing it behind them.

Don't go! she wanted to call out to Bella. Stay

here, we're safe in here. But her eyelids wouldn't open and her lips were sealed with exhaustion, and she slept.

CHAPTER 25

RACHEL WOKE SUDDENLY, EYES JERKING open, breathing like a frightened animal. Will watched her swallow, blinking, and then slowly look about her, checking the room which the twilight was swiftly turning to darkness. There was a lamp on the table, giving out a soft, golden glow, and he knew when she smelled the soup bubbling in a pot over the coals.

'Where's Bella?' she cried, trying to sit up.

'She's fine. Violet's lookin' after her. She's got two of her own, so she knows all about children.' He watched her coming to terms with that. 'Are you hungry?' And when she nodded, he began to clear the papers spread before him, stacking them together neatly and laying them aside.

'Are you sure she's all right?' Rachel asked again, something in her eyes almost like panic.

'Of course.' Then he went on matter-of-factly, 'Rachel, we have to talk about this.'

She suddenly became very still.

'We both know we can't live together any more. You know that, don't you?' His voice was quiet, almost pleading.

Slowly, she nodded her head, and sighed. 'I know.'

'Then, what's it about?'

Rachel gripped her hands together tightly. 'Will, I need you to help me. I helped you once, didn't I? And now I need you to help me.' She had rehearsed the words over and over to herself and yet now they sounded so false and contrived.

He frowned, and she hurried on.

'Mary Hymbury . . . my mother is returning to Sydney. I can't go with her, it would cause too much trouble for her. And I can't go back to Nerinbilly, either, not with Israel Potter there. I hoped you might let me stay here . . . until my baby's born.'

So, Will thought, that was it. The quicksand was working on him again and he looked away, pretending to think. It was ridiculous even to consider her request. She didn't belong here and he couldn't do his job properly with her here. And yet, it was true what she said. Once, she had helped him. He owed her a debt. If he paid it, she'd leave and they'd be free of each other.

Rachel watched him. He was thinking about it, and she could do no more. She was relying on his fairness, his sense of justice. And when he turned to face her again, she knew that she had been right to do so.

'All right.' Once the words were out, he knew he'd said the right thing. Whatever she had done, she was still his wife in the sight of God and man, and she was still his responsibility and no-one else's. Not Mrs McCrae's nor Mary Hymbury's nor even Frank Potter's. She was his responsibility, and she had known it, too, or why else come back to him now, after all this time?

'You can stay until the baby's born. I owe you that much, after what you did for me at Greengage. When I met you, I was goin' down fast. It was you who made me see what was happenin', and pulled me back. I'm grateful, Rachel, don't doubt that. I reckon I'd be dead now, if it wasn't for you. I've seen it happen with others.' He paused, thinking again. 'You'll have to stay here for the moment,' he gestured around the hut. 'There are no places in the married quarters just now and I can hardly throw out the Yellands or the Kemps, when you'll only be stayin' a short while. Anyway, a truckle bed will do me.'

Would do his back, too, Will thought wryly, but he supposed he had slept on harder. If things got too tough, he could always move into the stables with the horses and Joseph. But he'd rather not let Rachel know she unsettled him so much that he had to move out of his home.

'Thank you,' she said softly. 'I'm grateful for this, Will.'

He nodded, and the deal was struck.

Will spooned the soup into the bowl. Maeve was a great one for soup, and she had made this lot for him, but he wouldn't tell that to Rachel. And what, he wondered, would Maeve say when she heard that Rachel had moved in with him? Well, that would have to be dealt with when the time came. No use worrying about it now. At least Bella was happy, over there with Violet and her two brats.

Rachel was eating the soup with the thick slice of damper he'd cut for her. Will boiled enough water for the wash bowl, folded a towel near it, and put the soap down beside her on the table.

'Take your time,' he said. 'I'll just step out for a while.' He closed the door quietly behind him.

He gave Rachel an hour, to be on the safe side, before he returned with Bella. She was sitting on the edge of the bed in a long, white nightgown, a thick, knitted shawl about her shoulders, her toes curling on the bare floor boards. She had washed herself—all over if he judged by the state of the water she'd left—and apart from her hair, scraped back and held by a ribbon at her nape, she was as sweet as a daisy. The comparison stirred memories, but he quickly put them aside.

Bella had to be fed, and then Rachel brushed the child's curly hair and slipped her nightgown over her head. Bella was yawning and Rachel settled her down on the bed, close against the wall, kissing her soft cheek. She sat beside Bella, smoothing her hair, and sang, softly, a lullaby Will didn't recognise. Her voice was low and sweet and it stirred something inside of him, like a toothache. He moved restlessly, not wanting to let the past in. But it came anyway, sweeping down on him like a great bird.

After Will had left Rachel, he'd gone back to using his real name. Will Trigg seemed dead, and beneath that thin veneer Will Moody was waiting to take over. Solitary, single-minded, Will Moody was a better option when it came to surviving without Rachel. He'd come out of hiding, the killer. And it was easy to go back to doing what he did best. It even gave him a warped sort of pleasure, knowing how much Rachel would have disapproved.

And now, here she was. His wife. Back after all these years, if only for a short time. Could she cope with Will Moody, the man she had hated so much at Greengage she couldn't even bear his touch?

Rachel had finished singing; the silence was strangely alive with memories. Bella was asleep, her thumb in her mouth. I've missed so much, Will thought bitterly. I've been a father and didn't know it, and now it's too late. The life I've made for myself doesn't allow for Bella.

'Are you tired?' he asked Rachel sharply, to still his thoughts, but resentment lingered in his voice. 'I've more to write. Lie down and I'll try not to disturb you.'

Rachel lay down obediently and pulled the blanket up to her chin. Her stomach made a great mound under the covers and Will felt himself flinch.

'How long have you to go?' he asked her in that cold, expressionless voice she was growing to hate.

Her eyes slid to his, almost slyly, and away again. 'About a month,' she told him just as expressionlessly.

'Well, we'll have to face that when we come to it,' he muttered grimly to himself, and bent over his papers.

The bed was in the shadows at the edge of the lamplight and, feeling herself hidden, Rachel watched him. There was something magical in lying comfortable in the bed, gazing sleepily at Will. The expressions played over his face; the sudden frown between his brows, the quirk of his mouth. He'd rolled up his sleeves and his forearms were brown, the dark hairs barely visible against his suntan. Long fingers, ink stained, flexed as he wrote. She watched the muscles of his shoulders tighten beneath his shirt as he leaned forward, frowning at the papers before him. He'd taken off his boots—she'd watched him clean them and sit them neatly in the corner—and stretched out his stockinged feet, easing his long legs.

It was Will, it really was. She had imagined being with him all the way from Wattle Bank, but this was so much more. He was Will, and yet he was a stranger. The cold expression in his eyes frightened her; the familiar qualms set her stomach churning. How could she find a way through his hurt and anger and find again the Will she had married at Greengage four years ago? Was he still there to be found or had he changed beyond recognition? Had the man she had wanted back vanished entirely? Her thoughts spun around and around, until they no longer made sense at all.

Eventually she slept, her hand slipping off her breast to hang limply over the edge of the bed. Even Bella, turning in her sleep, could not wake her, and when Will finally stripped off his clothes and flung himself down on the hard little truckle bed, she hardly even stirred. It was Will who had difficulty sleeping.

His feet stuck over the end, and though he wrapped the blanket around himself, they soon felt like lumps of ice. And he wasn't used to sharing. Her breathing woke him several times in the night, bringing him up, his heart thumping, the adrenalin pumping as he made ready to fight the intruder. But each time he fell back against the hard pallet with a sigh. It was Rachel, no intruder. It was his wife.

Twice, she climbed out of bed to relieve herself, and almost tripped over him. And she took a long time to settle again, tossing and turning, sighing. As if the whole world were resting on her shoulders. Will pressed his forearm over his eyes. What was she worrying about? he asked himself irritably. He was the one who should be doing the worrying. She'd put herself in his care, hadn't she? All she had to do was sit tight and have her baby.

I should have made her go to the inn, he admitted to himself, deep in his heart. I should have insisted. But he also knew that he could never have turned her out. If he hurt himself by that weakness, then so be it.

Only a month. That was what she had said, wasn't it? One month, and she'd be leaving. Until then he'd just have to keep his distance, and that was one thing he was good at. Will sighed and lifted his arm from over his eyes to stare at the dark ceiling. Surely, he thought, in his innocence, things couldn't change that much, just because Rachel and Bella were here?

The dream came just before dawn. Rachel heard the voice, and as she drifted out of sleep, puzzlement turned to relief. Will's voice. And then, as sleep receded further, relief gave way to shock. For it was Will's voice, and yet something about it was wrong. 'Blood, there's blood,' he whispered. And then, his voice becoming a moan, 'Oh no, oh no.' His breath hissed out, and Rachel lay stiff, waiting for the dream to continue. Will turned his head, 'Watch out,' and his voice was strangled, 'there's a gun —' The last word was a shout, bringing him out of the bed and onto his feet. Rachel managed to get to her knees, reaching out a hand to grip his arm. At her touch, he cried out, going as stiff as a board, and his eyes, hollows in the faint dawn light, shone with terror.

'Will,' she breathed. 'Will, it's me. It's Rachel. Will, what is it?'

The terror in his eyes receded, and with a groan he put his head into his hands. Rachel struggled to her feet, putting her arms around him and they half fell, half sat onto the mattress. 'Just a dream,' he was saying. 'Just a dream.' As if he were trying to convince himself. Rachel held him, pressing his face to her shoulder as if he were her child rather than her husband. At last he took a shuddering breath and straightened.

Rachel realised that Bella was sitting at the bottom of the bed, eyes like saucers, and held out her arms. Bella crawled quickly into them and Rachel held her child, allowing the sensation of the little body against hers to comfort her. Finally, she felt able to look up at Will.

He was still sitting beside her. The feel of her seemed to have stuck to his skin, and he was having trouble clearing a mind still half blurred by sleep and the horror of the dream. Rachel's face was pale between the dark wings of her hair. He watched her eyes grow big. And then a rush of colour flooded her cheeks and she looked away as though she were embarrassed.

'I have dreams,' he said, the anger clipping his voice. 'Sometimes they're bad.'

Rachel nodded, her head still turned away, so that only her nose showed beyond the dark curtain of her hair.

The dreams were part of what he did for a living. It was as if his mind and emotions, which he controlled so rigidly during waking hours, ran amok in sleep. It was one of the reasons he preferred to sleep alone. Rachel, he remembered wryly, had been terrified of his dreams in Greengage. She had never held him then, as she did just now.

'I'm sorry if I frightened you and Bella,' he went on, calmer now. 'Put the pillow over your head next time.'

Rachel glanced sideways at him and he sensed she was going to ask questions. To forestall her, Will asked, 'Do you want something hot to drink?' and stood up, stretching until he felt the satisfying pull of muscle and sinew. 'I have to get up anyway.'

'You'd better put some clothes on first,' she said quietly. Beside her, Bella giggled.

It was only then that Will realised he was stark naked. He swore and dived for his breeches, hauling them on while Rachel and Bella gazed at their hands with studied care. He was angry, Rachel realised. He felt foolish. What would he feel if he knew that the sight of him had made her heart pound twice as fast as normal? The pale dawn light had turned the hard muscle of shoulder and thigh to marble. She'd called him beautiful once, long ago.

He still was.

Rachel sipped the tea he had made, watching the steam rise from the mug, and sitting quietly in the bed, soaking up the warmth before she need face the chill morning. Will—dressed now—pulled on his boots. 'I'll be out all morning,' he told her briefly, 'but I should be back by noon.'

She twisted the mug in her hands. 'I need to wash my hair.'

'You'll have plenty of time for that.' He went to look out of the window, frowning. The light showed up the weary lines around his eyes, the stern set of his mouth. Rachel hardly heard him speaking— 'Looks like a clear day. You can sit outside in the sun and dry it'—thinking how unhappy he must be. What right had she to upset his life? It was on the tip of her tongue to tell him she would go, when Bella said in her solemn little voice, 'You haven't kissed me goodbye, Father.'

Will laughed, and bent to give her a hug.

Rachel smiled and said nothing. She was here for Bella's sake, wasn't she? She sat there long after he had gone. She could hear voices outside. The Police Post was coming to life again, and Rachel was a stranger here, who must learn to find a niche for herself. Just now she was safe inside the hut, and, she reminded herself, Will would be back at noon.

Suddenly, she remembered that she needed to wash her hair before he got back, and with a gasp pushed herself out of the bed to begin her own day.

By noon, Rachel had washed her hair, and Bella's, and cooked Will's meal. He looked surprised when he came in and she wondered what he had expected to see. Both of them still in bed? Or maybe he had just hoped they would be gone.

'We'll need more rations,' he said, unbuckling his belt and unbuttoning his jacket. The sun was shining outside and Will was sweating from the hard ride back from Zachary Quills station, Emu

Downs. There had been a number of complaints about bushrangers to the east and Will was keen to follow them up. Quill had put him off.

'There are still several matters outstanding closer to home. Two servants absconded and Jarvis over at Hillside has been drinking and throwing his fists around again. The grey horse is still missing from Mr Paynter's run —'

Will knew he was right. It wasn't keenness to do his duty that made the prospect of riding away for a week or two so attractive. It was the thought of Rachel and Bella, and the confused tangle of his own emotions. Already, after only one night, he was beginning to realise that keeping his distance wasn't quite as easy as he had expected. When he'd woken up from his nightmare and found Rachel there, holding him in soft, warm arms . . . Something about her fresh, clean smell brought the past back with an unstoppable surge, and his body had responded. And then Rachel had turned to Bella and he'd had time to regain his control, damp down the desperate urge he'd felt to press Rachel back on to the bed and . . . Well, if his daughter hadn't been there things might have turned out differently. It wouldn't happen again. He'd make sure of it.

'Have you filled out the paperwork concerning your wife?' Quill had asked him, as if reading his mind.

'Not yet.' Will had taken all emotion out of his voice. 'She may not be stayin', once the baby's born.'

Quill had turned and looked at him, his brown eyes narrowing to slits. He was an intelligent man,

Quill, and Will felt uncomfortable before that questioning gaze. 'Indeed,' Quill replied at last. 'I thought that when we manage to get Yelland transferred back to Melbourne, you would be able to move to the married quarters. Can't be very comfortable for you at the moment?'

Will thought it was best to say nothing.

Quill shrugged. 'As you wish, Sergeant. Just let me know when she leaves.'

It wasn't until Will went out to his horse that he realised he was sweating as if it was midsummer rather than a mild spring day.

'More rations?' Rachel repeated now, interrupting his thoughts.

'Yes.' He avoided her eyes, and sat down to his meal. It was good. 'I'll take you across to the store this afternoon. God I'm hungry,' he admitted with a forced smile, and tucked in.

He was always hungry. She'd forgotten that—how he was always hungry. How many other things had she forgotten about him? The thought made her sad. If they had stayed together, they would have been wed four years now. So much time lost. They may as well be strangers.

Will was pleased with his meal. And despite his determination not to look, he noticed her clean hair.

She hadn't had time to bind it up, and had left it hanging loose down her back. Long, midnight black locks, curling damply at the ends. Like ink, he thought, drawn with the softly curving strokes of an artist's pen. Her skin seemed even paler against the black tendrils, although some of the tiredness had been smoothed away with sleep. But there were still hollows under her eyes, and she held her mouth straight and tight, as though she were no longer used to smiling. The girl of Greengage was gone and the knowledge hurt him, as if something precious had been stolen from him.

'Maybe you should rest this afternoon instead of comin' to the store,' he said abruptly. 'I'll ask Violet to mind Bella for you. Put your feet up, Rachel.'

He was being very kind, she realised. Was that because he felt sorry for her? Rachel winced at the idea—she didn't want his pity.

'No,' she insisted, 'I'm all right. Don't worry about me. I'm not here to be a burden to you.'

Why are you here then? he almost asked, but he changed his mind. Best not to ask. It would only get them further embroiled in the mess. Rachel would be gone soon and the less he knew about her life the better.

Already, his men were asking questions—he had one mounted trooper, Kemp, and one foot constable, Yelland, under his command. Strange, Yelland said, that he had never mentioned a wife before, and then one turns up, with one child walking and one on the way. Odd that. But Will had shrugged it off, fending the questions or just not answering them.

Yelland was the main problem. Kemp was just ribbing him in his usual half malicious, half friendly way. But Yelland was serious about it. 'Didn't even know you was spliced, Sarge!' he'd said, limping up. And, with a pretence at good humour, 'Or were you hopin' she'd lost your trail? Must be a pretty good tracker, eh? Maybe we can sign her on in Joseph's place?'

The two men sniggered.

'Your wife'd be a better black tracker, surely, Constable,' Will replied softly. 'She's half black with bruises already.' He'd walked away, knowing he shouldn't have said it. But Yelland's treatment of his wife infuriated him, and though he had tried to caution the man, Yelland just shrugged and told him to mind his own business. And Mrs Yelland was far too frightened of her husband to make any complaints. Now Yelland would only hate him more.

When he first arrived, Will had tried desperately to treat Yelland fairly, even though everything about the man filled him with repugnance. He knew the feeling was mutual, and the sooner Quill got Yelland that transfer the better.

The Police store turned out to be the locked room in the office building. Inside, the daylight was muted, but Rachel saw that it was much the same as the store at McCrae's Castle, packed with sacks and barrels, as well as the hardware of the Police Post. Here, a man could purchase new boots or a hat, a new coat or handkerchief, and here his weekly rations of flour, sugar and tea were doled out to him. There was a shelf of medicines, too—castor oil and something in a blue bottle that claimed wonderous results in settling the stomach. Rachel eyed them with interest, while Will sorted out their extra rations.

'Have you a cow?' she asked him, glancing about again.

Will felt his mouth tremble on the edge of a smile. 'Not on me, no.' Then, when she flashed him a doubtful look, 'We buy our meat, milk and butter from the general store back down the road. Jim McPherson has everythin' you could want, and then more. I'll have a word with him, if you like?' His eyebrows lifted questioningly.

'Thank you,' Rachel replied primly.

Will locked the door after them. When he turned, he saw that Kemp was standing behind him, and he had no choice but to introduce Rachel.

She smiled, giving him her direct rather disconcerting look. 'Constable Kemp.'

Kemp eyed her curiously.

'Constable Kemp is Violet's husband,' Will went on.

'Oh. Your wife has been kind enough to look after Bella for me.' As if, Constable Kemp later told his wife, it hadn't been near enough to a bloody order from her husband.

Kemp was a wiry little man, but his back was straight and his eyes didn't slide away from hers. His nose was bent slightly to one side, where it had once been broken, and there was a scar across his left eyebrow, cutting it in two. He looked as if he'd had a rough life.

'Sarge, can I 'ave a word?'

Will nodded, sending Rachel a glance which she supposed meant she should move along. She began to do so, but Bella dropped down to examine a black beetle making its laborious way across the dusty ground, and so she was still close enough to hear when Constable Kemp said:

'It's Yelland.'

Will nodded.

'I don't hold wif tellin' tales, but no-one likes Yelland and . . .'

Will sighed. 'Spit it out, Kemp.'

'The man's got a dangerous mouf on 'im.'

'What's he sayin'?' Will's voice was cold.

Kemp's voice dropped lower, beyond Rachel's hearing. Will listened, his head bowed, and then nodded brusquely. 'If I single him out, it'll look worse,' he said at last, reluctantly. He looked up, and noticed Rachel watching him. 'I'll deal with Yelland,' he said quietly. 'And thank you, Kemp.'

Kemp looked doubtful, but Will was already walking away.

Will walked quickly, and Rachel puffed to keep up with him. 'I didn't mean to cause you trouble,' she gasped, pulling Bella along behind her.

He didn't answer, but she thought uneasily that his silence was answer enough.

The subject was closed, and she bit her lip. They had reached the hut before she saw the man sitting on the ground beside it. A black man, in trooper's jacket and old canvas trousers, his bare feet white with dust. As they approached, he stood up, and Rachel noted that he was a short man, shorter than herself.

'Joseph,' Will said, and though he didn't smile, his grey eyes warmed.

'Boss.' Joseph glanced expectantly at Rachel. 'I came to meet your missus. Heard she was here. This her?'

And, when Will nodded, Joseph held out his hand. Startled, Rachel took it and felt as if her arm was being shaken off.

'How do you do?' he asked her politely, beaming at her.

'Very well,' Rachel answered him breathlessly.

'You come down from Wattle Bank, that right?'

Rachel nodded, 'That's right.'

For a moment Joseph's eyes seemed far away, and then he shook his head. 'Nice place that, missus.'

'Yes, it is. Do you know it?'

His smile mocked her, or himself. 'I know it.' He glanced at Will, 'Got work to do now, missus.' And he nodded, as his loose stride took him off towards the stables.

'He seemed very pleased to meet me,' Rachel managed.

Will said nothing, suddenly annoyed. He'd have to have a word to Joseph later. Joseph was the only one who knew the truth about him and Rachel. Will had told him, one night, when he'd found Joseph drunk for the dozenth time. It had seemed important for Joseph to know that Will'd once been chained to the grog, too, and that he'd pulled back from the brink. So Will had told him about Rachel. Joseph had been a good listener, and they'd forged a sort of friendship. Both loners, both out-casts, they had something in common. Not that Will's story had done much good. Joseph still drank as much as ever.

Rachel was watching him, wondering why he looked so irritated. It was like being with a stranger, she thought, feeling your way through each new moment, discovering how the other person thought or acted, what pleased them and what didn't. And then sometimes, like a revelation, she would see something of the old Will Trigg in him.

'Is Joseph a tracker?'

Will nodded brusquely. 'Came originally from Wattle Bank way. We're lucky to have him.'

'He must miss his home,' she said, remembering the look on his face. 'How did he come to be here?'

Will glanced at her then, consideringly. 'He was with the Native Police Corps until a couple of months ago. Have you heard of' em?' And, when she nodded, 'The idea was good, gettin' up a troop of blacks to keep order. If you send them into areas away from their own tribes, it's like old times for them, makin' war on the enemy. But the Native Police Corp's had similar problems to the rest of the police force. It's the same, white and black. Once the drink gets a hold on them, they're not much good at doing their job. Joseph was like that, but he's pulled back a bit since then. The Goulburn suits him better, I reckon.'

'I would have thought he was better off with his own family,' Rachel said, something in Will's eyes holding hers. 'Doesn't he have a family?'

'His family died a couple of years ago. The land they considered theirs now belongs to squatters. They didn't have their boundaries marked, you see, or put up fences,' he sounded sarcastic. 'There's nothin' Joseph can do about it. The squatters don't recognise any right to the land but their own.'

'His family . . . how did they die? I mean, they weren't murdered?'

Will smiled without humour. 'Murdered,' he repeated, turning the word over. 'Well, maybe. They died of smallpox. It's killed hundreds since the whites arrived in Port Phillip. That's what the blacks are dyin' of, disease not bullets. I'm not sayin' there haven't been incidents, but the blacks are dis-appearin' at a fast rate. Faster than any man could shoot them. Why, even a year ago the squatters were havin' more problems with sheep stealin' and spearings than they are now. I hear there are some squatters who don't bother to yard their sheep at night because the threat has gone. The blacks just aren't there—and they've poisoned the wild dogs with arsenic. The land belongs to the sheep.'

He sounded uncaring, merely stating facts. Rachel felt righteous anger stirring in her and some of the old passion was in her voice when she replied. 'You're talking as if you think that's how it should be!'

But Will shook his head. His eyes met hers, mocking her emotion. 'No, I don't think that's how it should be.' After a pause he went on, softly now. 'I've come across them dyin' in the bush, just lying down and dyin'. When I first saw it—an old woman and a child, it was, who had wandered off from the rest of the tribe, or sent away maybe when they saw they were sick. I wanted to help so bad . . . I wanted to take them in to the barracks, find a doctor . . . But I was with an old Corporal from the Border Police, and he told me there was nothin' anyone could do. They'd die, even if I took them to Melbourne and paid for the best doctor I could find. The smallpox and the syphillis was eating away at them, he said, and they couldn't fight it off. I didn't believe him then. I took that old woman and the child in to the Protectorate at Jim Crow. But the Corporal spoke the truth. There was nothin' anyone could do. The Protectors, they're the ones paid to help the blacks, but they can't do anythin'. And the squatters, well I think a lot of them do care more than you give them credit for, but there's nothin' they can do either. The whole thing is a tragedy. If I knew how to stop it, I would, Rachel.'

She was looking at him, and there was something in her eyes that startled him. Christ, he thought in amazement, she's looking at me like she used to, at Greengage. She's looking at me like I'm some sort of bloody hero.

'Don't,' he said sharply.

Rachel dropped her eyes. 'Don't what?' she asked him in a quiet, questioning voice.

He knew then that he must have been mistaken— a trick of the light—and shook his head. 'Come on,' he said impatiently. 'Come inside, and you can put your feet up.'

CHAPTER 26

RACHEL TOOK OVER THE COOKING. Will's stomach was her ally and she knew it. Besides, it was the least she could do. She kept the hut as tidy as possible, but with the three of them living in such a confined space things tended to get out of hand. Certainly, Will's rather austere living conditions could not survive. Did he cringe every time he came in the door? Rachel wondered. If he did, he kept his feelings to himself, just as he kept everything else to himself. Rachel got through her days well enough. There was always plenty to do. If she had wanted to, she could have pretended she was back at the Castle, or Down Farm, for the work was the same, and the sameness seemed comforting. It was the nights that bothered her.

With the baby so near, she hardly slept at all from the discomfort of her heavy body. And, lying awake, she found her thoughts revolving around the familiar worries of Will and Bella and herself.

The darkness became her enemy, just as Will had said it was his friend. All her fears and doubts came to keep her company in the darkness, and there were none of the chores she could do during the day to keep them at bay. Night after night, Rachel lay staring at the faint square of light from the window, and probed the details of her life, picking at it like an ill-stitched dress, torturing herself with her mistakes, wondering what she should have done differently. And then she would count the days left to her from the month Will had given her, feeling them rushing by, as unstoppable as a bolting horse. Panic gripped her, but she knew there was nothing she could do to force his acceptance of the situation. Will had made up his mind, and Will was like Mount Alexander; immovable. He was kind to her, yes, and considerate, but it was the sort of kindness and consideration one offered a stranger. There was a distance between them, as if he had put up an invisible wall. And although Rachel pressed her face against it, and searched with desperate fingers for some weakness, it held firm. Will stared back at her from the other side, totally inviolate and completely alone.

I want him to love me again, she admitted to herself in the darkness. I want to see that light in his grey eyes that used to be there whenever he looked at me. I want to feel his arms about me, holding me as though he'll never let me go. He used to seem so strong . . . and yet vulnerable, too, because he was as dependent upon my love for him as I was on his love for me.

Yes, the darkness was her enemy. Sometimes, she felt Israel's baby stretching inside her and wondered if it might not solve everything if she were to die giving birth. The idea would appeal, if it wasn't for Bella.

The Goulburn River flowed in a curve behind the Police Post, like a great half circle. Out of sight, where the riverbank butted into the river, was a small, rickety punt that travellers could use to pull themselves across to the other side. The main crossing punt, however, was further south, at Seymour and it was there the overlanders and the squatters took their sheep and cattle. The little punt was only fit for a man on horseback or a small wagon.

Rachel tried to go for a walk every day and more often than not she walked in the direction of the river. Trees grew thickly along the top of the steep, almost vertical riverbanks, between which the silent river flowed uninterrupted. The rippling water was the colour of gold, thought Rachel, with the occasional tree branch slipping along, half submerged beneath it. Dangerous, that was the Goulburn.

Rosa Yelland had come upon Rachel one day, gazing reflectively into the deep waters of the river.

Rosa's sly face, rather like that of her husband, assumed an ingratiating smile, displaying the black spaces which had once been teeth.

'Mrs Moody?'

Rachel smiled back. She didn't like Rosa Yelland. Rosa had straggling black hair and an unwashed body. Rachel found her dirt repulsive, but tried not to make her feelings too apparent. Besides she could understand a bit of dirt and grime; it was hard to be properly clean in a place like this.

Rachel could have forgiven the woman her dirt, if she'd been a nice person.

She wasn't.

Rosa stood beside her, smelling of rum and mutton, and peered into the river as if expecting to see something. There was an old native canoe pulled up almost on its end, the bark torn and rotten. Soon it would return to the earth from where it had come. Now that the punt was in place, no one had cause to use bark canoes.

'Sergeant Wheeler's wife used to stand here, just like this,' Rosa said, a strange look on her face. 'Many a time I've come across her, just like you are, starin' into the river.'

'Oh?' Rachel frowned. The words appeared to have some significance.

Rosa nodded her head, and leaned closer, breathing rum into Rachel's face. 'She drowned herself, poor soul.'

Rachel stepped back, suddenly nauseated by the other woman's closeness. Rosa, thinking it was her words which had repelled Rachel, smiled in what was meant to be a sympathetic manner.

They walked back to the post together. Rosa had five children, all as dirty and uncared for as their mother. Yelland spent most of his time down at the inn and Rachel, dislike him though she might, could understand his reluctance to come home.

Violet Kemp came out of her cottage as they approached and shouted a 'Good afternoon'.

'Got another shiner, I see,' she said to Rosa, hands on hips.

Rosa's mouth tightened. Surprised, Rachel realised that she did indeed have a black eye—she had thought it was just a thicker than usual coating of grime.

'Nothin' to do with you,' Rosa muttered.

'Maybe not,' Violet agreed heartily, 'but your noise is keepin' me and mine awake. Screamin' and yellin' half the night. Why don't you chuck him out?'

Rosa narrowed dark, angry eyes. 'You try feedin' five kids with no man and no money.'

Violet was unmoved. 'I'd rather starve than put up with that.'

Rosa muttered something uncomplimentary as she sidled away.

Violet shook her head at Rosa's departing back. 'She's a slut, but I can't help bein' sorry for 'er. Yelland is a bastard.'

Rachel agreed with her, but thought she'd better not say so. As the wife of the sergeant in charge of the Police Post, she found herself in a difficult position. The other two wives seemed to think she held as much power over their lives as Will, and took whatever she said as gospel truth. It was best to say as little as possible, and certainly nothing about her and Will's private affairs.

Violet, in contrast to Rosa, was a tall, robust woman, with a direct gaze and a dry sense of humour. Her apron was always clean and tied firmly around her broad waist and her two children always looked scrubbed. She viewed Rosa with contempt tinged with pity for her inability, or unwillingness, to alter her ways. Violet, as she told Rachel proudly, was the local nurse and midwife.

'Mr Quill couldn't get a medical man to come out here, and the nearest doctor is in Melbourne.

He reckoned I was the next best thing. It was me he wanted, when he took on Kemp. He told me so. Anyway,' with a grin, 'it brings in a few extra pennies.' Violet frowned. 'You'll be needin' me soon, or are you going down to the hospital in Melbourne? Left it a bit late, haven't you?'

'I'll stay here,' Rachel replied.

Violet nodded, viewing her with a professional eye. 'You need to rest up, Mrs Moody.' Rachel looked pale and thin, she thought. Whatever she had been doing these past months, since Will Moody came to the Goulburn, it didn't seem to have done her much good. Or maybe it was coming back to her husband that hadn't been beneficial for her body and soul.

'Your wife wants feedin' up,' she told Will roundly, when she met him outside the office. 'And she's got circles under her eyes as deep as the grave. She'll need all her strength when the baby comes, or she'll end up in one. I'm relyin' on you, Sergeant, to see she comes through it in one piece.'

Resentment simmered inside him. Relying on him, was she? Will glared at her, but Violet just glared back. Reluctantly, he grinned. 'You should have been the one to join the police, not your husband.'

Violet cocked her eyebrow. 'No good at takin' orders, Sergeant. Only good at givin' 'em.'

As Will walked slowly towards his hut—though it didn't feel like his anymore, by God!—Violet's words repeated themselves in his head. Hadn't he thought the same thing, when he first saw Rachel? And yet she was eating well and sleeping well . . . Or was she? Had he really taken much notice? To be honest, he'd tried not to look at her too closely.

And then there was Maeve.

Will hadn't been down to the inn since Rachel arrived. He didn't feel comfortable about it. Maeve had been asking after him—Yelland had told him so, eyeing him sideways. Will knew that he would have to go and see her, explain to her. The thought of it made him uneasy. He had never meant to let her get so close to him, but Maeve was a passionate woman. Somehow she'd slipped under his guard. She made him laugh, and that was something he hadn't done much of in a long time.

'You're too serious, Sergeant,' she'd mocked. 'Life's too short to be so serious. You need someone to teach you to enjoy it.'

'And you're the one, are you?' he'd retorted.

But she'd not been embarrassed in the slightest. 'I'm the one,' she agreed.

'I'm taken already,' he had said. He always said that, to keep women at a distance. After Rachel, there didn't seem much point in anyone else. Hannah had died and Rachel . . . well, Rachel's love had turned to hate. Two tries should be enough to convince a man he wasn't much good at keeping his women.

Instead of heeding his warning, Maeve had winked. 'I don't mind if someone else's had their spoon in the puddin'. Don't mean it doesn't still taste good.'

And he'd laughed, and while he laughed, she was grinning back at him, nodding.

Later, when he'd spent the night in her bed, she'd admitted she'd wanted him from the first. And he was flattered, because plenty of other men were after Maeve, and although she flirted and teased, she never asked them to her little room, as she had asked Will.

'I can't insult anyone,' she'd explained to him with a sigh. 'It'd be bad for business. So I have to play my little games with them, send them home happy, thinkin' that maybe next time they'll be lucky.'

'You're a clever woman, Maeve.'

Indeed, he knew he was a fortunate man. There were many others who would have changed places without a second thought. But it was he who Maeve had chosen, he who kissed that red, smiling mouth and clasped that golden body, and found all her secrets in the rum-scented dark. Occasionally, he found himself speaking to her as he hadn't spoken in years, but usually he let her do the talking. In Maeve, he had found something new and exciting, and if Rachel hadn't come back, perhaps Maeve would have been enough for him.

The thought took him by surprise.

Maeve *was* enough for him, he assured himself. Rachel was a temporary inconvenience. In a matter of weeks now, she'd be gone. What the devil was he thinking of? The ever present anger stirred, adding fuel to Violet's accusations, so his mood was not good as he opened the door to his hut.

Rachel had lit the lamp and the fire was giving off a pleasant, orange glow. The atmosphere was warm and stuffy and cluttered. She was stooping to the pot—he smelt something delicious and meaty cooking—and looked up with a tentative smile. Will was frowning, his mouth a forbidding line and she quickly turned away again, pretending not to notice.

Just as well, Will thought furiously. Just as bloody well! If she'd said anything he would have bitten her head off. He'd be damned if he'd let her back into his life again, laying waste to it. It was over. He'd waited a long time for her and she hadn't given him a thought. And now that he had found Maeve and begun to believe that happiness was again possible, here she was, back to spoil it for him. The fury, simmering inside him, bubbled up. He felt his control begin to slip.

A pair of little arms gripped him around the thighs. Startled, Will looked down, and his dark emotions dissolved. Bella! He smiled with relief and lifted her up. At least with Bella there were no complications. He would miss Bella more than he dared to imagine.

'How are you, darlin'?' he asked her, but didn't really listen to her long recital of the day's activities. He was watching Rachel.

She was bending over the hearth, and paused to push the damp tendrils of hair back from her face— the heat of the fire had her flushed and per-spiring. She straightened then, pressing both hands hard to the small of her back, as though to give it extra support. Will watched her arch her body, so that her back was like a bow, and her stom-ach jutted out beneath the thick folds of her skirt. The bodice strained across her swollen breasts, and sweat stains made half circles under her arms.

Suddenly Will was so furious he wanted to smash something. He wanted to swing his fists around, breaking everything in sight.

As if aware of his inner turmoil, Bella had stopped

talking and edged away from him. Will clenched his hands on his thighs.

'Sit down before you fall down,' he said between gritted teeth. 'I'll do that.'

Rachel looked at him wide-eyed, her mouth slightly ajar. He was frowning again and he looked angry. Very angry. Her heart began to thud, as she searched her mind desperately for what she might have done wrong. But he had wrenched out a chair and, with an iron grip on her shoulders, pushed her down hard into it.

Bella giggled nervously.

'I don't mind—' Rachel began haltingly.

'Well I do!' he shouted. She jumped. 'How do you think it feels to have Violet Kemp telling me I'm workin' you to death?'

So that was it. He was upset because he'd been made to look unkind. Rachel sighed. 'She doesn't understand,' she told him quietly. 'I'm perfectly all right.'

But Will, stooping to the hearth, shot her a look from under his fringe of dark hair. 'You don't look all right,' he snapped. 'Do you eat, Rachel? You're too thin.'

'I eat,' she whispered.

'Do you sleep then?'

Her eyes slipped away and she shrugged. Rachel waited, tense, for him to berate her. But he only made an impatient sound and began to dish up their meal. In his hurry, he slopped it onto the table. Rachel opened her mouth, caught his eye, and closed it again. How could she tell him the truth?

That sometimes she thought of dying. And that

if it weren't for Bella, and the worry of her, she might even imagine death her friend. Will would not have her back, she knew that now. There was no use pretending she could somehow wheedle her way around him. He was too hard for her. And at night, as she lay in the darkness, unable to sleep, she faced her own mortality.

They ate in silence and afterwards Rachel settled Bella for sleep. The soft murmurs of his wife and daughter flowed over him and Will allowed his thoughts to drift. The anger was in hiding again, deep inside. It frightened him, that anger. It had hardly bothered him at all, until Rachel came back. Could he possibly turn into another Yelland, lashing out at his wife and children for his own shortcomings and inadequacies? The idea was unpleasant to say the least. He had never felt like hitting Maeve; there was only one thing he wanted to do to Maeve . . .

'Will?'

Will looked up sharply, realising Rachel had been calling his name and he hadn't answered her. He wondered, for a moment, whether he had 'Maeve' printed on his forehead, and then told himself not to be ridiculous—Maeve was his business, not Rachel's.

Rachel was stroking Bella's head—the child had fallen asleep in her usual place on the bed. Dark curls softly framed the little heart shaped face, smoothed now of all cares as she dreamed pleasant dreams.

'Will, can you promise me something?' She was fixing him with her dark eyes, bewitching him, he thought uneasily.

'Promise you what?' he countered coldly.

'If something happens to me when the baby's born, do you promise to look after Bella?'

'What could happen?' he asked her suspiciously.

'I could die,' she said matter-of-fact.

A hollow opened in the pit of his stomach, and he stared at her in horror.

'I just . . . sometimes I think . . .' she swallowed, squeezing her hands together in her lap. 'You asked me if I slept well. I don't, Will, I don't sleep well. And that's one of the things that worries me in the night. It's something I have to think about . . . plan for. I would rest better if I knew you would take care of Bella if anything happened to me.'

'Ah, Rachel, don't,' he whispered, as if he couldn't help himself. Surprised, she looked up and saw that he was genuinely distressed. 'You don't want to think like that,' he went on, his voice recovering. 'You'll be fine.'

She shook her head, her face hard with determination. 'You can't know that. Women die. Ask Violet Kemp. I know what it's like to be alone, Will. I know. Bella needs you.'

He shook his head, trying to clear his mind. 'She'd be better off with your mother,' he said, forcing his anger up from its hiding place. 'What do I know of children? I couldn't care for her properly, Rachel.'

'You don't understand,' she whispered, and her voice was muffled because she had bowed her head. 'She doesn't want anyone else.'

And in a quiet, weary voice she told him about Bella running away and the terror of those hours when they had thought she was lost forever. And then what Bella had said, when finally she was brought home. When she had finished there was a long silence. 'Why didn't you tell me this before?' he asked curiously.

Her chest was rising and falling so fast he was concerned and then the words burst out of her, garbled and almost incoherent, but he got the gist of them. She thought it was her fault. She and Mary had been so caught up in each other, she hadn't had much time for Bella. And that morning—the morning before she ran away—Rachel had snapped at her.

Will sighed.

'You see now, don't you?' she demanded of him. 'If something happens to me, then it's you she wants, Will. And don't tell me a father can't bring up his daughter, because I know differently!'

Will straightened his shoulders. 'All right,' he said softly. 'If anythin' happens to you, then I'll look after her.'

The strength went out of her. There was a tremendous sense of relief; Will would be there. He would take care of Bella. And whatever he might think or feel for Rachel herself, she knew he loved Bella.

'You still haven't told me why you didn't mention this when you first arrived,' he said after a moment.

She half smiled, shifting on the bed to ease her back. 'I was afraid you'd think I was using it against you, to force you to let me stay. I didn't want to use Bella like that. I hoped . . . I don't know what I hoped,' with a shake of her head. 'Just that somehow everything would come right.'

He said nothing and she didn't dare look at him.

Rachel shifted her weight again, reaching around to try and rub the ache in her back. Will watched her, knowing he should offer to rub it for her, but he couldn't. He dared not. If he touched her . . . he was afraid to touch her.

The knock on the door startled them both. Rachel straightened, looking around with curious eyes. Will began to rise to his feet, but the visitor didn't wait for an answer. The door was flung open, and a buxom blonde stood quivering on the threshold, her face glowing with fury, her blue eyes brilliant with tears.

'You bastard, Will Moody!' she shouted without preamble. 'I thought you were a man, but you're no different to all the other bastards. So I'm to be abandoned, am I? Because your wife comes home like a run away cat havin' kittens? Well, I won't have it, do you hear me? I won't have it!'

Her voice was of the carrying kind. Doors all over the Post opened and interested faces peered out. Will grabbed at the flailing arms.

'Maeve, shut up for Christ's sake —'

Her bosom swelled with so much indignation, Rachel thought it might pop right over the top of her dress. 'After all we've been to each other, you tell me to shut up. And you,' she glared around his shoulder at Rachel, 'I know all about you, so don't pretend you're innocence betrayed. He's not your man any more, do you hear me? He's mine! You go back to whatever hole you crawled out of and leave Will alone.'

Rachel stared at her, open mouthed.

Will shoved Maeve through the doorway and into the darkness. Outside, Rachel could hear him talking fast in a low voice but not what he said. However, Maeve did no more shouting, and after a time Rachel heard footsteps retreating towards the inn.

Will came back inside, and closed the door. His grey eyes avoided hers, as he smoothed back his hair. 'That was Maeve,' he said.

'Yes.'

'She's bit of a hot-head,' he added. 'You shouldn't take too much notice of what she says.'

It was an understatement. Rachel put her head into her hands and her shoulders began to shake. Will groaned aloud, and took a step towards her, at a loss what to say after Maeve's performance.

'Rachel, it's nothin'. She didn't mean the half of it, she never does. She just likes makin' a scene—enjoys it.' And then, as he touched her shoulder and bent closer, he realised she wasn't crying after all. She was laughing.

'Rachel!'

His shocked voice made Rachel lift her face, pink and crumpled, tears of laughter streaming from her eyes. She gasped, 'W-what a woman.'

'It's not funny,' he said reprovingly, but suddenly laughter was winding its arms around him, too, and he found himself chuckling as she covered her face again, shaking her head.

It took several minutes for Rachel to recover, and then when she glanced at Bella and found her still fast asleep it nearly set her off again.

'I'm sorry,' she told Will at last, her voice husky from mirth. 'It wasn't really funny. It was just the way she burst in, I suppose, when we were talking so seriously. It was a bit like a play, wasn't it?'

Will gave a wry grin. 'I hope everyone enjoyed it.'

Rachel grimaced, thinking of the gossip. While they had laughed, they had felt almost comfortable with each other. Now the silence grew awkward again—Rachel knew Will was watching her, waiting for her to speak.

'Is she nice?' she managed. 'I mean, when she isn't carrying on like that?'

He narrowed his eyes at her, as though he were turning the question over in his mind, searching for hidden traps. 'Nice enough,' he told her at last in a cautious tone. Then, 'Rachel—'

But she shook her head sharply, fixing him with a look. 'It's all right. I don't expect you to . . . that is, I know I came here and forced myself on you. At the time it seemed the only thing I could do, after Bella, and . . . Well, I don't expect you to stop seeing Maeve. I should have made that clear in the beginning.'

Will knew he should be relieved. He should thank her for her generosity. Instead, there was that anger deep inside him, burning away with a bright, orange fire, and he knew with despair that he would have preferred it if she had ranted and raved and acted the jealous wife—rather like Maeve had done. He wanted Rachel to be jealous. Just as he was jealous—so hurt and angry and jealous it was tearing him apart. He couldn't bear knowing that it was not his child inside her. He wanted to kill her for that. He wanted to kill Israel Potter.

Rachel stood up, straightening her back carefully. Her dark eyes met to his, full of gentle mockery. 'Anyway, our marriage is all over with now, isn't it,

Will? If it wasn't for Bella, we wouldn't need to see each other ever again, would we?'

Did she know how he felt? Was she making fun of this agony inside him? Will searched her face for some hint of sadistic enjoyment, but she turned away, not waiting for an answer, and began to fold Bella's discarded clothes.

'If you want to go down to the inn any night, please do,' she went on conversationally. 'You don't have to worry about Bella and me. I want you to carry on with your life as if we weren't here.'

The fire inside him was burning brighter. She was giving her permission for him to visit another woman, and she could be so uncaring about it. 'I will,' he managed, his voice hardly above a whisper.

'Good!' She said it as if she were relieved they had come to a mutual understanding.

Should he say 'thank you' and head off after Maeve? She'd given him her blessing. The only problem was, he didn't want to go.

Rachel was humming. Glancing sideways at her, Will saw that she was beginning to prepare for bed. Head bent, she was unbuttoning the bodice of her dress, a lock of hair falling forward into her eyes. Impatiently, she tucked it behind one ear, frowning as she concentrated on the fastenings that held the dark cloth across her bosom. He watched her, fascinated; he couldn't help it. The bodice gaped slightly as she progressed, and Will saw her chemise, with a thin line of lace scalloping the neckline. And there, above it, the opulent swell of her breasts. The plump, white curves were suddenly so seductive. He'd always loved her breasts. How many times had he caressed them, kissed them, run his tongue across their peaks . . . Will swallowed.

Suddenly, as if sensing his gaze, Rachel looked up. For a long moment her eyes held his, dark and secret, before he looked away. He didn't look again until he heard her slip into bed and then he blew out the lamp and undressed quickly and savagely, throwing himself down onto his own bed.

'Goodnight, Will,' she said, her voice friendly. Sisterly, he thought bitterly.

He didn't answer. He didn't dare. And this time it was Will who tossed and turned all night, and Rachel who slept peacefully until dawn.

CHAPTER 27

AFTER MAEVE'S VISIT, RACHEL FELT as if things between her and Will had changed in some way. And yet she couldn't quite decide how. He had taken some of the worry from her shoulders with his promise in regard to Bella, but there was more to it than that. Something in his eyes, perhaps, when he looked at her, something in his manner. He was almost awkward in her presence, and she wondered, at first disbelieving and then with a surge of hope, if Will's barricades were coming down.

He still kept his distance. He rarely touched her, and then it was accidental or a formal taking of her arm. And he spoke to her only when necessary, preserving his silence. But there was something . . . Occasionally she glanced up quickly and caught him watching her. He always looked away, but just for an instant there was an expression in his eyes— was she mad to think it?—something like need or want or even desire.

'Desire!' she whispered hysterically to herself. How could a man like Will desire a woman so pregnant she was like a ship in full sail! And yet the hope grew, and she blossomed with it. Her pale face acquired a flush, her eyes shone, and her skin, sensitised by the coming child, tingled whenever he was near her.

Violet noticed the change in her. 'You're lookin' better, anyhow,' she said, giving Rachel one of her thorough, searching looks.

Rachel smiled, her face lighting up in the old way. 'I feel better.'

'Now you just need to get yourself a bigger hut.'

Rachel's smile faded. She'd like nothing better, but there was Will . . . Will hadn't mentioned her leaving again, not since she had told him about Bella. But neither did he say he had changed his mind. She could ask but asking would force him to give an answer, and what if it wasn't the answer she wanted to hear? Better to remain silent, better to hold onto her hope, because it was all that she had.

'You need to get rid of Maeve,' Violet added thoughtfully. 'But it won't be easy, not now that she's got 'er hooks in 'im.'

'He doesn't love her,' Rachel said quietly, and knew it for the truth. If he had loved Maeve, he would never have laughed at her or left her to walk home alone.

Violet frowned. 'Love or not, she's got a powerful attraction.'

And Rachel had seen enough of Maeve to know just what that attraction must be. Yelland, Rosa's husband spent hours hanging over his drink just watching her. Not, said Violet, that she looked at Yelland. Will was the one she'd chosen out of all of her admirers.

That evening, at the inn, Maeve was busy exercising her particular attraction on Will. The place was full and as noisy as usual—there were always men passing through or employees of the local landholders willing to drink and spend their money. Maeve had found herself and Will a quiet corner in which to talk, while Sean served the drinks. Sean was, so Maeve said, her 'dogsbody' and quite devoted to her. He did whatever was asked of him with a smile. Good natured and good humoured, everyone liked Sean and overlooked his peculiar, wrinkled little old-young face.

While Sean shrugged off the customers' jibes with a grin, Will leaned closer to Maeve and explained about Bella's request to see her father. And, after some probing from Maeve, Rachel's promise to leave after the baby was born. Maeve was contrite, begging his pardon, her blue eyes soft and hot, all at the same time. 'Come to my room after closing,' she told him, bending close, so that her bosom was resting against his arm. 'Poor Rachel won't mind.'

So it was *poor Rachel* now, he thought mockingly. As for the invitation . . . he was tempted, but that was as far as it went. Perhaps it was the thought of Rachel, waiting, that stopped him, and the knowledge that he'd have to face her with Maeve's scent all over him. Or perhaps it was simply because Maeve no longer appealed to him. That was a shock, but true enough. He looked at her voluptuous curves

and blonde curling hair, and . . . nothing happened.
Well, not exactly nothing. He admired what he
saw, but it went no deeper than that.

Maeve was cross with him when he made his
excuses, but Will knew he could tease her around
next time. And he hoped she didn't realise that his
feelings had undergone any sort of major change.
He didn't want to hurt her, she didn't deserve that.

In the end, he was glad to get outside, away from
the smoke and the stink of ale and rum. Sometimes, when he came here, he felt as if he couldn't
face stepping inside. But then the stubborn pride
in him would force his feet over the doorstep, just
to prove to himself he could do it, that he could be
in such a place and not take a drink. Because Will
hadn't taken more than one sip of the stuff since he
gave it up in '39.

Will grinned wryly, remembering that one sip.
He'd taken it by accident, down in Melbourne,
thinking it was water and too busy listening to the
talk to notice until it was too late that someone
had slipped spirit into it. He'd spat it out to the
great amusement of the taproom and, later, had lay
in his bed, sweating, craving the taste as he hadn't
done in a long time. In the end it came down to
a simple choice. He could sink back into the mire
he'd been in when Rachel found him, or he could
make something of his life. For that was the gift
Rachel had given him, whatever else she may have
done, and lying shivering alone in his bed, Will had
chosen to accept her gift.

Outside the Pride of Erin, the chill spring air
refreshed him. Will breathed deeply. He loved the
night. Above him, the cold stars shone in their

millions against the dark sky. He could see Orion diving headfirst over the eastern horizon while Pegasus galloped low in the north. Sagittarius, the centaur, was in the west and the Southern Cross shone brightly due south. He knew them, had used them to find his way in the darkness, they were friends. But tonight their beauty struck him afresh, as if he were looking at everything with new eyes.

As he neared his hut, unconsciously his step quickened. Inside, Rachel was sewing, seated by the fire in her nightgown and shawl, her dark head bent close to the lamp. She looked up with an anxious smile. He had a terrifying urge to reach out and smooth back a lock of hair that had fallen on her cheek, and bending place his mouth against the warm, soft crease between her jaw and her neck . . .

Abruptly, he turned to remove his jacket, forcing himself to empty his mind and concentrate on what he was doing. He knew now, what he had stubbornly refused to know before. There was no more pretending, and no more hiding from it. It was Rachel he wanted, even the way she was. No wonder Maeve no longer appealed. Will Moody had fallen in love with his wife, despite the fact that she was carrying another man's child, despite the fact that he had promised himself he would never forgive her and perhaps never could.

'How was Maeve?' she asked him sweetly.

'She was fine.'

'You don't sound very happy. I thought seeing her would make you happy.'

'Leave it, Rachel,' he said shortly.

Wisely, she did.

He pulled off his boots and sat down, stretching

his legs out under the table, carefully avoiding hers. The dying fire flickered at the corner of his eyes, its heat warming him, soothing him. Contentment settled over him, try though he might to hold it back, and his eyes rested fondly on Bella's peaceful, sleeping face.

'Will.'

'Hmm?' he grunted.

'Would you go and fetch Violet?'

'Hmm,' he said, and then lifted his head and stared back at her as the full meaning of her words penetrated.

'I was waiting for you to come home,' Rachel told him in a soft, worried voice. 'I hoped it would be a long time before I needed Violet, but I think you'd best fetch her now.'

Shock rendered Will motionless. And then he jerked to his feet. His boots, where were they? 'Why the devil did you let me take off my boots?' he snarled at her.

Rachel either didn't hear him or ignored him. She was busy dealing with a contraction, not fierce yet, but strong enough. Somewhere beyond the lamplight she heard Will swearing as he pulled on his boots.

'You said a month,' he burst out, accusingly.

Rachel felt like laughing, but knew better. 'A baby comes when it's ready,' she explained gently, 'not when the calender says so.'

'A month is a month!' he muttered, and went out, leaving the door swinging open. Rachel took a calming breath. She stood up, stretching her back, trying to ease her tense muscles. Don't be afraid, she told herself. Violet will be here in a moment.

Don't be afraid . . .

Voices were drawing closer. A lantern swung, the light careering wildly over the dark buildings outside. Will, frowning, was back, but behind him loomed not the capable bulk of Violet but the slight, bedraggled Rosa Yelland.

Rachel stared at Will, fear rendering her speechless.

'Violet's gone out to Mrs Watkins,' Will said harshly, his eyes searching hers. 'Her husband sent in for her a few hours ago. Kemp thinks it can't be too much longer. This is Mrs Watkins's sixth, he says.' He didn't say what else Kemp said, about it just slipping out after that many times. He hadn't thought it particularly funny.

Rachel bit her lip, trying to hide her anxiety. She trusted Violet, everything would have been so much better if Violet had been here.

'Rosa says she'll help.'

Rosa. Rachel turned and had a good look at Rosa. Her face and hands were still filthy, and as she drew nearer, Rachel could smell the rum on her. With a shaking breath, she said, 'No!'

Will stared at her as if she'd gone mad. 'What do you mean, "no"?'

'She's dirty. Look at her hands. And she's drunk. I don't want to die from her filth.'

Rosa didn't have to be told twice. With a savage look, she turned and fled, slamming the door after her.

Slowly, Will put down the lantern. Such things hadn't occurred to him. Why should they? He'd never had anything to do with midwives and babies. He'd thought that Rosa would do, that any woman would do.

'What now?' he asked her.

'We wait.' She bit her lip as another hard contraction tightened, like an iron band, about her middle. It was worse than the last and she couldn't help but cry out. 'Will!' she gasped. He caught her outstretched hand in his, feeling the desperate strength of her fingers as she gripped him. As the pain eased, she drew a slow, deep breath, then pushed back her hair and met his eyes, trying to hide the lurking fear in her own.

He was watching her and she could see that he wished he was somewhere else. Well, she didn't blame him for that. She wished *she* was somewhere else! But he was here and they would just have to make do until Violet arrived.

'Perhaps you should move Bella out of the bed,' she suggested.

He arranged some blankets over by the hearth, in the warmth of the dying fire and carried his daughter to the nest he'd made. She didn't wake, hardly stirring as he set her down. When he'd finished he turned back to Rachel.

She was still watching him, judging his usefulness to her. He sensed she was afraid. Will remembered suddenly how he and poor dead Hannah had laughed about their own child. 'Will you make a good midwife, Will?' she had asked him, smiling, and he had joked and said he would. But now that the chance had come it was no joke. Oh, he'd seen horses foal, he knew what was what, but this was Rachel. And he felt useless.

She must have known it, for she smiled, kindly, and said, 'It's all right. We'll manage all right. Sometimes the only help a woman has is her husband and it's enough. Come here now, Will, and help me walk. They say it helps if you walk; makes the baby come more easily.'

He slipped his arm about her and she clung for a moment, gasping, as another pain wrenched at her, then laughing as it subsided.

'I'd forgotten how it felt. God is kind to women like that . . . or maybe he mocks them with a lesson they can never learn.'

They walked around the table, slow steps, pausing as each contraction overtook her. These seemed, even to one as inexperienced as Will, to be getting fiercer and more frequent. Rachel's face was white and damp, her hair soaked at the temples. He found a cloth and wrung it out in cold water, pressing it to her brow. The next pain made her groan and grip his arm so tightly he winced. 'Bed now,' she breathed, when she was able.

Will slid his arm under her knees and lifted her up, taking the two steps required to the bed. Gently, he lay her down on the old quilt she'd spread over the mattress. Already another pain was coming, and she caught his hand, turning her face away. He saw the corded muscles of her throat and knew she was trying hard not to scream.

'It's all right.' He heard himself murmuring her own words. 'It's all right.'

Her hand relaxed. Her face was shining with sweat, beads of it dotting her upper lip, and she was breathing deeply through her mouth. Will felt a terror such as he had never known, not even in the worst days in Vandemon. If she should die now, when he had only just discovered how much he still loved her and wanted her ...

Another contraction was starting. Will gripped her hand, stroking her face and smoothing back her heavy hair, while she lay gasping, gathering strength. Her eyes were closed, and he wondered if she even knew he was there, cocooned as she was in her own pain. As it eased, he trickled some water onto her lips and she swallowed, managing a smile.

'Will,' she croaked, 'help me.' The dark eyes opened, fixing on his; he felt his stomach drop away.

'You know I will, Rachel,' he whispered.

The next pain was building, getting worse. This baby, Rachel realised in despair, wasn't going to wait for Violet Kemp. Will helped her pull herself into a more upright position. Gasping, she said, 'I have to push. But you need to look for me, Will. You need to tell me when you can see the baby's head.'

The pain was back again, gripping her body, and she clung to him, groaning with the effort. He wondered, with growing panic, whether the baby would rip her apart before it was ever born. 'Will?' Rachel gasped out, asking him the question again.

His shirt was sticking to his back, and he knew that he was sweating as much as her. He took a breath.

'Will?' panic now, trembling in her soft whisper.

He slid his strong arm around her shoulders. She was warm. She was his Rachel and she needed him. Gently, he eased the nightgown up over her hips. Her creamy skin shone with sweat, and where it stretched over her belly he could see the hardening of another contraction, forcing the baby downwards. Rachel was groaning again, caught up in her private pain. He stroked her thigh, waiting for it to pass, and then bent to look. He knew his face blanched, he couldn't help it. 'I don't know if . . .' he muttered. Another contraction and Rachel cried out, struggling to push her baby out into the world. This time when he looked he realised he could see something. Excitement gripped him. 'I think . . . Christ, it's the head!'

'Good,' she breathed. 'That's good.'

Will was leaning over her now and she felt him supporting her with his arms, lifting her forward to ease the pain in her back. Rachel gripped his shoulders, her face resting against the hollow of his throat. There was comfort in his arms; suddenly she didn't feel alone.

He hadn't been there when Bella was born. Perhaps it was only right he should be here now. The justice of the situation made sense to him.

'Come on,' he whispered. 'I reckon one more push. You can do it now. You can do it, darlin'.' With a cry, he felt her body surge and looking down realised the baby was almost born. He reached out, supporting the head with his hand as Rachel gathered herself again for the final push. And then suddenly he was holding a tiny bloody scrap of humanity. For a brief moment the baby lay still in his hands, as exhausted as its mother. And then it turned its head to the side, making little mewing sounds; the eyes opened and he was certain the baby looked at him, directly at him, for what seemed to Will a very long time. Something inside Will moved, a feeling he had never felt before, comprised of wonder and exhilaration and other deeper emotions for which he had no name.

Rachel was lying back, gasping, and looking like she'd ridden into battle. 'Will?' she whispered, without opening her eyes. 'Will?'

'It's all right,' he said. 'Everything's all right.' And he lifted the baby, still attached by the umbilical cord, and settled it gently against her side, safe in the crook of her arm. 'A girl,' he told her, and grinned.

Rachel touched the baby's cheek, and her mouth trembled. 'Oh, Will,' she gasped. 'Oh, Will . . .' they smiled at each other in amazement, and in that moment it was as if the baby really was his.

His and Rachel's.

The door opened. Violet marched in. Completely caught up in the moment, Will was stunned by the intrusion. Violet swept a professional glance over the scene and began to roll up her sleeves. 'Well, you've left me little enough to do, Sergeant,' she said loudly. 'But I'm here now. Heat me some water.' It was the same voice of command he used with his men. He didn't argue with her, he just went to do her bidding. Bella was huddled by the hearth and stared at him with enormous eyes, and he wondered how long she'd been awake.

Behind him, he heard Violet saying, 'You didn't need me after all, did you? Your husband's done just fine.' And she turned and met Will's eyes briefly, her own full of speculative amusement.

Will stoked the fire into life. He hadn't realised so much time had passed—it was nearly out. 'Come here, Bella,' he whispered to his daughter. 'You look frozen.'

She edged nearer and he lifted her up onto his

knee. Her feet were colder than a Greengage winter and he warmed them both in one big hand. 'It's all right now,' he breathed. 'Everything's all right.' But he didn't know whether he was reassuring her, or himself.

Violet came at last to fetch the water, and helped Rachel to wash and change into a clean nightgown, and brushed her hair. She rolled the soiled bedding into a pile and tossed it near the door. And then at last Rachel, spick and span again, was ready for them. Violet held out a hand for Bella's, grinning.

'Come on, lovie,' she said. 'You've got a sister over here waitin' to meet you.'

Apprehensively, glancing back at Will, Bella went. She perched herself carefully on the bed beside Rachel, and the two dark heads bent over the bundle in her arms. With a sigh, Will rose to his feet, hesitating. Violet looked at him, and then made a face.

'Sergeant?'

He came and stood by the bed, and Rachel looked up at him, trying to smile. She looked as normal now, apart from her pallor and the dark hollows under her eyes—Violet had done her job well. The baby in her arms was clean too, red faced and dark haired. Suddenly all Will's anger came back with a rush. This was Israel's baby. How could he ever love it as he loved Bella?

Rachel looked away. She must have seen what was in his eyes; he couldn't hide it. But all she did was smooth the red cheek with one gentle finger, and say, 'Thank you, Will. And thank you, Violet. 'I'll not forget either of you for your kindness this night.'

Violet gave a snort of laughter. 'I didn't do much, Mrs Moody. I reckon I'd better watch my back, or the Sergeant here will be takin' over my job!'

Will grimaced. 'No fear of that, Violet.'

'Ah well,' Violet teased, 'at least you'll know what to do next time.'

At that, she told her husband later, Will Moody looked positively wretched.

Will hardly knew the baby was there.

In the morning when he rose it would be sleeping beside Rachel—Bella had moved to the bottom of the bed, in a nest of blankets—and when he returned for his midday meal, it would be tucked up in the crib Violet Kemp had loaned them, or else lying on a rug on the floor, wriggling and waving its arms and legs. At night, again, it would be asleep, and whenever Rachel did anything for it, changed it or fed it, she always did so as far away and as quietly as possible.

He found that he could ignore it almost completely. And he wanted to ignore it. He never gave it more than a quick glance, and never touched it or held it or spoke to it. The sight of it did something to him, inside—like a clenching fist—and it was easier to pretend it wasn't there than to allow the hidden emotions to surface.

One of them was anger, he knew that, and then there was hurt and resentment and grief . .

. a whole range of things that Rachel just wasn't strong enough to deal with. Besides, he hardly understood himself what was wrong with him. When the baby had been born, he hadn't felt angry. There had been wonder and joy. It had been a joint effort, and for that brief moment as he sat beside his wife with the child in her arms, he had felt an overwhelming sense of contentment. It was only later, as he stood by the bed, that the other feelings had surged to the surface. And a disappointment so keen he still hadn't come to terms with it.

Violet Kemp was often there, even popping in sometimes in the evening to admire the baby. She and Rachel would sit, their heads closer together, and he heard their laughter and their soft chatter. Women's talk, he thought scornfully. That's what Joseph called it, when Will left them to it one night and went and sat with him in the stables.

Joseph's brown eyes squinted at him in the lamp light, and Joseph's teeth flashed strong and white as he grinned. 'You scared of those women, Boss? You hidin' out here with me?'

Will grunted, closing his eyes and leaning his head back against the hard stall.

'They frighten me, too, Boss,' Joseph soothed. 'That wife of yours, she really frightens me.'

Will opened one eye and looked at him. 'Why is that?'

'She's got eyes like river pools, Boss. Deep. They'd drag you down into them, if you looked too long. Like a big fish. Swallow you up!'

Will snorted, and didn't answer.

'But maybe you want to be swallowed up, eh Boss?'

Maybe he did. Maybe that was the trouble. He wasn't fighting Rachel or Maeve . . . he was fighting himself. 'You talk too much,' he muttered.

Joseph grinned and said no more. He would have liked a swig of the rum he was so fond of, but he knew Will Moody didn't like him drinking. Said it would rot his innards and his brain. He knew that was true and that Will Moody cared what happened to him. But sometimes he just needed to forget that once this had been his country, and that no man, white or black, had been his 'boss'.

'Dear little mite,' Violet was whispering, back inside the hut. She glanced at Rachel out of the corner of her eye. Will Moody had closed the door hard as he left, as though something was churning within him. Apart from darting a quick look after him, Rachel had said nothing. There was something strange about the Moody household, Violet had often thought it.

Rachel crept around her husband as if she wanted to be invisible, and he let her. In fact, if the rumours were anything to go by, he acted as if he were still a single man.

'Heard Maeve was boasting down at the inn,' Violet whispered to Rachel. 'She says Will Moody feels sorry for you and that's why you're here.'

Rachel shook her head. Will had said nothing about her leaving, although it was over a month now since she'd had the baby and therefore a month beyond the time she should have been gone. Was he just allowing her to build up her strength? She didn't for one moment believe he had forgotten their arrangement.

Violet sighed with exasperation. 'I'll give you

some advice, Rachel,' she said. 'Men soon crumble if a wife turns on the tears. He'll do anything you want then.'

Rachel looked at Violet and wondered if that was how she kept Kemp in line. Somehow, she doubted that Kemp, tears or not, would dare do anything Violet didn't want him to.

When Violet had gone, Rachel changed the baby and sponged the tiny, wriggling body before putting on its nightdress. It was one of Bella's with tiny pink flowers on the collar. She touched the delicate embroidery with her finger, smoothing the silk thread backwards and forwards. The baby stared at her with big blue eyes, watching her intently. Rachel knew she was its whole world. She had not meant to love her new daughter, indeed she had been certain she would not. But somehow, when Will handed her the baby, love gripped her wounded heart, and had only grown since then.

She felt no disloyalty in loving the baby. She loved Bella as much as ever. This was a new love, and there was room enough in Rachel's warm heart for them both.

Not so Will.

She knew that.

Apart from that one wonderful moment when he had placed the baby in her arms, Will behaved as if it didn't exist. He'd returned to his cold corner, watching her like a stranger. She was frightened that if the baby intruded on him too much, he would tell them it was time to go, but fortunately the baby was good.

Of course, Bella loved her sister. The baby reminded her of Maggie. The little girl hung over the crib, watching it sleep, and smiling when it woke. Rachel felt her child's loneliness like an ache in her heart. Bella was so solitary. She played with the other children, but preferred to be on her own. She sat for hours, playing with her doll, or just watching the world around her. Rachel had begun to wonder if she had done the right thing, after all, in bringing Bella to Will.

The uneasy thought had forced her to take more notice of the pair of them, and Rachel had taken to observing Bella's face, when Will came in. It relieved her of her doubts. The child lit up, often jumping to her feet with a broad grin. And Will, no matter how harassed he seemed or how distant, always stooped to lift her up high in his arms. Sometimes, when he sat down, Bella would climb onto his knee, curling her little body against him. His arms slipped around her without him seeming to notice it, and he would go on with whatever he was doing.

At least Bella has found herself a father, Rachel told herself. Even if the new baby has none.

CHAPTER 28

I T WAS A WARM AND sunny afternoon. The sky was blue, and parrots of green and red, drunk on the nectar, were screeching and squabbling in the flowering gum trees by the river. Like, Will said wryly, station hands, clutching their wages and heading for the local grog shop. He had had to break up a fight down at the inn during the night. Sean had came pounding on his door to tell him that some station hands had arrived from a sheep run to the north and were busy drinking themselves blind. When Will returned, he was so tired, he had fallen immediately into his bed, only to awaken before dawn in the throes of one of his nightmares. Rachel had tried to comfort him, but he'd walked to the door and opened it, standing silhouetted against the pale sky. He'd stood there for a long time, until she had eventually fallen asleep again. This morning, he had had to go out straight after breakfast—there was an assigned servant to be arrested for insolence and refusing to work.

'Two of the more serious offences in the squatters' handbook,' Will told Rachel, with a lopsided smile. The man had been locked up on the property, so it wouldn't take long to collect him and bring him back to the watch-house. Then it was up to Quill to charge him, so that Will could arrange for him to be escorted down to Melbourne Gaol.

'Three months imprisonment, probably,' Will said. 'Quill's favourite number.'

'Is he fair?' Rachel asked.

Will shrugged. 'He's fair. Does his best. I don't suppose it's an easy job—I wouldn't want it—havin' to decide whether or not a man should be locked up and for how long.'

Rachel stacked the plates ready to be washed. 'You make decisions too.'

He was quiet for a moment, and then he mocked her softly with, 'You mean with my finger on the trigger?'

But she shook her head, not looking at him. 'No—yes! I don't think you pull the trigger unless you have to. You're not a cold-blooded killer, Will. You never were. Killers don't care about anyone but themselves. I think you care too much. Why else would you dream of what you've seen and done over and over again?'

His breath was locked in his throat and it took him a moment to answer. 'You didn't always feel like that.'

'No,' and now she did look at him.

He didn't know what to say. What did she mean? There was something different in her dark eyes, half shy, half defiant. Was he imagining it, or was there an invitation in the curve of her lips, the way she was leaning forward towards him? Will's hand twitched, and in a moment he knew he'd be touching her, drawing her against him.

Joseph filled the doorway. 'You comin', Boss? Mrs Moody,' he added with a nod. Will turned and followed him without a word.

Rachel released her breath slowly. She wasn't sure whether she was glad or sorry that Joseph had interrupted them. What if Will told her, as he had before, that it was over between them? What if he left her no choice but to leave immediately? Joseph had saved them the need for an answer, and by the time Will returned it would be, if not forgotten, then tucked away, hidden, and they could pretend it had never happened.

The afternoon slipped away, and Will still wasn't back when Maeve knocked on Rachel's door.

The two women stood staring at each other. Rachel hadn't seen Maeve properly the night she came to rant and rave at Will. She saw her now, and what she saw made her heart sink like a stone in the Goulburn.

Maeve was beautiful. Thick, blonde waves of hair spilling over her shoulders, a smiling red mouth, pale blue eyes. Her bosom swelled over the low neck of her dark green gown, while her waist in comparison was tiny. She was older than Rachel, a good ten years older perhaps, and there was a wealth of experience in the glance she gave her.

If Rachel saw a beautiful blonde, Maeve saw a slim young woman with ivory skin and big dark eyes. Pretty, Maeve supposed, but rather worn down. She must have been beautiful when Will married her—in fact he had said she was, Maeve remembered uncomfortably—but Maeve felt she had the edge now.

Only a matter of time, she thought with relief, and Will would be back. He was very bitter about the baby; it was eating at him under that calm surface he showed to the world and that didn't fool Maeve. No, Rachel wouldn't be around for much longer, but there was no harm in giving her a bit of a hint. Maeve smoothed the green gown over her hips, and prepared herself to be magnanimous,

'May I come in?' she asked smiling prettily.

Without a word, Rachel stepped back to let her in and closed the door behind her.

Maeve looked about curiously at the crowded little room. It was tidy, as tidy as it could be under the circumstances, but she knew it must be driving Will mad. She nodded at Bella, who was staring at her unsmilingly from the hearth, and spotted the baby in its borrowed crib.

'Can I see her, Mrs Moody?' And, when Rachel nodded, went to lean over the crib, saying, 'Poor little thing,' in such a compassionate voice it set Rachel's teeth on edge.

What, Rachel wondered, between anger and despair, had Will been telling her?

'I've come to apologise for that night,' Maeve went on, watching as Rachel bent to tuck the shawl closer around the stirring baby, trying to lull it back to sleep.

'There's no need,' said Rachel. She gestured for Maeve to be seated and put the kettle on to boil. The baby started to cry, and Rachel stooped to lift it up, holding it in the crook of one arm while she continued to make the tea.

'Oh no, let me!' Maeve insisted on taking the baby. She tickled the little face, smiling down, all bright eyes and gleaming hair until the baby stopped its cries to gaze up, fascinated. Just like most of the men in the district, Rachel thought wryly.

Rachel poured the tea. She had discovered some proper teacups in the store, only one of them chipped, and yesterday she had made a cake so that she could entertain Violet in style. Violet had been impressed. Maeve wasn't, taking such things as her due.

'I haven't any children of my own.' Maeve went on. 'A sadness to me, Mrs Moody. Although I've time yet. But then, you know, Will may not want any more.' And she glanced disparagingly about the room.

Rachel froze. Had Will said something? Did he complain to Maeve, and yet say nothing to Rachel? Such under-handedness did not seem in character, but then how did she know? Will was her husband in the eyes of the law, but they had not lived together as such for four years. With an effort, she moved her hand towards the cup and rested it there, trying not to let it shake.

Maeve sipped her own tea delicately, her hand rock-steady. Her nails were well-kept, rounded and pink. 'I'm sorry if I've hurt your feelings, Mrs Moody,' she said with an open smile. 'Will and I always think it's best to be honest about everything, and that's how it should be, don't you think? Before you came back, I was expecting him to move in with me at the inn. We've even talked about him resigning here, and helping me to run the place.' It was true, they had talked about it, and Will had given no firm answer. He'd been reluctant to throw in his lot with her. However, Maeve being Maeve, she was positive could persuade him to it, given time.

'I need a strong man about the place,' she went on chattily. 'Oh, I have Sean, I know, but what use is he in a barney? It was all but decided, and then you came along for your little holiday . . .' She pulled what was meant to be a playful face. 'I know you don't intend staying on permanently, Mrs Moody. I know that. Will told me you'd be leavin' after the baby was born. But now . . . well, he's too soft-hearted to tell you to go.' Maeve sighed, as though enlisting Rachel's sympathy in the matter. 'And you know,' leaning forward confidentially, 'your staying here is making him so miserable. I had to explain to him that no woman would stay and make a man unhappy, not on purpose. Because you and I know, Mrs Moody, what Will must be thinking whenever he looks at your baby. Well I didn't know what to say to him, to ease the hurt. Only your going can do that. So I said that I was sure you'd be moving on just as soon as you could manage it. I was right, Mrs Moody, wasn't I? You are leavin' very soon?'

Her head was tilted to one side, her smile sweetly enquiring, but her blue eyes were hard. And the words, spoken with that soft, sweet Irish lilt, were poisonous.

Rachel forced her expression to remain still and calm. She supposed she should be charitable and try to understand Maeve's position. Since Will had moved to the Goulburn Maeve had had him to herself. Perhaps it was just as she said and Will had been preparing to move into the inn with her, until suddenly Rachel was back and Maeve's cosy little house of cards had come tumbling down.

She should be charitable, but at the moment Rachel didn't feel very charitable. She just felt angry. She was sure—well, almost, that Will didn't love Maeve. She had seen Will in love and it wasn't the way he was behaving now. For a moment, Rachel felt like telling Maeve so, but common sense made her bite her tongue.

'I don't expect Will to give up any of his old friends,' Rachel said coolly. 'And so I have told him.'

Maeve narrowed her eyes. This, Rachel could see, was news to her. 'Well.' The pretty smile became rather forced and hard. 'I'm so glad to hear that! So you won't mind, when Will stays over at the inn? Just to help out, that is, Mrs Moody.'

Their eyes locked. Rachel shook her head. She bent to cut the cake, handling the knife very carefully. She would have liked to plunge it through Maeve's bosom, deep into her heart.

Maeve took a slice, biting into it, her eyes triumphant. 'I have a proposition to put to you, Mrs Moody,' she said, licking crumbs from her fingertips. 'I haven't mentioned this to Will because I don't want him to feel beholden to me. You see, I have a bit of money put by—not a lot, mind, but enough. I would be pleased to lend some to you, on the condition that you leave Will and promise me you'll never come back. Now, you're a woman of good sense, Rachel. Will doesn't want you here, you know that, and the money would see you to Melbourne and keep you until you found work or . . . well, whatever you decide to do. What do you say?'

Rachel said nothing, Maeve, she thought bitterly, must love Will very much to be willing to buy off his wife. Perhaps she should take the money and leave them to it. If Will was as unhappy as Maeve said . . . Something brushed her arm, and startled Rachel looked down into Bella's grey eyes. The little girl pressed closer against her, sensing the turmoil in the room and seeking security. Rachel smoothed a dark curl behind her daughter's ear. 'You can't mean you're wantin' to stay on when your husband does not want you?' Maeve persisted, impatient now and unable to hide it. 'Surely you have more pride than that?'

'Your offer is very generous,' Rachel cut in, her voice rough. 'I need to consider it carefully. It's not a step I can take without thinking about it . . . leaving Will, I mean. He's come to depend on me . . . to keep house, you understand. And he loves Bella.'

Bella stared unsmiling at Maeve, making the other woman nervous. She rose, setting down the cup. 'I understand, Mrs Moody. But don't wait too long, will you? Thank you for the tea and cake. I'll call again soon for your answer. Good day.'

Rachel stood at the door, watching Maeve stroll down the track towards the inn as if she had all the time in the world. She was beautiful and much sought after . . . and she wanted Will. Rachel wished viciously that a bolt of lightning would strike her dead.

After a moment, sensing someone watching her, Rachel looked up. Constable Yelland was leaning lazily against the wall of the stables. He stared back at her and then he smiled. It wasn't a nice smile.

Rachel stepped back inside Will's hut and slammed the door.

Violet called on her after a decent interval. 'A

right bitch that,' she muttered to Rachel regarding Maeve. 'Why'd she come?'

'I think she was apologising in advance,' Rachel said thoughtfully. 'For taking Will off me.'

'The cow!' Violet cried. 'Will wouldn't take her over you, Rachel. He wouldn't.' But her eyes slid away, not quite meeting Rachel's despite her loud denials. Rachel couldn't blame her. Maeve was very beautiful.

'No one likes the bitch,' Violet went on comfortingly. Then thought, wryly, that that wasn't exactly true. The men liked her, it was only the wives who hated her, and for obvious reasons. As for Will, no one could deny he was a good looking man. Until Maeve came along he had shown no interest in other women, and although plenty had looked long and hard, Will Moody had kept to himself. Maeve had made a set at him from the first. Even when she found out he didn't drink, she didn't care. She said she respected him for that and it was his company she wanted, not his custom.

Oh, Maeve was beautiful, and there was no doubt Will was flattered. But Violet had always thought there was something mysterious about the Sergeant. He didn't talk about his past, although there were stories and rumours. And he'd never mentioned a wife, but when Rachel turned up that day, she and Will had sort of fitted together.

As if they belonged.

And Violet was damned if she was going to let Maeve spoil it.

Will had finished his supper. Rachel cleared away silently, keeping an eye on the baby in its crib. Bella, even more quiet than usual, sat by the hearth, holding her doll tight against her. She'd been like that since Maeve left this afternoon and although Rachel had tried to talk with her, the little girl would say nothing, tightening her lips and turning her face away. In the end Rachel had given up and left her alone, hoping that she would work things out in her own way.

Will had noticed her silence. For a time he'd just watched her, sitting back in his chair with his long legs stretched out in front of him. 'Come here, Bella,' he said at last, softly, and held out his hand. 'What's the matter?'

The hand proved irresistible. Bella came, slowly, scuffing her feet on the bare boards. Rachel stopped what she was doing, watching.

'You're my father,' Bella said gruffly, and there was a hint of desperation in her voice . . . and fear.

It caught at Rachel's heart, but Will didn't hear it or if he did, didn't realise what it meant. 'I am that, darlin'!' he joked.

'You don't want us to go away, do you?'

The laughter died in his eyes. Dread filled him but he kept it at bay, turning to look at his wife where she was standing by the table, her face shadowed by the fall of the lamp. Had Rachel decided the time had come for her to leave? 'No, I don't want you to go away,' he managed. 'But I can't make you stay, Bella, if your mother doesn't want to.'

Bella shook her head, her little face screwed up with misery. 'It was the lady said it. The lady said you want us to go away.'

Will was frowning now, looking for an explanation. Rachel made an uneasy gesture. 'Maeve visited us today,' she told him quickly. 'I wouldn't have told you . . . I didn't realise Bella knew what she . . . I mean Bella doesn't quite understand the situation.'

Anger trembled inside him but again he hid it, smiling at Bella and lifting her onto his knee. 'I don't want you to go away, Bella, no matter what the "lady" says. All right?'

Bella nodded, her face burrowed into his chest. 'You don't hate Baby, do you?' she whispered, her voice shaking.

By God, what had Maeve been saying? If she thought she could come up here, upsetting his little girl, she had made a sad error of judgment. 'No,' he said stiffly. 'I don't hate her.'

It satisfied Bella. She snuggled closer. He looked up at Rachel again. There was something in her expression, something that made him narrow his eyes and wonder what else Maeve had said.

He waited until Bella was asleep, hiding his impatience. When she was finally tucked into her nest of blankets, he pulled on his boots and went to the door.

'I won't be long,' he said, over his shoulder.

Rachel merely nodded, not looking at him, bending closer to her sewing as though it held her entire attention. It was only after the door closed that she laid down her work and sighed, glancing to the baby sleeping in the crib.

'He's gone to see Maeve,' Rachel murmured dryly. 'To "help out".'

Thoughts of Will and Maeve began a dull ache inside her. I won't think of it, Rachel told herself. But the image kept returning, growing in detail, until it was almost as if she were a third occupant in Maeve's bedroom. That greedy red mouth on Will's, that enormous bosom flattened to his broad, brown chest . . . Rachel shuddered and stood up, moving restlessly to the window.

The moon was out, leeching all colour from the trees. There was no breeze and everything was so still. The silence made her edgy. I'm his wife and yet I have no rights, she thought indignantly to herself. He can tell me to go at any time . . . I'm sure he only lets me stay because of Bella. And I hang on to that, praying it will be enough, and that one day some spark of what he used to feel at Greengage will rekindle. So I let him go to Maeve, and force away the images of him holding her, pretending I don't care. When I do. I do care!

There had been no talk of the married quarters, although there was so little room for them here. Will said nothing about Constable Yelland's possible departure, although Violet had told Rachel all about it and how much trouble Will had been having with the man. Rachel would be glad to see the Yellands go. Rosa hadn't spoken to her since the night Rachel insulted her, and Yelland himself . . . well, she found him repulsive and rather frightening. Sometimes she met him about the Post and, although he nodded politely, there was a look in his eyes that was at once sly and malicious. Once she was certain he whispered 'bitch' as she walked away, but when she spun around he was nodding and smiling, his eyes wide and innocent. Rachel didn't say anything to Will; she was always afraid to draw attention to herself in case it hardened his resolve to send her away. But if he really was as unhappy as Maeve would have her believe perhaps the decision had been made for her?

Rachel closed her eyes, and leaned her brow against the cold glass. Was Maeve comforting him now? Telling him that soon Rachel would be gone, soon they could be together? And yet she had felt so certain that Will did not love Maeve. Could she be wrong? The cold glass soothed her aching head, stilling the whirl of thoughts inside it. There had been times, lately, when Will looked at Rachel, that she thought he might be beginning to love her. Her heart knocked hard against her ribs. Was she mistaken in that look? Was it just a case of wishful thinking? Was Will simply feeling the echoes of times past?

Well, whatever he thought of Rachel, Will loved Bella, there was no mistake there. And the baby?

The baby! she repeated to herself angrily. She didn't even have a name yet.

Rachel sighed, and moved back to the light of the lamp. She was being stubborn about the name, she knew that, but Rachel was determined it must come from Will. He wouldn't be able to pretend the baby didn't exist if he named it. The trouble was time was running out. Violet kept asking, and Rachel kept saying they hadn't decided yet.

Rachel sat down and put her head in her hands. Oh, Will, she cried silently. I'm wishing you home again.

'You're a hard man, Will Moody,' Maeve teased him, her fingers dancing lightly up the buttons of his jacket. 'Such a sweet little baby!'

Will's eyes narrowed. He had been intending to confront her with his knowledge. In fact, the two hours he had sat in the corner, watching her laugh and joke behind the bar, flirting with her customers and glancing at him to see what effect it was having, had been spent in deciding exactly what he was going to say to her. However as the time passed, the edge of his anger had dulled, and Will changed his mind. Better to let her do the talking.

Maeve swept one fingertip across the line of his jaw, where the rough stubble grated against her skin. 'I went to see your wife today, Will. Poor thing. So pale and skinny. Doesn't look well, does she? I feel sorry for her, Will, just as you do. But we can't blame a sweet little baby for what its mother's done, now can we?'

Will said nothing, watching her. The wrath he felt towards her began to burn again, but apart from a slight glitter to his grey eyes it didn't show. Maeve had no right to go and upset his wife and daughter. They were his business. Maeve couldn't know that he was not like Rachel—Maeve's side of the argument didn't even enter into his thoughts. He saw things in black and white, right and wrong. And tonight, Maeve was clearly in the wrong.

It seemed that Maeve was oblivious to Will's thoughts. She smiled again, a gleam of excitement in her eyes. The inn was closed, but Will had stayed.

That in itself was a triumph for her. Will hadn't been down here for weeks, which meant that nasty little visit to Rachel had been worth it. With a studied yawn, Maeve raised her arms above her head, arching her body voluptuously. She knew Will was watching her, and knew she looked her best tonight in the red dress, with her curls tumbling loose from the ribbon at her nape. Will wanted her, he'd proved that often enough, and after tonight he'd be all hers again.

'She understands about us, you know,' she went on softly, persuasively. 'She doesn't expect you not to see me. Perhaps it's a relief to her, Will, to know you won't be askin' her to be a wife to you proper, hmm?' And she laughed her low, husky laugh, teasing him and exciting herself.

Her dress had slipped off one shoulder, and he saw the place where her breast swelled, so full and soft. He knew it was an invitation. Once he would not have thought twice about accepting and tumbling her onto the bed. Now he didn't move.

'Don't go up there again, Maeve,' he said softly.

Maeve laughed as though he had made a joke, and pouted up at him. 'I'm sorry. I wanted to help. At least you don't have to worry any more about staying here with me. She knows about us and she doesn't care. She said so.'

Had she? That made him even more furious, but he held it back. This was Maeve, he reminded himself. The woman who had made him laugh again and helped to soothe away his pain. Beautiful Maeve, who had chosen him from all the other men in her orbit.

'Perhaps you mean well,' he began slowly, 'but

this has to stop. I won't stay here with you, not any more. I've a wife and child at home. They're my responsibility, Maeve. That's what I've come to tell you.'

Maeve's smile switched off, like a candle snuffing. She looked as if she doubted she had heard him right. 'You won't stay . . .' she began. The colour flooded her face. 'Why the bloody hell not? Are we speaking of your wife here, Will, the woman who had a brat by another man? Or the bloody Virgin Mary?'

'You're upset,' he said coldly, and now the glitter in his eyes was plain to see.

'Yes, I am upset! I thought I meant something more to you than a quick poke, Sergeant Moody. Instead it seems you're just like every other man I've made a fool of myself over. I hate you, do you hear me? Go back to your slut of a wife and I hope she leaves you again. Because she will, you'll see. She will!'

He turned and walked towards the door. At the sight of his back, fear gripped her so hard it was like a cramp in her stomach. She ran after him.

'Will, oh Will, I'm sorry. I didn't mean it. I'm just so frightened for you. I don't want you to be hurt again. She told me today she wasn't staying, she said she'd be off soon. She doesn't want you, Will, but I do. I do!'

There were tears in her voice, and her pain ripped at him, breaking through the anger. Will stopped and took a deep breath, then he turned and put his arms about her. She lifted her face blindly and he kissed her willing mouth, long and deep. His body tightened, but he knew it was the same response he'd feel from kissing any attractive woman. Whatever love he had felt for Maeve was gone.

'Will?' she murmured, holding him closer, pressing her warm body to his. 'Will?'

He caught her upper arms, and he had to grip her hard, bruisingly hard, to put her away from him. She gazed up, bewildered, disbelieving. 'I have to go,' he said. 'Thank you, Maeve, for everythin' you've done. I won't forget.'

Maeve's head was spinning. What could she say?

She'd said everything, she'd offered him everything. And still that hadn't been enough to sway him from that black-eyed witch. She couldn't believe it. Jealousy and anger choked her, and she swallowed convulsively, sure she was going to be sick.

Will touched her bright hair, gently, like a blessing. 'Goodbye, Maeve.'

When the door closed it was all she could do not to howl like a dog. She spun around, biting down on her fingers. The tears were streaming down her face.

The door to the taproom creaked and Maeve froze. Suddenly the tears were icy on her cheeks and her heart was beating like a military drum. A shadow limped closer, and Yelland eyed her up and down. He gave her the benefit of his evil smile.

'What do you want, you crippled bastard!' she shouted in fright.

But Yelland's smile didn't shift. 'Don't be like that Maeve,' he said. 'I might be able to help you.'

'Help me?' she shouted. 'The only way you can help me is to send that witch back to hell where she came from!'

Yelland's smile broadened. 'Is that all?'

Maeve's eyes narrowed and suddenly her anger fled, for what she saw in Yelland's face kindled hope inside her. But before she could speak, Sean appeared in the shadows behind him.

'You all right, Maeve?' he murmured, his voice soft, his wrinkled little face full of concern for her. He loved her, she knew that. He would always love her, and in her way she loved him. But it wasn't the same as Will, it could never be like Will.

Gaze on Yelland, Maeve nodded slowly. 'Yes, Sean. Go to bed now. I'll lock up.'

Sean hesitated, but even as he paused, Yelland closed the door on him with a final click.

Will walked slowly through the darkness, up the track towards the Police Post. Towards Rachel. Should he believe Maeve? Had Rachel really said those things? He had no illusions about Maeve, but Rachel had never said she would stay—in fact she had agreed in the beginning that she would go.

The hut was in darkness and he entered quietly. It was a cool night and he moved to stir the coals into glowing life, holding out his hands to their warmth. He could hear Maeve's voice reverberating in his head, but it was something he had known he had to do. And now it was done. Will had a sense of burning his bridges, of suddenly floating free. It was frightening, and yet exhilarating at the same time.

Rachel woke to hear him moving about, removing his boots and his belt, the soft slither of his jacket and shirt, the creak of the chair as he sat down. She knew all his sounds—she could picture him in her mind. The image of him, naked, was still there in all its glory. Sometimes when she lay thinking of him, a warm glow would envelope her. Rachel knew what it was. It had been the same at Greengage. She just had to think of him and the need would be there.

How Maeve would sneer if she knew Rachel was lusting after her own husband!

The chair creaked again as he stood up and suddenly his step sounded closer to the bed. Rachel held her breath. He didn't move, just stood there, and she lay there watching him and wondering what he was thinking. Had Maeve persuaded him at last to tell her to go? Was he searching for the right words? Rachel trembled, her breath catching in her throat like a trapped bird. I won't beg him to let me stay, she told herself desperately. I won't . . .

The bright moonlight outside the window gave the room a ghostly glow. Some of it had spilled over the sill to the bed, illuminating Rachel's hand where it rested on the sleeping baby beside her. It was so long since Will had really looked at the baby, he was surprised by the change. The little face had lost its crumpled newborn redness and had become smooth and plump. Long dark lashes swept rounded cheeks. A tip-tilted nose, and rosebud lips, slightly parted. The dark hair had thinned, but there was enough for Rachel to tie one curl on top of the baby's head in a pink ribbon, which made Bella laugh.

The baby stirred, and Will watched as the rose-bud mouth opened. It gave a soft cry, and then again, louder, turning to the side and searching for Rachel, snuffling like a little animal.

'Shh.' Rachel's hand was there, soothing, rocking, trying to lull her daughter back into oblivion. The baby would not be pacified, her movements growing more frantic. Rachel sat up and Will knew she was looking at him, wondering what was wrong with him.

'Is she all right?' he asked softly.

'Just hungry.'

She hesitated, as if expecting him to turn away as he usually did whenever she dealt with the baby. But this time he didn't move and the baby's cries grew louder. She gave up trying to work him out and fumbled with her nightgown. Will saw the full curve of her breast with its dark nipple as she drew the baby in against her. The hungry mouth searching and fastened on, sucking with quick, desperate motions. The baby's eyes closed in ecstasy and it curled close into Rachel's body.

For the first time since the moment the baby was born, Will felt himself softening towards Israel's daughter. He stood and watched Rachel and the baby, and let the pain begin to heal.

'Will?' Rachel's voice was quiet, drowsy. The baby's sucking was slowing, growing erratic. She was nearly asleep again.

'What?'

'She has to have a name.'

For a moment he didn't know what she meant. And then he did. Suddenly Maeve's words came back to him. Another man's baby. Maybe Maeve was right, maybe Rachel would run off and find someone else. Anger and resentment filled him again where a moment before he had been at peace, and he turned to walk away. 'It's your baby, not mine,' he said coldly, over his shoulder.

She didn't reply. Soon, he heard her changing the baby and settling it again in the bed. His bed. Will undressed and lay on the truckle, staring at the ceiling.

He shouldn't have said that. He'd thought he had more self control. She would probably be gone in the morning. Will turned his head to the side and looked at the shape of the bed, silhouetted against the moonlit window. You're a bastard, Will Moody, he told himself bitterly, Maeve was right about that. Serve you right if she does go and leaves you all to yourself. Just as you did to her.

The choice was his, and suddenly he knew it. And knew what he had to do.

Rachel stirred to the morning light shining into her face and the aroma of hot tea. She opened her eyes and saw that Will was already dressed. She had lain awake so long after she had fed the baby last night, upset by what he had said, that she had slept late.

'I'll have your breakfast in a moment,' she gasped, beginning to rise, but Will shook his head.

'It's all right. I have to go.' In fact he was already at the door, his hand on the latch. He paused. 'Call her Hannah,' he said, without turning. And closed the door softly behind him.

Rachel stared at the door, not knowing whether to laugh or cry. Hannah, after his beloved dead wife. Hannah! She bent to the sleepy baby, kissing her warmly on one soft, flushed cheek. 'Good morning, Hannah,' she whispered.

CHAPTER 29

I T WAS AS IF WILL had surrendered. And he'd done it the morning he decided on Hannah's name. At least, that was what Rachel felt. Since the dreadful moment they had met again at McCrae's Castle, Will had been fighting her. The hurt and anger had been there inside him, and even though he said nothing it was as if he were shouting at her. And the fight had continued here, at the Police Post, until the morning he decided on Hannah's name.

When he came back at noon, Rachel wasn't sure what to expect. She was struggling to make the meal. Hannah screamed every time Rachel put her down, so that she was forced to hold the baby in one arm and work with the other. Will took one look at the situation, reached over and lifted Hannah into his own arms, and vanished outside.

Rachel stood, frozen, the spoon dangling from her hand. Mary Hymbury's words flashed into her head, and she wondered, with a sense of suffocating terror, whether Will was going to do as Mary's husband had threatened to do: Take the baby out into the bush and leave her there. Slowly, on stiff legs, she went to the open door.

Her shoulders relaxed. The white look left her face and she smiled. Will was sitting on the ground, leaning against the wall of the hut. He was holding Hannah crooked in one big arm, so that she rested against his broad chest. The baby had stopped crying, probably from sheer surprise, and was staring at Will with wide, unblinking blue eyes. Quietly, Rachel turned back to the hearth.

Will touched the tiny hand with his finger, and her fingers clung with surprising strength. 'Well, Hannah,' he murmured, 'looks like you and me have to make the best of things. What do you say to that?'

Hannah gurgled in reply and her mouth curved into a smile. Will sighed.

'She likes you,' Bella said with a grin, when they sat down to their meal.

Will grinned back, and his voice held soft mockery, 'Ah, Bella, all the ladies do.'

Rachel gave him a long look. 'Maeve does, anyway.'

The grin faded, and he looked at her hard. 'Maeve had no right to come here yesterday, and so I told her. She won't do it again.'

'How can you be sure?'

'Rachel, I'm sure,' he said sharply. 'It's over between Maeve and me.'

Rachel blinked at him, wondering if she was hearing him correctly. Her hands were shaking, but she hid them under the table. 'Over?' she whispered.

Will nodded slowly, still watching her. 'I told her

so when I saw her last night.'

'But . . .why?' she managed. Something in her throat seemed to be strangling her voice.

He looked at her for a moment more, and then dropped his eyes back to his plate. 'I won't have Bella upset,' he said quietly.

Feeling as if she was floating on air, Rachel choked back a few spoonfuls of her meal. Will had finished with Maeve, for Bella's sake . . . and yet there had been something in his eyes, something that gave her hope. He didn't say any more and neither did she, but there was a difference about him. It wasn't until after he'd gone again that she realised what it was. The barricades she had sensed between them were gone. The war was over; Will had surrendered. That was what was different. She'd actually felt as if he were there, in the room, with her. Not locked away in some cold distant sphere. Will was back again.

Rachel put her head in her hands and wept.

Will rode over to Emu Downs, after Quill had finally issued the warrants for the bushrangers. They'd held up a station to the north-east of the Post, terrorising the occupants and stealing money and supplies as well as guns. Others reported seeing three or four men racing their horses and firing guns in the air. Obviously, these bushrangers were out to have a good time.

'It doesn't appear as though they're trying to

be inconspicuous,' Quill said, lifting his eyebrows. 'Will you need extra men to make an arrest?'

Will shook his head. 'Kemp and Joseph should be enough.'

You couldn't help but admire the man, Quill thought. It was no wonder he radiated confidence— he rarely failed in his duty. He seemed to be able to think like the outlaws he pursued, a handy attribute in his line of work. If things had turned out differently, perhaps Will Moody might have been a bushranger himself.

'You're still residing with your wife, Sergeant Moody? I thought it was a temporary situation.'

'It's permanent, as far as I'm concerned.' Will reached into his jacket and brought out a thin sheaf of papers. 'Here's the paperwork.'

Quill took the crackling sheets. 'And is it permanent as far as your wife's concerned?' he asked, and half smiled as his normally efficient, unemotional Sergeant suddenly looked a lot more human.

Will ran an agitated hand through his hair, searching for the right words.

Quill took pity on him. 'It's all right, I'll deal with these,' and he tapped the papers. 'When are you riding out after the bandits?'

'May as well make it tomorrow mornin'. The sooner we go, the sooner we get back.'

A strange thing for Will Moody to say, Quill thought later. Sergeant Moody had never before begrudged time spent in the pursuit of justice. Quill remembered the look on the man's face when the subject of his wife had come up, and smiled. He'd never admitted it, but he'd always been rather in awe of his Sergeant. It was nice to know he was as capable as any man of floundering in love.

'We'll be leaving at dawn,' Will explained to Rachel that night. 'I can't say how long we'll be gone. It could be a few days . . . or it could be a few weeks.'

'I see.' She looked down, avoiding his eyes.

'You'll manage?' He wished she'd look at him; he desperately needed to know what she was thinking.

'I'll have to.' She was a trooper's wife now, and this was the cold reality of it. She must wait until he returned . . . if he returned.

Bella's voice piped up. 'It's Christmas soon, Father.'

His eyes softened. 'I'll be back long before then, don't worry.'

'You'll be careful?' Rachel whispered, and then bit her lip as though annoyed with herself for saying it. But she was looking at him, and what he saw in her eyes warmed him, almost as if she had put her arms around him and held him tight.

'I'll be careful,' he told her softly. 'I've got somethin' to come back for now, haven't I?'

The morning was clear and cool, but the blue sky promised a warm day. Wattle birds gave their raucous cries in the gum trees by the river, competing with the more melodious song of a magpie. The air of the Post hummed with activity, as the horses were saddled, an extra horse loaded with supplies, and the men made ready. Will slid his carbine into the saddle holster and checked the pistol at his belt. The familiar way in which he handled the weapons frightened Rachel—they belonged to the other Will. The sight of the pistol in his hand reminded her of that terrible day in Greengage when she had learned of the man he had been.

'Are we ready?' Will murmured to Joseph. Joseph nodded, and grinned at Bella as he swung himself up into the saddle.

Will lifted his daughter for a hug and a kiss, before turning to Rachel. She'd been preparing herself for this moment. Violet had told her what being a trooper's wife meant. 'No use in clingin' and blubberin', she'd said. 'They don't need that. You've got to pretend everythin's business as usual, even if you're breakin' up inside.'

Rachel had prepared herself for this moment. But when she looked up at him all the preparations she'd made turned to dust, swirling beneath the horses' impatient hooves. She didn't know what to say.

Perhaps Will didn't either, because he wrapped his arms around her and bent his head. She felt his lips, warm and desperate on hers, and then he'd released her. He didn't look again as he mounted his horse and led his men out. Rachel felt light-headed. It seemed as if she'd said goodbye so many times to so many people, but this time she knew it was different, because her heart had gone with Will.

If Rachel hadn't already known how firmly Will had melded himself back into her life, his not being there made it obvious. The old, familiar sense of loss and aloneness assailed her. She moved through the next few days like a ghost; doing everything she must, chatting with Violet, caring for the children. But she wasn't really there.

It was on the third day that she came back to earth. That was the afternoon that Maeve called on her.

She looked the same, Rachel thought, but there was a new resolve in her eyes. 'Mrs Moody.' Maeve's smile was completely devoid of friendliness, even the false kind. 'I've come for my answer.'

Rachel stood in the doorway to the hut, Bella peering around her skirts. It would be polite to ask Maeve in, but she wasn't going to and besides, she doubted Maeve would accept.

'Come now,' and Maeve's mouth curled, 'you do have an answer, don't you? I'd like to hear it. You've thought deeply on the matter, I'm sure.'

Rachel nodded slowly. 'I've thought on it, yes, and I have to decline your offer.'

Maeve nodded, but other than a certain tightening about her jaw, she seemed unaffected. 'Well, you're makin' a terrible mistake, but there's no point in me tellin' you that now, is there?'

Rachel shook her head. 'No point at all.'

Maeve's blonde hair flashed in the sun. 'Very well then, Mrs Moody. You've made your decision, and I've made mine. Good day to you.'

And she turned and walked away, quickening her steps into long strides as she reached the track to the inn.

The visit played on Rachel's mind, but for reasons other than the obvious. Perhaps it was that Maeve, on the few occasions they had met, had struck her as being so passionate and hot-blooded. The Maeve who had stood at her door just now was cold, and that coldness sent an answering chill through Rachel.

The following morning, Rachel was fetching water when Yelland approached her. She watched him limping towards her and hesitated, feeling uncomfortable, as she always did when he was near her.

'Mrs Moody' Yelland's smile was irreproachable, but his narrowed eyes told another story. 'No word yet on the Sergeant?'

Puzzled she shook her head. 'No. Should there have been?'

'No." Yelland shifted onto his good leg, easing the twisted one. It was paining him, but nothing of his discomfort showed in his face. He watched Will Moody's wife trying to guess what he was up to, and it amused him. She was a looka—trust that bastard to have a wife like this, while he was yoked to Rosa. It was just another point against him, in Yellands's opinion.

He glanced up at the blue sky. 'Nice day, Mrs Moody.'

She stared at him in silence and he felt like laughing aloud. 'Yes,' she managed at last. He watched her make a decision, drawing herself up slightly before she spoke. 'Is there something you want to say to me, Constable Yelland?'

He turned to her, his eyes wide with surprise. 'Why no, Mrs Moody, Just passin' the time of day.'

'Well, I have things to do, so if you'll excuse me—'

'If I had a woman like you at home, I wouldn't

be leavin' her here alone.'

She'd taken a step, and now turned and stared at him. Her eyes were enormous. 'What did you say?'

His smile curled up. 'Then again the Sergeant knows I'm here to protect you, don't he, Mrs Moody?'

She whirled around and fled. He stood watching her, laughing softly to himself. A shiver of excitement ran over his skin. This would be different to hitting Rosa, Rosa who never fought back. He had a feeling this one would fight back. And afterwards . . . he wanted to be there when Will Moody found out. He wanted to see his face. He wanted to see him suffer.

It was the fifth afternoon of Will's departure, and Rachel was in the middle of the washing. Hannah was asleep in her crib, and Bella was out playing with Violet's and Rosa's children. At first, they had run around outside Rachel's hut, screaming and laughing, but now the children's voices had faded. Rachel didn't notice. She was enjoying the peace and quiet, resting a moment at the wash board to ease the ache in her arms.

She had puzzled over Yelland's behaviour for some time, before finally putting it aside. She wouldn't let him upset her; he surely wouldn't be here much longer. And as for Maeve . . . well that was over. Will had seen to that.

She missed him.

Thinking of Will, Rachel didn't hear Rosa approaching, until suddenly the shadow fell across her and Rosa was there.

Rosa Yelland had hardly spoken two words to her since the night Hannah was born, but now there was nothing of the usual sly hatred in her dark eyes. The thin lips were working and Rosa was twisting her hands, picking at her apron with dirty nails.

'Rosa? What is it?'

Rachel, concerned, stepped closer and laid her own hand over Rosa's. She noticed then the black eye, proof of Yelland's affection. It looked new. A shiver of rage went through her at the thought of the man.

Rosa glanced over her shoulder. 'Is Bella here, Mrs Moody?'

Whatever Rachel had expected to hear, it wasn't this. 'Bella?' she glanced about, as though her daughter would be standing in plain view behind her. 'I. . . why do you ask?'

Rosa bit her lip and then took a sharp breath. Her voice trembled. 'Yelland told me last night that Maeve was planning to take Bella.'

Rachel shook her head, disbelief uppermost. 'Maeve take Bella? But why?'

Rosa shrugged. The dark eyes narrowed and slid sideways. 'Sergeant Moody pissed 'er off. Maeve, I mean. She's killing mad, that's what Yelland says. Maybe she thinks if Bella was out of the way, he'd come back to 'er.'

Rachel jumped, as a dozen or more parrots streaked, screeching, across the sky. Their colours were so bright they hurt her eyes. Terror had momentarily rendered her speechless. 'No,' she whispered. 'It makes no sense. Besides,' looking about wildly, 'Bella is playing with the other children.'

Rosa shook her head slowly. 'No, she ain't. Mine are at home and Violet Kemp's taken her two down to McPherson's store. And I saw Maeve a few minutes ago, goin' towards the river.'

Rachel took a step, halted, cried out, 'Watch Hannah!' and began to run. Her skirts hampered her and she held them out of the way. She felt her heart pounding with the effort. The edge of the bush was there before her, and she plunged into it, the sudden change from sun to shade forcing her to pause until her eyes adjusted. A bird flew up from its investigation of the leafy ground. Rachel thrust aside branches, not allowing herself to think. She reached the great thick trunk of a red gum, centuries old, and clung there, catching her breath. The river was just ahead; she could smell the water and hear the drone of cicadas in the trees.

Rachel held her breath, trying to still the pulsebeat in her ears, listening. Nothing. Carefully, Rachel moved forward until she reached the curving riverbank. It dropped away steeply before her, down to the swirling golden water. The level of the Goulburn had dropped over the past month—there'd been little rain. Below her, on the steep bank, the old canoe had rotted further, soon it would be dust. Something rustled in the scrub and was still, listening with her.

'Bella?'

Her own voice startled her with its edge of panic. The memory of Bella's brush with death at Wattle Bank was still too close. Terror was crowding

Rachel like a pack of wild dogs, but she held it back, calling again.

'Bella!'

Her voice echoed around the sweeping curve of the river, mocking her. A mosquito whined in her ear and she brushed it away. Perhaps she should try further down where the punt was? Would Maeve go there? The thought of Maeve, with Bella, brought dread bubbling to the surface again. She remembered how strange Maeve had seemed two days ago, how cold and, yes, determined.

Dried leaves crackled behind her as someone took a step, Rachel spun around, hope and relief in her soft cry. Yelland was so close her hands brushed his chest.

'Oh!' She jumped with fright, and then took a deep breath. 'Constable Yelland. Did Rosa send you? My daughter . . . have you seen Bella?'

He took her upper arms in a firm grip. Perhaps he thought she was going to over-balance. 'No. I haven't seen her. Is she missing?'

Rachel tried to think coherently. 'Yes. I thought your wife must have sent you. She said . . . I hardly know whether to believe it, but she said that Maeve had a plan to take Bella . . .' she stopped, her eyes opening wide at him. 'But she said you told her it was so!'

He said nothing. For a moment they stared at each other, as Rachel tried to come to grips with this new development. And then Yelland smiled, his sly face full of humour.

'It's not Bella you should be worryin' about, Mrs Moody,' he told her quietly.

Despite the humid warmth of the day, Rachel

felt chilled. His smile broadened. Don't show him you're afraid, she told herself. Pretend you're not afraid. 'Oh?' she replied calmly 'Perhaps we could go back to the Post and speak to your wife.'

But he wasn't deceived. As a crow feeds on carnage, he fed on fear, and he sensed it in her now. He took a deliberate step forward and, perforce, Rachel took one backwards. She felt the drop of the river-bank at her back, inches from her heels.

'Maeve thinks you're a witch,' he told her, still smiling, 'but I don't believe in witches.'

Rachel tried to pull her arms away from him, but his grip only tightened, brutally. She would never have thought him so strong. 'Let me go or I'll scream,' she said. She should be angry, but the fear was draining away any fury she might have felt.

'I don't care if you do,' he retorted. 'Maeve and I have already decided, witch. You're goin' to drown yourself in the river.'

Rachel stared back at him, her throat dry 'Why would I—' she managed hoarsely.

Yelland smiled. He was enjoying this, just as he knew he would. And when he was finished here, he'd go back to the inn and Maeve would be so grateful . . . he was looking forward to seeing just how grateful she could be.

'Rosa said she's seen you around here a lot,' he told her conversationally. 'She reckons you've been thinkin' about that silly cow who threw herself in the Goulburn in the autumn. Wheeler's wife. She'll say how unhappy you are and that she thinks it's been on your mind.'

Rachel was shaking her head. 'This is quite ridiculous,' she burst out. 'There's no reason for it!'

'No reason?' he repeated, mocking her, hating her. He took another step forward, pressing his body against hers, but she couldn't retreat. There was no where left to go. The river bank was very close now. Glancing over her shoulder, Rachel could see the swirl of the golden water.

'Before you came 'ere Maeve was happy . . . I was happy. So it follows that with you gone, Maeve can 'ave Will Moody back again and when she persuades him to leave the police, then I can go back to being in charge. Just like before. And it'll be a pleasure to see him go, witch, because I reckon there's no-one in this world I hate more than Will Moody.'

The truth of it was there in his eyes, and she couldn't pretend any more. 'Will won't go back to Maeve,' Rachel whispered. 'He's finished with her. And they'll never let you stay here . . . they want you gone. Quill is trying to have you transferred back to Melbourne.'

He frowned, but almost at once dismissed it. 'No. With you dead, Maeve'll have her way, and so will I.' His fingers tightened, and she saw the deadly intent in the hard, determined line of his mouth.

'No!' With a gasp, Rachel tried again to pull free, at the same time kicking at Yelland's legs. But it was too late. Yelland gave a sudden thrust, releasing his grip on her, and Rachel was falling backwards into empty air. She screamed, her hands grabbing for some hold, desperate to save herself. And then there was only blue sky, whirling dizzily above her. Her foot caught on some bushes on the bank and her shoe came off. And then she hit the water, hard, with a great splash.

And went under.

It was cold. That was her first thought. It was icy cold. Then she was rising up through it, floating to the surface with the air in her skirts buoying her up. She splashed her arms into the water swirling about her. So cold, Rachel gasped. Her wet hair was blinding her, but she stretched her hands towards the bank, grasping at the almost vertical incline that was just too far away. Yelland had made sure of that: his push had sent her a good two yards out into the river.

Yelland! The thought made her look up, and Rachel saw him above her, leaning forward slightly, watching. His face was a white mask. The fact that he was standing there, waiting, made it so much worse. She knew that he would stay there until she drowned and nothing she could do or say would make him come to her aid.

Her skirts were filling with water. Rachel kicked frantically, feeling her other shoe come off, and sink. But even as she kicked and struggled, willing herself to survive, she knew it was no good. Her skirts were no longer her life buoy. As the water filled them, they were becoming so heavy, dragging her slowly down to certain death. The tug of cloth and petticoats was like the weights they used in the store, to measure flour, all tied about her waist.

With a cry, Rachel went under.

It took a superhuman effort to force herself up again, gasping and choking, her arms pounding through the water, her legs kicking amongst the strangling folds of her skirts. Through the blur of exhaustion and splashing water, she saw Yelland, still above her.

Oh God, it was so unfair! Rachel thought, and tried to scream, but her throat had closed up with panic and terror. It was so unfair to die now, when Will loved her again! When everything was coming good, after all these years alone. So unfair . . . she slid down beneath the surface again, knowing it would be the last time, and as she did so something hard nudged her in the back.

Again Rachel tried to scream, but again no sound came, only air bubbles rising. She thrust her hands out, clawing at this new aggressor, and broke her nail on rough wood. A snag. And a sizeable one by the feel of it. It was floating just below the surface, propelled along by the river currents.

Blood was thumping in her head, her lungs were bursting. Rachel caught at the branch and pulled herself closer. Her fingers grappled, searching. The snag felt like part of a tree trunk, struck by lightning perhaps, and split in two. There was a thick piece of trunk, with a large branch still attached—it was the branch which had dug Rachel in the back.

She was losing strength. Soon it would be too late. But God or fate or whatever had given her this chance, and she must make use of it. Rachel fastened her hands firmly around the branch, bracing herself for a last mighty effort. And then she hauled herself upwards, the muscles of her arms screaming from the leaden weight of her skirts. But she was coming up, she felt herself ascending as the tree branch held firm. Rachel's lungs were bursting. She had to breathe . . . she had to breathe . . . she . . . Rachel gasped, expecting her lungs to fill with water, and found instead that her head was above it.

For a moment all she could do was breathe. Great gulps of sweet air filled her lungs. Her head was spinning, dizzy as a top, and she shook it slightly, clearing the wet hair from her eyes, not daring to remove her hands from their grip around the snag.

'Shit!'

The savage voice channelled her thoughts. Rachel swung her head, trying to focus on her surroundings.

Yelland had seen her. When Rachel's head had appeared, floating, above the water, he had thought he was losing his mind. That she was indeed a witch! Until he had realised the truth, and that the rest of her must be being supported just below the surface.

'Shit,' he said again. His face was as colourless as hers. He limped along the curving bank above her, following the path of the snag as it was drawn downstream by the current of the river. Rachel saw him fumbling with his belt. He swore again when he realised his pistol wasn't there. Sobbing with relief, Rachel clung on, her fingers beginning to lose all sense of feeling in the cold water. The rough wood of the split trunk was jagged, pieces of it digging into her breasts through her clothes, and there was a raw scrape on her collar bone, where she had torn skin while she was hauling herself up.

She could hang on, she told herself, but a voice in her head mocked her. As the cold water sucked the strength from her arms and fingers, she knew that at most she had another ten minutes. And then Yelland would be granted his wish.

A splash behind her startled Rachel so much that she nearly lost her grip. The shift in balance caused the snag to roll in the water, like some huge living creature. Rachel screamed, clinging on, forcing the branch to roll back again by pitting her own weight against it. Slowly, slowly it did so, righting itself, steadying.

Another splash, closer this time. Rachel gritted her teeth. Carefully, she moved her head, turning it so that she could see Yelland as he found another stone to fling into the water close beside her. She prayed that his aim did not improve, taking long deep breaths, calming herself.

He was screaming at her, furious at her for being still alive. 'Die, you fuckin' witch!'

The words did not affect her, other than to strengthen her resolve to live. He was hysterical, hopping around like a great shabby crow, looking for things to throw at her. She realised then that she was almost adjacent to the place where the bank swept out into the river, beyond which was the punt. That was why Yelland was so upset. If she reached the punt, she may be able to pull herself out.

Something struck her on the shoulder. It went numb and Rachel's fingers almost lost their grip. She began to scream, beyond all thought now, desperate to survive. She was screaming so loudly, it was a moment before she heard the other sound, clanging through the bush.

The bell at the Post. Someone was ringing the bell.

Wildly, Rachel looked around her. No Yelland. Had he left her? Or was he lurking about, ready with some other scheme to upset her precarious hold on life? Oh God, had he gone back for his gun?

The idea gripped her insides, making them writhe and squirm like a spadeful of worms.

'Will,' she breathed, even knowing how pointless it was to call on him. 'Will!'

The bell had stopped ringing. Its echo faded to a deathly silence. Rachel lifted her head sharply, suddenly aware that the water had been lapping at her lips. She was getting weaker. Soon she wouldn't be able to hold her head above the water any more. The riverbank seemed to be slipping by so slowly . . .

Rachel opened her mouth to scream again, and nearly choked as a voice called out to her from the bank.

'Rachel! Hang on, oh God, hang on!'

Violet, her eyes like saucers.

Rachel's heart was beating madly, and she watched as slowly, slowly, the bend in the river gave way to the place where the punt crossed it. The banks were lower here, and the gradient gentler. And there it was.

The punt.

A rectangle of planks fastened together and made reasonably watertight. It was drawn up to the river-bank. Rachel was gazing at it so intently she did not realise there was a figure on the bank. A man, standing there. Rachel sobbed, thinking it was Yelland, but almost at once she realised her mistake. It was Sean, from the inn. He jumped onto the punt, and grasped the rope used to propel it over the water. With hard, sure strokes, he was pulling it

out into the middle of the river. Rachel watched
it moving, slowly, across the sluggish current, and
into her path.

Sean was trying to look reassuring, but Rachel
sensed he was as terrified as she. 'Just hold on,' he
told her quietly. 'Here we go now, here we go . .
.' The snag bumped into the punt. Rachel felt it
begin to roll and screamed. Sean leaned over the
edge and stretched out his hand to grab hers. She
hardly felt his grip, her own was so numb. She
knew she could not hold on to him, but despite his
thin body, Sean was strong. He heaved Rachel up
onto the side of the punt, rolling her over and over,
so that she lay on her back on the rough planks,
her wet skirts twisted and dripping darkly about
her. She was exhausted, panting with great sobbing
breaths. But safe.

'There now,' he murmured, and his voice was
shaking. He peered down at her, eyes creased to
slits. A tear ran down his cheek.

With a great effort Rachel gathered her strength
into a whisper. 'My children? Where are my children?'

'Safe, never you mind,' Sean assured her. 'They
never meant to harm your children.' He patted her
awkwardly on the shoulder, his fingers gripping.

'You knew,' she wasn't even sure if she'd said it
aloud.

Sean's unhappy monkey face looked even more
unhappy. 'She's a bloody fool and no mistake. I
knew there was something up, Mrs Moody, I've
known for days. And then, today, I got the truth
out of her. She suddenly realised, I think, what was
going to happen to you. It was real, not just pre-

tendin'. She's a good woman, really. Your husband made her lose her mind for a time, but it's over now, and she's sorry for it. I came running up here fast as I could. I met Violet Kemp on the way and left her ringin' the bell. I thought it might be too late, until I heard you screamin'.'

'Yelland?'

Sean's eyes darkened. 'He's evil, that one. Like the devil, waitin' in the shadows to steal away your soul. He almost had Maeve's, but she realised the wrong of it in time.'

'Where is he?' Rachel looked around, as if expecting to see Yelland smiling at her from the bank. She shuddered so uncontrollably, Sean took off his jacket and wrapped it around her, holding her in his arms.

'He's gone. It's all right now, Mrs Moody. You're safe, thank God you're safe.'

His voice trailed off.

It was only then that Rachel allowed herself to cry, hot tears streaming down her cold cheeks. And it didn't surprise her when Sean joined in.

CHAPTER 30

'HERE YOU ARE,' VIOLET PRESSED the hot mug into her hand. It was supposed to be tea, but the reek of rum nearly knocked Rachel over.

They were in Violet's cottage and Violet had stripped her and wrapped her in various blankets and shawls, until Rachel had finally stopped shaking. Now she was just angry.

'Yelland's gone.' Mr Quill had just come in, his face full of concern. 'One of the horses is missing, and I presume he's taken it. McPherson up at the general store spotted him earlier and said he was heading north.'

Violet looked positively savage. 'If I ever get me hands on him—'

Quill ignored her. 'His wife says he forced her to say what she did, under threat of violence.'

Violet snorted. 'Well, that's probably true enough!'

'I'll send her down to Melbourne as soon as possible. I doubt Yelland will be back for them and we can't support his family for him.'

Rachel was silent, breathing the steam from the

mug. The tip of her nose had turned red from the heat and her dark hair was drying, curling at the edges. She had undergone a terrifying experience, and was still coming to grips with what would have happened if Sean hadn't come to her aid. After Rachel had been saved, Violet had heard Bella yelling from the Yelland cottage and gone to investigate. Rosa had been unable to sustain her calm under Violet's bullying tactics and told all—how she was supposed to keep Bella 'safe' until Yelland had finished with Rachel. That was one thing in Maeve's favour—she had been adamant that the children must not be harmed.

'What about Maeve?' Violet asked now, belligerently. 'It's all very well to say she's sorry—'

Quill shook his head. 'Maeve is genuinely repentant and Sean is doing his best to lay the blame on Yelland. It depends on whether Mrs Moody wants to press charges.'

Violet opened her mouth, but Quill held up a hand for silence. 'I might add that Maeve's licence will be coming up in a few months and it's up to me to decide whether or not it's renewed. I've already told her it won't be. She can complain all she likes. I'm the only law around here, and I've made up my mind.'

'Well . . . good!' said Violet lamely, and plumped back into her chair.

Rachel managed a smile. 'Do you think anyone will find Yelland?' she whispered—her throat was raw from screaming.

Quill tried to look confident. 'I'll put out the word. We'll be looking for him. He can't stay hidden forever.'

Rachel nodded, but in her heart she didn't believe they would catch him now. The thought of Yelland watching her drown flashed into her mind and she hastily sipped the scalding tea.

'How are you feeling?' Mr Quill asked her gently. When they had dragged Rachel Moody from the river, she'd looked like nothing more than a drowned rat. But she had insisted on walking to Violet's cottage, despite the tendency for her legs to wobble. A brave woman, this one.

'I'm all right now,' she said, and lifted her chin.

'Your husband has some leave due to him,' Quill went on thoughtfully. 'When he gets back, I'll suggest he makes use of it.'

Rachel smiled properly this time. 'Thank you,' she murmured. Her hands closed hard around the hot mug and tears shone in her eyes. For the first time her voice wavered. 'I hope he gets back soon.'

Rosa Yelland had returned to Melbourne. Rachel had been a little sorry for her in the end, but not Violet.

'She meant you to die, just like her husband and Maeve. She deserves all she gets.'

'But her children—'

'She went whining to Quill before she left. He paid her the wages owin' to Yelland. No, you just be glad they're gone and you've got their married man's hut!'

The hut. When she and Violet went to inspect

it, Rachel discovered the remains of a garden at the front. Perhaps the unhappy Mrs Wheeler had tended it, but since then the Yellands had let it die from lack of care . . . and water. Apart from a few hardy geraniums, grimly hanging on, there was mainly dust. The building contained three rooms. A main or sitting room with a hearth, a small bedroom and a larger bedroom. All of it was, quite simply, filthy.

'Disgustin'!' Violet hissed, holding her nose. 'Pigs live better' an this!'

The floor was inches thick with dirt and grime, and Rachel doubted the hearth had been cleaned out since the Yellands arrived, choked as it was with ash. Certainly, the soot covered the walls and the chimney, and there were scorch marks on the dirty sacking they had used as a hearthside rug. The bedrooms were just as bad, the one belonging to the children stinking of urine. The mattress reeked too, but Violet was sure a good airing would see it right.

The first thing Rachel did was throw open the windows. And then they started at the door and cleaned all the way through, forced to use a shovel in places, to clean away the muck. It took all day and at the end of it they were covered in filth, their hair and clothes reeking and their bodies aching with effort and limp with exhaustion. But it was worth it. The place was unrecognisable. The walls glowed and the floor could have been eaten off. Rachel drew a deep, satisfied breath as she looked about her.

'I'll get our things moved over in the morning,' she said. Then only one thing would be missing—

Will. She missed Will so much. She wouldn't feel right until he was with her again. At night she lay awake, needing him to blot out the horror of the river and her brush with death.

Involuntarily, Rachel's eyes shifted beyond the sitting room, beyond the bedroom door. There was a double bed there, the dull brass polished and gleaming softly in the fading light. Rachel found her eyes returning to it again and again. Excitement caught in her throat. What would Will say, when he saw it? But stronger than her nervousness concerning Will's reaction, was her own need to have done with pretence. She wanted to be with him in that bed, she wanted his arms about her and his mouth on hers. She wanted him as much as she ever had and almost dying had only strengthened that desire.

'The Sergeant will appreciate this,' Violet was saying. 'Probably goin' slowly mad in that other hut. If it'd been any other man, he'd 'ave tossed Yelland out long ago and moved in himself. But that's not Will Moody's way, is it, Rachel?'

'No.' Despite his dislike of Yelland, or perhaps because of it, Will would have been scrupulously fair.

'No word of Yelland yet,' Violet went on. Mr Quill had sent a letter to the Police Post on the Murray, but there had been no answer, and with Yelland gone, and Kemp and Will away, there was no-one to go riding around the district searching for Yelland. 'Probably heading for Yass or Sydney,' she went on. 'Although I can't imagine anyone wantin' to hire Yelland on as labour, no matter how desperate they are.'

Rachel shuddered. 'No.'

Violet patted her shoulder awkwardly. 'He's gone, Rachel. He can't hurt you now. And neither can Maeve,' and her eyes gleamed. They had had word that Maeve and the faithful Sean had packed up and left for Melbourne two nights ago. Rachel knew that she owed Sean her life, and Maeve too, for confessing the plan—although if it hadn't been for Maeve there would have been no plan to confess— but she just wanted it forgotten. So that she could begin to live the life she had almost lost.

Their new quarters had begun to look like home to Rachel, a real home. It was a long time since she had had somewhere she could call her own. Greengage, that had been hers, although the memory of poor Hannah was always there. Otherwise, she had lived in other people's homes and relied upon their kindness or her own hard efforts.

Violet had made some biscuits. Bella munched on one, while Hannah lay kicking on the floor, gurgling to herself, as the sun circled through the doorway and the day drew on.

What would Will say when he saw the changed accommodation? Perhaps he preferred the old place? Not as it was now, but how it had been when he was there alone. Austere, uncluttered, unencumbered. That was Will Moody. He had created the sort of solitary existence he craved, and now she was forcing him to be a husband and a father. She was looking at the possibility of their beginning a new life together, but maybe that was something Will Moody could not do.

Just as she longed for his return—as she had longed for him ever since she was thirteen and he had ridden into her life on a dark, stormy Midsummer's Eve—she also dreaded it. Just as she was afraid of what she would see in his eyes, she still had to see what he felt about her. Even if it was the worst thing possible. I won't live a lie anymore, she told herself fiercely. I did that once before, hiding my face from the truth. This time I know the truth and I still want him. But he must want me, too.

Rachel smiled to herself. Hannah, at her feet, was trying to roll over and when she couldn't began to howl in frustration. Bella had gone outside to play with the two Kemp children. Lately, she had begun to lose some of her need for solitude, as though she were finally settling in to her new life. I was right to come here, Rachel told herself firmly. No matter what it cost, I was right.

Sometimes, Rachel thought of Suzy and George in Melbourne. And Sarah and Thomas, up at Nerinbilly. Their lives had all taken such different turns. Rachel missed them very much, but she knew in her heart that, if she had to, she could live her life without them. She very much doubted that she could live, or would want to live, without Will.

Will was back.

Rachel and Violet hurried outside to watch the dusty, weary threesome ride into the Post. Being so big, Will stood out above the other two. Rachel's eyes ran frantically over him, seeking some hurt. Other than looking tired, the lines on his face more pronounced, and his clothes grubby from hard riding and camping out, he appeared to be in one piece. Rachel felt herself go limp with relief and then her heart began to beat at a rapid pace.

Two prisoners, their hands bound before them, rode with the troopers, and a third, bundled in a blanket, hung dead over his saddle.

Will dismounted, taking his time to issue instructions to Joseph and Kemp. And then he was looking around, straight at her. He quickly looked down, but she saw the curve of his mouth and knew he was smiling. Rachel's heart filled to over-flowing. Will murmured a last comment to Joseph, and began to walk towards her. He was looking full at her now and there was no mistaking the blaze of satisfaction in his eyes. Bella ran to him, and he lifted her high into the air, making her squeal. 'I need a bath,' he said with a grimace, moving towards the old hut.

'Will!' Rachel's voice burst out in a rush. 'The Yellands have gone. I moved us into their place.' She had no intention of telling him the whole truth until he was rested. She was a little afraid he would turn around and jump onto his horse again and set off after Yelland.

He took another step before he could stop, his tired mind finding difficulty in coordinating his legs. And then he turned and peered at her through narrowed grey eyes.

'I didn't think you'd mind,' she added, and tried not to let her voice drop to a whisper.

He opened his mouth to say something, and then closed it again. He sighed, letting Bella slip to the ground. 'As long as it's got a bed, I don't care if we live in a trunk,' he said, and followed her to their new home.

She'd watered the geraniums and they were looking healthier. In her more optimistic moments, she planned to make a proper garden, with pink roses and white lilies, lifting their faces to the summer sun.

Rachel opened the door, and heard Will behind her. Inside, the space was neat and clean and tidy. Hannah was asleep in the crib in the corner, thumb jammed in her mouth. Will glanced about without speaking, unbuckling his belt, placing the pistol and holster out of reach on top of the cupboard.

'Where's the bed?'

Rachel pointed out the doorway to the bedroom, and he walked over and looked in. He stood with his back to her, and she noticed with a tingling shock that there was a white strand of hair at his nape, unmistakable amongst the black. She had never noticed it before, and the sight of it now made her tremble.

Will turned to look at her over his shoulder. 'Where's my bed?'

Rachel met his eyes without flinching. 'Violet was here. She just assumed we would be sharing it.'

Silence. He was watching her and she felt as if all her hopes and fears were written on her face and he was reading every one. But all he said was, 'I'm goin' to have a wash,' and walked past her, back out of the door.

Rachel let out her breath and set about preparing him some food. He seemed to be away a long time, and by the time he returned the meal was ready and Hannah was awake. Will's hair was wet and still dripping, and he was wearing clean breeches and an old shirt. Something of the deadly tiredness had gone from his face, but his eyes were still narrowed, as though the light hurt them.

'You caught the bushrangers,' she said, sitting down beside him with the baby in her arms.

'Yes.' He took a mouthful. 'I missed your cookin', Rachel.'

She laughed. 'I doubt that's a compliment after mutton and damper over a campfire.' He grinned back and kept eating. Rachel shifted Hannah into a more comfortable position in her arms, while Bella sat as close to Will as she could manage. 'What becomes of the prisoners?'

'Two'll be sent down to Melbourne. The other one goes into the ground.'

Shock at the callousness of his words widened her eyes. 'What happened?' she whispered, forcing the words out. She had to know. No secrets, she reminded herself.

He shrugged and met her look appraisingly, and she realised he had been waiting for her to speak. Probably waiting for the recriminations. 'They didn't want to give themselves up when the time came. We persuaded two of them, but the other one preferred to die. I can't blame him for that, Rachel. Gaol for some men is as bad as dyin'. And he was a convict already, so he would have ended up at one of the secondary punishment places—

Port Arthur or Norfolk Island. Men draw lots there for their mates to kill 'em. Better off dead.'

'So you did him a kindness?' she breathed, and something of the old Rachel glittered in her eyes.

'No,' he replied, struggling to keep his voice level. 'It was his choice, not mine. But when a man comes at me, firin', I don't take risks with my life. I've got a family to consider, haven't I?'

She had no argument. He was right, she knew he was right, and yet anger at such waste of life remained with her.

Will was watching her and shook his head, a reluctant smile curling up one side of his mouth. 'Do you think I don't feel sorry, too? Do you think I don't keep the memory of it with me, as I keep the memory of all the men I've killed? But there was no other way. It was me or him and the odds were on my side.'

She nodded. 'I know,' she said, 'I know. Eat your meal, Will.'

He hesitated and then turned back to his food. After he finished, Will rose and, touching her head briefly, staggered into the bedroom. When Rachel peeped in later he was asleep, sprawled sideways across the bed, as if he'd just collapsed into unconsciousness. He'd removed his boots, but that was all.

She stood a moment, watching him. He'd done his job and done it well. She was proud of him, she told herself. Forget the man who had died. Be grateful that it was not Will dead, wrapped in a blanket and slung over his horse. Just be grateful that Will was alive.

The afternoon wore on, and she fed Bella and Hannah their supper, settling the baby for the night.

Bella curled up in her bed in the other room, and by the manner in which she was forcing her tired eyes to remain open, Rachel knew her daughter had an important question to ask her.

'Will my father have to go away again?'

Rachel smiled and caressed her warm cheek.

'That's his job, darling. Sometimes he has to go away.'

'He goes out to shoot bad men.' Bella informed her knowledgeably, her eyes closing at last. Rachel bit her lip, wondering what Violet's children had been saying. It was ironic that Rachel had grown up on the side of the hunted and now her daughter was on the side of the hunter.

The long evening waned to darkness. Outside, the night was still, with only the occasional bark of a dog, and an owl calling eerily. Inside, the cottage was so silent Rachel could hear her own heart beat, muffled in her ears.

Will must have been in the saddle for days on end to sleep so deeply and so long. He pushed himself too hard; he expected too much of himself. She wondered if he did it so that he wouldn't have time to feel. Had dedication to duty taken the place of the drink, in blunting his emotions?

Rachel yawned and knew the moment had come. She couldn't put it off any longer. Besides, she admitted to herself, she wanted to sleep in the bed beside Will, she wanted that very much.

Will had moved, rolling onto his side to face away from her. At some stage he had pulled a blanket half over himself. Rachel watched him as she undressed and slipped on her voluminous nightgown. The cloth was cool against her flesh, pleasant on such a warm night. She brushed her hair, slowly, feeling the bristles catch and then slide through the heavy curls. The action was soothing and sensuous.

She left her hair loose, like a bride.

Rachel blew out the candle and with slow, cautious movements, slid into the bed beside Will. And lay, listening to the steady rhythm of his soft breathing. Rachel forced herself to relax, stretching out her legs, straightening her clenched fingers one by one, and then turned onto her side, cupping her palm under her cheek. Will seemed a lot bigger, lying beside her. She watched the broad expanse of his back move gently with each of those steady breaths. One leg was bent slightly at the knee, and she knew the muscles of thigh and calf would be hard even in sleep. His dark hair lay silky against the back of his head. Rachel remembered suddenly how shocked she had been when she saw the white amongst the black. It was a sign of Will's mortality and she didn't like it. She didn't like it at all.

With a shaking hand, Rachel reached out to touch that single, white strand.

He woke in an instant, rolling over and catching her wrist in a brutal grip. Rachel was too startled even to cry out, and lay, staring back into his eyes. Slowly, the cold, hard grey of them softened into recognition. His fingers loosened their hold and Rachel let out a shaky sigh.

Will's eyes shifted, noting the tumble of dark hair on the pillow, the neat buttons of her nightgown which hid so much and yet revealed more in the curves beneath it. The thought of her had sent him riding for home at a cracking pace. Even during the few hours here and there he'd allowed for sleeping, he'd spent staring up at the star-filled sky, wide awake. She'll be there, he told himself. She has to be there. Because if she isn't, there's nothing left for me on the Goulburn.

As soon as he had reached the Post, he'd looked for her, half blind with exhaustion, squinting through the glare for the one face that really mattered. And when he found her, his relief was almost shocking in its intensity. He'd pretended to linger, giving orders to his men, praising them . . . anything so that she wouldn't guess how much it meant to him that she was there. By the time he turned back to her he was in control again. Himself again. Until she told him about the married quarters.

And he'd seen the bed.

And now the dream was reality and Will knew he had finally lost the battle with his self-control.

Something deep inside Rachel began to tremble as Will's eyes came back to hers. She felt the bed move as he shifted his weight to lean over her, looking down at her out of the shadows. The tension in her was such that when his mouth touched hers she cried out, softly. The kiss was gentle, a mere brush of his lips, as if he were testing her response, but at her cry his kiss deepened. Slowly, slowly his hand slid up to close over the full, warm curve of her breast, squeezing gently. Rachel gasped beneath his lips.

Will bent his head, and began to undo the little buttons of her bodice with unhurried ease. Rachel watched his fingers, struggling to breathe. His face was so close to hers that when he glanced up their eyes were only inches apart. For a moment they gazed at each other as if they were meeting for the first time. And then Will parted the edges of her nightgown and buried his face against her soft flesh. Rachel held his head hard against her, twisting her fingers in his thick soft hair. She felt his mouth close over her nipple, and the joy of it made her tremble so badly he felt it and lifted his head.

'Rachel?' he whispered. 'Tell me to stop, and I will. Rachel?'

But she pulled his face down to hers, silencing him with her kiss. He needed no further encouragement. His hands grazed the tips of her breasts, moving down to close on her waist. His thigh slid between hers, and Rachel pressed against him, arching her back. His breath was hot in her ear, as he whispered, 'It's been such a long time . . .' Rachel shivered, her hands sliding over his shoulders and around the thick column of his neck. The last time, he remembered, he'd taken her in sleep, tricking her body into accepting something her mind would not. He'd been in love with her then and he was in love with her now. Time had changed nothing after all.

Will was gathering the folds of her nightgown, pulling it up and over her head, and her hair floated free, like ink across white shoulders and breasts.

Her dark eyes shone and she smiled with trembling lips.

Rachel pulled at his shirt and he let her take it off him. Now she could touch him too, smoothing the hard, curving muscles of his chest, pressing her face into the hollow of his throat. It was like a thousand dreams she had had since he left, when always the bliss of finding him had vanished upon waking. Only this was no dream, this was real.

Will slid off his breeches, tossing them onto the floor, and suddenly the slowness, the dreamlike quality was gone. He gathered her into his arms, kissing her while the silk of her hair tangled about them. His big hand spread warm over her back, drawing her body even closer to his until they were pressed so hard together she felt only his bare skin.

A tear rolled down her cheek, and he caught it with his tongue, kissing her damp lashes, kissing her soft mouth. 'Don't cry,' he murmured. 'It's all right, darlin', it's all right.'

He kissed her again, deeply, and she felt him positioning his body above hers. The muscles of his thighs and buttocks were bunching, gathering strength, and then he was inside her. Rachel cried out, lifting her hips to draw him in still further. Passion gripped her, but it was more than that. The empty space that had existed in her heart sprang open, and Will was there, filling her. At the same time, she heard his voice, as Will Moody shattered, and she grasped him in her arms.

He slept afterwards, holding her tight, but Rachel lay awake, her thoughts drifting. So many things had come between them, so many people had kept them apart. None of it mattered now. It felt perfect just being here, clasped against Will. He was hers and she was his, and it had always been so. She knew it now more than ever, just as she knew that alone, she had been only half alive.

Her arms tightened about his waist and she placed kisses under his jaw, breathing him in. Never again, she told herself. I'll never loose you again. He stirred, his hand cupped her cheek, his thumb brushed the curve of her lips, and his sleepy mouth claimed hers. 'Rachel,' he murmured, his voice deep with satisfaction. The same satisfaction that had been in his expression when he saw her waiting for him earlier. He opened one eye and smiled at her, as if they shared some vast secret, before closing it again, and laying his head against her breast with a sigh.

CHAPTER 31

IT WAS A BEAUTIFUL MORNING. The sky was a calm blue lake, with boats of fluffy white clouds floating across its surface. A magpie caroled in the trees by the river, singing a song just for Rachel. Or so she felt. The Post was very quiet this morning—Kemp and Joseph were resting up. Rachel watched Violet chasing one of her children, promising dire retribution. And then she was gone, and the magpie was singing again, and Rachel couldn't keep the smile off her face.

Will could hear her out in the other room, moving about with her usual light step. He lay in the half light of the bedroom, enjoying the soft bed and the knowledge that he had nothing to do and nowhere to go. And the memories of the night.

She couldn't have pretended passion like that. Just as she had been unable to pretend in the smithy's cottage at Greengage. She was his again, his sweet young wife, so in love with him her eyes shone with it whenever she looked at him. And he had been her hero, perfect, incapable of any wrong.

Will smiled wryly to himself at the thought. Well,

it hadn't turned out that way, had it? He was certainly no hero and Rachel was no longer the sweet young wife she had been.

But was that such a bad thing?

Last time their love had been unable to withstand the cold, hard truth. This time, founded on truth, it should stand as solid as a rock.

Rachel was bending over the hearth when she heard his step behind her. 'Are you hungry?' she asked him without turning. 'You slept so long, but I didn't like to wake you.'

He didn't answer. Should she turn? And yet she was suddenly afraid to, shy of what she might see in his eyes. His warm hand touched her shoulder and lay there. She stiffened.

'Rachel?' It was a question.

His hand tightened. 'Where're Bella and Hannah?' he asked, glancing around the empty room.

'Violet took them for an hour or two,' Rachel replied nervously. 'I've done the same for her. Gives us both a break.' Then, even more nervously, 'Will?' For he had slid his other arm around her waist, drawing her slowly back against him. She felt his body shudder. He was laughing at her!

He nuzzled at the place between her neck and shoulder, which he'd been dying to kiss for weeks. Rachel shivered and her hands, bunched into fists to hit at him, lost their strength. Slowly, he turned her in his arms. The stubble on his jaw and his tousled hair gave him a dangerous look. He cupped her face in his hands, the callouses rough against her cheeks, and tilted her face to his.

'Come back to bed with me, Rachel.'

Rachel's eyes widened. 'Now?'

'Now,'

Will's mouth moved over her cheekbone, warm and seductive. Rachel closed her eyes, her breath quickening. His lips brushed hers and clung for a moment. And then suddenly he had released her, stepping back. Rachel felt herself swaying towards him, before she could stop it. As if he were her lode-stone. Her eyes flicked open. He looked very serious suddenly, as if he were about to pronounce sentence on her, and she went still, waiting.

Will felt his heart beating like a drum. 'There's still somethin' between us,' he said softly, 'and you can't pretend there isn't.'

'I'm not the girl I was.' Her voice was a whisper.

'I'm not the same man. Does it matter?'

Slowly, she shook her head.

'Ah, Rachel,' and his face was suddenly naked in all his love and pain. 'Am I a Moonraker to feel like this? Tell me the truth. Do you feel it too?'

'I feel it too,' she whispered. Everything was happening so quickly, her head was spinning. She stepped forward to press her cheek against his chest and closed her eyes. His heart was beating, slow and steady, and she slowed her breathing to match. His arms came naturally around her.

'Have I felt like this all along?' he murmured, as if to himself. 'Or is it new? All I know is that I thought my heart dead all this time and now it's started up again.'

Rachel smiled. 'I've missed you so much, Will,' she said. 'Nothing's the same when you're not here.'

He tilted up her chin and kissed her hard. 'Do you love me again, Rachel?' he demanded.

'I've always loved you. Even when I was hating

you, I loved you.'

He smiled against her lips. 'You know what I mean.'

'Am I older and wiser, is that it? Well, I am. I am, Will. Don't ever leave me again.'

The last was said in a rush and her arms clung with all her strength. He closed his eyes, letting the feel of her wash over him, and told himself: Never.

Violet sat fanning herself with her straw hat, watching Rachel slyly. She'd brought the children back and, for politeness sake, Rachel had asked her to stay for a cup of tea. Violet had been more than willing, but, after a while, came to the conclusion that Rachel's mind really wasn't in the same room as her body.

She began sentences and forgot the ending, or else she stood, staring into space, until Violet cleared her throat and brought her back to the present.

'You sickenin' for something, Rachel?' Violet asked her at last, curiously.

Rachel pushed back an untidy strand of hair— that was another thing, her usually neat chignon was all askew, wisps and dark curls sticking out everywhere. 'No, I don't think so,' she smiled vaguely.

Behind her the bedroom door opened. To Violet's dismay, Rachel started violently. What was wrong with her? What was there in the sight of her husband to make her jump like that? Had Will

Moody threatened her, or hurt her? Violet narrowed speculative eyes at him.

Will had pulled on his breeches, but his shirt was unbuttoned, and he was barefoot. There was a sense of total contentment about him, as if he hadn't a care in the world. Violet had never thought of Will in that way before. He was usually so serious, so intense. But here he was, smiling lazily at her and, yes—she swore it was true to her husband later—humming under his breath. He came over to the hearth and leaned one shoulder against the mantle-piece.

Rachel swallowed. Her face was turned unnaturally in Violet's direction and Violet was sure it was by design, so that she didn't have to look at Will. But he was looking at her, his eyes sliding up the straight line of her back to the neat white collar buttoned at her nape and the soft, untidy chignon spilling over her shoulders. There was something in his eyes . . . Violet couldn't quite place it.

'You've made the place nice,' Violet went on, shifting uneasily in her chair. 'Better 'an that little cupboard you had before, eh Sergeant?'

Will smiled again. A sort of slow smile that, Violet admitted secretly to herself, made even her hardened heart flutter. 'Much better.'

Rachel was pretending to examine a spot on her cuff and her cheeks were pink. God, she was in a state. What had the big bastard done to her?

Violet's husband laughed when she told him. 'You great silly lump!' he called her. 'Our Sergeant's 'appy, that's all. 'E's a lusty man and 'e's got a warm, pretty armful of a wife. You weren't there when 'e turned for 'ome—never seen a man ride so 'ard and so fast! I reckon them prisoners were glad to see the inside of the watch-'ouse.'

Will rode over to see Mr Quill in the afternoon. When he arrived back he came straight to the quarters. Rachel knew that he'd heard about Yelland because his face was white and she saw the muscle flicking in his cheek. But it was his eyes that frightened her. They blazed with an icy fury she had never seen before.

Rachel went and put her arms around him, holding on tightly, feeling his big body trembling.

'Tell me,' he said. And, when she hesitated, 'I mean it, Rachel. Tell me!'

So she told him about the time in the river, her voice wavering despite herself, and as the story unfolded, Will turned to iron.

'He's gone,' she whispered. 'Will, he's gone.'

His hands gripped her shoulders and he held her away, looking down into her face. 'There's nowhere he can go, that I won't find him. And when I do, I'll kill him.' It was like a vow, and it frightened Rachel.

Will could see it frightened her but he didn't care. He pulled her back into his arms and just held her there, savouring the feel of her. When Quill had told him what happened while he was away, Will had wanted to go and look for Yelland immediately. He'd strode back and forwards across the room, making Quill nervous. But Quill had calmed him down and made him see sense.

'He'll turn up. They always do. Someone will recognise him and turn him in. And as for Maeve . . . she's long gone. Don't go looking for her, Sergeant.'

Will shook his head, looking sick. 'Christ, I wouldn't trust myself to!'

'Go home to your wife,' Quill told him gently. 'And thank God for your luck, Sergeant.'

Will sighed, running a hand through his hair. He looked drained. 'I don't feel I can thank you enough for what you did, sir—'

'It was Sean saved your wife, not me.'

Remembering Quill's words, Will held Rachel tighter. The shock would pass, and the rage, too. But he was patient. He could wait until he found Yelland, and when he did he would deal him Will Moody's kind of justice.

The letter came near the end of January 1844. The weather was hot, a north wind blowing dust and the smell of burning across the Goulburn District. Everyone hated the north wind and tempers frayed. Will had broken up a fight at the inn— reopened and renamed 'The Young Queen'—and there had been problems on a few of the sheep runs with one shepherd assaulting another and a bullock driver dropping dead after spending his entire quarterly pay at the inn. Will was tired and seriously thinking of agreeing with Quill that he needed some leave.

The letter was waiting for him when he returned to the cottage and he sat by the window and read it, with Rachel watching him surreptitiously as she went about her work. He read in silence and when he finished he was frowning. He sat for a long moment staring into space and Rachel had to say his name three times before he heard her.

'Will, is everything all right?'

His smile was lopsided. 'It's from Frank.'

'I know. Are the children well?'

'Nothin' wrong with the children, Rachel,' and he reached out a hand. Rachel smiled and came to take it. He drew her onto his knee, kissing the top of her head and squeezing his arms about her. 'You smell good.'

Rachel laughed.

He kissed her again, and sighed. 'Frank is marrying Greta Redcliffe.'

Rachel turned her head and stared at him in silent disbelief.

He smiled back wryly. 'I know. That's what he says here in his letter. He's marryin' her and Israel has left Nerinbilly. He's living up on the northern run and Frank doesn't think they'll ever speak to each other again.'

Rachel didn't know what to think. She swallowed. 'I can understand, I suppose. Frank is the better man, by far. But if what you thought was true, and Israel did that thing for her, surely she would marry him?'

Will touched her cheek with a gentle finger. 'Well, perhaps I was wrong after all. You know him better than I do. Don't you?' with a lift of his eyebrow.

Slowly, Rachel nodded her head. 'He's devious and cunning, Will, but he's no murderer. He's not the sort to give himself up for love, you see—he doesn't believe in it—and only love would have made him kill Greta's husband for her.' She bit her lip, and looked at him sideways. 'What else does Frank say?'

Will sighed. 'He wants us to come to the weddin'. We're his oldest friends, he says. And the children are lookin' forward to seeing you, and Bella of course.'

'But . . .where is it to be?'

'At Nerinbilly. They've arranged for some Reverend from Melbourne to be there.'

'But . . . Israel?'

Will shook his head. 'I doubt he'd make an appearance from what Frank says. And anyway,' and his arm tightened, 'you don't have to be frightened of him, Rachel. I'll never let him, or anyone else, hurt you again. You know that, don't you?'

His grey eyes were serious and sincere, and Rachel took a deep steadying breath. 'I know,' she answered him softly. They sat a moment in silence. Bella's voice came from the other room, telling Hannah a story; the buzz of a fly faded towards the window. It was so peaceful. Rachel drew a deep breath.

'I can't take Hannah,' she said at last.

'Why not?' and there was an edge to his voice now. 'She's part of our family and he wants us to come as a family'

'But—'

'But what?' He sounded angry, and no longer

able to disguise it.

Rachel stood up and moved away from him. 'I don't want you to feel embarrassed,' she admitted.

'Embarrassed?' he repeated. Warily, she looked at him, scanning the taut line of his jaw, the narrowed grey eyes. 'Embarrassed is the last thing I feel when I look at Hannah.'

Her skin tingled with foreboding. 'Will,' she breathed.

But there was no stopping him. The cold man, the calm man was disintegrating before her eyes and fear shot through her as he rose to his feet, his eyes full of fury. This was anger he had held back for a long time and now there was no stopping it. He did not want to stop it. If he was ever to make the new beginning he so desired, there were words he must speak. He only hoped Rachel was strong enough to bear them.

'I waited for you,' he said. 'But you couldn't even write a bloody letter!'

'Will . . . don't you see? It was as if you were dead. I was so hurt, I felt like you were dead. Can you understand? And then . . . after Israel, when I wanted to find you, it was too late.'

He dismissed the excuse as though it was too feeble for him to listen to. 'I loved you,' he went on. 'But you thought love meant takin' someone else into your bed. Was that easy for you, Rachel? To forget everything we'd had together and let Israel Potter into your bed . . . into your body . .' his voice broke at last, and he turned his back on her.

Rachel lifted a hand to touch him, and then didn't dare.

'I was lonely,' she whispered, feeling the tears

warm on her cheeks.

'Lonely?' He turned and looked at her, and she wished he hadn't. How could he love her, when he looked at her like that? 'Don't you think I was lonely? Don't you think I longed for you so much that I burned and ached?'

'You left me.'

'Because you couldn't accept me for what I was. You wanted me to be a hero and I'm nowhere near that. What was the use of stayin', when you couldn't even look at me anymore?'

Rachel sank down into the chair—she didn't think her legs would hold her any longer. 'I asked you to wait,' she reminded him, staring up into his tight, angry face. 'But you wouldn't give me enough time.'

'What was the use of time, except to make you hate me more?'

'You can't punish me for being too young to understand!' she cried out. 'I had to learn, Will. And I have. I have learnt. I'd never do such a thing now. You're not perfect, I know that, and neither am I. But don't pretend to me that it's all my fault. You left me and I had Bella on my own, and I had to think of her then. I had to be sure she was fed and clothed. I couldn't run away, not like you did.'

He rubbed his eyes. 'You didn't run away from Israel Potter, did you Rachel?' and his voice was weary.

'What about Maeve?' she snapped, dark eyes flashing. 'How did you think I felt, knowing you were down at the inn with her? Weren't you betraying me, with Maeve?'

He shrugged his shoulders. 'That was after I

learnt about Israel Potter. Nothin' much seemed to matter then, and if I could find some happiness with Maeve, then I felt I deserved it. But she was only ever a surrogate for you, Rachel.'

'I'm sorry,' she whispered at last. 'I was so lonely for you, Will. I was wanting you, and he seemed . . .' she bowed her head. 'I thought I saw you in him. But I was wrong. If I could turn the time back I would. I would!'

Rachel put her face in her hands. After a moment she felt his fingers, gentle, on her bowed head, stroking her hair.

'Ah Rachel, Rachel,' he whispered. 'I love you, I do. It's just the thought of you and him . . . Sometimes I feel so betrayed and so angry. I love you, but as for the rest . . . it'll take time.'

He squatted down before her and lifted her face, his eyes full of longing as they gazed into hers. 'Hannah feels like my child. Israel'll never be her father, not like I am. You know that.'

'Yes.'

'We're goin' to Nerinbilly. I have leave. And we'll take Bella and Hannah, and whatever happens . . . we'll deal with it when the time comes.'

She clung to him then and felt him clinging to her.

CHAPTER 32

T HE WEATHER STAYED HOT AND, although excitement kept Bella from noticing, the baby grizzled from the heat and the constant jolting of the wagon. Will stopped as often as he could, but Rachel knew the less they stopped the sooner they would reach Nerinbilly, and some kind of civilization.

Not that she hadn't enjoyed sleeping under the stars with Will, lying with her head resting on his shoulder and his arm around her. Every day with him was another day she had once thought she would never have, so every day with him was special.

From the Post, they travelled through thick bush-land and ironbark forests, until the land grew hillier, and they turned towards the bulk of Mt Camel. The sun sank, making mauve shadows on the rounded sides of the mountain, softening the harsh summer landscape. White cockatoos flew in clouds, while pink and grey galahs swept across the sun.

One night they found shelter at a station. The

hut was basic and the overseer rough, but he stinted them nothing of what he had. Rachel settled the children and lay down to sleep in the little private room the overseer had made with some calico sacks slung on a rail. It was very late before Will joined her.

'Another homesick Vandemonian,' he said by way of apology.

Rachel glanced at him, trying to read his eyes in the faint light thrown by the mutton fat lamp in the other room. 'Are you homesick, Will?'

He shrugged. 'Sometimes. There's a feelin' about a place you come from; you belong to it. The Aborigines know that.'

'Do you think we'll go back?'

'I don't know. Maybe.'

What was left for them in Vandemon, Rachel wondered. Some sweet memories, but bad ones, too, and bad dreams. Did Will long for the smithy where he had worked with his father and the cottage his mother had ruled? Perhaps it was that which drew him, the thought of a happy home. She smiled and touched his cheek, thinking: I can give him that. There's no need to go searching for it.

Will turned at her touch. Suddenly he reached into the pocket of his jacket and drew something out. He stretched out his hand, palm up, and she saw that there was some object resting on it. It was round, the casing dinted and tarnished, and had definitely seen better days.

With a gasp of shock, Rachel recognised the watch she had given to Will at Greengage when they were married. Her eyes held a question.

'I've carried this with me all the years we've been apart,' he told her quietly. 'It doesn't work any more. I fell on it, when my horse stepped into a hole one night. Here,' and he flicked open the case with his thumb nail.

Rachel took the watch carefully and held it close. She didn't need light to know what she would see. Herself, painted in minature. Or rather, the girl she had been. Clear eyed, young, her hair a dark cloud. Signor Rossi had done well, for he had caught the stubborn tilt of her chin, that certain intractability in her that was to be her and Will's downfall.

'If I couldn't have the real thing,' he told her, 'at least I had this.'

Gently, Rachel closed the watch, smoothing the damaged case with her finger. Tears stung her eyes, but she didn't let them fall. She and Will had moved on from the day when this was painted. Life had taught them both some hard lessons, but they had come through it all, and they were together again.

'It'll be all right, won't it?' she whispered. 'Will?' And he put his arm around her, holding her close.

The home station at Nerinbilly was an improvement on the hut Rachel remembered. A long rectangular building, with a low, sheltering verandah at the front and a neat path between two rather austere flower beds. It looked slightly incongruous, surrounded as it was by the old yards and huts and station buildings, but Rachel knew that, given time, it would age and begin to fit in with its surroundings.

Bella was jumping up and down with excitement. Will swung her to the ground with a grin. And then footsteps clattered on the verandah and the three Potter children were there, suddenly shy, but smiling.

Rachel hugged them all, gazing at them in wonder. Young Frank was so tall and Matty was dressed like a prim young lady. Victoria was still plump and pretty and looking more like Martha.

Sarah's excited blue eyes met Rachel's across the touseled fair heads and the two women hurried to embrace. 'I'm so pleased to see you,' Sarah whispered, her cheek damp on Rachel's. 'You and Will.' And her fingers squeezed Rachel's, hard, before she turned to Will and held out her hands. He swallowed them up in his own.

'Will!'

Frank Potter came from the direction of the barn, his boots sending up little spurts of dust on the bare ground. He looked bronzed by the sun, his uncovered hair bleached. The two men shook hands. Will narrowed his eyes, looking about the place. 'You've done well for yourself, Frank.'

Frank's smile wavered slightly. 'Well, as to that . . . Everything has a cost.' Then he turned to Rachel, bending to kiss her cheek. 'The children miss you,' he murmured, 'we all miss you.'

Bella grinned at him and he patted her dark hair. 'This one's grown.'

There was a question in his eyes. Rachel leaned over the wagon and lifted the sleeping baby into her arms. Hannah lay against her like an angel, dark curls waving in the faint, warm breeze, a flush in her velvet cheeks. Frank looked at her and his smile was suddenly full of regret.

'She's a beautiful child, Rachel.'

'We've called her Hannah,' Will said quietly. 'I've two daughters now.'

Frank glanced up at him sharply and then his face relaxed into a proper smile. 'I'm glad. Come inside! Greta's waiting.' He went to turn, and then hesitated, glancing back at Will and Rachel. The kind blue eyes were serious. 'I hope you will both wish me happy, although I am already happy . . . so happy!' He shook his head, as if he could hardly believe what he felt. 'I want no misgivings and no lectures.'

Will shook his head, glancing sideways at his wife. 'I don't know about Rachel, but I think you're old enough to make up your own mind.'

Rachel forced herself to smile, and then the smile became genuine as Frank peered anxiously into her face. 'I wish you happy, oh of course I do!'

Frank sighed with relief, nodded, and led the way to the verandah.

Sarah put her arm around Rachel. 'I've missed you,' she murmured softly. 'It's not been the same.'

'For me either.'

'You're happy?'

Rachel smiled her beautiful smile. 'Oh yes.' She paused, her hand on the verandah pole—a young jasmine was making hard work of climbing it. 'Is Greta living here then?'

Sarah nodded. 'They're husband and wife in all but the blessing. Happened while Israel was here. Greta took a hard look at both brothers and decided

Frank was best. She crawled into his bed one night and that was it. That was about two months ago. Israel's gone to the northern run and we haven't seen him since, but I heard he was livin' hard and drinkin' harder, and the men he's got up there are worse than him. Meanwhile, Greta looks like a cat with cream.'

'Is she . . .' Rachel bit her lip. 'Do the children like her?'

Sarah shrugged. 'Well enough. Mainly because she lets them do what they like, as long as they don't bother her too much. She's no mother . . . not like you, Rachel.'

They had reached the door, and had to stop their whispered conversation. Inside, Rachel could hear Frank's voice, unnaturally loud and jolly, and then Will's deeper reply. Sarah led her into the sitting room. Greta Redcliffe was there, looking up at Will, her arm clasped firmly in Frank's.

'—good of you to come,' she was saying, with her pussycat smile. She was the same, Rachel thought. Her auburn hair might be bound in a neat chignon, and her dress might be new and fitted to her slim curves, while the tilt of her face might be more assured. But in essence she was the Greta Redcliffe Rachel had known at McCrae's Castle, and with whom she always felt so uncomfortable. Secretive, that was the word for Greta.

The green eyes turned to her, considering, and Greta held out her hand. 'Rachel. You look very well. How is the baby?'

All polite, all proper. But something shifted in the green eyes and Rachel knew that Greta was pretending, for Frank's sake.

'We've arranged the wedding for Saturday,' Frank was saying. 'Mrs McCrae and Hazelwood are coming. We thought we'd make a day of it, eh, Greta?'

Greta smiled sweetly up at him. Rachel felt Will's fingers slide into hers, locking, and looked up. He lifted his eyebrows slightly, questioningly, before Frank spoke to him again and he turned to answer.

Eventually, Sarah showed her to their room, and Rachel sank down onto the bed with a groan and closed her eyes. 'Oh, that's good!'

Sarah laughed, watching her. Rachel was like a flower. At Greengage she had been lovely, but now she had a new maturity, as though a bud had opened into full bloom. She had put on weight and her face was flushed and beautiful, the dark hair gleaming despite the dust and tangles. Happiness had done that to her, and for Rachel, Will was happiness.

'What do you do at Nerinbiily, Sarah?' Rachel asked, her eyes still closed, savouring the soft bed and the stillness after the wagon. Beyond the window there were the usual voices and bleating of sheep, the everyday business of the station, but it was soothing because she knew she didn't have to do a thing.

'A bit of everything,' Sarah shrugged. 'I look after the children, of course. There's another woman to cook and clean—Catherine, her name is. Thomas teaches the children and keeps Captain Potter's books for him.'

'You sound as if you're settled here for life.'

Sarah nodded. 'Oh yes, we're settled. Even Greta hasn't been too bad. Although maybe she's just on 'er best behaviour, until the wedding.'

Rachel pulled a face. 'She used to run Redcliffe's with an iron hand, so they said . . .' her voice trailed off, remembering what Will believed about Greta. Best not to mention that to Sarah; things would be hard enough for her without believing her new mistress was a murderess! Besides, Will might be wrong. Rachel was sure he was wrong about Israel, so why could he not be wrong about Greta, too?

'Rachel?'

'Hmm?'

Sarah smiled at her friend, as Rachel lay half asleep. 'I'm glad you and Will are together again.'

Rachel's lips curled, though her eyes stayed shut. 'So am I.'

'Tired?' Will brushed her cheek with one finger. Rachel smiled. 'Yes.'

He kissed her, letting his lips trail over her throat, while his fingers unbuttoned her bodice with firm deliberation. 'What did you think of Greta?' he asked her.

The smile faded. 'I don't like her. I can't help it.'

He kissed the tip of her nose. 'She's not like you, darlin'. But maybe she has some good points?'

Rachel said nothing.

He laughed. 'Frank likes her.'

'Frank's taste in women isn't so good.'

'Hmm.' He leaned back on one elbow, considering that.

'If she really cares for him, Will, then I'll try and

like her. But I'm worried it's all for what he can give her, like Martha. Not for what he is.'

Will's smile was lopsided. 'She's what he wants. He tells me he's bought her a grey mare for a weddin' gift. Cost him a small fortune.'

'Do you still think—'

'I've no proof that she ever had anythin' to do with her husband's death, you know that.'

'But what if she did? Is Frank next?' She was angry now, dark eyes flashing.

He touched her shoulder with gentle fingers. 'I thought you might have a few things to say in her favour. Sold to a man twice her age, a drunkard . . . violent with it. Perhaps she had reason to do as she did—if she did.'

Rachel blinked at him. 'Is there ever a reason for murder?'

His fingers tightened. 'I can't tell you that. You used to think there was.'

She sighed and rested her head against his chest, listening to the beat of his heart. 'I don't know. Perhaps there is a reason. I could understand it if she hit him over the head or . . . or picked up a gun and shot him, to protect herself. But to arrange for someone else to take the blame . . . ? It's cold blooded, Will.'

He stroked her hair, nodding. 'Maybe, and yet there's nothin' we can do about it.' His voice deepened. 'Now come here.' And he rolled over, taking her with him. He smiled up at her, half closing his eyes. 'Kiss me.' he murmured.

'Just a kiss?' she teased.

'A kiss to start with and then we'll see how much time we have before they call us to supper.'

Supper was an informal affair. Greta spoke little, sitting back and allowing Frank to hold the floor. He and Will had a lot to talk about, and Rachel put in an occasional comment. And all the time she was aware of Greta sitting there, listening, her face a polite, smiling mask.

How can Frank love her? she asked herself. She was so much younger than him, but apart from that, she was devious and sly. Did he see none of that? But Frank, she thought wryly, was one of those men who saw what he wanted to see. He had married Martha, after all.

After the meal, Rachel searched out Sarah on the pretence of checking on the children and found Thomas with his wife in the kitchen. He looked up with a smile and rose to take her hands. He was thinner, Rachel decided, but otherwise much the same. The gentle brown eyes warmed.

'Captain Potter keeps me busy,' he said, in answer to Rachel's question. 'It might take a few more years, but he'll do well here at Nerinbilly.'

'And Israel?'

Sarah and Thomas exchanged glances.

'I went over there last month,' Thomas replied quietly. 'The men were all drunk and Israel was the drunkest of the lot. I had a look around—before he ordered me off. The place is a shambles; yard fences falling down, roofs leaking and probably sheep missing. The only way to fix it is to sack the lot of them and hire more men. And get rid of Israel.'

Rachel frowned. 'Difficult, when he owns half the run.'

'Impossible,' Sarah murmured.

Thomas shook his head. 'It could be done, but Captain Potter won't do it. He feels he's wronged his brother enough already. He won't interfere.'

'So you think he really intended to marry Greta?' Rachel asked curiously. 'Israel I mean?'

Thomas looked thoughtful. 'He thought he did. She kept him guessing, that was the thing. He was never sure of her.'

Sarah nodded. 'I doubt his heart's broken. More likely it's his pride. She's bested him and he don't like it. Probably never happened to him before.'

'Well, she's made Captain Potter happy,' Thomas went on. 'He's head over heels!'

Rachel and Sarah exchanged a glance. Frank Potter deserved to be happy, neither of them would deny him that, but the two women were not sure Greta was the one for him.

Mrs McCrae and Hazelwood arrived the next day. Mrs McCrae looked just as large and imposing, wearing a new and rather terrifying bonnet. Hazelwood, his craggy face beaming, shook Frank's hand. Mrs McCrae, who seemed to prefer to forget what she knew about Greta, embraced the girl and offered her congratulations.

'What will you do with Redcliffe's?' Hazelwood

asked, cocking an eyebrow.

'We'll run it from Nerinbilly,' Greta said promptly. 'If necessary we can put in an overseer.'

'Maybe Israel can handle it.' Hazelwood's face wore an innocent look.

There was a silence. Greta's mouth hardened. 'Israel has chosen to go his own way, despite all that Frank has done for him.'

Frank touched her shoulder gratefully, but his face was weary. 'No, my dear, we are as much to blame as Israel. This time it is I who have wronged him, and badly.'

There was an awkward silence.

Mrs McCrae turned to Will and said in a hearty voice, 'And how's life on the Goulburn, Sergeant Moody?'

Will told her.

Hazelwood winked at Rachel, and murmured, 'Is the young fella expected to come to the weddin', Mrs Moody?'

Presumably, the 'young fella' was Israel. 'He's been asked, but so far no-one's heard,' she whispered back. 'Better for everyone if he doesn't.'

Hazelwood searched in his pocket for his pipe and then thought better of it. 'Could get nasty if he does. Might need to call in your 'usband.' The old eyes mocked her.

Rachel lifted her chin. 'Will is a guest not a police guard.'

Hazelwood sniffed. 'Though if Israel Potter had any sense, he'd stay well away from Will Moody, after the thrashin' he got last time. I 'eard he was flat on his back for a week.'

Rachel felt a savage satisfaction. 'He deserved it,'

she said.

Hazelwood laughed.

A warm hand touched her back and she looked up with relief as Will moved to stand beside her.

'Heard you had a bit o' trouble over your way,' Hazelwood said to Will. 'Bushrangers, was it? Heard one of them was Scanlon, the bolter. Nasty.'

Will nodded. 'That's right, it was Scanlon.'

'Did you get him?'

'We got him.'

Hazelwood looked as impressed as Hazelwood could look. 'Put up much of a fight?'

'Yes, he put up a fight.'

'Kill him, did you?' and Hazelwood smacked his lips, prepared for the details.

Will glanced at Rachel. 'Yes,' he said shortly, and changed the subject.

Later, Mrs McCrae demanded to see Hannah, and duly admired her.

'Awkward situation, this,' she said, settling herself in the chair in Rachel's room.

Rachel pretended not to understand.

'A pity Captain Potter decided on Greta Redcliffe. There are so many other more suitable girls.'

'He seems happy.'

Mrs McCrae shook her head. 'All that trouble over Redcliffe's death.' Then, looking up, 'They found him, you know.'

Rachel blinked. 'Found who?'

'Big Mary's husband. They found him. Dead, unfortunately. Natural causes. But the powers that be decided to let Redcliffe's death rest there. As good a place as any! I don't expect your husband will be very pleased. He thought Greta had a hand in it, didn't he?'

'My husband never arrested anyone, and it's not his business any more.'

Mrs McCrae shrugged. 'Well, the matter's been laid to rest, whatever the truth of it. And I always had a lot of sympathy for Greta Redcliffe. To be honest, I'm glad to see her come out of it so well.'

Rachel said nothing, only pursing her lips slightly. Mrs McCrae knew the girl disapproved of Greta, but then the two were poles apart. She ran a shrewd eye over the younger woman, and nodded to herself. Rachel looked in fine fettle. Love! she thought, with a pang. Amazing what effect it could have. Well, Rachel deserved her happiness. By all accounts it was Israel Potter who was getting his comeuppance these days.

The wedding day dawned hot.

The minister had arrived the night before. Since leaving Melbourne, he'd married, baptised, and said prayers over graves at a rapid rate. He was glad of a warm meal and a soft bed.

Rachel dealt with excited children and Will had gone to keep Frank company. The wedding was set for eleven o'clock and the sitting room was decked out with flowers, which were already starting to wilt, and branches of gum leaves. It looked as festive as they could make it, but the heat was sweltering.

It was nearly eleven when Sarah came seeking

Rachel. 'Greta wants to see you,' she announced, eyes curious.

Surprised, Rachel went with her. Greta was dressed in a pink dress, the flounces and bows decorating it making her look a little like a party cake with icing. The face she turned to Rachel was calmly smiling.

'I thought we should talk, Rachel,' she said, when Sarah had closed the door. 'Frank is very fond of you, you know.'

Rachel met the green eyes curiously. 'I am fond of him.'

'Frank will expect us to be friends.'

Taken aback, Rachel said nothing.

'You don't think that's possible, do you?' Greta asked her quietly.

'I would make my best efforts to be friends with whoever Frank married—' Rachel began.

Greta's smile thinned. 'You think I'm not good enough for him, don't you? You think I'm marrying him for what I can get?'

'I wouldn't presume—'

'You would presume,' Greta retorted, the green eyes hard. 'I don't know why you set yourself up so high. After what you did, I wonder your husband took you back.'

Rachel felt her face colour. 'My life is my business,' she replied, keeping her voice even with difficulty.

But Greta ignored her. 'You see, we're more alike than you'll admit! We should thank God for men like your husband, and Frank, who can love and forgive. I never thought I'd find a man like Frank. I thought they were all the same—like Israel.

Smooth and lying, after the one thing. You know what he was like, Rachel. That's something else we have in common.

'My husband was a beast, do you know that?' And when Rachel didn't answer, was too shocked to answer, 'I hardly knew him before we married. I had just arrived in Melbourne, everything so strange and suddenly I was wed to a man so much older than me. My parents needed the money. I was only a child, but I grew up. Oh, I grew up! Redcliffe took me to a hut in the middle of nowhere, in the middle of nothing. And there I was, frightened out of my wits. The shepherds were rough and rude. I hid from them most of the time. I thought Redcliffe would protect me, but he laughed at me. He said my cooking was bad, he said I was ugly. He went to the native camp whenever he could—he preferred his women "well done", he said. And I let him do that to me. I thought I must accept my fate, that it was God's will. That was what I had been taught, all my life. To bow to God's will.'

Rachel found her eyes caught and held by Greta's. The picture the other woman had drawn her was appalling by any standards. 'Was there no-one you could turn to?' she breathed.

Greta shook her head. 'No-one. And so it went on. I tried very hard to do my best. I thought, if I could only do my best, and please him, everything would be all right.' Finally, she looked away, playing with a hair brush. Her long fingers turned it over and over, smoothing the fine silver handle. It was beautiful. A gift from Frank, Rachel supposed.

'One morning,' Greta went on at last, 'I woke up, after he had almost killed me with one of his drunken beatings, and I was bleeding—I was carrying a child, did I mention that? And as I lay and felt my child's life drain away, I became very angry. The anger was like a fire inside me and it was telling me I must fight. So I fought, though sometimes fighting meant hiding in the bush until Redcliffe sobered up. And I grew to realise that he was frightened of me. Of me! If I stood up to him and looked him in the eye, if I showed him I wasn't frightened of him, then I was the winner, not him. Oh, he still hit me, but he didn't enjoy it any more. And that made a difference.'

Rachel knew her face was white. There was a smell of lillies in the room, from Greta's posy. It was suddenly so strong, it was almost sickening. Rachel went to the window and took a deep breath.

'You don't have to tell me this,' she managed.

'I want to. I want you to know that I love Frank. He's set himself against Israel, because of me. Not that Israel ever loved me—he doesn't know what the word means. But for a time, I loved him.' Her smile grew wistful. 'He was . . . Well,' with a shrug, 'you know what he was.'

'You chose the better man,' Rachel said, turning back to face her.

Greta's smile could have lit up the night. 'I know.'

'Frank deserves to be happy. Martha . . . his late wife, they didn't get on so well.'

Greta nodded. 'I know, he's told me. He was very unhappy, just as I was unhappy. We have no secrets.'

For the first time since they'd met, Rachel found those green eyes perfectly transparent.

'Frank understands,' Greta went on quietly. 'He has forgiven me, Rachel.'

She means, Rachel told herself firmly, that he's forgiven her for Israel. But her heart was thudding, and she felt curiously light headed. Because there was something in Greta's eyes that Rachel did not want to see.

Rachel's voice sounded rusty. 'What does he forgive?'

Greta only smiled, and her skirts rustled as she rose and moved across the room. 'I think it's time now. Shall we go?'

The sitting room was full of expectant faces. Greta walked to where Frank stood, waiting, and he took her arm. His lined, still handsome face was flushed, and his eyes sparkled. Rachel moved quietly to Will, and slipped her hand into the crook of his arm. He was suddenly so solid and safe. She leaned against him slightly and felt her calm returning, as the Reverend began the service.

The words rolled over her. Why, she asked herself with a shiver, had Greta made her the recipient of such confidences? They had never been friends. Perhaps Greta saw in Rachel someone who might understand, someone who had been through her own troubles and found happiness. But if what Greta had said was true, her life had been much worse than Rachel's, worse even than she had imagined. Rachel closed her eyes a moment, remembering Greta's smooth, untroubled face— like the moon, but with the moon's subtle and devious powers.

The memory teased her again, of Greta's smile at McCrae's Castle, when Hazelwood swore that the blacks had killed Redcliffe. The secret smile. Why had she smiled? Surely it could only have been because her plan had worked, because she was free at last of the man she had loathed, and still had what was lawfully hers.

'All right?' Will was watching her, frowning slightly. Perhaps she was pale—she had a right to be pale after what Greta had said.

'Yes,' and she smiled, to show him it was true. Suddenly she knew that she would not tell Will. What was the point? Greta had admitted nothing. One could not convict a person because of a look in their green eyes, or a smile.

The sound of footsteps on the verandah outside distracted Rachel. She glanced behind her. There was a figure in the doorway. A man was leaning against the door jamb, a shadow against the glare outside. She frowned; there was something familiar in the way he stood, the tilt of his head . . . Rachel felt her blood freeze for the second time this morning.

Israel.

She had not meant to speak aloud and only realised she had done so when she felt Will stiffen beside her, and turn to look in the same direction.

It *was* Israel. He had taken a step into the room, brushing by Sarah and Thomas. He looked awful. Unshaven, gaunt, his eyes bloodshot. Like those shepherds who have been alone for too long and turned a little mad. Frank and Greta, unaware, were listening to the minister, their expressions earnest. When Israel spoke, they swung around, pale with shock and guilt. Almost as if they were expecting to be punished.

'I told you your taste in women was bloody awful, brother.'

Frank forced a smile to his lips, ignoring the insult. 'Israel. You're very welcome here.'

'Am I, Frank?' Israel's blue eyes turned on Greta, and briefly, a blaze of anger lit them. She flinched, as if he had physically struck her, and then straightened, her green eyes narrowing like the cat she had always reminded Rachel of. For a long moment they stared at each other.

'I've come to give you what you deserve,' Israel said quietly.

The silence in the room was so thick, it was like a solid thing, holding them all in their places. Israel slid his hand into his jacket. Even as Rachel felt Will's arm go taut, and knew he was about to spring, Israel's hand came out. He was holding a small silver flask, and he lifted it high into the air.

'I drink to the bride and groom,' he said, and took a long swig. And then he looked around him at the stunned faces, and laughed.

There was an echo of nervous laughter, and the releasing of held breaths. Frank nodded, smiling with obvious relief, perspiration shining on his face, and Greta slowly smiled back. Israel could have said anything he wanted, they knew that, but instead he had decided to be magnanimous. In a nervous voice, the minister continued with the service.

'Bloody fool,' Will muttered.

Rachel took a deep breath and turned back to the bridal couple. And wished she hadn't. Israel had caught sight of her and he had a stupid grin on his mouth. As she watched with growing dismay, he made his way to her side and she realised he'd been drinking.

'To beautiful Rachel!' he announced in what he thought was a whisper, lifting the flask again.

Rachel said nothing, feeling the blood rushing into her face, and refusing to meet his eyes. Beside her, Will was a statue. She didn't dare glance his way.

Hazelwood muttered, 'Come and sit down, matey,' but Israel waved a hand irritably.

'Sit down? Not yet, not yet. I'm talking to Rachel.' He gave her a sentimental smile. 'You know, Rachel, I'm glad Frank's got Greta. I thought I was angry, I really did. And then this morning I woke up, and told myself: This is their wedding day. And do you know what? I felt as if someone had lifted a boulder off my chest. I felt free again! And that's something I haven't felt in a long while. But by God, now I do, I mean to stay that way.'

Rachel stared at him in amazement. 'You mean after all you've said and done to make them miserable, you're glad Greta's marrying Frank?'

He nodded. 'I would have left her anyway. I'm not made for marriage.' He leaned closer, breathing rum fumes all over Rachel. 'I don't envy Frank, you know. She's a demon, that one. Got claws like a wild cat. Tear his back to pieces.'

Shocked, Rachel laughed; she couldn't help it.

'Not like you,' he added.

The blue eyes were suddenly gazing into her own, so longingly, so lovingly. Rachel felt her heart hammering with fright. Involuntarily, her eyes swung to Will and she felt as if he'd struck her. He couldn't have heard what Israel had said, but he was thinking the worst. His face was rigid with fury.

With a soft cry, Rachel turned and fled. Out of the room, out onto the verandah and into the hot glare of the sun. Behind her, she heard Sarah's call, but she kept moving, her strides quickening, running from Israel . . . and from Will. She didn't know where she was going, only that she must get away. The sun's rays burned her dark hair and her shoulders. She felt it prickling her skin as she rounded the side of the barn, half blinded by tears. And ran into someone coming the other way.

'Shit!'

Rachel stumbled, almost falling. She began to apologise, her lips trembling, but something about that voice stopped her. Israel and Will were forgotten in an instant. Slowly, she lifted her head, not believing, telling herself it couldn't possibly be true.

But it was.

The man was Yelland.

CHAPTER 33

YELLAND HAD REGAINED HIS BALANCE, grimacing as he put his weight on his twisted leg. 'Why don't you watch where you're goin', you stupid bitch?' he snarled, and looked up. Rachel saw his expression freeze, almost comically.

Shock was giving way to terror, and with a cry, she spun around to run. He was quicker. He caught her arm, swinging her back against him. 'No, you don't,' he grunted. His hand went over her mouth. It stank of sweat and horses, and she gagged. Rachel swung her elbow back, trying to jab him in the stomach, but he twisted to avoid her, returning the blow with interest.

For a moment, Rachel was too winded to do anything. He gripped her elbow, forcing her along beside him, until they reached the stable. And then he pulled her in and closed the door. Here it was cool and dim. The sounds from the men's hut were muted; she could hardly hear them above the drumming in her head. Frank had given his employees rum to celebrate his wedding and they were well away by now. Usually the horses were kept out in the yard, or fenced in the paddock, but today there was a mare stabled here. Rachel remembered suddenly that Will had told her Frank had bought a gift for his bride—a grey mare.

The animal looked ghostly in the dim light. Someone had spent time grooming the fine coat and combing the silver mane and tail. Rachel watched as Yelland slipped on the bridle, jerking the head down when the mare moved uneasily. She was not used to rough treatment and her eyes rolled.

'What are you doing here?' Rachel gasped, finding her breath at last.

'I could ask the same,' he said. Then, lifting on the saddle, 'I came with Israel Potter. I've been workin' for him . . . if you call it work.'

'From what I've heard you'd fit in nicely there,' Rachel managed. The painful dizziness was going; soon she would be able to straighten.

Yelland gave her his evil grin. Then he reached into his belt and produced a pistol, pointing it in her direction. 'I could kill you now,' he told her, musingly. 'But Will Moody would come after me. So I'll take you with me. He'll still come after me, but at least then I'll 'ave something to bargain with.'

The same pride which had come to her aid on the river bank was there now, making Rachel straighten her back and lift her chin, refusing to show him how afraid she really was. If he expected her to beg, then he would be disappointed.

Yelland tightened the girth strap viciously, making the mare dance about her stall. And then he turned and grabbed Rachel's arm, jerking her to her feet. With one hand holding the gun to

Rachel's back, and the other the bridle, he moved towards the stable door. Slowly, he cracked it open, and peered outside. When he was sure there was no one about, he opened the doors wide and, forcing Rachel to mount the mare, climbed quickly up behind her. The feel of his body against hers made her stomach squirm, but she remained still, waiting.

She should try to escape now. She should jump down and run . . . but the pistol barrel was hard and cold in her side and she knew she wouldn't get far. She must stay alive. As long as she was alive, surely there was a chance of getting away, or of Will finding her?

Yelland kicked the mare into a trot and set its head to the north, in the direction of Israel's run. Desperately, Rachel glanced over her shoulder. Just then, she saw Sarah, a pale wraith in the shadows of the verandah. Sarah appeared to see her, too, for she shouted and waved her arms, and then she was running down the steps and along the path. But her voice was already far away, and before Rachel could respond Yelland was riding down into the valley and a stand of trees swallowed them up.

Yelland kicked the mare into a faster stride, avoiding the rough tree trunks, turning her out onto the open ground again. His body smelt and Rachel swallowed, feeling terror hovering on the edges of her mind, trying not to let it take hold. Concentrate, she thought, and said the first thing that occurred to her.

'Don't you want to know about your wife and children?'

He laughed. 'They'll be all right. Rosa's good at managin' on her own. Can't say I miss 'em at all.'

'No, you're right. They're better off without you.'

He jabbed her ribs so viciously that she cried out. 'What 'appened to Maeve?'

Rachel took a breath, trying to ignore the savage ache in her side. 'She and Sean packed up and left. It was Sean who saved me.'

Yelland grunted. 'She turned coward, did she? Well,' he shrugged, 'what can you expect? Women always renege on their promises.'

They were in open country now, rolling hills and gentle valleys, but ahead was more forest, and that was the way Yelland was heading.

'Where are we going?' Rachel asked him.

'That all depends,' he sneered, 'on your 'usband.' Then, softly, 'I almost wish he would follow us. I'd like to kill 'im. This is 'is fault, all of it.'

'How can it be his fault?' she said. The viciousness in his voice frightened her.

'He sets himself up too high,' Yelland retorted. 'I'd like to bring 'im down, so I would. If I can get as far as Yass, I reckon I'll be safe.'

'You'll never be safe,' Rachel murmured, and there was a grim satisfaction in saying it. 'Will Moody used to be a bounty hunter. He took twenty-five men in Vandemon. Do you think he can't take you?'

He was quiet—she could almost feel the waves of shock reverberating through him—but when he spoke again, the bravado was back. 'Even so, I reckon I can make Yass—I've a head start and a fast mount.'

'What about me?'

'Didn't I tell you?' and his voice was full of suppressed laughter. 'I'm leavin' you at Israel Potter's run.'

She didn't believe him. He would never leave her, not alive, anyway. Rachel wondered whether she could leap from the horse without being killed or badly injured. But even if she survived the fall, Yelland would only return for her. Or shoot her. She glanced over her shoulder again, but saw nothing. Only the midday sun, boiling in a blue sky cauldron, and the shadowless trees standing silently, their drooping grey leaves offering little shade.

'You better 'ope he don't follow,' Yelland said. 'I might let you live, if he leaves me alone.'

Hope flared, but she damped it down. He was playing with her. Remembering the river, and his pitiless face, she knew he would kill her as soon as it became necessary. There was no kindness in Yelland, none of the morals found in ordinary men. If Will was looking for a murderer, then he should look in Yelland's direction.

They rode on in silence. Rachel felt her skin burning beneath the hot sun. The sweat was running down her back and between her breasts. She thought of Bella and Hannah but forced them from her mind. It did no good to let her fears overcome her. She must remain strong and alert, she must prepare herself for every chance that came her way. She must . . .

The sensation came in a rush, overwhelming her. And, even before she turned her head, Rachel knew. Behind them, the shadows were longer, although the sun still boiled. But as she gazed fixedly at the slope they had just ridden down, Rachel saw a movement. A shadow. Someone slipped between the tree trunks and then out onto the open ground at the bottom of the hill.

Rachel must have made some sound, for Yelland's head jerked around and he swore softly and foully. He dug his heels into the mare's sides, but even as he did so Rachel knew with a sense of elation it would do no good.

Will was catching up to them.

She glanced again and was positive he was gaining ground. He was riding low against his horse's neck, almost as if he were part of the animal. It dashed across the land, its strides smooth and even. He was getting closer all the time; Yelland's mare with its double load was tiring, despite Yelland's unrelenting pace.

There was a thick belt of trees ahead and Yelland, knowing he had no chance of outrunning Will on the open ground, was heading in that direction. Rachel turned back and saw that Will had straightened. And then she saw the shape of his carbine, as he lifted it to his shoulder and took aim. The shot rang out, like the crack of a whip, echoing around the valley. Rachel was sure she heard the bullet whistle by them.

Yelland cursed, huddling lower, gripping Rachel so hard she could hardly breath. She wondered why he didn't fire in return and then realised that the pistol's range was far too short and too inaccurate. Will had the advantage with his carbine.

They reached the trees. Yelland jerked the mare to a halt—the forest was too dense to allow entry on horseback. He slid to the ground, dragging at Rachel. 'Get down,' he snarled at her, his fingers digging into the flesh of her thigh. She saw the sweat on his face and sensed his fear. His eyes were flickering everywhere. Her own heart was racing, but she said nothing, letting him force her in front of him, holding her body before his like a shield.

Will had halted too, some yards away, with the sun at his back. He was a dark shadow, so still, waiting. Impossible to see his expression, impossible to read his thoughts. Rachel held her breath.

'Stop followin' or I'll kill her!'Yelland shouted.

Will's horse shuffled slightly, tossing its head. 'Let her go, Yelland.'

'Not likely. You'll kill *me* then.'

Rachel, dizzy, was sure she heard Will laugh. 'I'm going to kill you anyway. I owe you for the river. But there are many ways of killin' a man, Yelland. If you don't let her go, you're going to suffer.'

'You're the one who'll suffer.' Yelland shook Rachel so hard she stumbled and almost fell. The shot came out of the sun, sending Yelland's pistol spinning. Rachel heard his indrawn breath and then he was dragging her into the trees, running as best he could with his crippled leg.

Branches slapped her face, twigs scraped at her. She held up her hands, trying to protect her eyes. The trees grew so close, she scraped against their rough trunks and the bark tore at her clothes. Yelland dragged her along, uncaring of her safety. She realised that his hand was bleeding, where Will's bullet had sliced through the flesh. The blood ran down his fingers, dripping into the dried leaves.

Rachel tripped and fell, losing her shoe. For a moment, she lay, trying to catch her breath. Then Yelland struck at her. 'Get up, bitch.' But in that second of silence, Rachel had heard someone behind them, following. Slowly, painfully, she sat up, looking at Yelland. His face was white, his mouth twisted in fear and hatred.

'No.'

'Get up!' and he wrenched at her arm, trying to haul her to her feet.

'He's going to kill you,' Rachel burst out. 'It doesn't matter about me. It's you he wants.'

Yelland's eyes fixed on hers and she flinched at what she saw in them. And then he was gone, pushing wildly through the scrub, forcing his way further into the dense bush.

Slowly, Rachel pulled herself to her feet. There was blood on her hand, where a nail had torn, and more on her cheek. She could hear the fading sounds of Yelland's retreat, but beyond that . . . nothing.

He made no sound, but suddenly he was there, stepping out of the shadows. Rachel went to run to him, sobbing with relief, but he put out a hand, and she stopped, almost falling. Grey eyes slid over her, taking everything in with a sort of emotionless practicality that chilled her to the bone. 'Are you all right?' he asked her.

She managed to nod, swaying, longing for him to hold her and comfort her.

'Will?'

But he was already looking past her, head tilted as he listened to the faint sounds Yelland was making. She saw that he was carrying the carbine in his hand, lightly balanced. An extension of his own body. 'Stay here,' he said, and walked past her.

'Will!' Terror spread dark wings over her. 'Will?' and it was a question, as if she were no longer sure it really was him. She thought he wasn't going to answer, and then he turned and looked at her, impatience in the tightening of his jaw. Hurry up, he seemed to be saying. I've a job to do.

'Stay here,' he repeated. 'I'll be back for you.'

And then he was gone.

She stood, breathing through her mouth. I must stay here, she thought. Yelland is evil and he deserves all he gets. But Rachel knew in her heart she couldn't stay behind; it was not in her to do so. With a groan, she began to follow.

No matter how carefully she moved, she could not be silent. Twigs snapped, leaves rustled. But she tried, following along in the direction Yelland and Will had taken. There was a stitch in her side, and twice she had to pause until it faded, breathing deeply, pressing her hands to the ache.

What am I doing here? she asked herself. I have no place here. This is Will's business. If I go back and wait, he will come and take me home. And I need never know what he's done. I need never know . . . but once before Rachel had hidden her head, like a child under the bedclothes, and it had been a mistake. So she pushed onwards, ignoring the dread that fluttered in her mind.

'Like to hurt women, do you Yelland?'

The voice was sudden, but quiet, somewhere to her right. Rachel stopped, rigid. In front of her came a crashing of brush, as though someone were running blindly.

Then the voice again. 'You can't get away.'

'Leave me alone, you bastard!' Yelland sounded shrill, ahead of her.

'Like you left Rachel alone,' said Will.

'It was Maeve's idea! Go after Maeve! I didn't—'

There was a shot. Yelland screamed, a sound between rage and terror. The hairs rose on the back of Rachel's neck. She realised she was clinging to a low branch, her nails digging into the green young wood.

'I'm going to kill you,' Will Moody said softly. Savagely. 'But you're goin' to suffer first. Just as you made Rachel suffer.'

Another shot. Rachel jumped. Yelland screamed again, this time in agony.

'Bastard,' he moaned. Rachel realised he was coming towards her now, disorietated, turning back on his own tracks. Quickly, she stepped behind an old, blackened tree trunk. Once, a bushfire had roared through here, but it was long ago, and most of the bush had regenerated. The old trunk remained, pointing jaggedly to the sky. She stilled her breath, crouching down half inside the trunk, hidden where new trees, spindly and weak, were trying to find their way towards the sun.

Another shot, close to Rachel. It echoed about them, and she gasped, cowering further into her hiding place. She heard Yelland scream again, like an animal. Sickness was churning in her stomach. And then he appeared, clinging to a branch a few steps in front of her, looking wildly behind him.

He had deteriorated. His trousers and shirt were torn and filthy, and there were scratches and cuts on his hands and face. He was limping even more than usual. Rachel saw the blood staining his sleeve, a great, dark patch of it.

'Where are you, you bastard?' he gasped.

The shot was so close, Rachel screamed. Bark flew off the branch of a tree beside Yelland. He jerked away, yelling his head off. There was something horrifying in seeing a man reduced to near madness like this. Will was playing a cruel game with him, letting him think he might get away, that there was hope, when really there was none.

'I'm over here.'

Yelland spun around, because the voice was behind him, in the direction he had just come from. He began to back away, towards where Rachel was hiding, stumbling on the uneven ground. Rachel could hear his breath sobbing in his throat.

And then she saw something move at the corner of her eye and turned, too shocked to cry out. Will stood in the shadows. 'Come on then,' he said quietly. 'Come and get me. Or do you only fight women?'

Yelland moaned as he realised Will was not where he had thought and lurched forward. He fell, and tried to get up, but he'd done something to his leg. Rachel watched as he attempted to push himself along with his good leg and his arms, scrabbling in the leaves and dirt like some obscene crab.

'Please, don't hurt me! Don't hurt me!' His voice rose sharp and high.

'Oh, I'm goin' to hurt you. I'm goin' to hurt you so much that you'll beg me to shoot you . . . in the end.'

And finally, Will stepped forward into Yelland's view.

'You're a bloody monster!' Yelland gasped, his mouth wide open. He was frightened, almost too frightened to move, although he made an attempt to drag himself around to face Will. By comparison, Will was hardly out of breath, untouched by the whole episode. There was, thought Rachel, no pity in his eyes. There was nothing.

And then, so quickly Rachel jumped, he lifted the carbine and aimed.

Yelland screamed, thinking he was about to be shot. And, when the gun wasn't fired, he whimpered, cringing on the ground, his hands over his face. Will was waiting, calculating just the right moment. And then, as Rachel sensed Yelland's terror returning to manageable bounds, Will fired. The bullet ploughed into the ground by the man's head. A stone spun up, striking him on the cheek.

Yelland fainted, his head falling back, his eyelids fluttering. Blood trickled down his face. This time it was Rachel who screamed.

She bowed her head into her arms, doubling over. She wanted to crawl further and further into the tree trunk, she wanted to sink into the earth. This was not Will, this could not be Will. And yet she knew without doubt that it was Will, the Will she had never known, and he was cold and cruel, every bit as savage as the men he had pursued. She could hear her voice, a whisper that repeated itself over and over again.

'Please, please, please . . .'

Slowly, Will lowered the gun. Rachel's voice had turned into a sob now; he heard it faintly at the edge of his mind and it bothered him, made him uncomfortable. He wanted to concentrate on Yelland, it was important he deal with Yelland . . . Yelland was silent, either still unconscious, or pretending to be so. He had suffered, but it was only just that he suffer, for Rachel. Will knew he had to kill him; he had always meant to kill him. But there was Rachel's voice again, sobbing, frightened. What was she frightened of? He wondered impatiently. He had everything under control. He touched her shoulder, meaning to comfort, but she cried out, starting with fear. And it was only then that he realised, with a feeling of amazement, that she was frightened of him.

He put a hand to his eyes, the shock clearing his mind. And he knew, as if Rachel had spoken it aloud, that if he killed Yelland she would never lose that fear of him, of Will Moody. It would always be there, behind her smile. And just as he had had to make a choice once before, so he must make one now.

'It's over.' Will spoke quietly, his voice hoarse and strange. He put his arm around her, helping her up. 'Come on.'

She swung around, looking to Yelland, but he lay as before. Unconscious, but alive . . . thank God, alive!

'Come on,' he repeated, and pulled her to her feet. He moved to walk back the way they had come, and then hesitated, as if he'd remembered something.

'Wait here.'

She staggered, holding on to a young sapling, and obediently waited. Thinking he had gone back for his gun. But when she turned, he was standing by Yelland. He stood a moment, unmoving and then he put his boot on Yelland's leg, below the knee, and pressed down with all his weight. Rachel heard the bone crack, before Yelland shrieked in shock and agony. His body went limp and still among the leaves and debris.

'I can't risk him getting away,' Will said matter of factly, and looked up to meet the horror in his wife's eyes.

Somehow they got back to the edge of the forest. Rachel's legs weren't working properly, but she wouldn't let him help her. Tears were running down her face—she felt quite dead inside. There was nothing to say. She had seen Will Moody now and she knew. And what she knew frightened her, and sickened her, and terrified her, all at the same time.

And he knew it.

'I gave you justice,' he said, as she stopped ahead of him. 'An eye for an eye . . . remember?'

'That's not justice,' she managed, swallowing, her voice shaking. 'That's savagery. What you did makes you as bad as Yelland!'

'I don't see it that way.'

And he didn't, that was the thing. He saw it as retribution for Yelland's attack on Rachel. An eye for an eye, in the old biblical sense. In his own way, Will had avenged her.

'You broke his leg,' she whispered, and tried not to cry.

'He would have got away.'

'In God's name, couldn't you have tied him up!'

He said nothing. The sun was still shining, as if nothing had happened in the shadows of the forest. Rachel lifted her face to the blue sky, wishing she could feel warm again. What she had just seen had changed her forever. And she wondered, desperately, if she could live with it. If she could live with Will.

'I'll take you back to Nerinbilly.' He sounded

tired, suddenly so very tired, as if he understood at last that he had broken more than Yelland's leg. 'Sarah'll look after you.'

Sarah? Not him? Not Will? Through the myriad of emotions came a new fear, negating all the rest. Rachel's world narrowed alarmingly as she faced the prospect of losing him again.

'Will?' she whispered.

He drew a deep, shuddering breath. 'I wanted to kill him. I could have killed him so easily . . . so easily. But I didn't. I didn't do it. Do you know why?' And, when she shook her head, 'Oh, not for any reasons of pity. I don't pity Yelland. I didn't kill him because I knew you wouldn't love me any more. But I think that maybe you won't anyway.'

He turned to look at her then, his eyes full of despair. With a cry, Rachel put her arms around him and he pulled her hard against him, dropping his head to her shoulder. 'Oh Rachel, Rachel,' he said, over and over again, as if it were a prayer that could pull him from the darkness, back into the light.

RACHEL

1853

EPILOGUE

IT WAS MIDSUMMER'S EVE.
She hadn't said anything. Only, after supper, she'd slipped out into the darkness to gaze at the stars. The creek, below in the valley, moved sluggishly. It had been a dry summer. Not like the river at Richmond, where the ducks swam and Will had come riding like a ghost.

It was long ago.

Frank and Greta were doing well at Nerinbilly, Rachel had had a letter only last week. The gold rush at nearby Bendigo diggings had meant high prices for meat and grain, and Frank had grabbed the opportunity with both hands. Greta had had another baby, this time a boy, and they were going to call him Will. Martha's children were grown so big. Young Frank was at school in Melbourne, and Matty and Victoria had been promised a place at one of the young ladies' academies.

Well, thought Rachel, they had worked hard, and deserved their success. Even Greta. They had never become friends, but they had a certain respect for each other. And Greta had made Frank happy, there was no doubting that.

As for Israel, he had grown tired of the northern run and moved to Sydney. There was talk of a political career for a time, but that faded. Last Rachel heard, he had travelled further north, into the unexplored country. Always searching, always looking, though for what, perhaps even Israel didn't know.

The northern run had been taken over by Thomas and Sarah. They lived there now and were buying it from Frank Potter. They had never had any children; Sarah's only sadness—but she spoilt Frank's children as if they were her own. Suzy and George had ended up rich. Rachel smiled, remembering when she had seen them in Melbourne last year. George had opened a store on the goldfields at Ballarat and made a fortune. They now owned a carriage and four, and Suzy took great pride in driving about in it, all done up in her silks and satins, looking for all the world like a duchess. Until she opened her mouth.

Violet? Well, she had remarried after Kemp had been killed while escorting a prisoner to Melbounce. Her new husband was much like Kemp and Violet ruled that roost just as she had ruled the last.

And that left Will.

He'd resigned from the police and gone back to his other trade. They had bought a blacksmithy on the road to Melbourne—Rachel still had the money from the sale at Greengage, plus the interest accumulated over the years. Will had done well enough, though it was only now, with the gold rush, that he'd begun to see the fruits of all his labours. The number of people passing through from Melbourne to the gold fields was endless. There were fortunes to be made, but Rachel thought that it was people like she and Will who would make them, rather than the poor diggers.

They were happy.

Only, sometimes, she would remember the close, crowded forest and the killer. They did not speak of Yelland, there were some things it was better not to speak of, even for those who had no secrets. They had had no more children. Rachel had longed for them, but it was not to be. Will said it was better so. He laughed and claimed the memory of Hannah's birth would live on with him until his dying day, and he didn't want to repeat it. But there was a gentleness in his eyes when he said it, remembering. Bella grew more like him every day, until sometimes Rachel thought it was Bella who ran the house and not her mother. Hannah . . . well, Hannah was a dreamer. Soft and gentle, she gazed into space, weaving her fantasies. 'She's like you,' Will said, but Rachel wondered.

She looked up at the stars again, breathing the warm, still air. It was a moment before she realised she was no longer alone, that Will was there, behind her. His arm slid around her waist, pressing her to his side. He rested his cheek against her hair.

'Are you makin' wishes?' he teased her.

'I've none to make.'

'Would you have nothin' different then?' and although he smiled, and teased, she sensed it was a serious question.

'I made my wish long ago, it hasn't changed.'

He squeezed her gently in his strong arms, thanking her for the answer. 'Come inside, darlin',' he whispered. 'There are too many ghosts out here.'

He was right. Rachel leaned against him, and slowly they walked back together.

ABOUT THE AUTHOR

Kaye Dobbie has been writing professionally ever since she won the Big River short story contest at the age of eighteen. Her career has undergone many changes, including writing Australian historical fiction under the name Lilly Sommers, to romance written as Sara Bennett and published in the US and Australia. Her books have been translated into many languages. She is currently writing under her 'proper' name, Kaye Dobbie, and is published by Harlequin Mira in Australia and Weltbild in Germany. Kaye lives on the central Victorian goldfields with her husband and three very important cats.

Sign up to her Newsletter for the latest:

www.kayedobbie.com

www.facebook.com/KayedobbieAuthor